BATMAN
NIGHTWALKER

THE GRAPHIC NOVEL

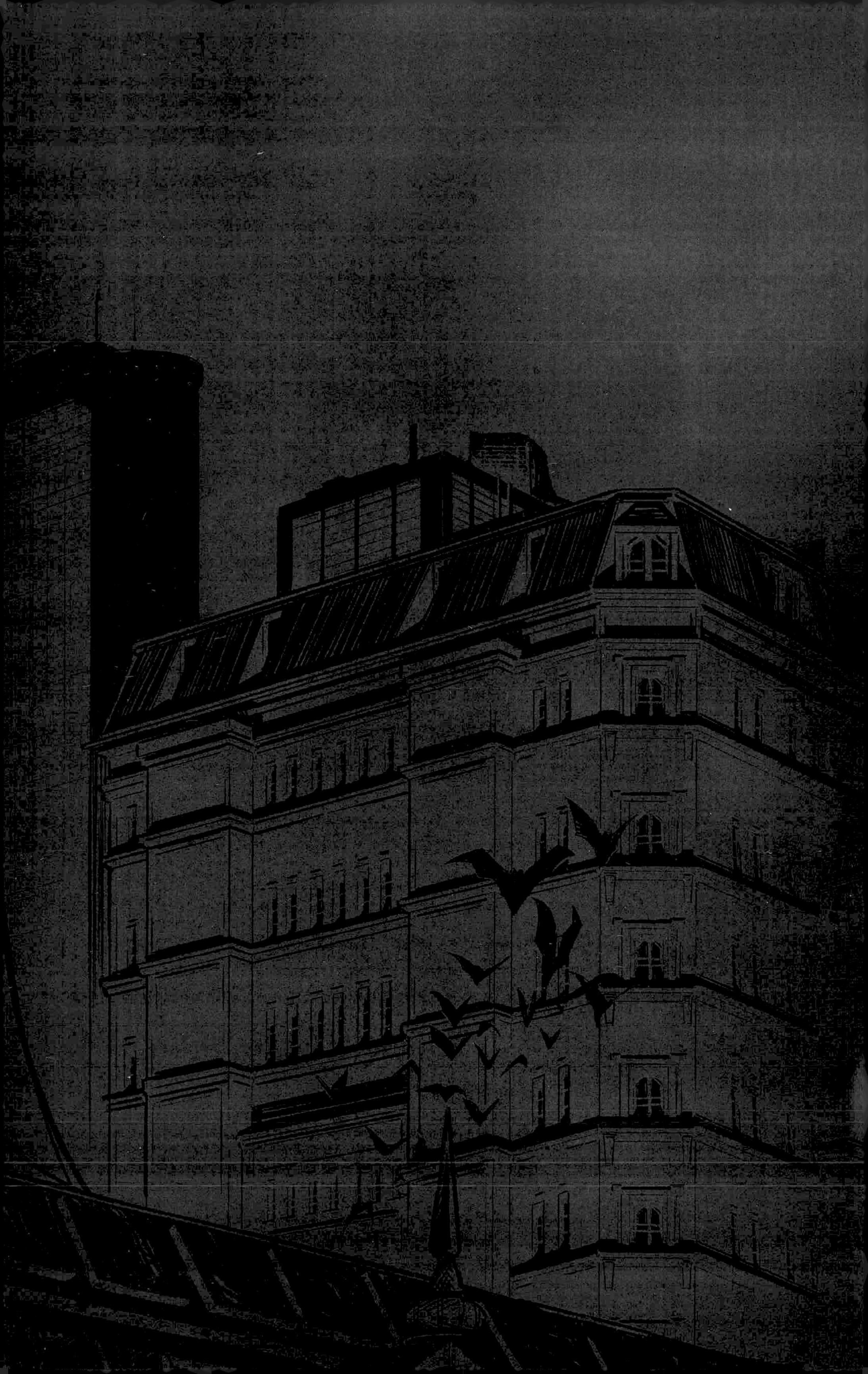

BATMAN
NIGHTWALKER
THE GRAPHIC NOVEL

BASED ON THE NOVEL WRITTEN BY
MARIE LU

ADAPTED BY
STUART MOORE

ILLUSTRATED BY
CHRIS WILDGOOSE
WITH **CAM SMITH**

COLOR BY **LAURA TRINDER**

LETTERS BY **TROY PETERI**

BATMAN CREATED BY
BOB KANE WITH **BILL FINGER**

LAUREN BISOM Editor
STEVE COOK Design Director – Books
AMIE BROCKWAY-METCALF Publication Design

BOB HARRAS Senior VP – Editor-in-Chief, DC Comics
MICHELE R. WELLS VP & Executive Editor, Young Reader

DAN DiDIO Publisher
JIM LEE Publisher & Chief Creative Officer
BOBBIE CHASE VP – New Publishing Initiatives & Talent Development
DON FALLETTI VP – Manufacturing Operations & Workflow Management
LAWRENCE GANEM VP – Talent Services
ALISON GILL Senior VP – Manufacturing & Operations
HANK KANALZ Senior VP – Publishing Strategy & Support Services
DAN MIRON VP – Publishing Operations
NICK J. NAPOLITANO VP – Manufacturing Administration & Design
NANCY SPEARS VP – Sales

DC Comics, 2900 West Alameda Ave.,
Burbank, CA 91505

Printed by LSC Communications,
Crawfordsville, IN, USA. 8/23/19.
First Printing.

ISBN: 978-1-4012-8004-8

PEFC Certified

This product is from
sustainably managed
forests and controlled
sources

PEFC

PEFC/29-31-337   www.pefc.org

Library of Congress Cataloging-in-Publication Data

Names: Moore, Stuart, adapter. | Wildgoose, Chris, artist. | Trinder, Laura,
   colorist. | Peteri, Troy, letterer. | graphic novel adaptation of: Lu,
   Marie, 1984- Batman: Nightwalker
Title: Batman : Nightwalker / novel written by Marie Lu ; adapted by Stuart
   Moore ; art by Chris Wildgoose ; color by Laura Trinder ; letters by Troy
   Peteri.
Other titles: Nightwalker
Description: Burbank, CA : DC Comics, [2019] | "Batman created by Bob Kane
   with Bill Finger."
Identifiers: LCCN 2019021229 | ISBN 9781401280048 (paperback)
Classification: LCC PZ7.7.M657 Bat 2019 | DDC 741.5/973--dc23

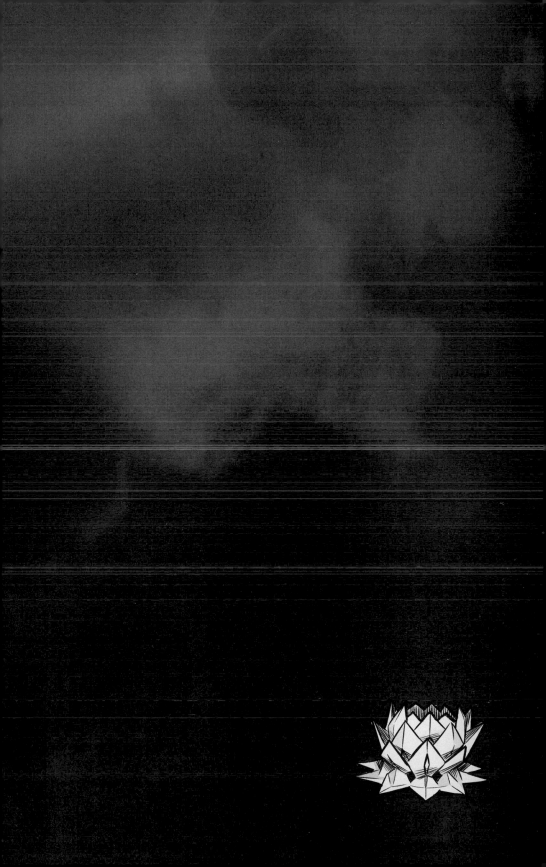

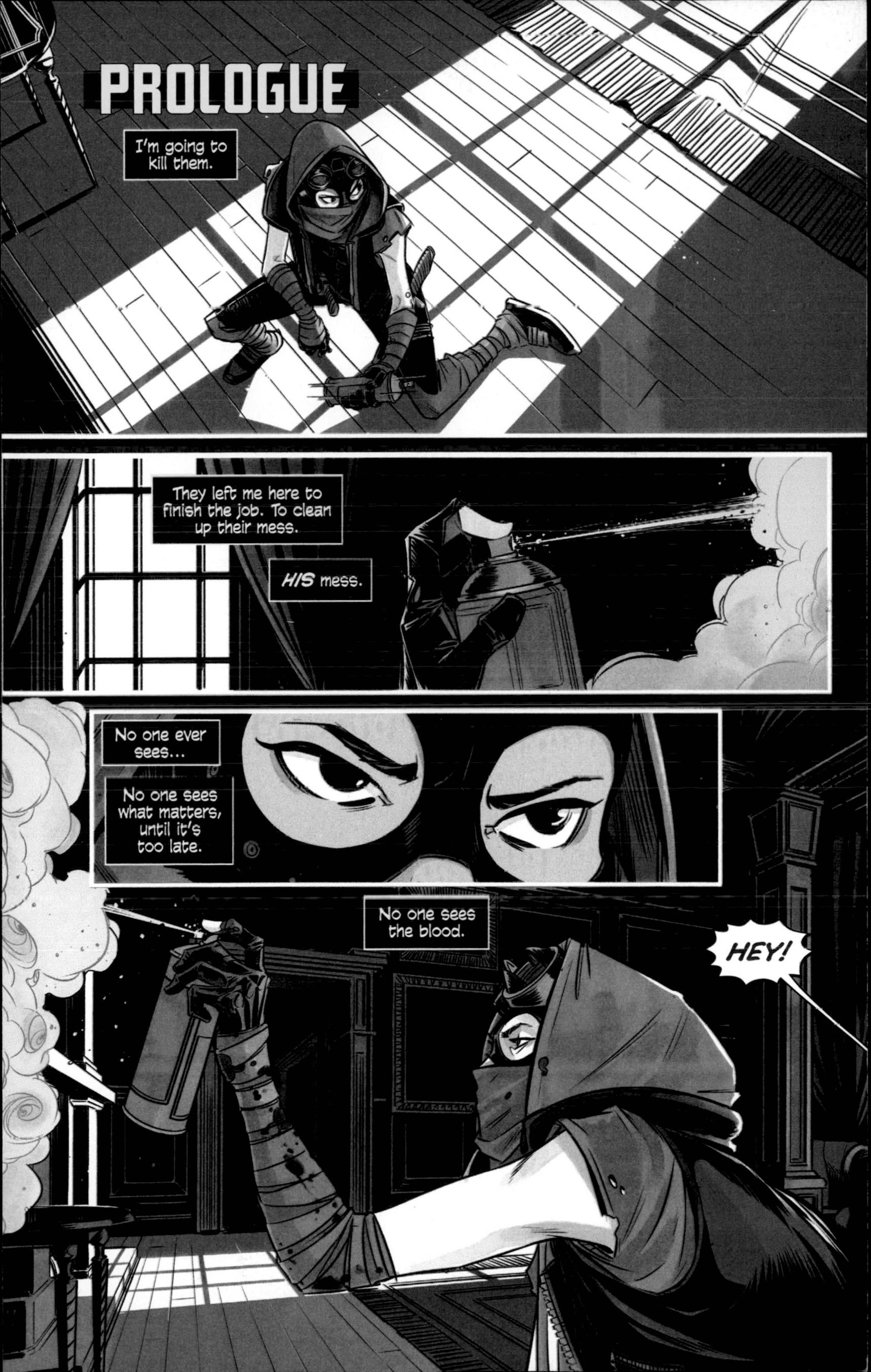
PROLOGUE
I'm going to kill them.
They left me here to finish the job. To clean up their mess.
HIS mess.
No one ever sees...
No one sees what matters, until it's too late.
No one sees the blood.
HEY!

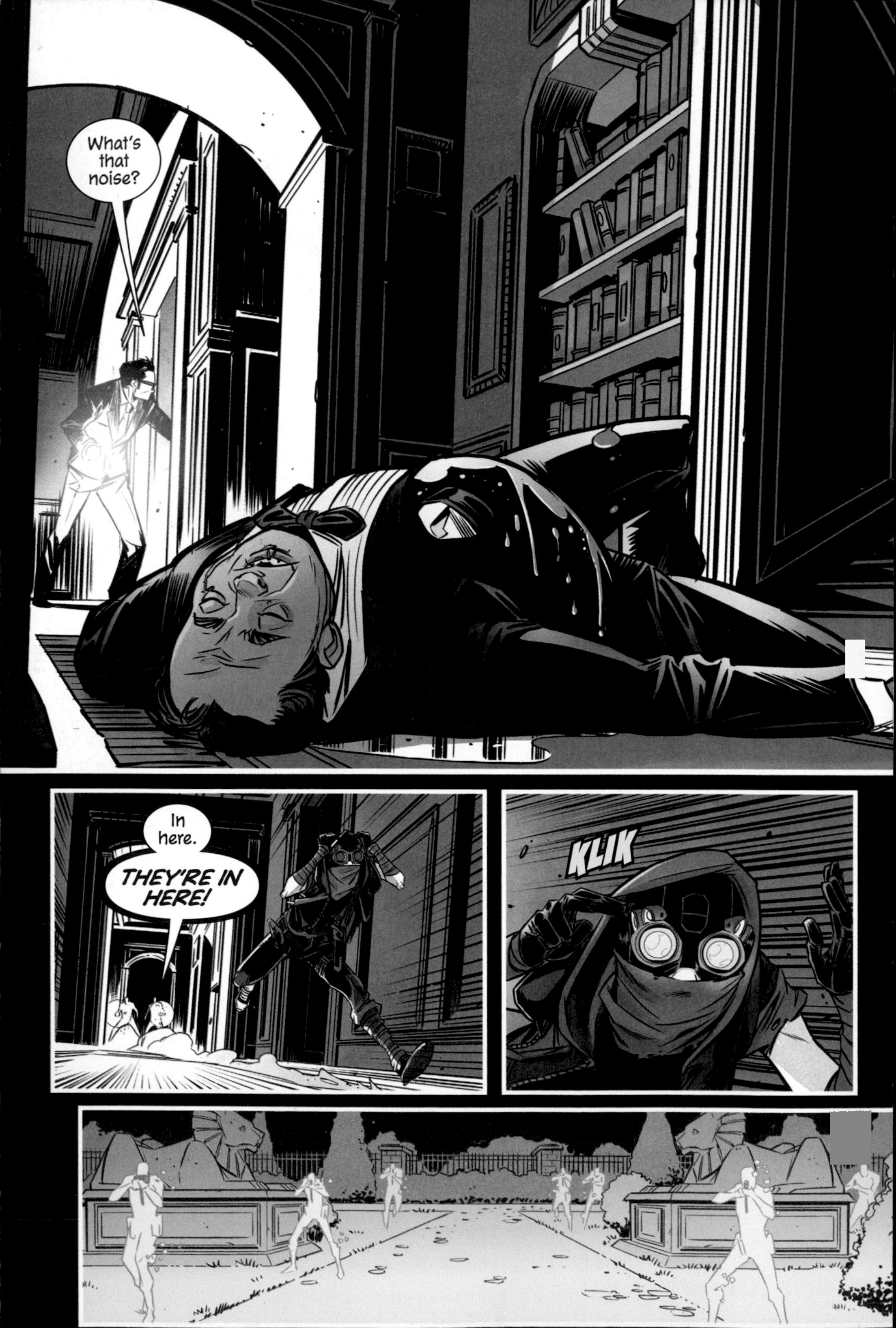
What's that noise?
In here.
THEY'RE IN HERE!
KLIK

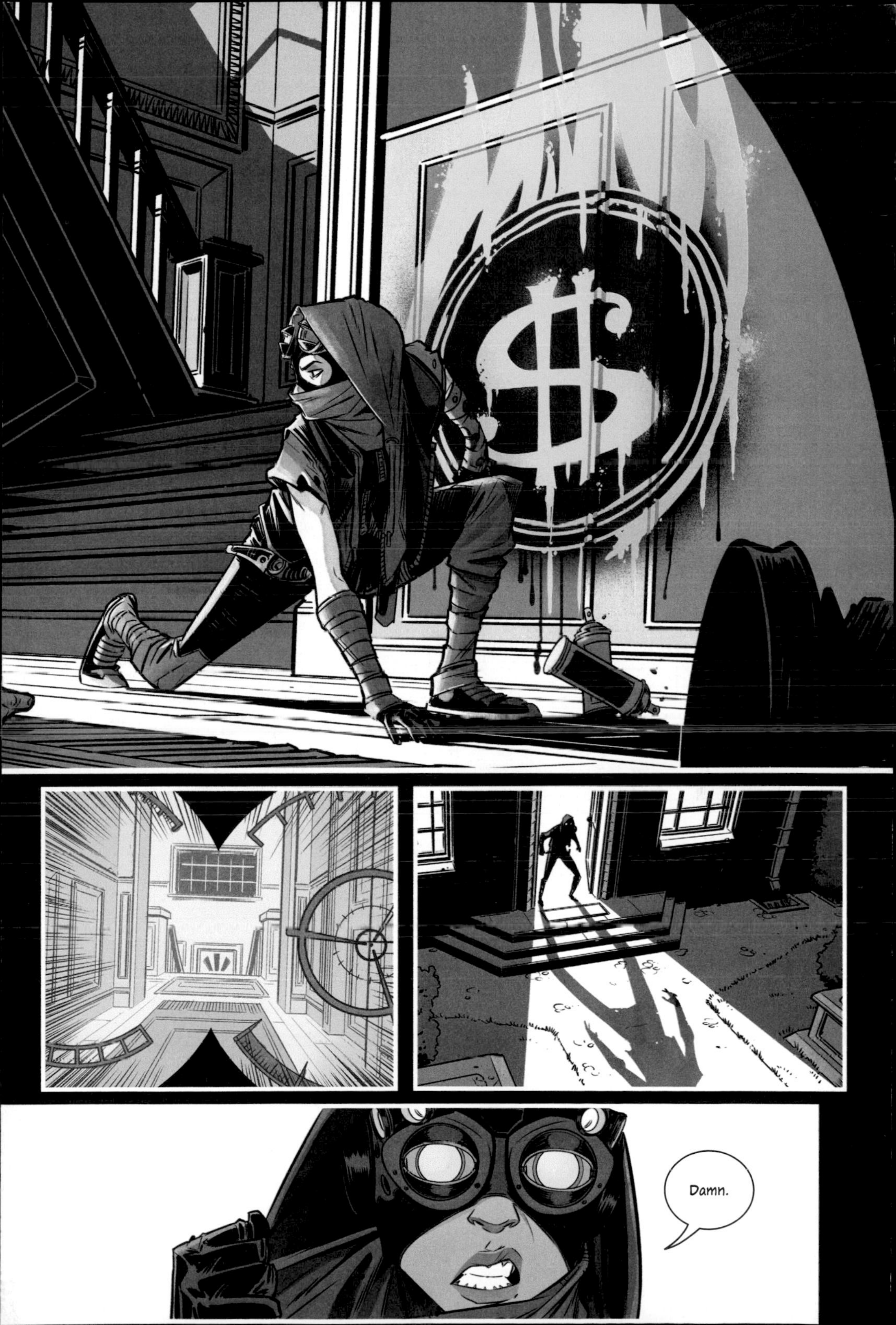
Damn.

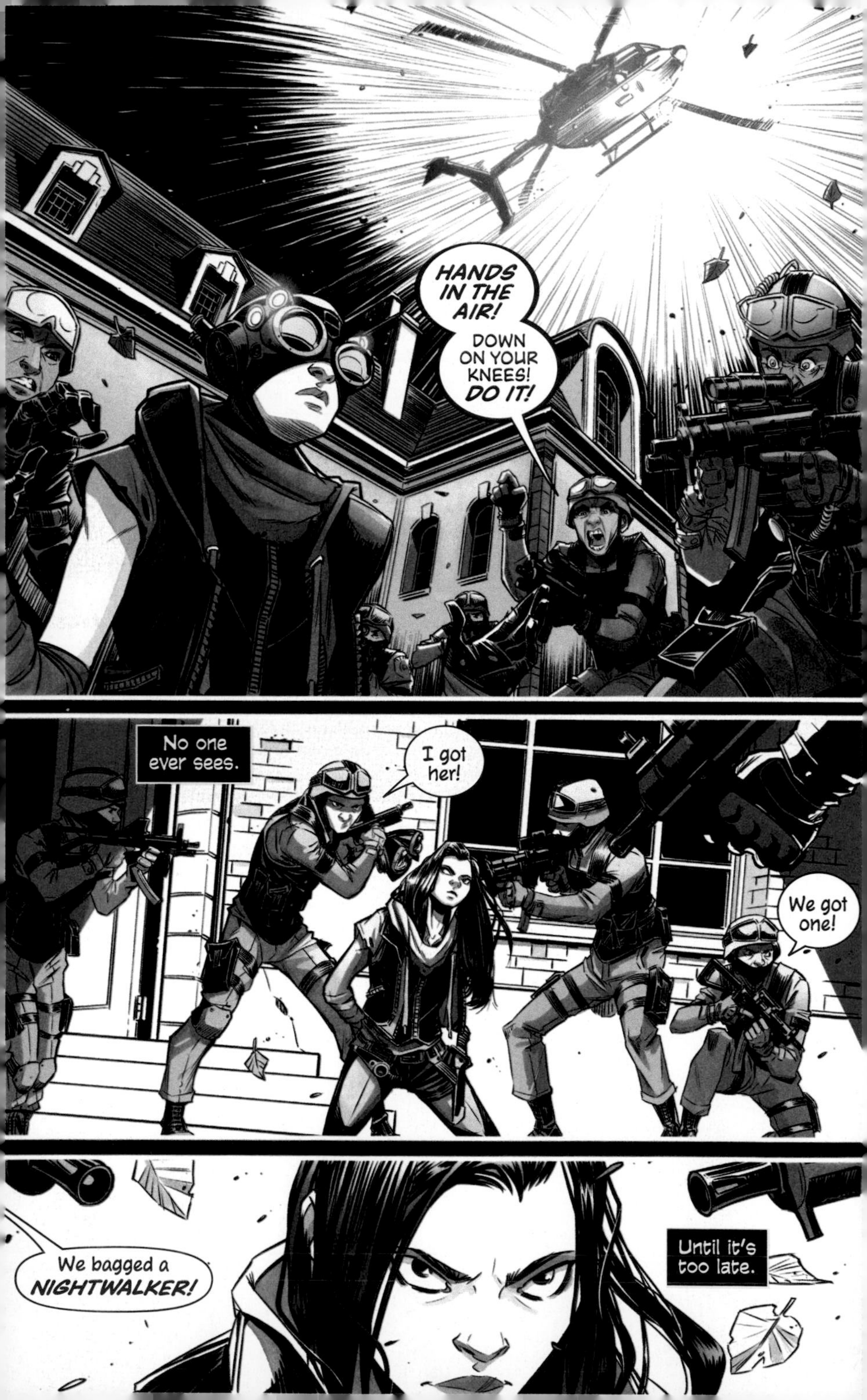
HANDS IN THE AIR!
DOWN ON YOUR KNEES! DO IT!
No one ever sees.
I got her!
We got one!
We bagged a NIGHTWALKER!
Until it's too late.

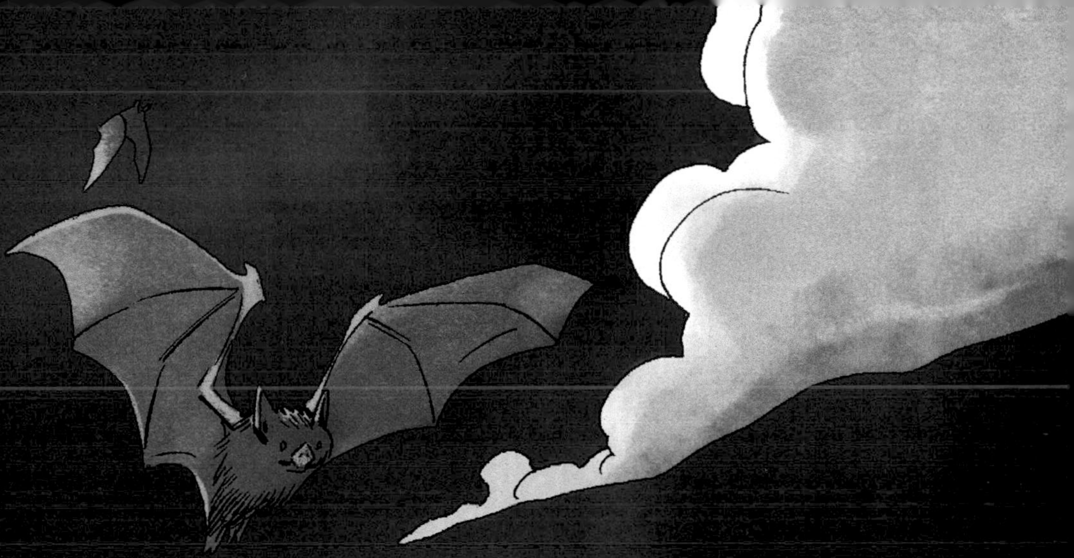

PART ONE

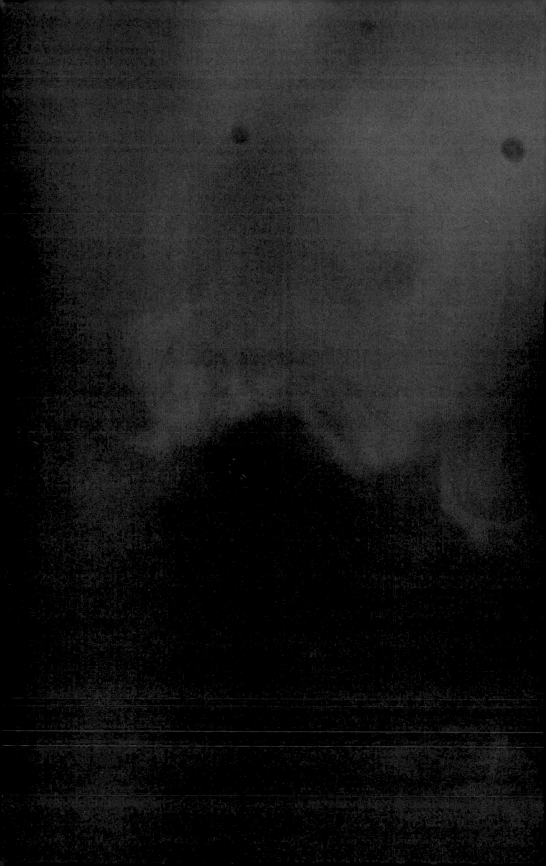

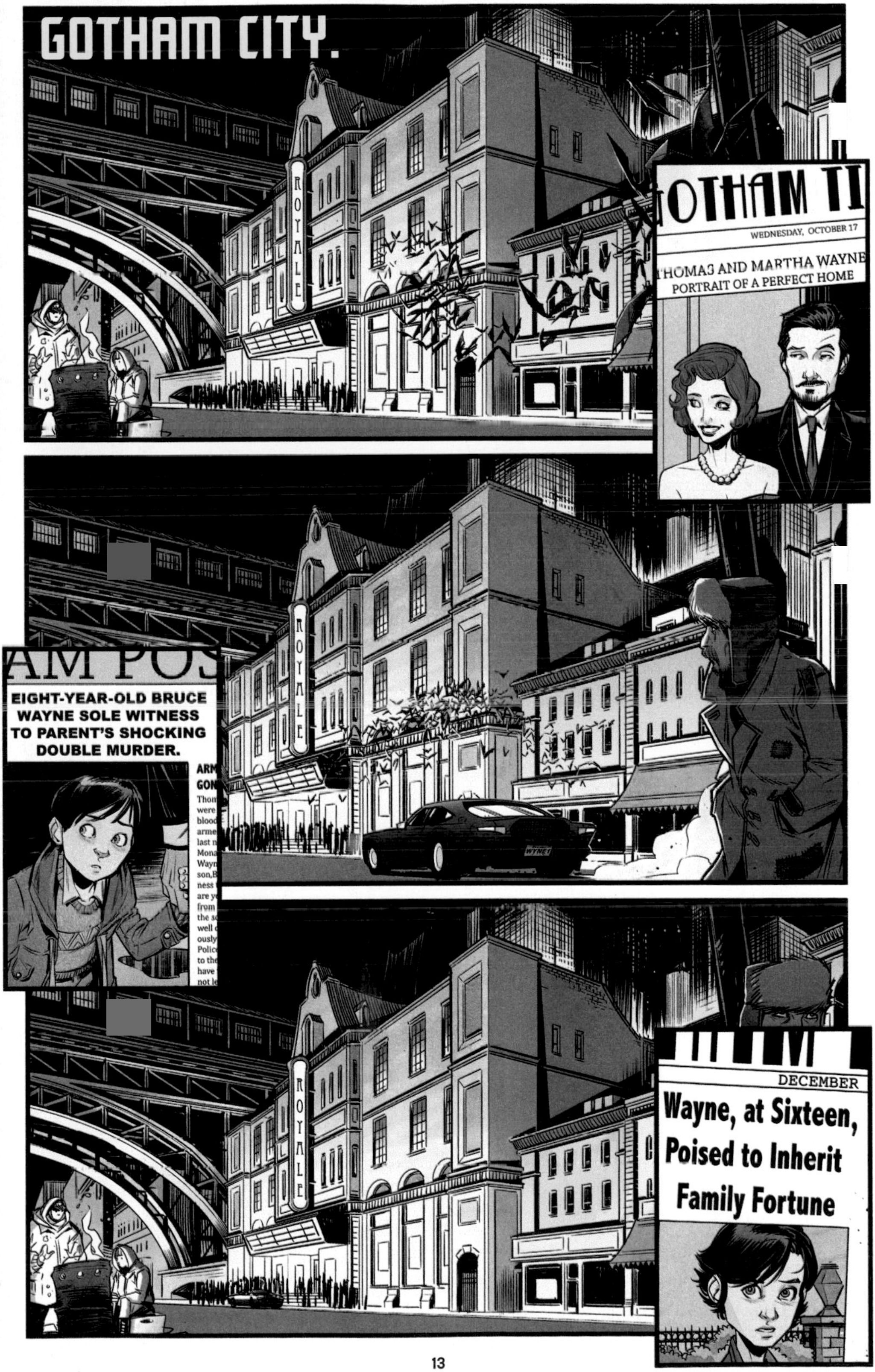
GOTHAM CITY.
GOTHAM TI
WEDNESDAY, OCTOBER 17
THOMAS AND MARTHA WAYNE
PORTRAIT OF A PERFECT HOME
AM POS
EIGHT-YEAR-OLD BRUCE WAYNE SOLE WITNESS TO PARENT'S SHOCKING DOUBLE MURDER.
DECEMBER
Wayne, at Sixteen, Poised to Inherit Family Fortune

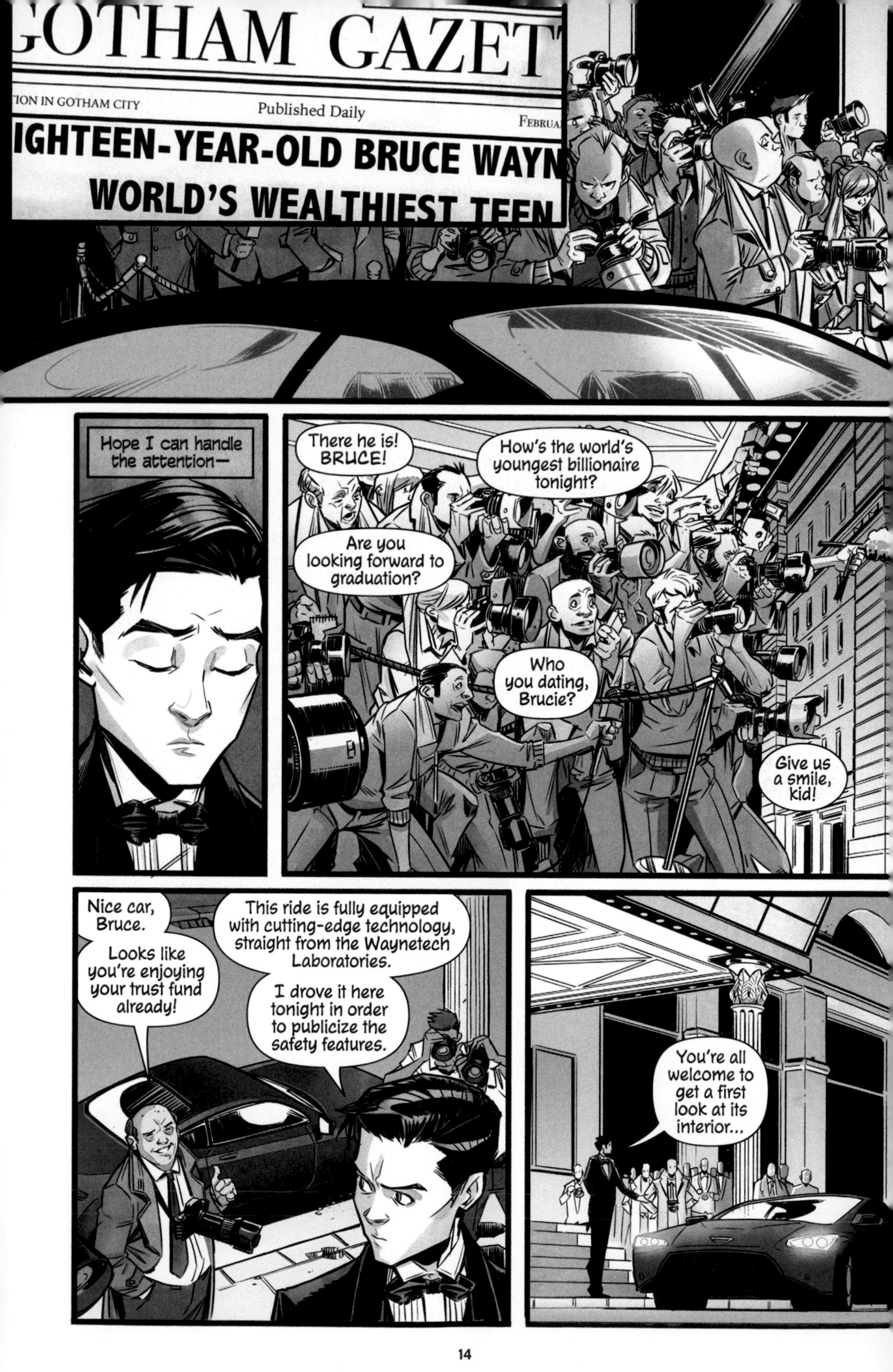

GOTHAM GAZET
TION IN GOTHAM CITY
Published Daily
FEBRUA
IGHTEEN-YEAR-OLD BRUCE WAYN
WORLD'S WEALTHIEST TEEN
Hope I can handle the attention—
There he is! BRUCE!
How's the world's youngest billionaire tonight?
Are you looking forward to graduation?
Who you dating, Brucie?
Give us a smile, kid!
Nice car, Bruce.
Looks like you're enjoying your trust fund already!
This ride is fully equipped with cutting-edge technology, straight from the Waynetech Laboratories.
I drove it here tonight in order to publicize the safety features.
You're all welcome to get a first look at its interior...

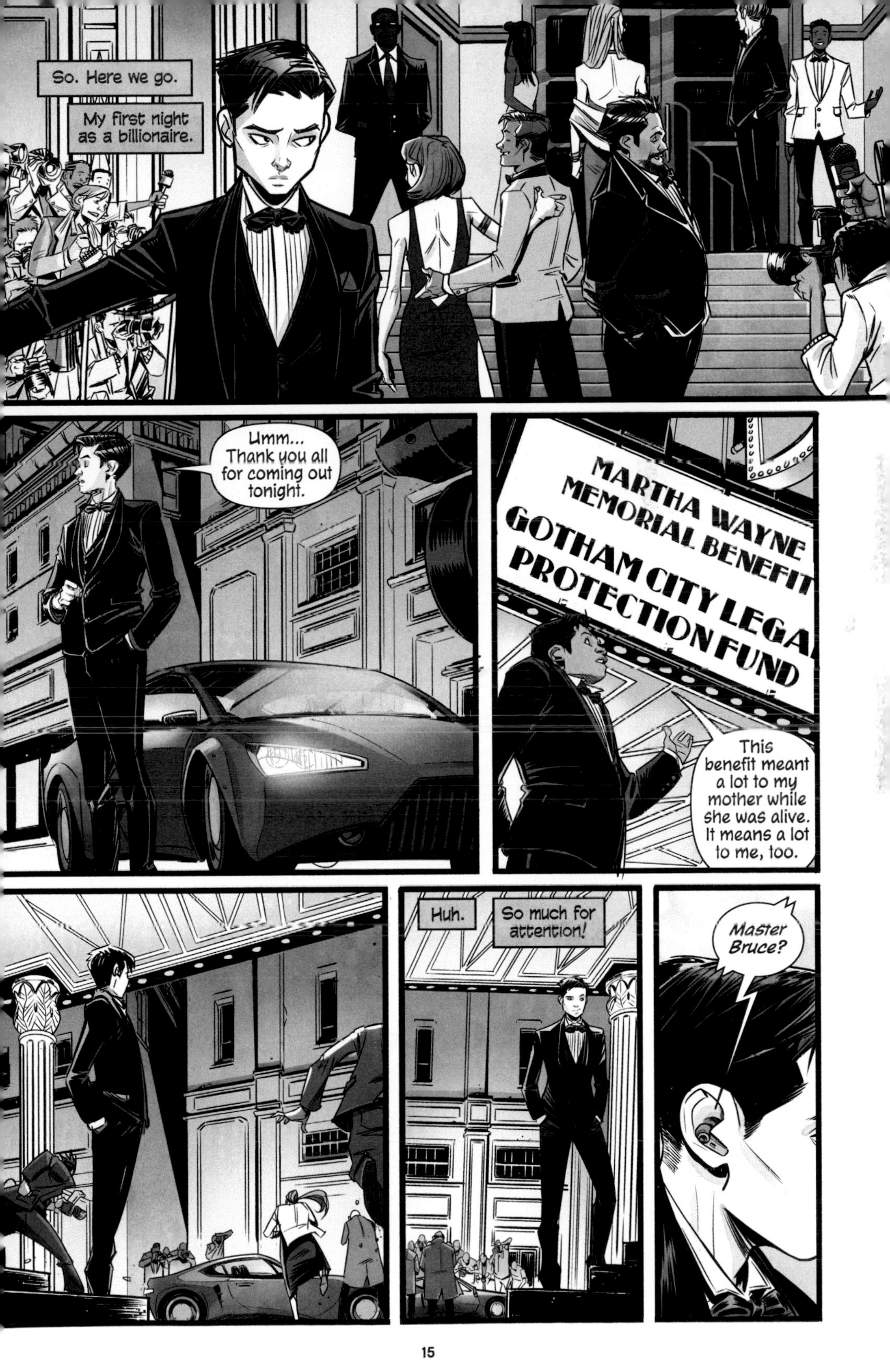
So. Here we go.
My first night as a billionaire.
Umm... Thank you all for coming out tonight.
MARTHA WAYNE MEMORIAL BENEFIT
GOTHAM CITY LEGAL PROTECTION FUND
This benefit meant a lot to my mother while she was alive. It means a lot to me, too.
Huh.
So much for attention!
Master Bruce?

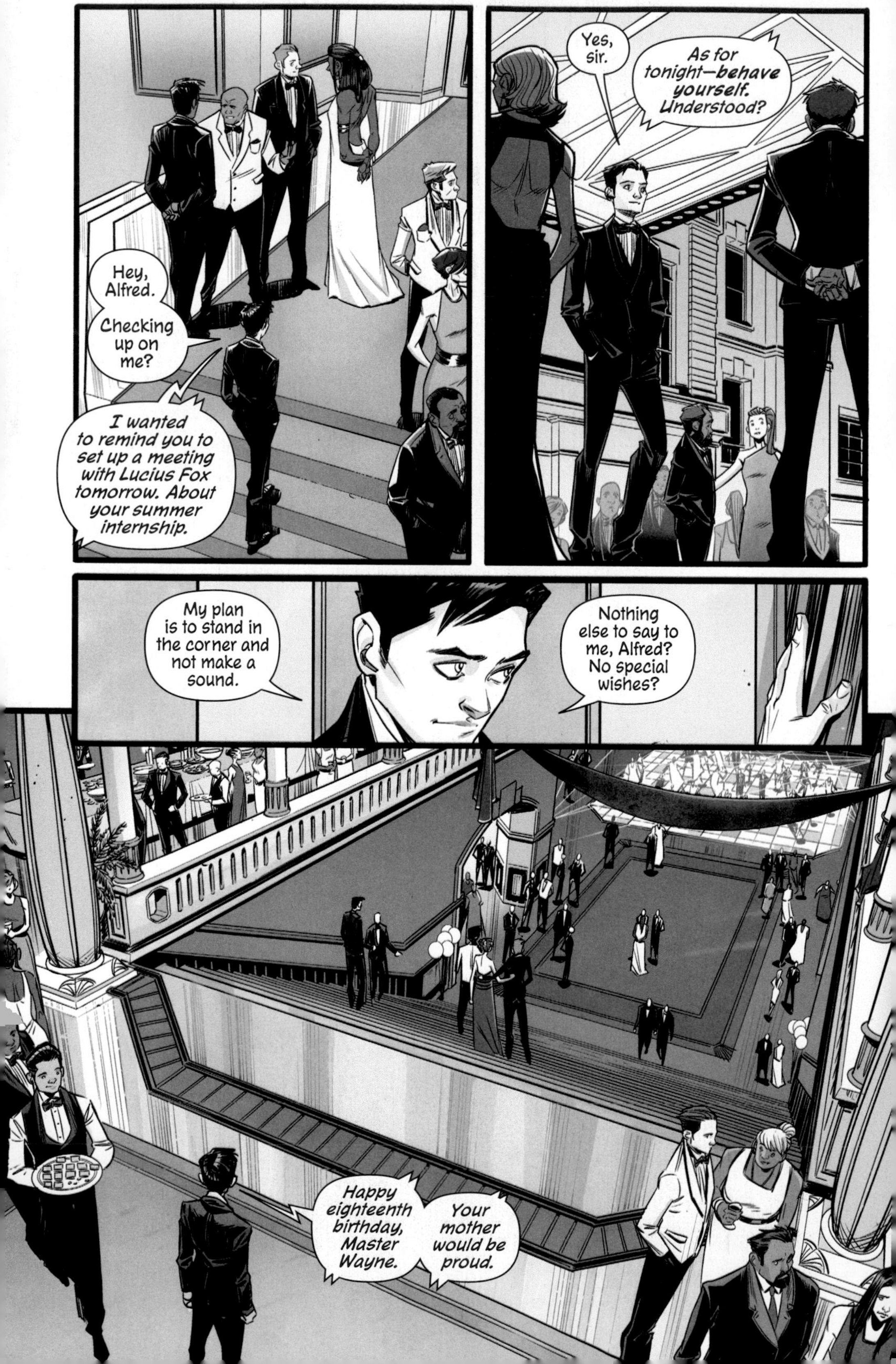
Hey, Alfred.
Checking up on me?
I wanted to remind you to set up a meeting with Lucius Fox tomorrow. About your summer internship.
Yes, sir.
As for tonight—behave yourself. Understood?
My plan is to stand in the corner and not make a sound.
Nothing else to say to me, Alfred? No special wishes?
Happy eighteenth birthday, Master Wayne.
Your mother would be proud.

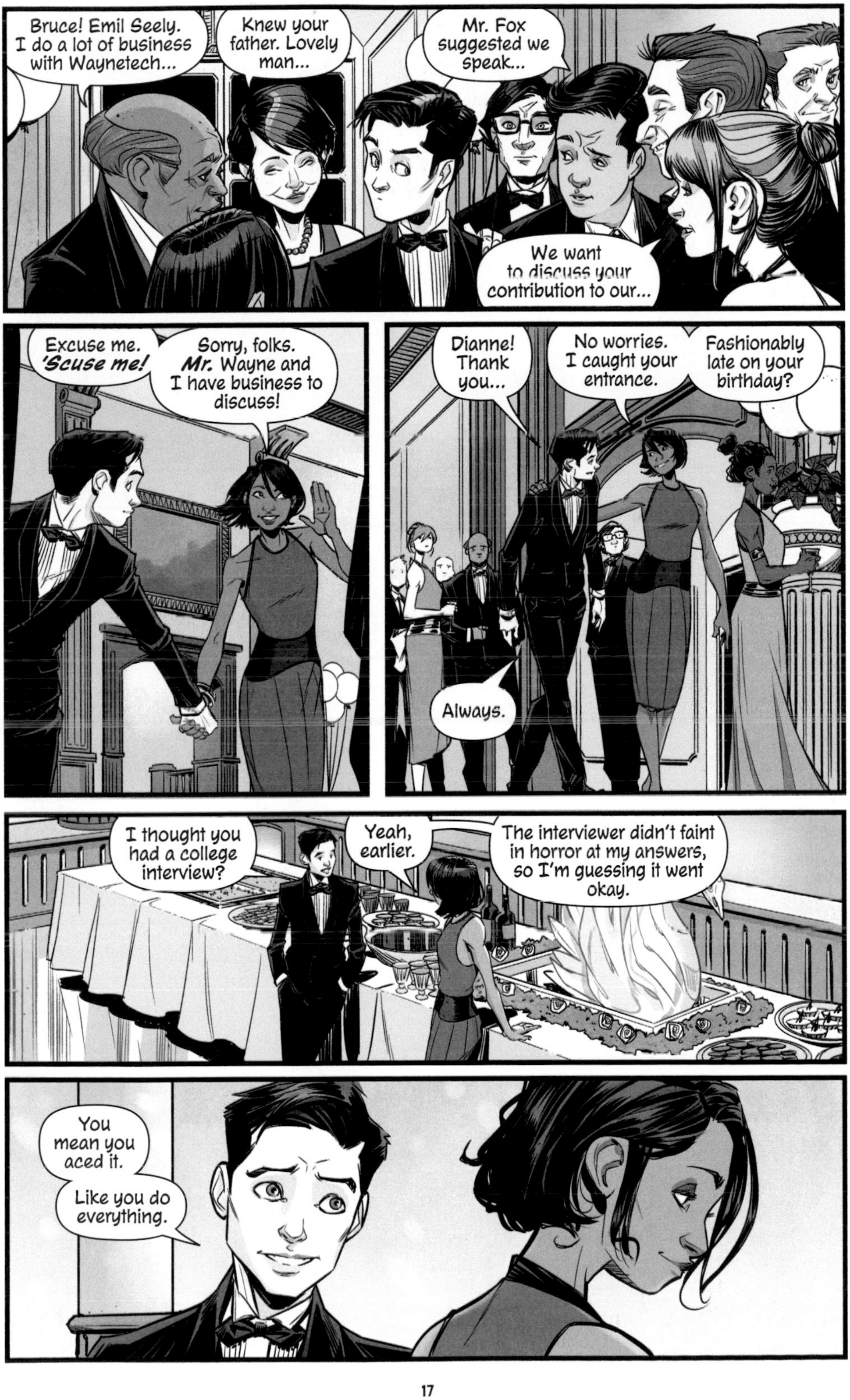
Bruce! Emil Seely. I do a lot of business with Waynetech...
Knew your father. Lovely man...
Mr. Fox suggested we speak...
We want to discuss your contribution to our...
Excuse me. 'Scuse me!
Sorry, folks. Mr. Wayne and I have business to discuss!
Dianne! Thank you...
No worries. I caught your entrance.
Fashionably late on your birthday?
Always.
I thought you had a college interview?
Yeah, earlier.
The interviewer didn't faint in horror at my answers, so I'm guessing it went okay.
You mean you aced it.
Like you do everything.

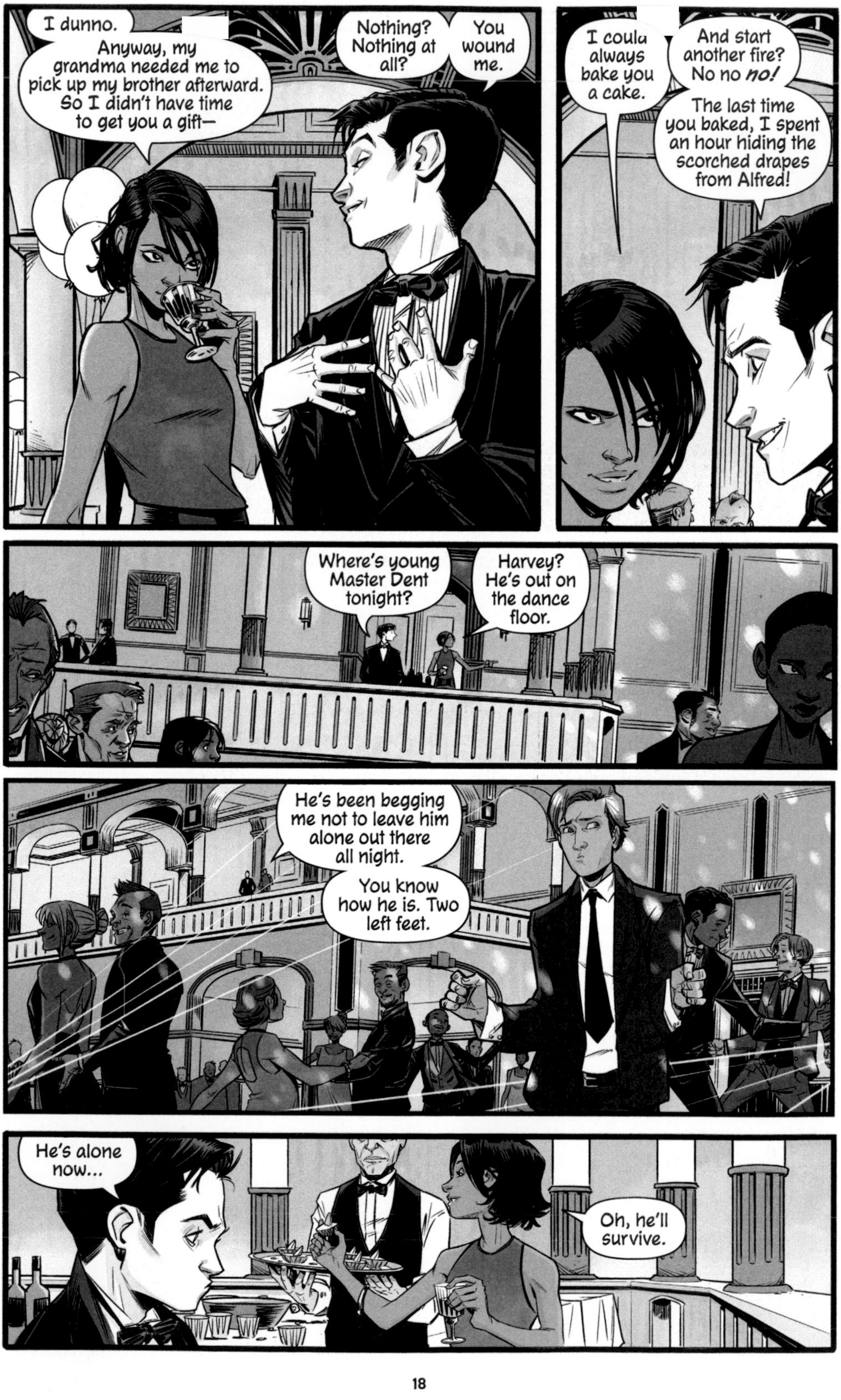
I dunno.
Anyway, my grandma needed me to pick up my brother afterward. So I didn't have time to get you a gift—
Nothing? Nothing at all?
You wound me.
I could always bake you a cake.
And start another fire? No no *no!*
The last time you baked, I spent an hour hiding the scorched drapes from Alfred!
Where's young Master Dent tonight?
Harvey? He's out on the dance floor.
He's been begging me not to leave him alone out there all night.
You know how he is. Two left feet.
He's alone now...
Oh, he'll survive.

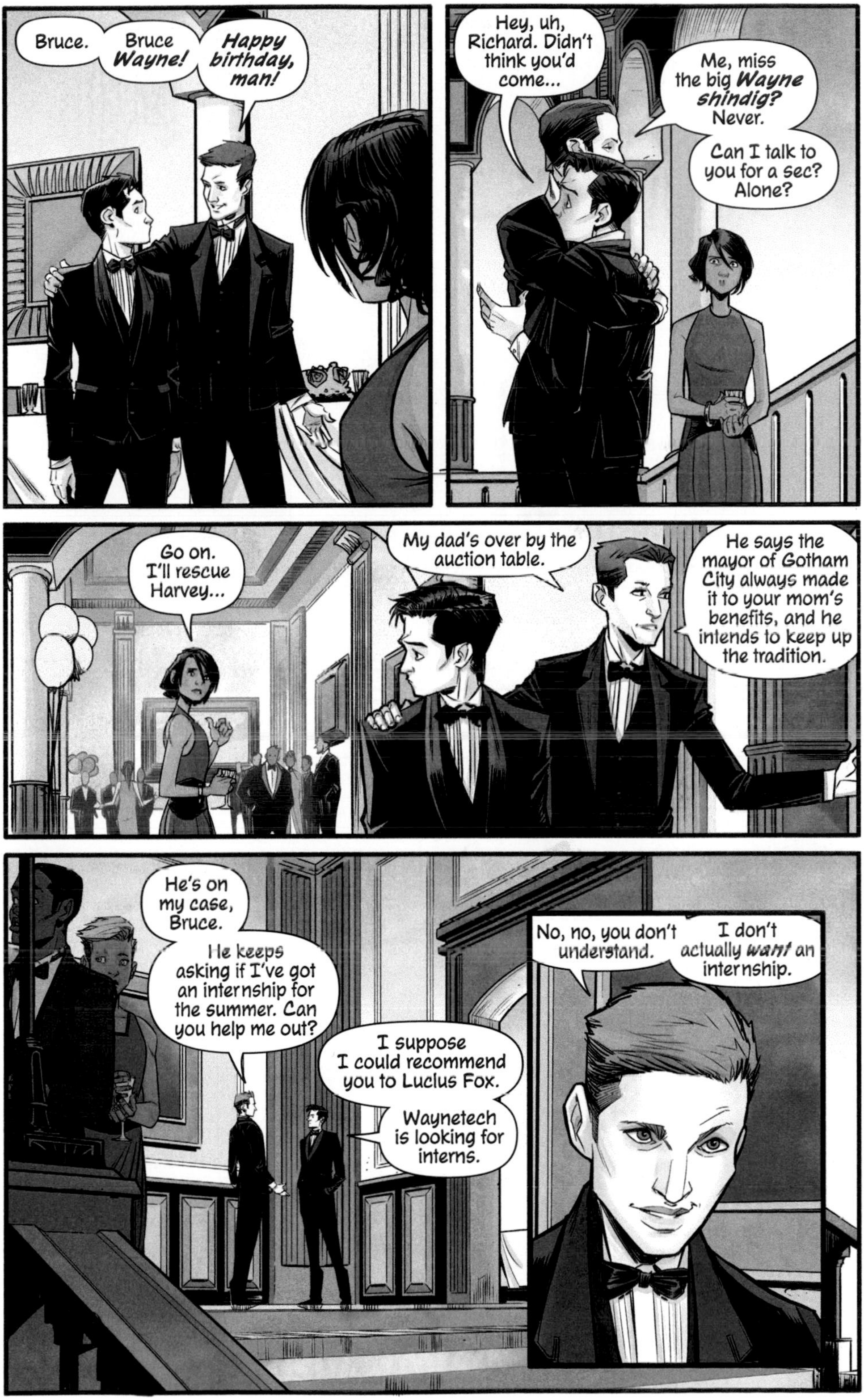
Bruce.
Bruce Wayne!
Happy birthday, man!
Hey, uh, Richard. Didn't think you'd come...
Me, miss the big Wayne shindig? Never.
Can I talk to you for a sec? Alone?
Go on. I'll rescue Harvey...
My dad's over by the auction table.
He says the mayor of Gotham City always made it to your mom's benefits, and he intends to keep up the tradition.
He's on my case, Bruce.
He keeps asking if I've got an internship for the summer. Can you help me out?
I suppose I could recommend you to Luclus Fox.
Waynetech is looking for interns.
No, no, you don't understand.
I don't actually want an internship.

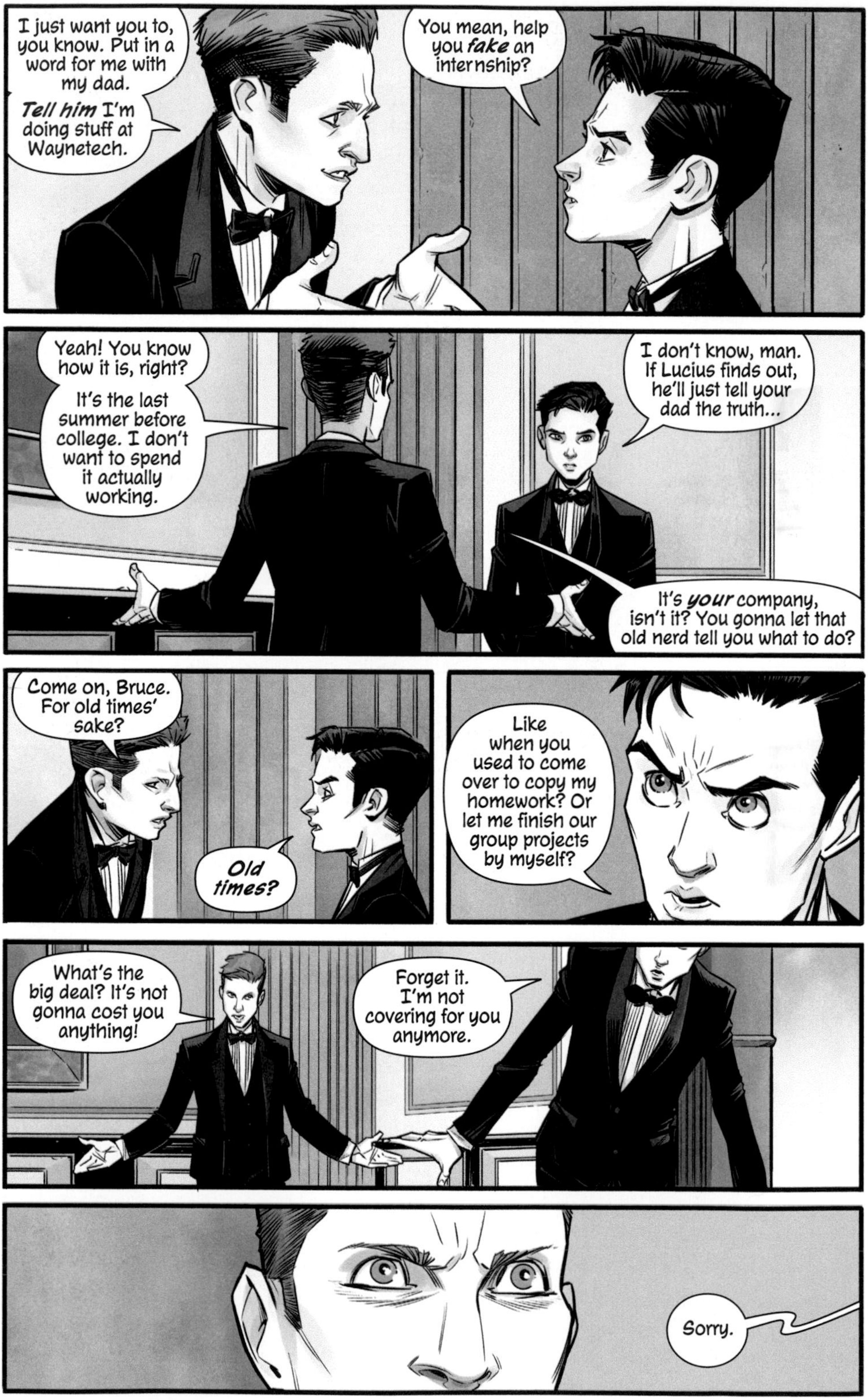
I just want you to, you know. Put in a word for me with my dad.
Tell him I'm doing stuff at Waynetech.
You mean, help you *fake* an internship?
Yeah! You know how it is, right?
It's the last summer before college. I don't want to spend it actually working.
I don't know, man. If Lucius finds out, he'll just tell your dad the truth...
It's *your* company, isn't it? You gonna let that old nerd tell you what to do?
Come on, Bruce. For old times' sake?
Old times?
Like when you used to come over to copy my homework? Or let me finish our group projects by myself?
What's the big deal? It's not gonna cost you anything!
Forget it. I'm not covering for you anymore.
Sorry.

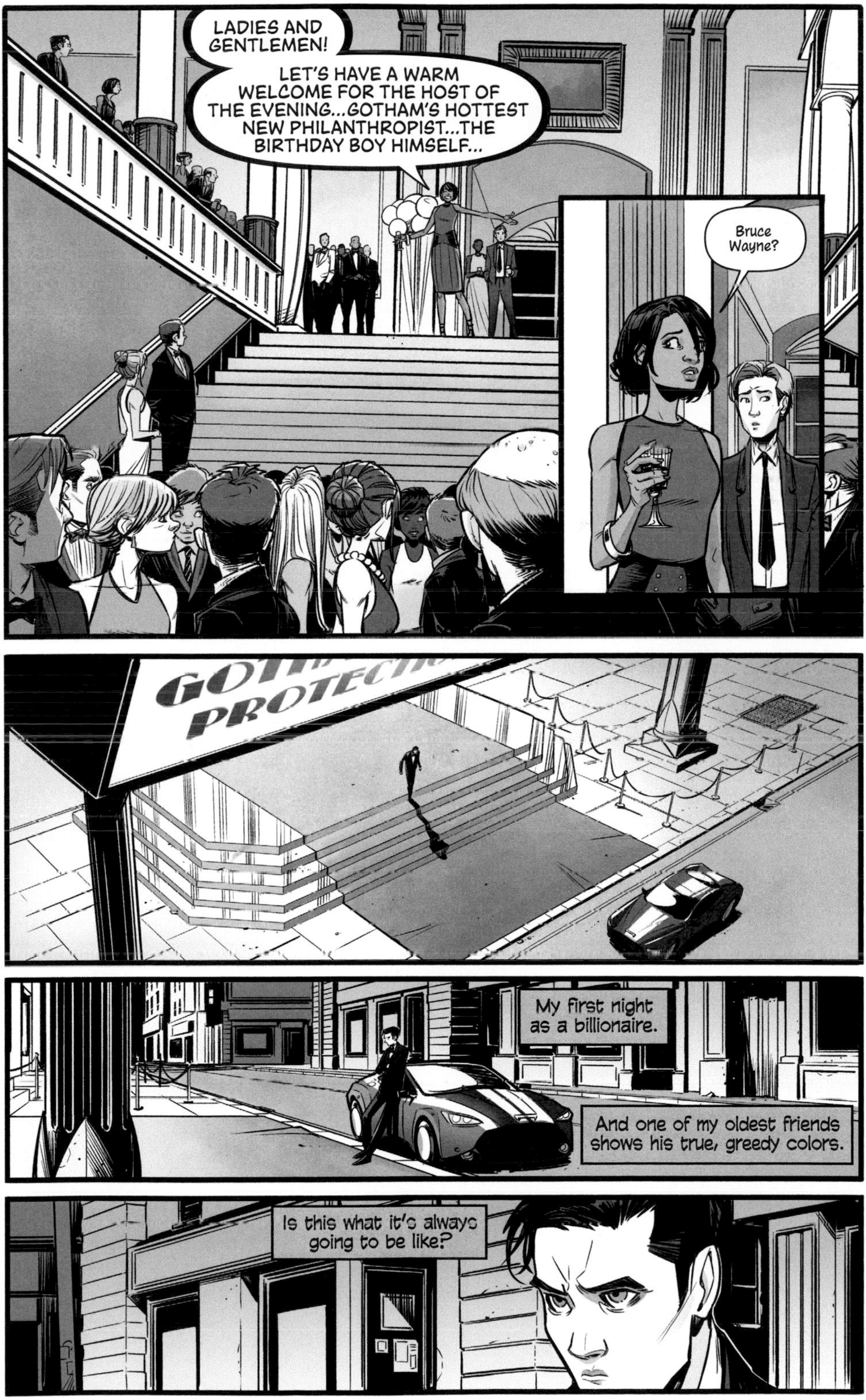
LADIES AND GENTLEMEN!
LET'S HAVE A WARM WELCOME FOR THE HOST OF THE EVENING...GOTHAM'S HOTTEST NEW PHILANTHROPIST...THE BIRTHDAY BOY HIMSELF...
Bruce Wayne?
PROTECTI
My first night as a billionaire.
And one of my oldest friends shows his true, greedy colors.
Is this what it's always going to be like?

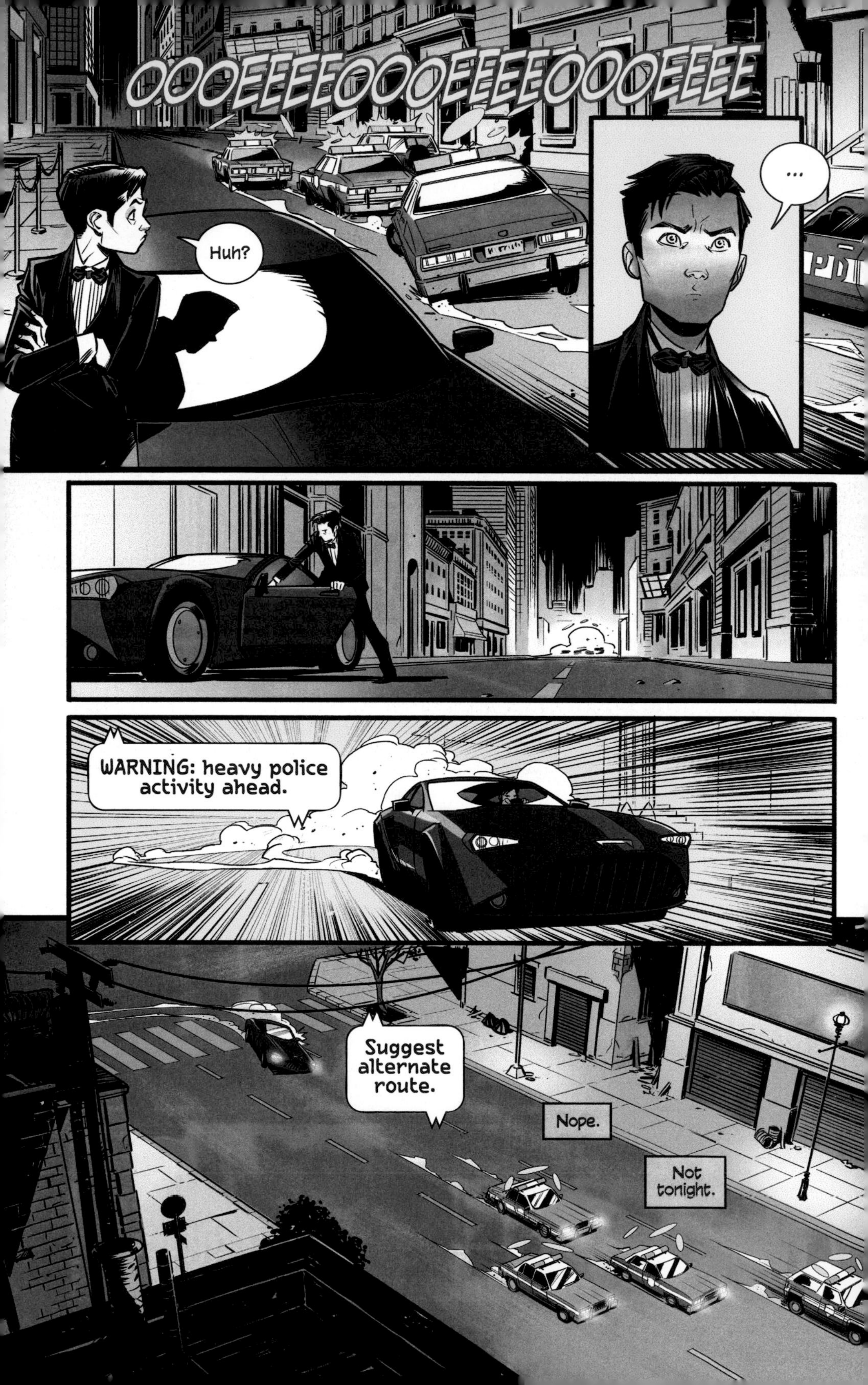
OOOEEEEOOOOEEEEOOOOEEEE
Huh?
...
WARNING: heavy police activity ahead.
Suggest alternate route.
Nope.
Not tonight.

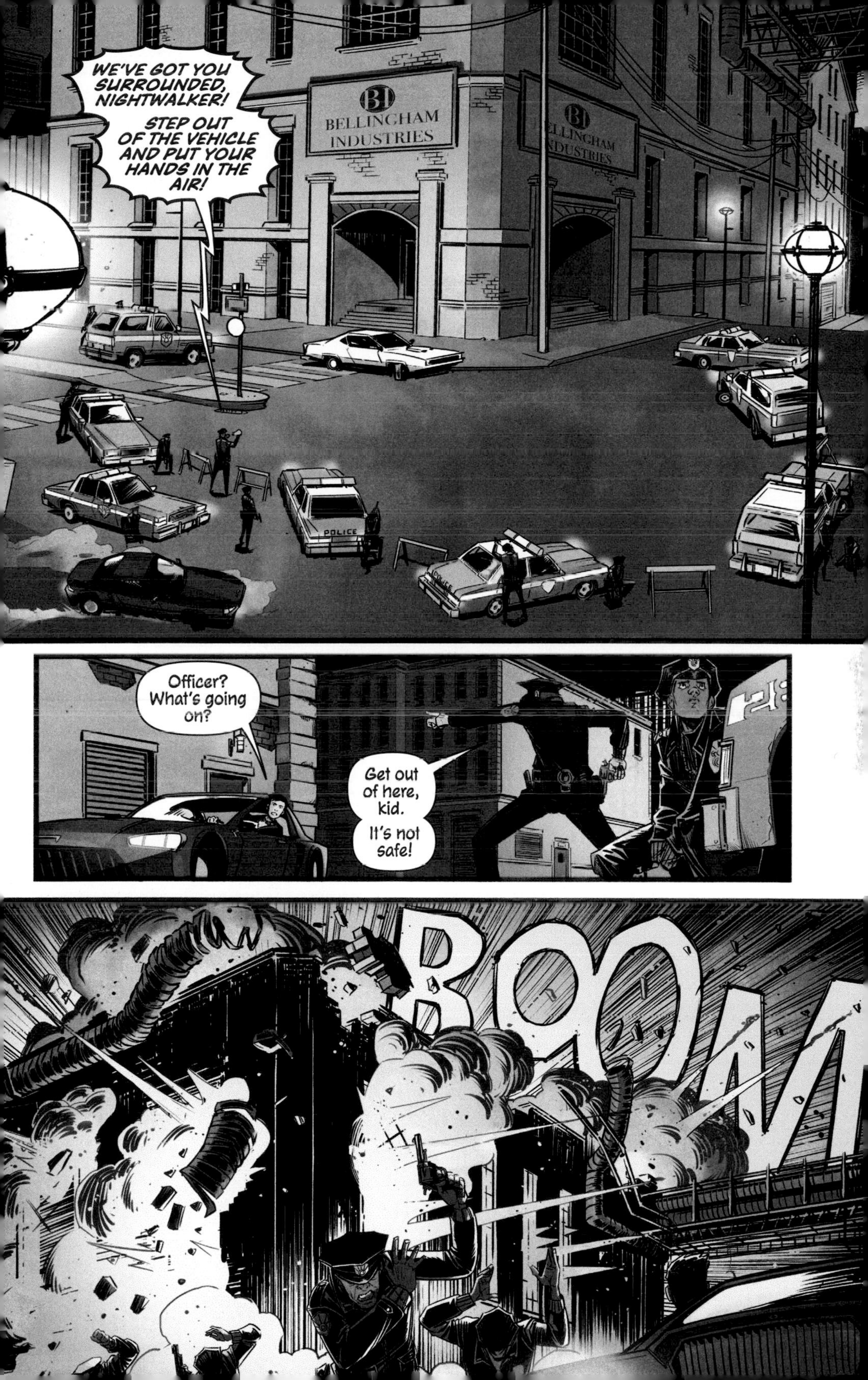
WE'VE GOT YOU SURROUNDED, NIGHTWALKER!
STEP OUT OF THE VEHICLE AND PUT YOUR HANDS IN THE AIR!
BI
BELLINGHAM INDUSTRIES
POLICE
Officer? What's going on?
Get out of here, kid.
It's not safe!
BOOM

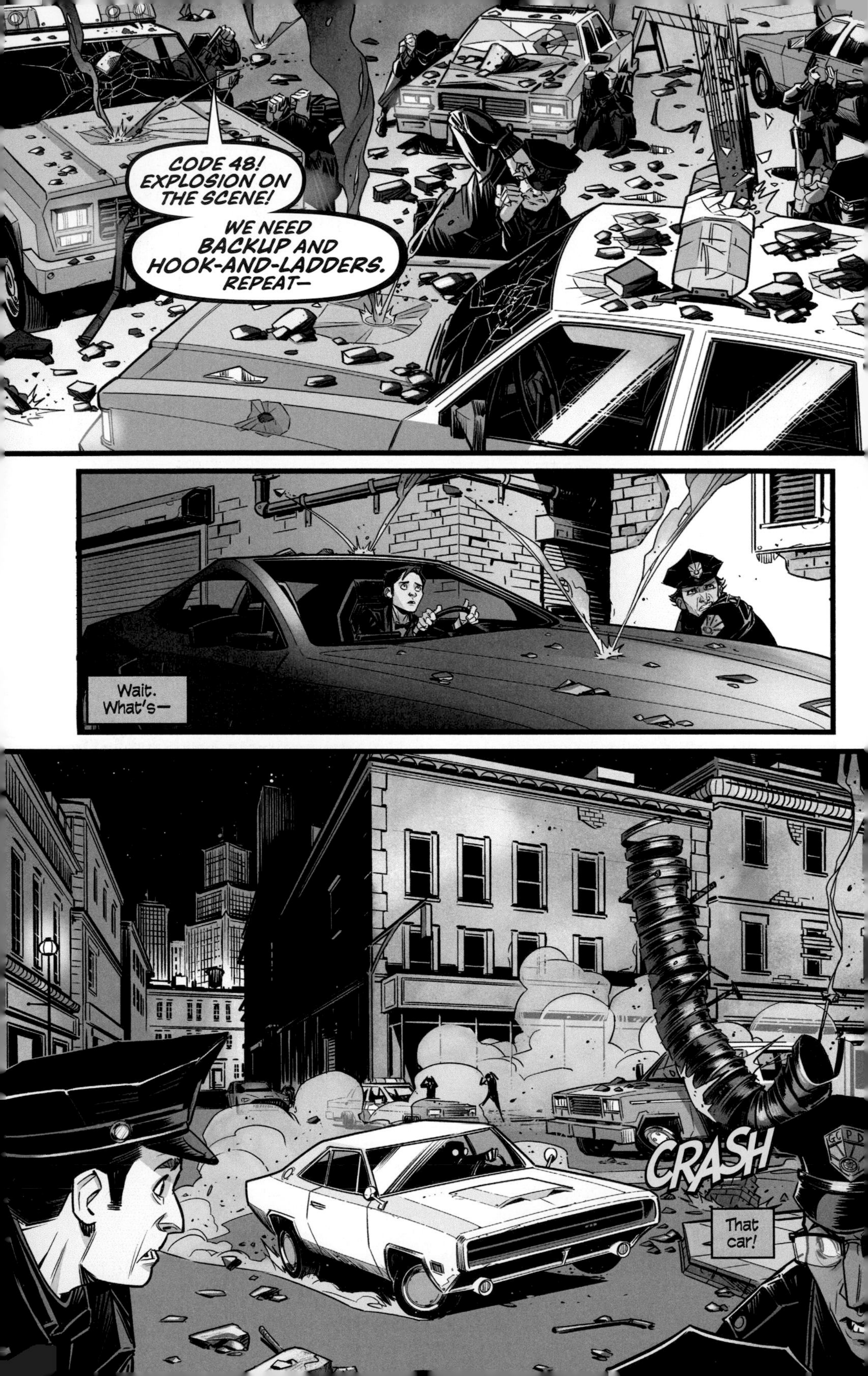
CODE 48! EXPLOSION ON THE SCENE!
WE NEED BACKUP AND HOOK-AND-LADDERS. REPEAT—
Wait. What's—
CRASH
That car!

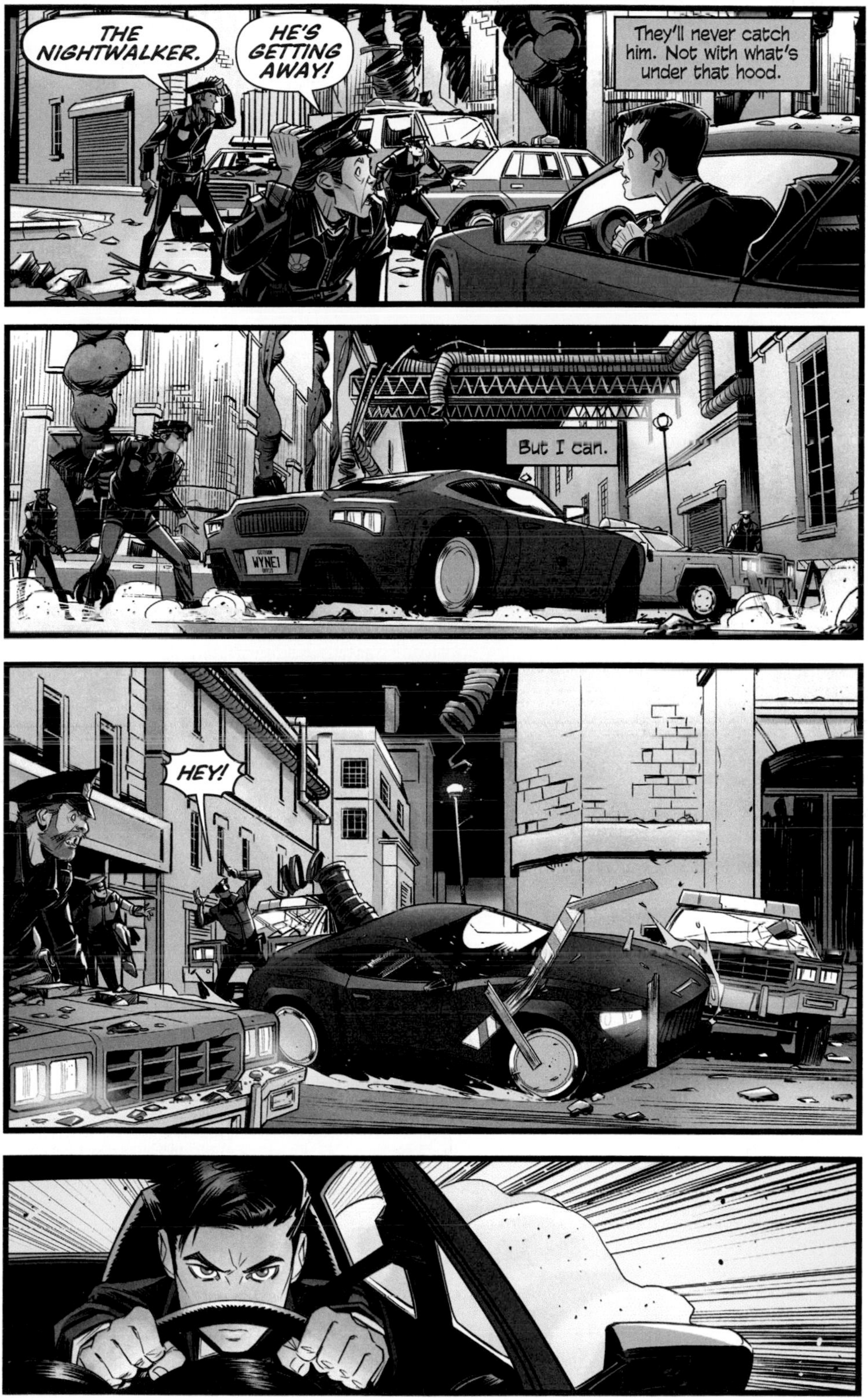
THE NIGHTWALKER.
HE'S GETTING AWAY!
They'll never catch him. Not with what's under that hood.
But I can.
WYNE1
HEY!

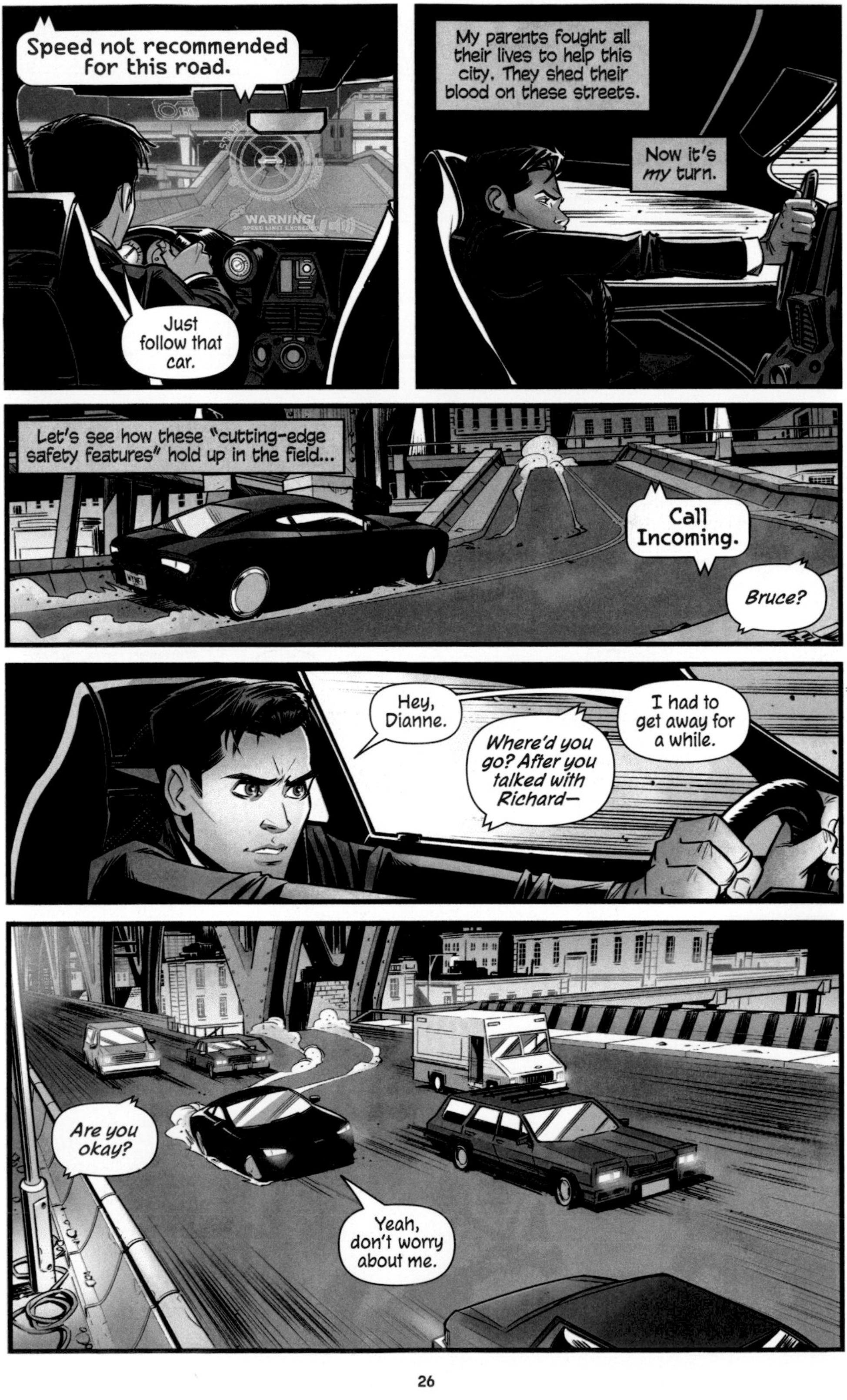
Speed not recommended for this road.
WARNING!
SPEED LIMIT EXCEEDED
Just follow that car.
My parents fought all their lives to help this city. They shed their blood on these streets.
Now it's *my* turn.
Let's see how these "cutting-edge safety features" hold up in the field...
Call Incoming.
Bruce?
Hey, Dianne.
Where'd you go? After you talked with Richard—
I had to get away for a while.
Are you okay?
Yeah, don't worry about me.

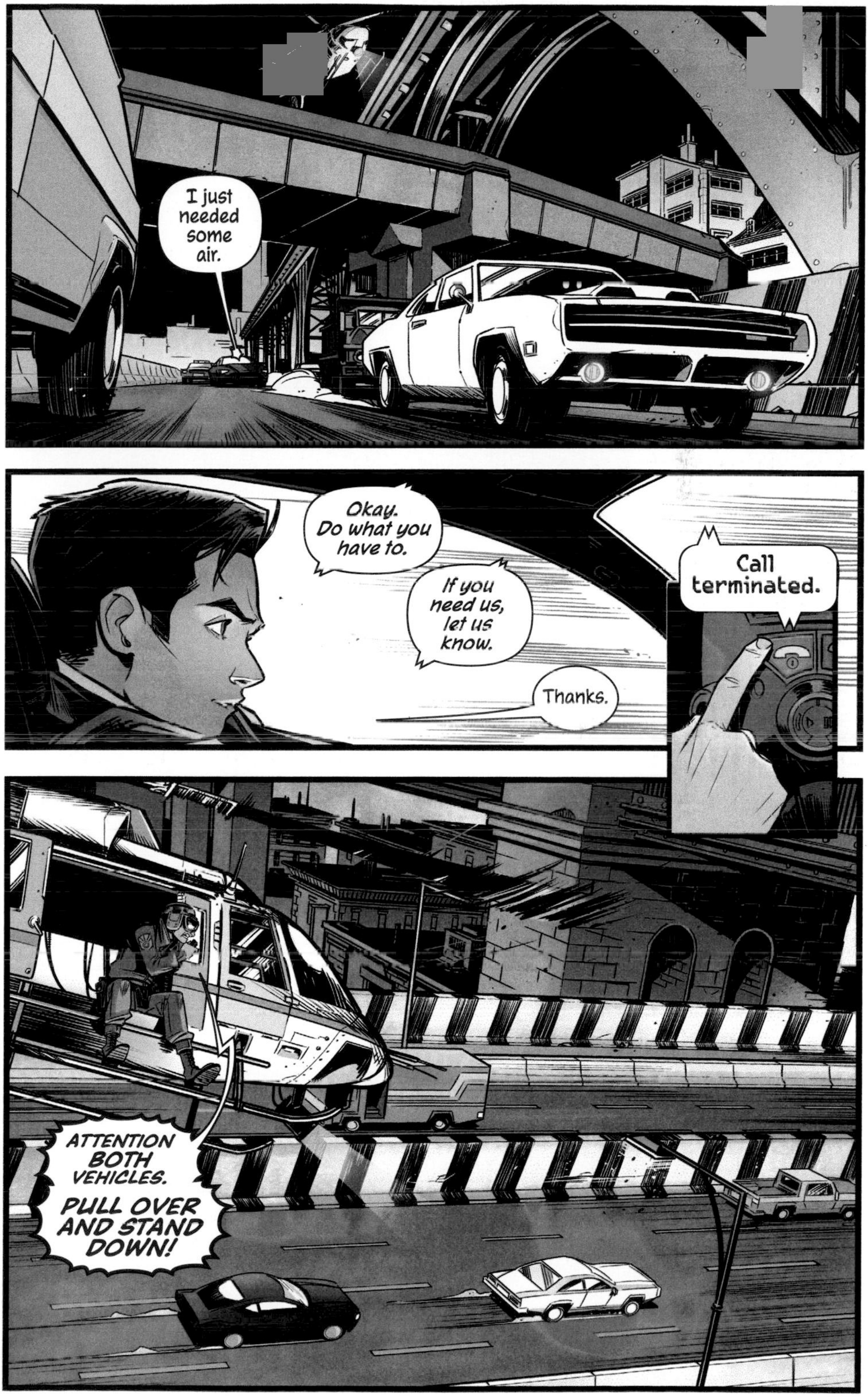
I just needed some air.
Okay. Do what you have to.
If you need us, let us know.
Thanks.
Call terminated.
ATTENTION BOTH VEHICLES.
PULL OVER AND STAND DOWN!

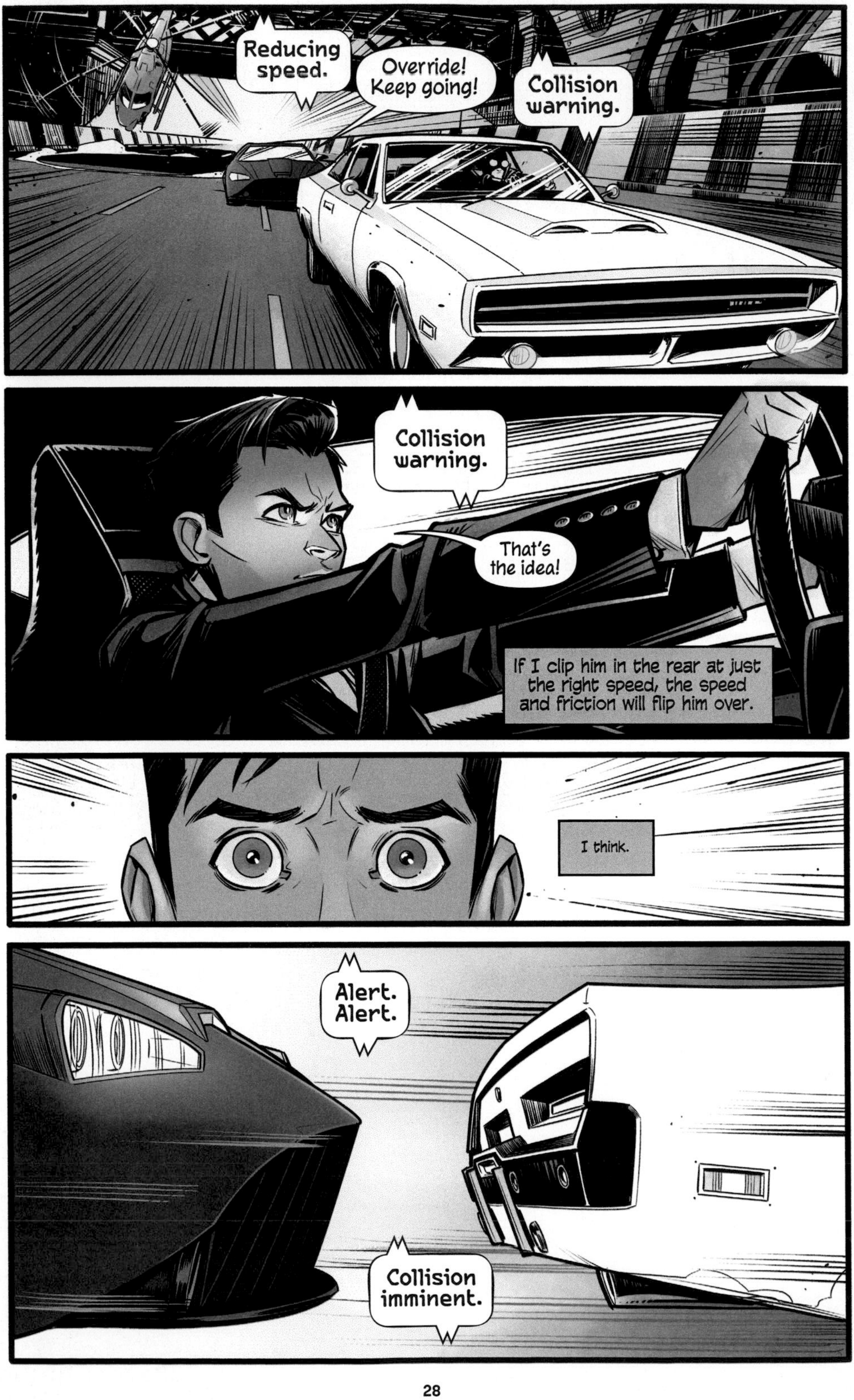
Reducing speed.
Override! Keep going!
Collision warning.
Collision warning.
That's the idea!
If I clip him in the rear at just the right speed, the speed and friction will flip him over.
I think.
Alert. Alert.
Collision imminent.

SCREEE

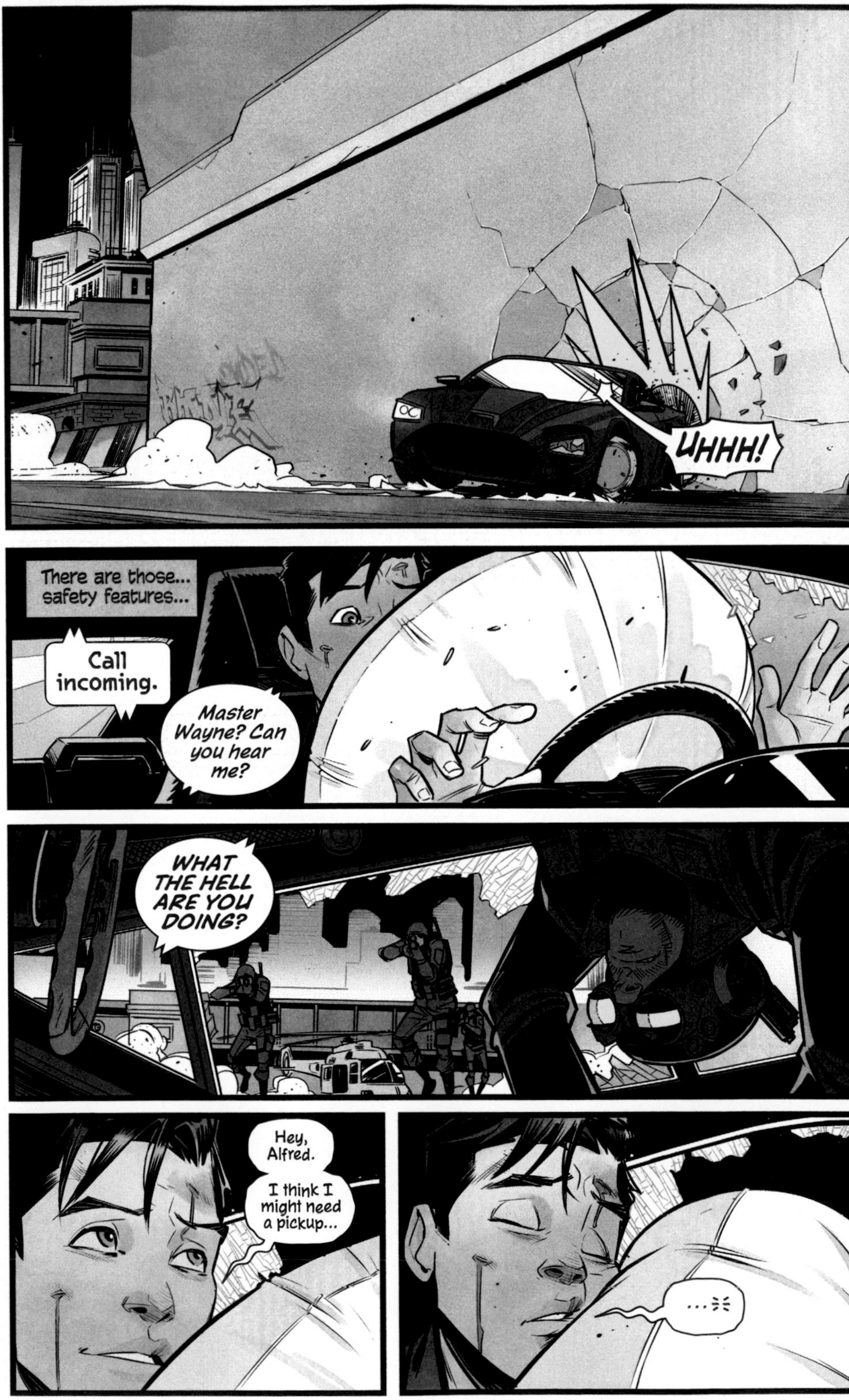
UHHH!
There are those... safety features...
Call incoming.
Master Wayne? Can you hear me?
WHAT THE HELL ARE YOU DOING?
Hey, Alfred.
I think I might need a pickup...
...

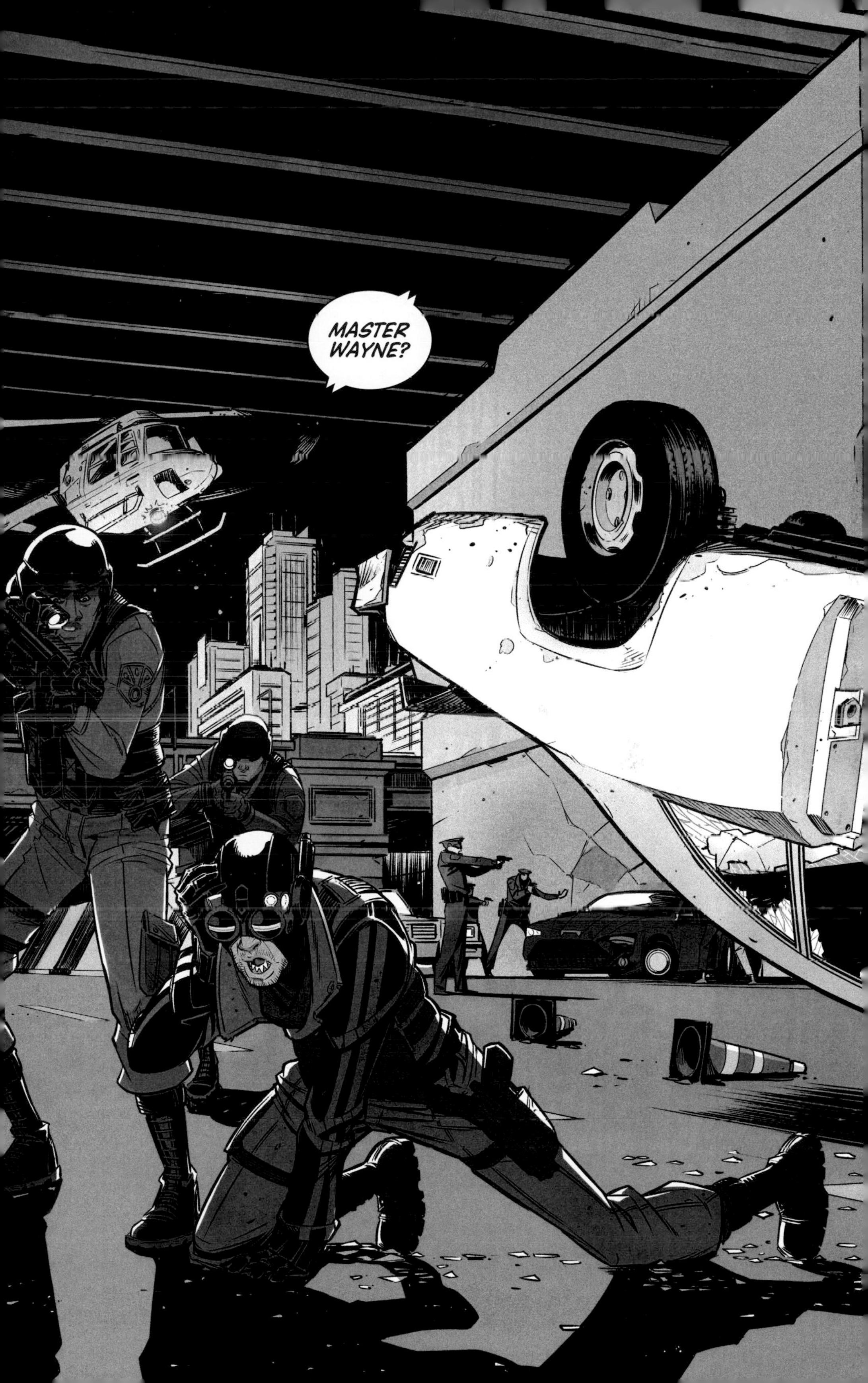
MASTER WAYNE?

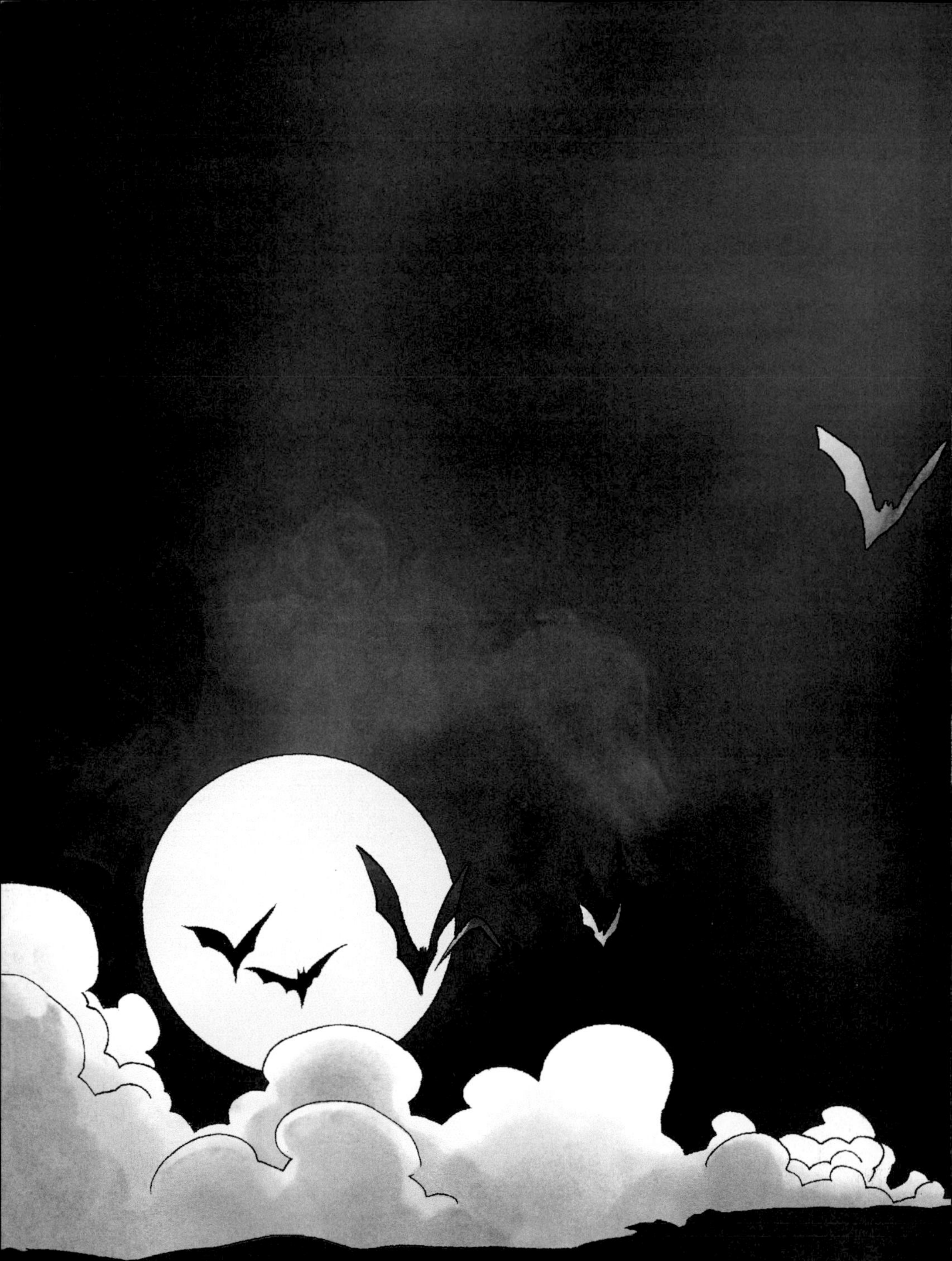

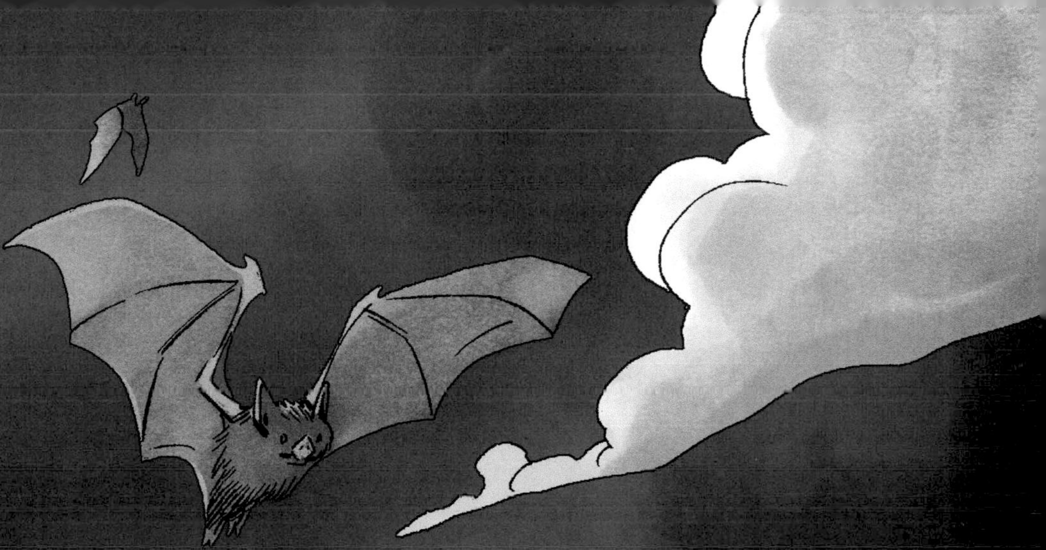

PART TWO

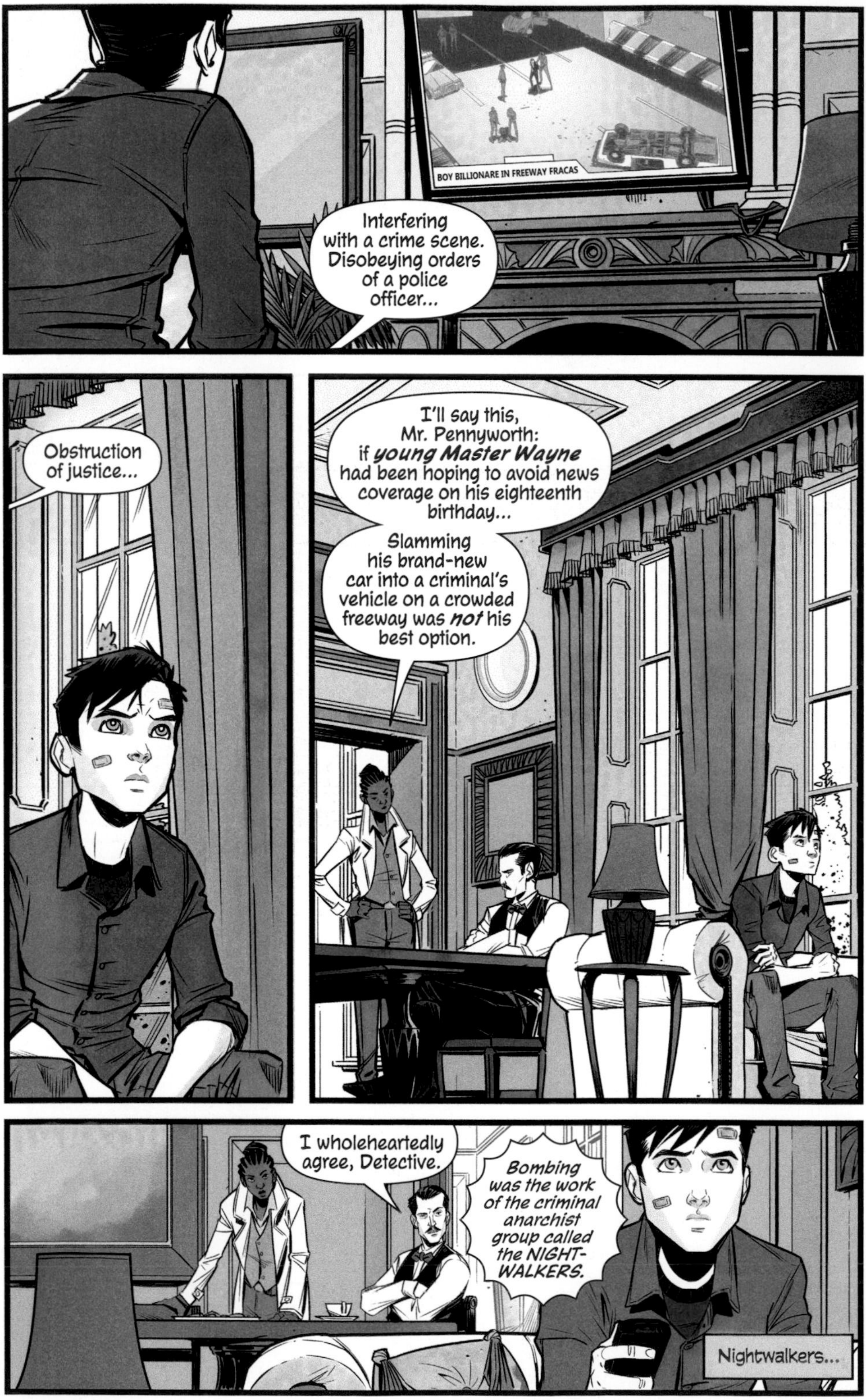
BOY BILLIONARE IN FREEWAY FRACAS
Interfering with a crime scene. Disobeying orders of a police officer...
Obstruction of justice...
I'll say this, Mr. Pennyworth: if *young Master Wayne* had been hoping to avoid news coverage on his eighteenth birthday...
Slamming his brand-new car into a criminal's vehicle on a crowded freeway was *not* his best option.
I wholeheartedly agree, Detective.
Bombing was the work of the criminal anarchist group called the NIGHT-WALKERS.
Nightwalkers...

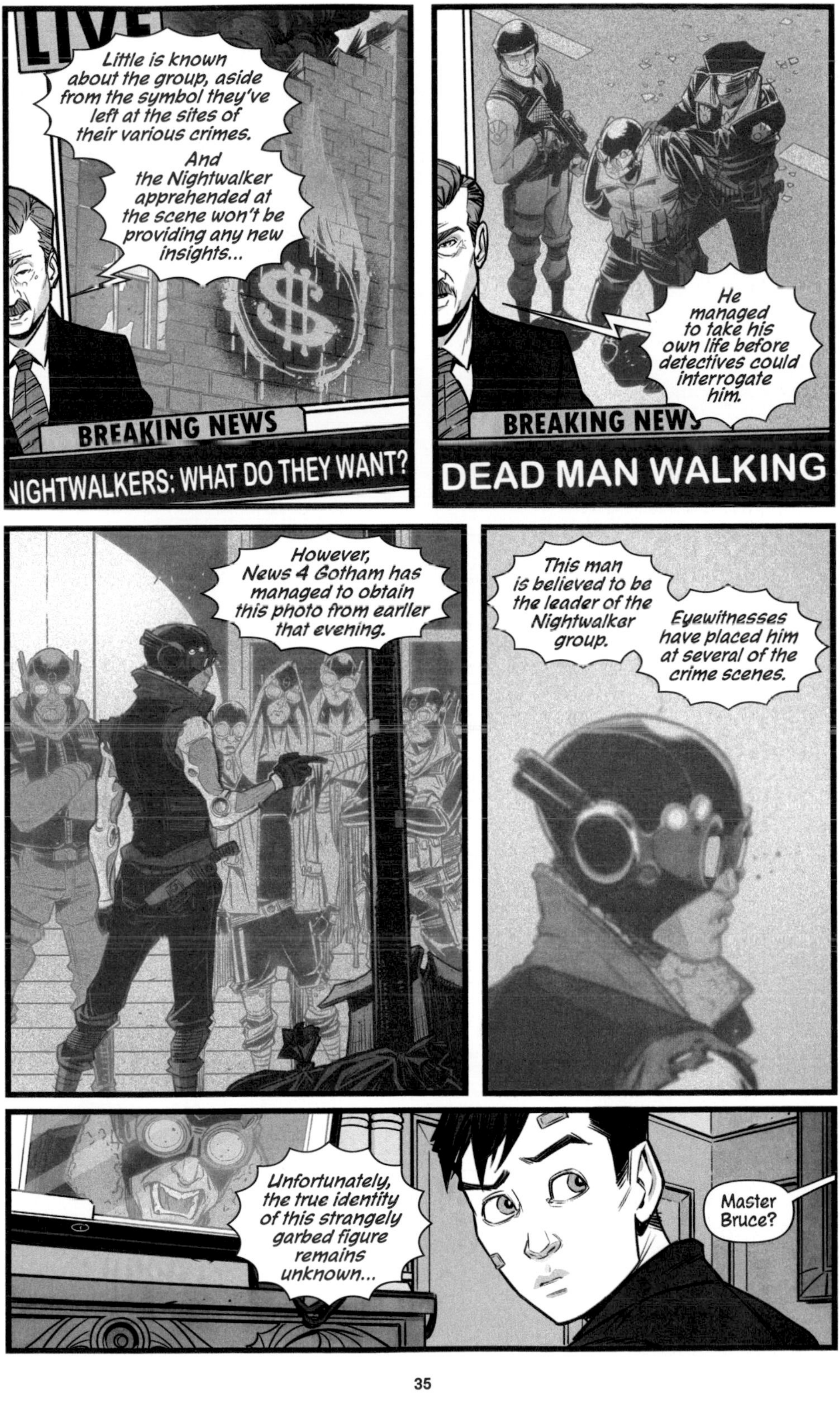
LIVE
Little is known about the group, aside from the symbol they've left at the sites of their various crimes.
And the Nightwalker apprehended at the scene won't be providing any new insights...
BREAKING NEWS
NIGHTWALKERS: WHAT DO THEY WANT?
He managed to take his own life before detectives could interrogate him.
BREAKING NEWS
DEAD MAN WALKING
However, News 4 Gotham has managed to obtain this photo from earlier that evening.
This man is believed to be the leader of the Nightwalker group.
Eyewitnesses have placed him at several of the crime scenes.
Unfortunately, the true identity of this strangely garbed figure remains unknown...
Master Bruce?

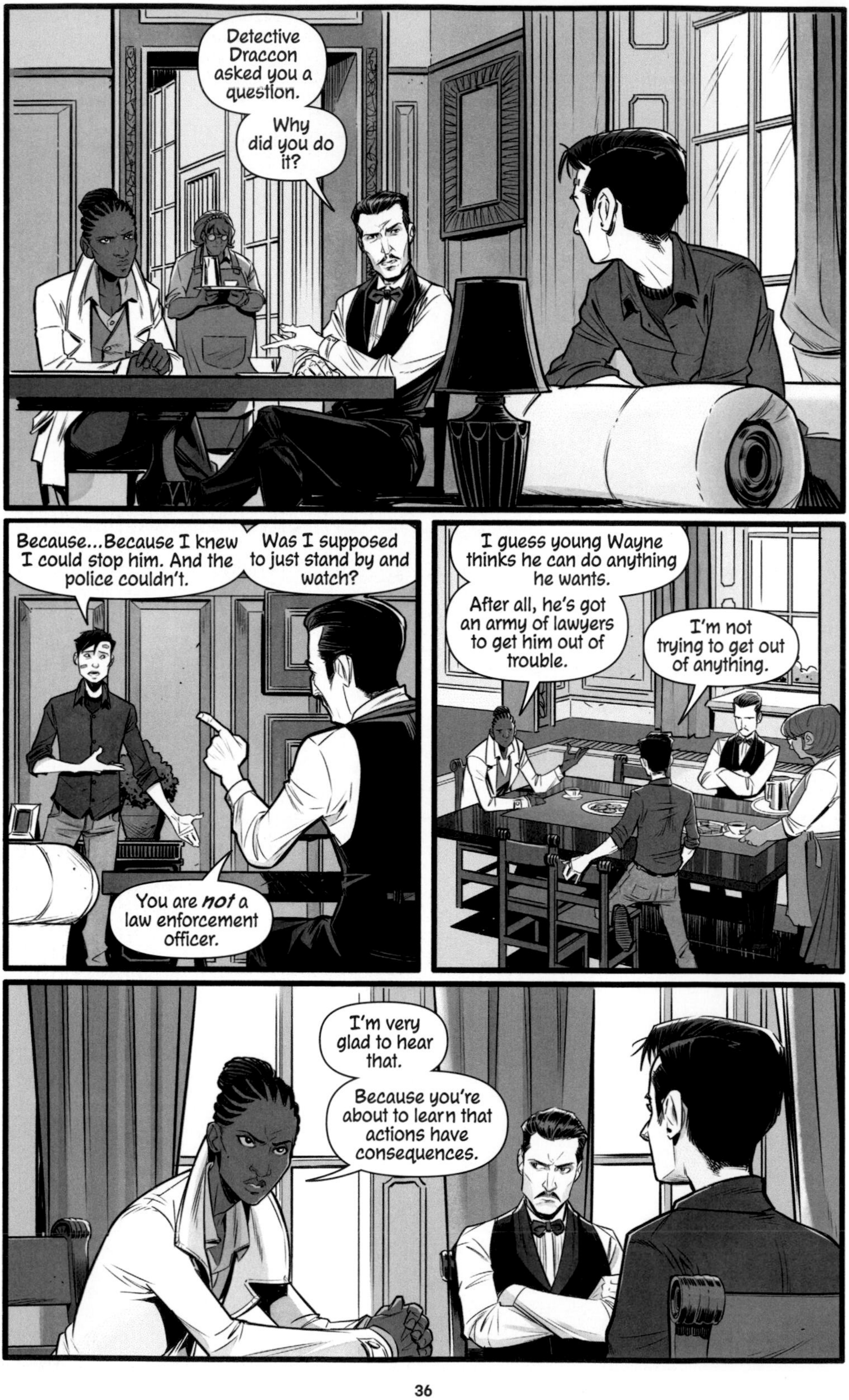
Detective Draccon asked you a question.
Why did you do it?
Because...Because I knew I could stop him. And the police couldn't.
Was I supposed to just stand by and watch?
You are *not* a law enforcement officer.
I guess young Wayne thinks he can do anything he wants.
After all, he's got an army of lawyers to get him out of trouble.
I'm not trying to get out of anything.
I'm very glad to hear that.
Because you're about to learn that actions have consequences.

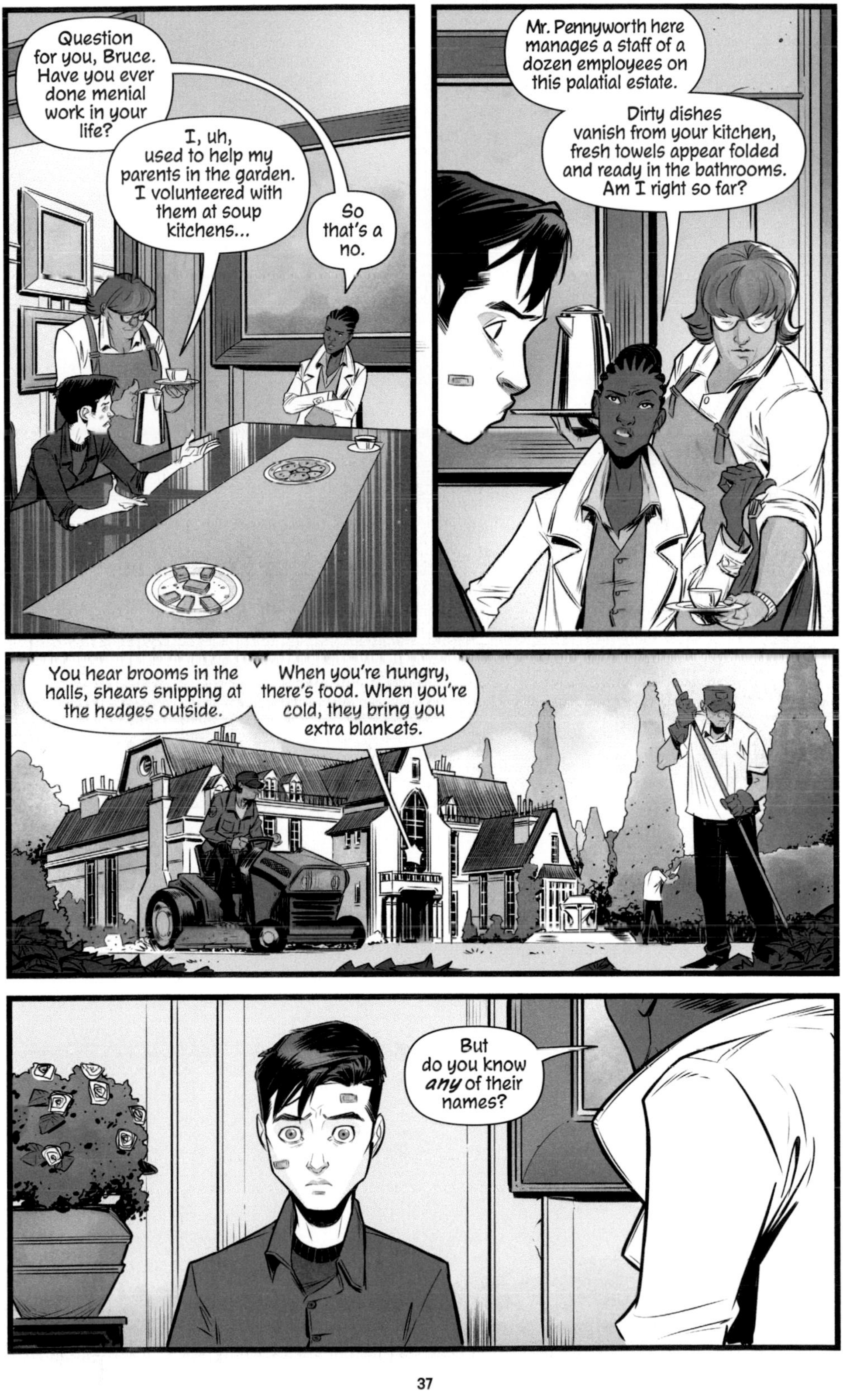
Question for you, Bruce. Have you ever done menial work in your life?
I, uh, used to help my parents in the garden. I volunteered with them at soup kitchens...
So that's a no.
Mr. Pennyworth here manages a staff of a dozen employees on this palatial estate.
Dirty dishes vanish from your kitchen, fresh towels appear folded and ready in the bathrooms. Am I right so far?
You hear brooms in the halls, shears snipping at the hedges outside.
When you're hungry, there's food. When you're cold, they bring you extra blankets.
But do you know *any* of their names?

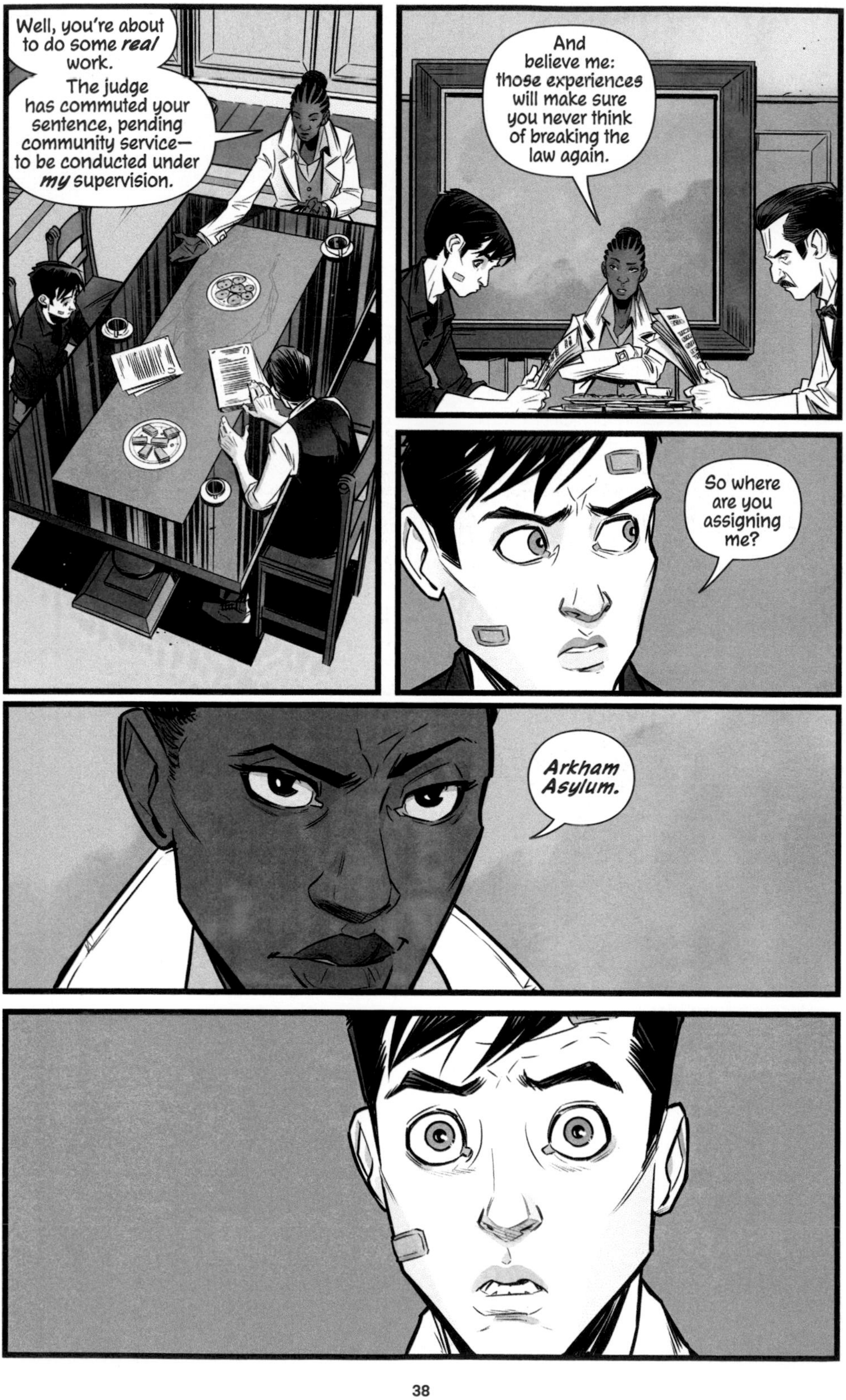
Well, you're about to do some *real* work.
The judge has commuted your sentence, pending community service— to be conducted under *my* supervision.
And believe me: those experiences will make sure you never think of breaking the law again.
So where are you assigning me?
Arkham Asylum.

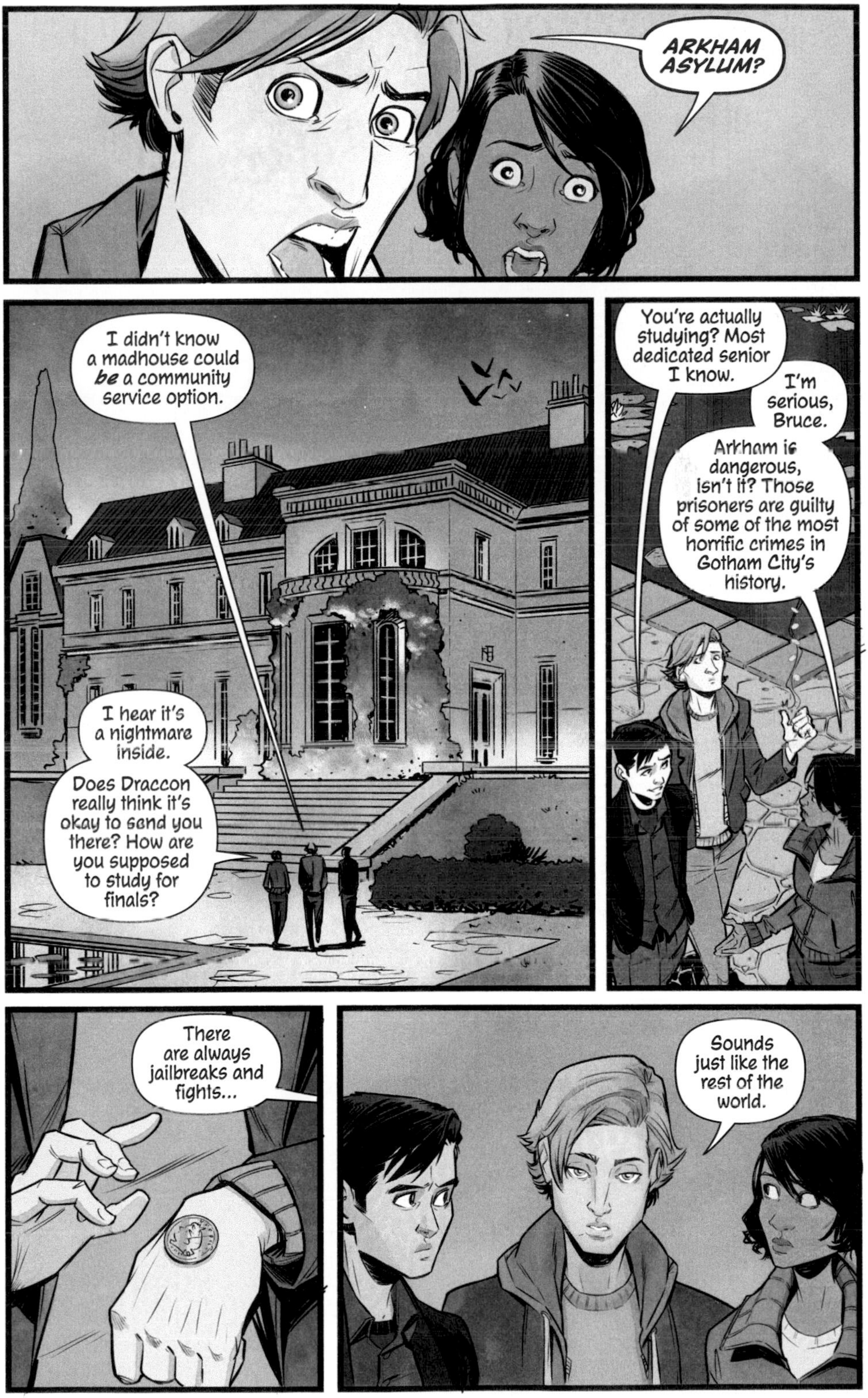
ARKHAM ASYLUM?
I didn't know a madhouse could *be* a community service option.
I hear it's a nightmare inside.
Does Draccon really think it's okay to send you there? How are you supposed to study for finals?
You're actually studying? Most dedicated senior I know.
I'm serious, Bruce.
Arkham is dangerous, isn't it? Those prisoners are guilty of some of the most horrific crimes in Gotham City's history.
There are always jailbreaks and fights...
Sounds just like the rest of the world.

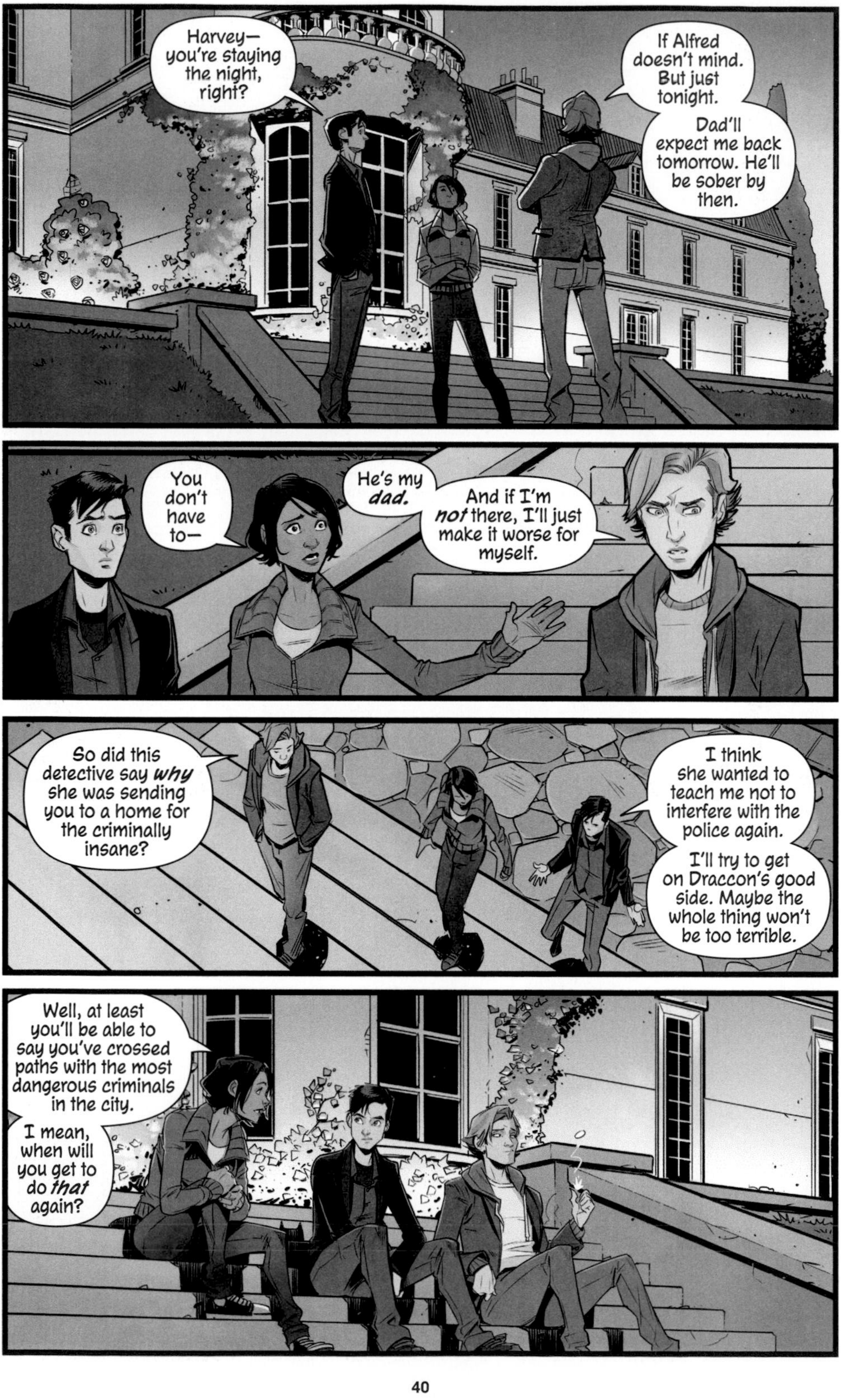
Harvey— you're staying the night, right?
If Alfred doesn't mind. But just tonight.
Dad'll expect me back tomorrow. He'll be sober by then.
You don't have to—
He's my *dad.*
And if I'm *not* there, I'll just make it worse for myself.
So did this detective say *why* she was sending you to a home for the criminally insane?
I think she wanted to teach me not to interfere with the police again.
I'll try to get on Draccon's good side. Maybe the whole thing won't be too terrible.
Well, at least you'll be able to say you've crossed paths with the most dangerous criminals in the city.
I mean, when will you get to do *that* again?

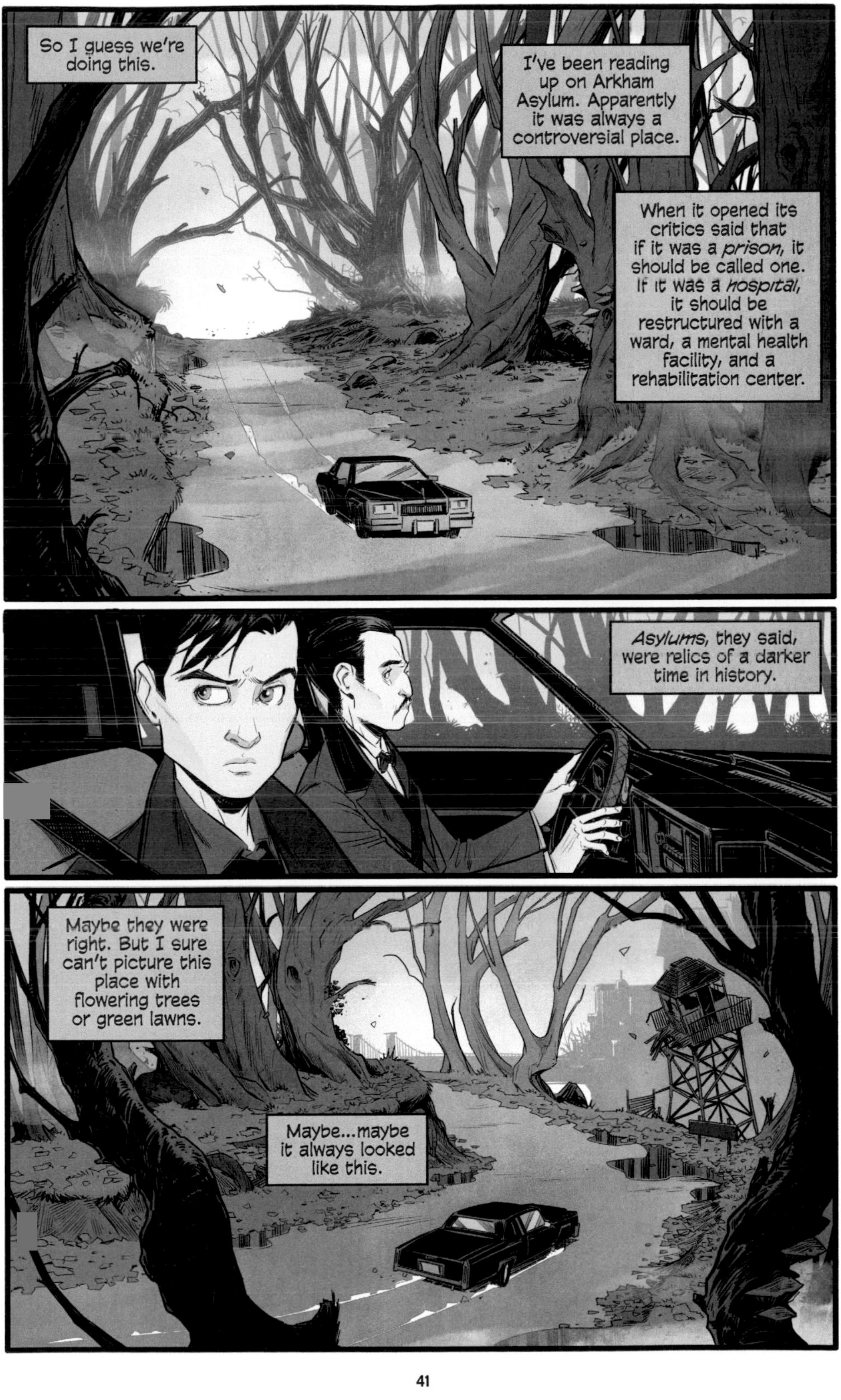
So I guess we're doing this.
I've been reading up on Arkham Asylum. Apparently it was always a controversial place.
When it opened its critics said that if it was a *prison*, it should be called one. If it was a *hospital*, it should be restructured with a ward, a mental health facility, and a rehabilitation center.
Asylums, they said, were relics of a darker time in history.
Maybe they were right. But I sure can't picture this place with flowering trees or green lawns.
Maybe...maybe it always looked like this.

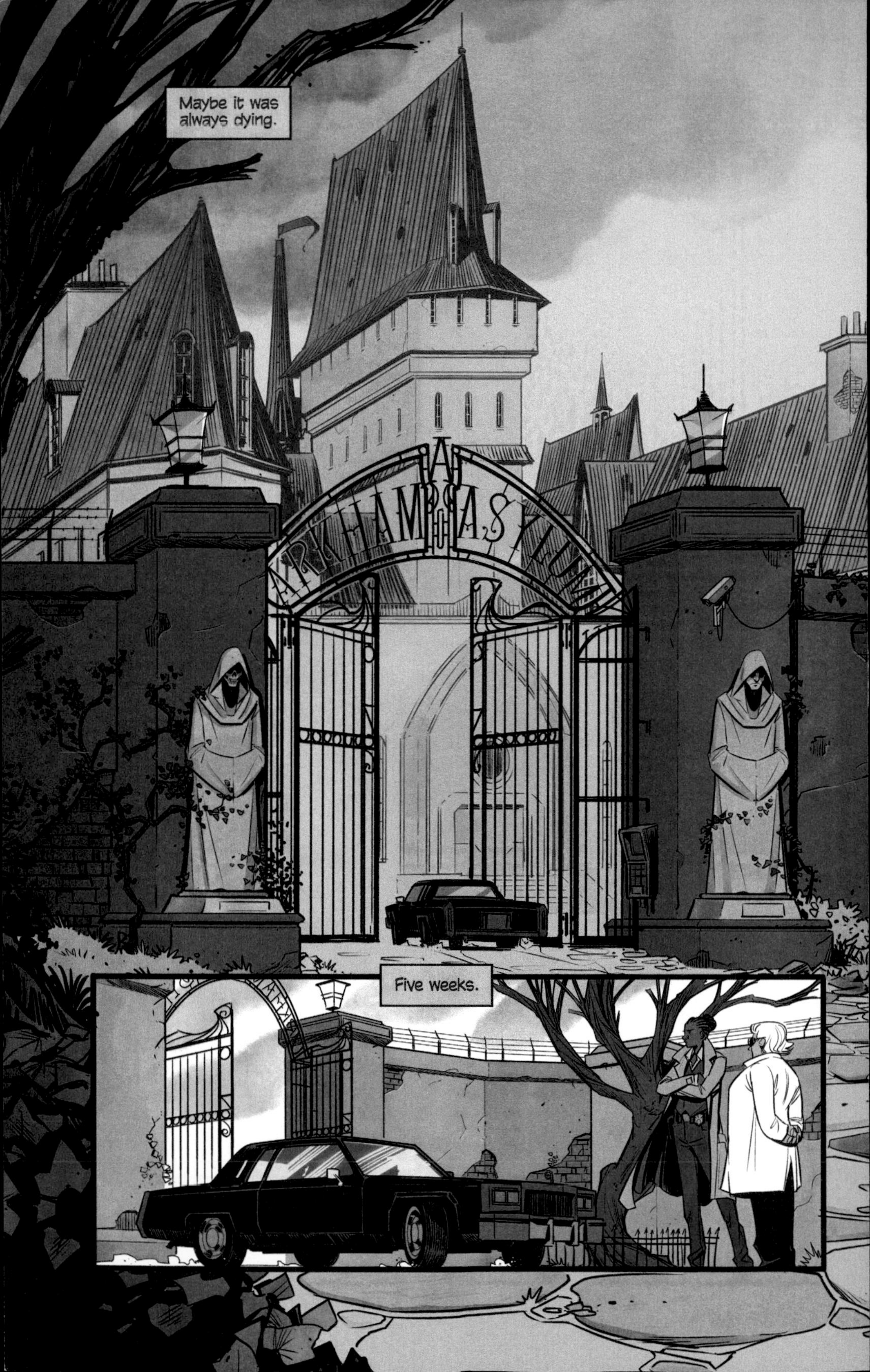
Maybe it was always dying.
ARKHAM ASYLUM
Five weeks.

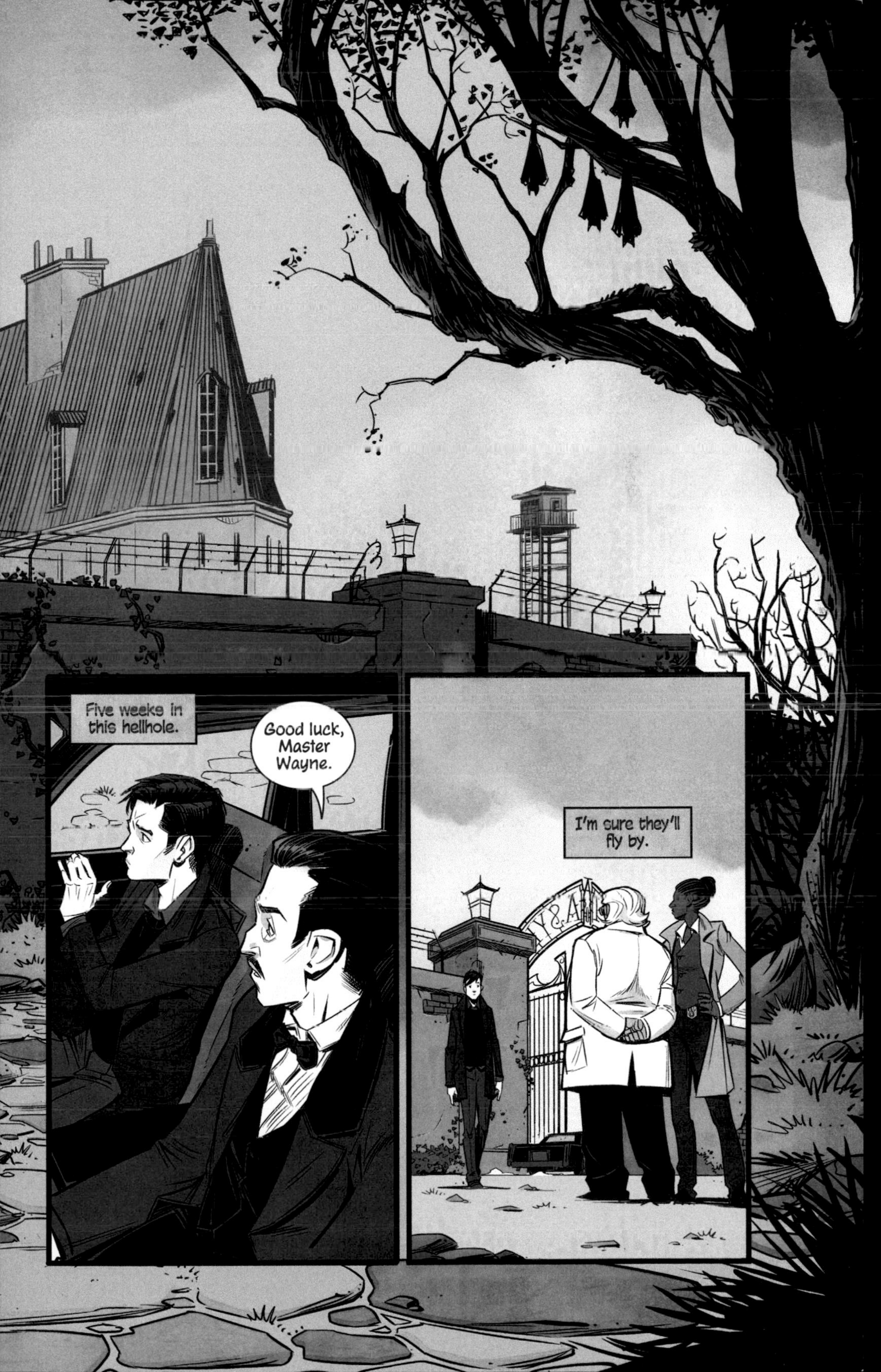

Five weeks in this hellhole.
Good luck, Master Wayne.
I'm sure they'll fly by.

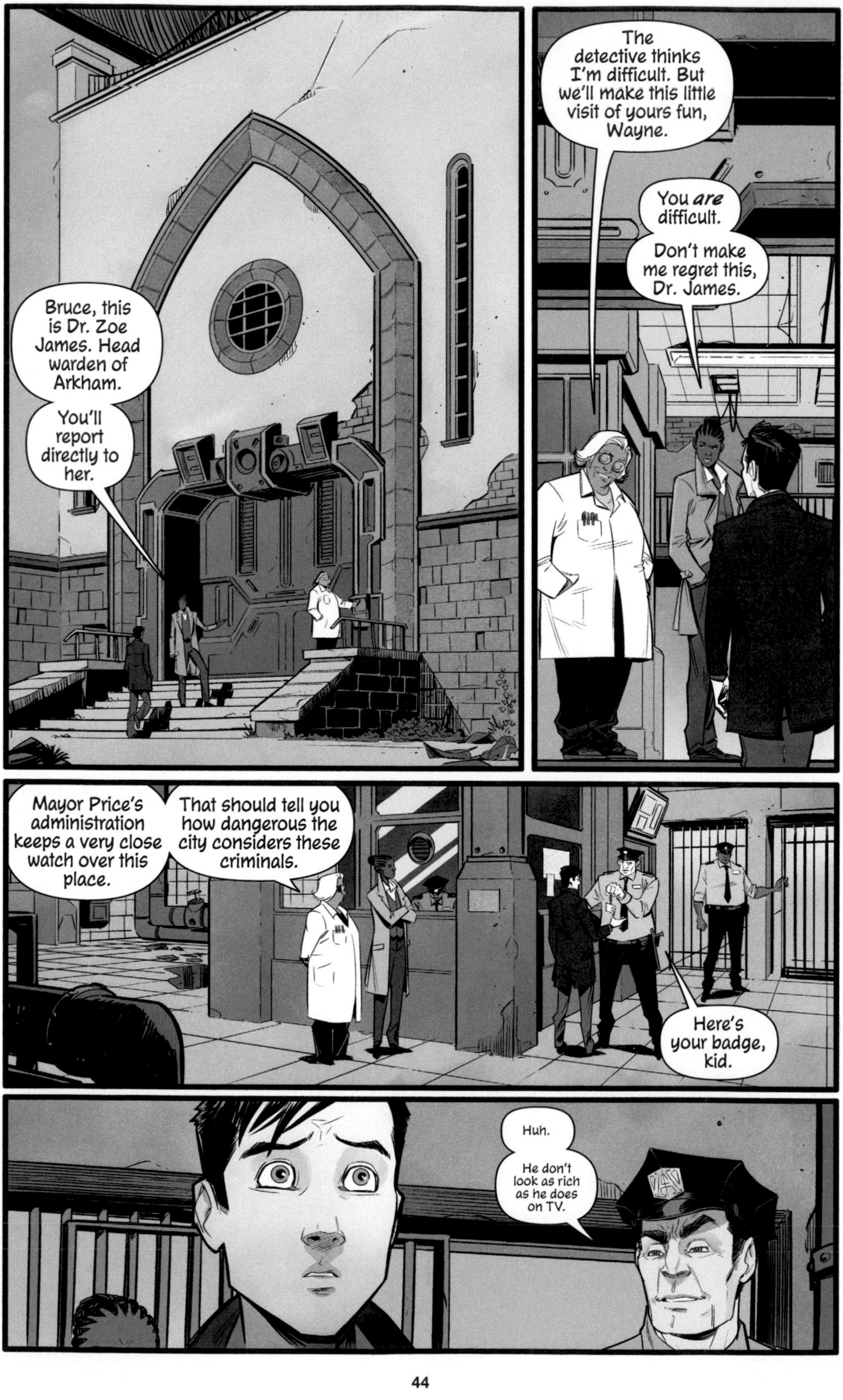
Bruce, this is Dr. Zoe James. Head warden of Arkham.
You'll report directly to her.
The detective thinks I'm difficult. But we'll make this little visit of yours fun, Wayne.
You *are* difficult.
Don't make me regret this, Dr. James.
Mayor Price's administration keeps a very close watch over this place.
That should tell you how dangerous the city considers these criminals.
Here's your badge, kid.
Huh.
He don't look as rich as he does on TV.

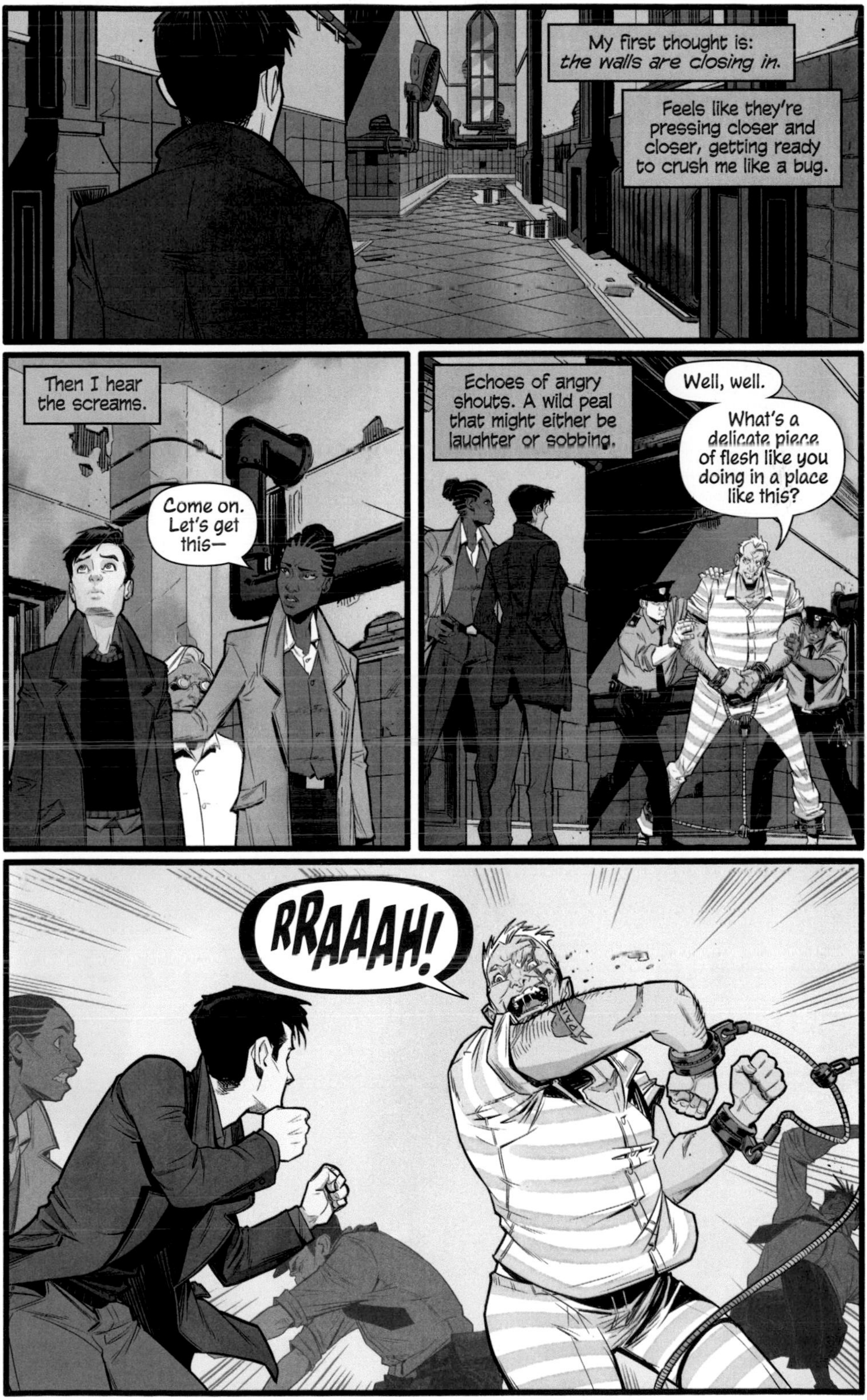
My first thought is: *the walls are closing in.*
Feels like they're pressing closer and closer, getting ready to crush me like a bug.
Then I hear the screams.
Come on. Let's get this—
Echoes of angry shouts. A wild peal that might either be laughter or sobbing.
Well, well.
What's a delicate piece of flesh like you doing in a place like this?
RRAAAH!

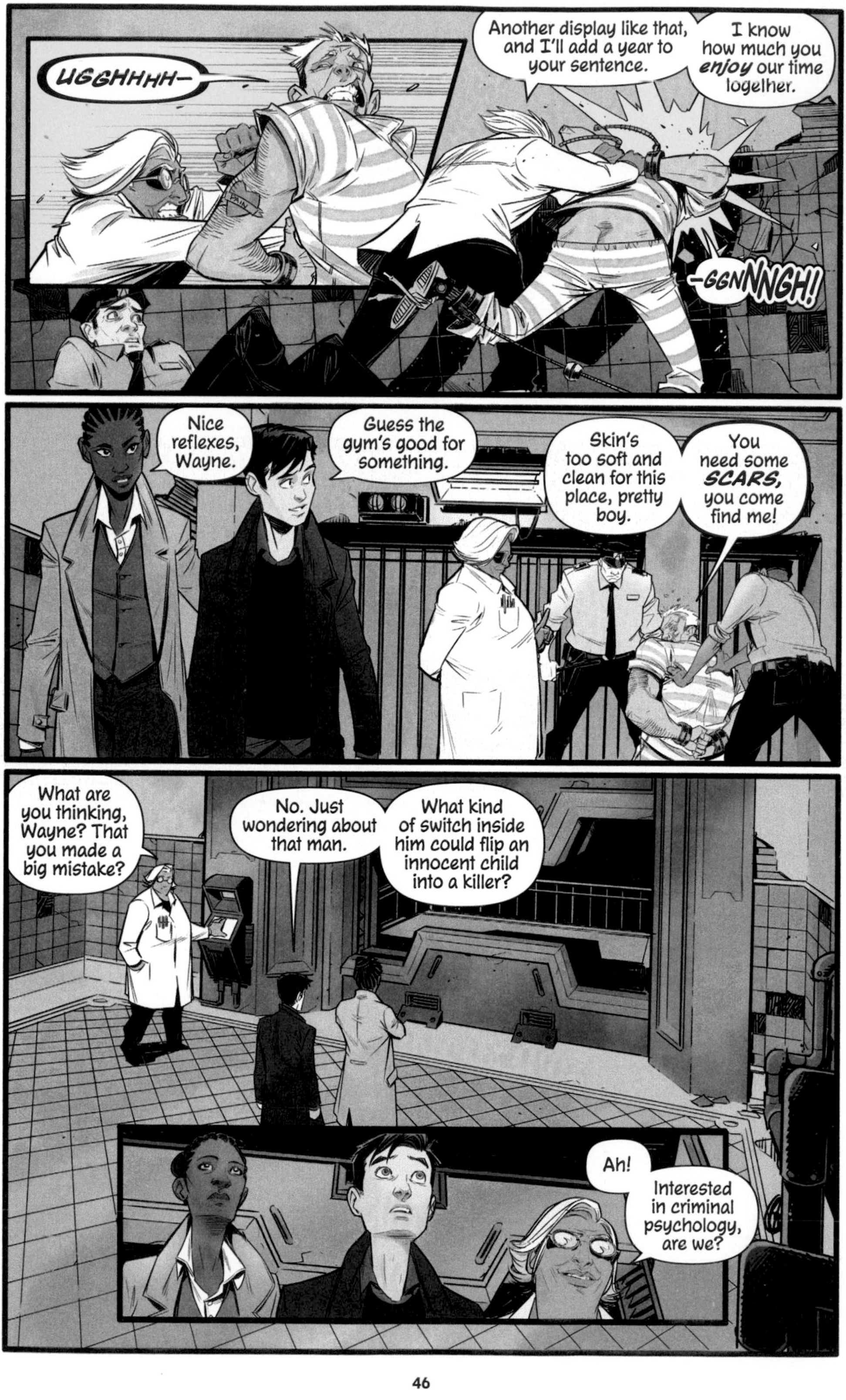
UGGHHHH—
Another display like that, and I'll add a year to your sentence.
I know how much you *enjoy* our time together.
—GGNNNGH!
Nice reflexes, Wayne.
Guess the gym's good for something.
Skin's too soft and clean for this place, pretty boy.
You need some **SCARS,** you come find me!
What are you thinking, Wayne? That you made a big mistake?
No. Just wondering about that man.
What kind of switch inside him could flip an innocent child into a killer?
Ah!
Interested in criminal psychology, are we?

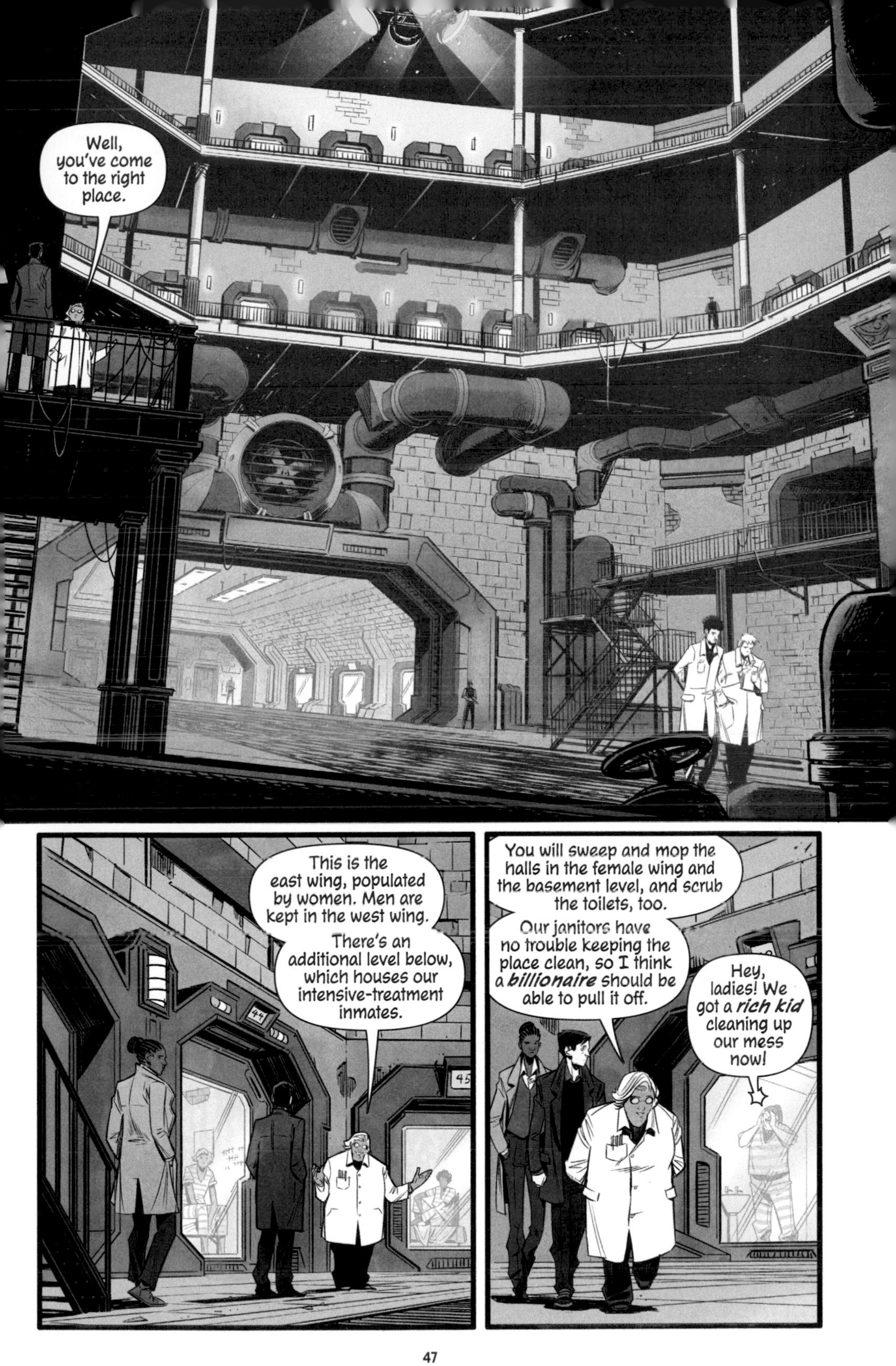
Well, you've come to the right place.
This is the east wing, populated by women. Men are kept in the west wing.
There's an additional level below, which houses our intensive-treatment inmates.
44
45
You will sweep and mop the halls in the female wing and the basement level, and scrub the toilets, too.
Our janitors have no trouble keeping the place clean, so I think a ***billionaire*** should be able to pull it off.
Hey, ladies! We got a ***rich kid*** cleaning up our mess now!

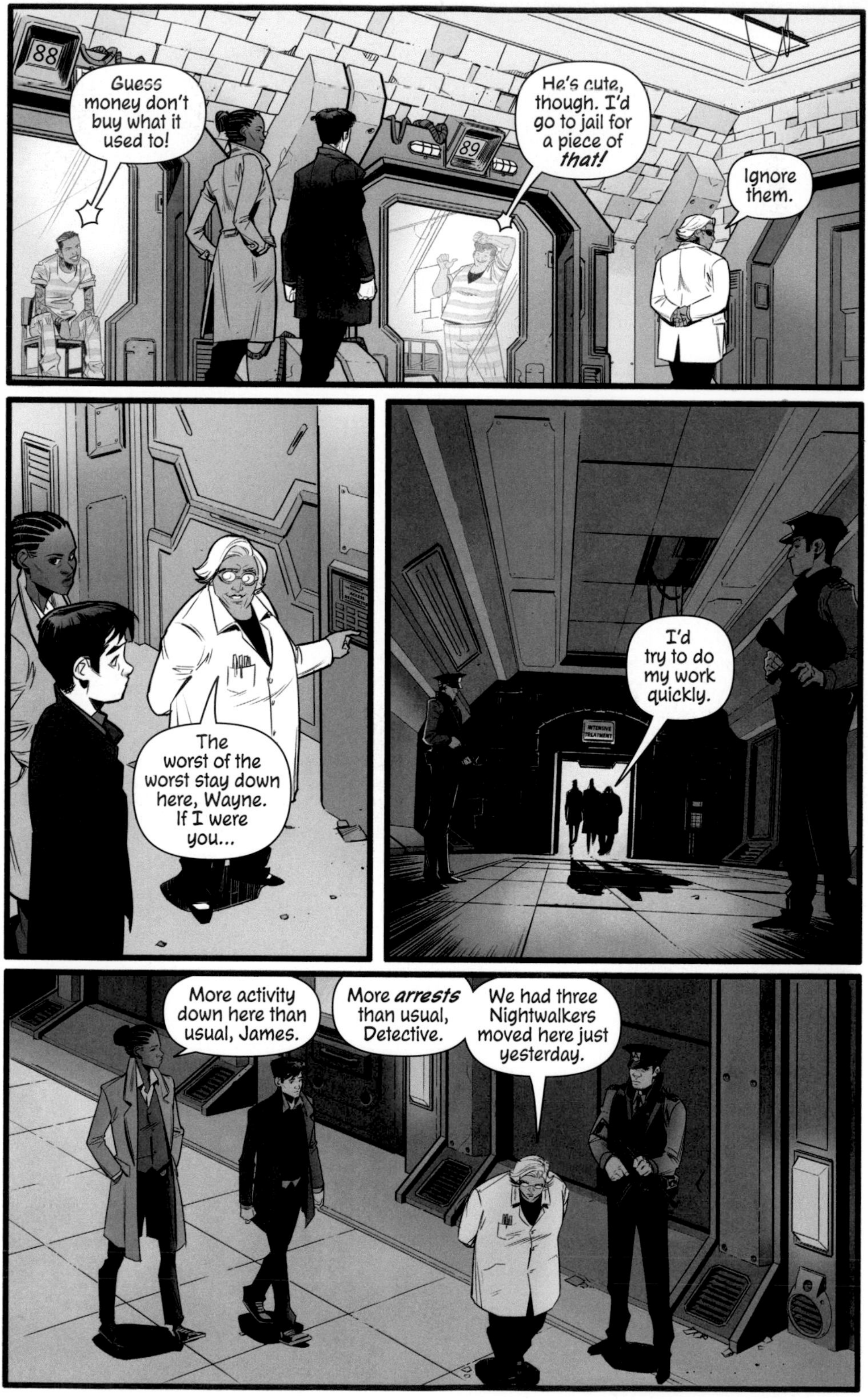
Guess money don't buy what it used to!
He's cute, though. I'd go to jail for a piece of *that!*
Ignore them.
88
89
The worst of the worst stay down here, Wayne. If I were you...
I'd try to do my work quickly.
INTENSIVE TREATMENT
More activity down here than usual, James.
More *arrests* than usual, Detective.
We had three Nightwalkers moved here just yesterday.

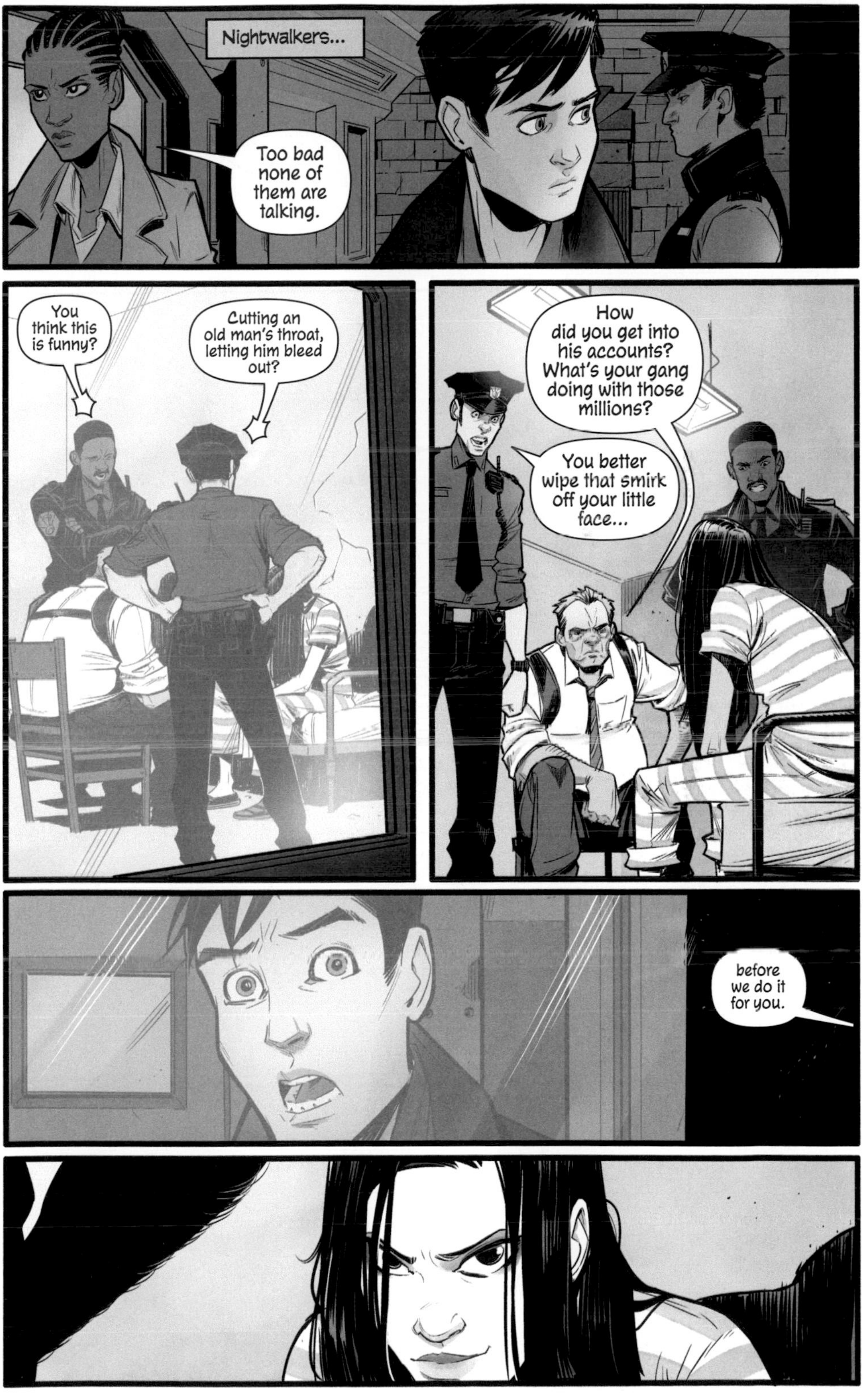
Nightwalkers...
Too bad none of them are talking.
You think this is funny?
Cutting an old man's throat, letting him bleed out?
How did you get into his accounts? What's your gang doing with those millions?
You better wipe that smirk off your little face...
before we do it for you.

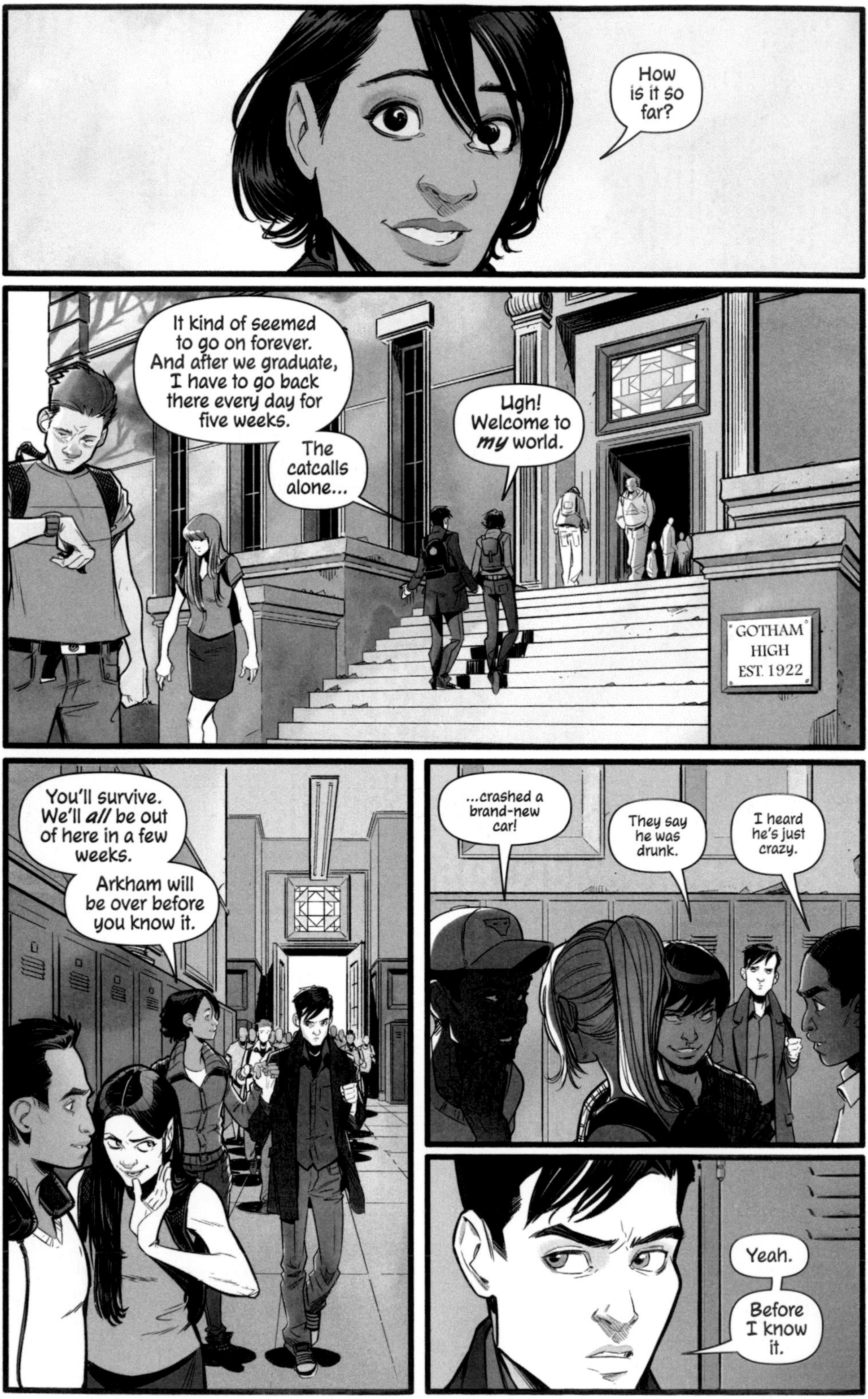
How is it so far?
It kind of seemed to go on forever. And after we graduate, I have to go back there every day for five weeks.
The catcalls alone...
Ugh! Welcome to *my* world.
GOTHAM HIGH EST. 1922
You'll survive. We'll *all* be out of here in a few weeks.
Arkham will be over before you know it.
...crashed a brand-new car!
They say he was drunk.
I heard he's just crazy.
Yeah.
Before I know it.

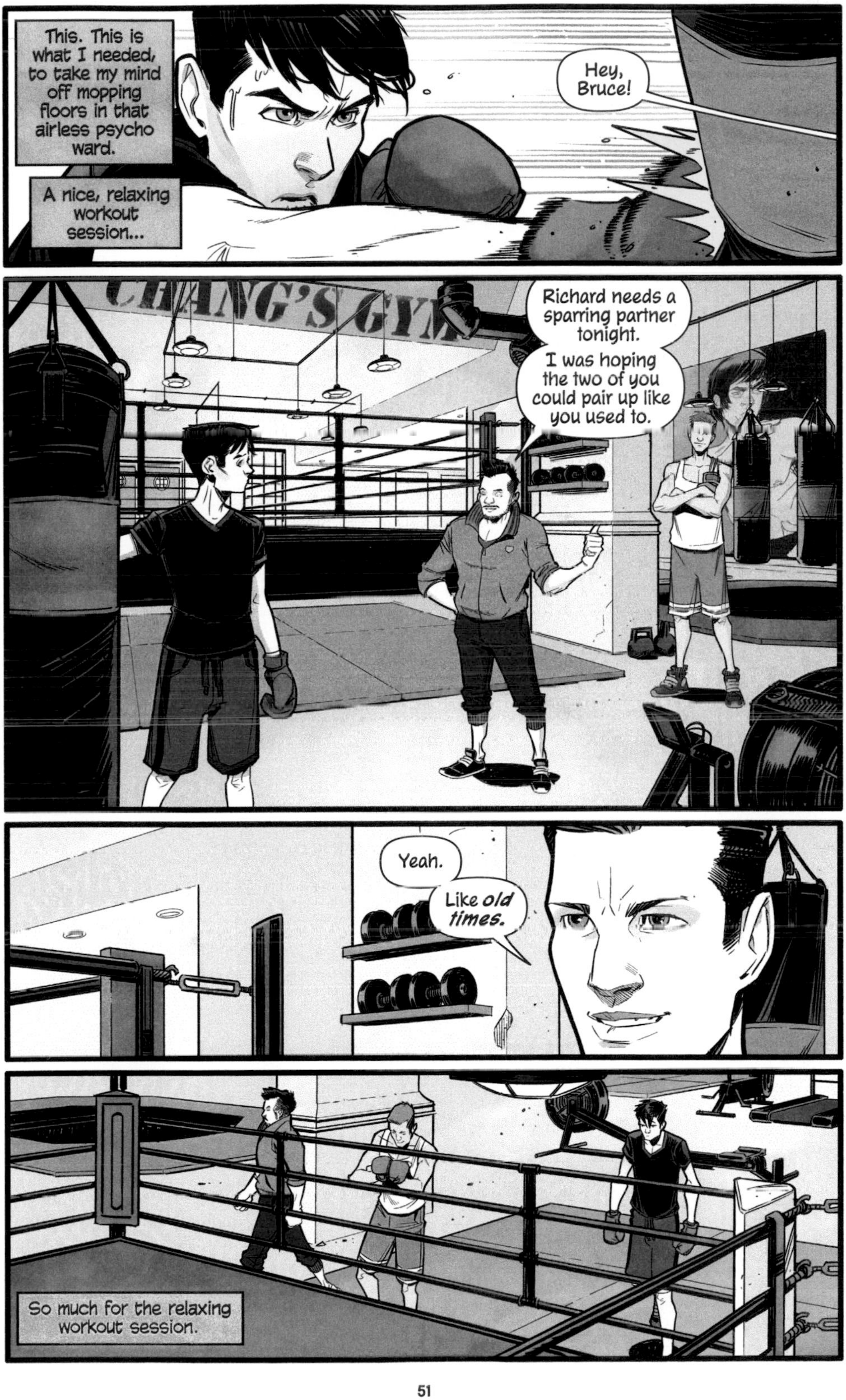
This. This is what I needed, to take my mind off mopping floors in that airless psycho ward.
A nice, relaxing workout session...
Hey, Bruce!
CHANG'S GYM
Richard needs a sparring partner tonight.
I was hoping the two of you could pair up like you used to.
Yeah.
Like *old times.*
So much for the relaxing workout session.

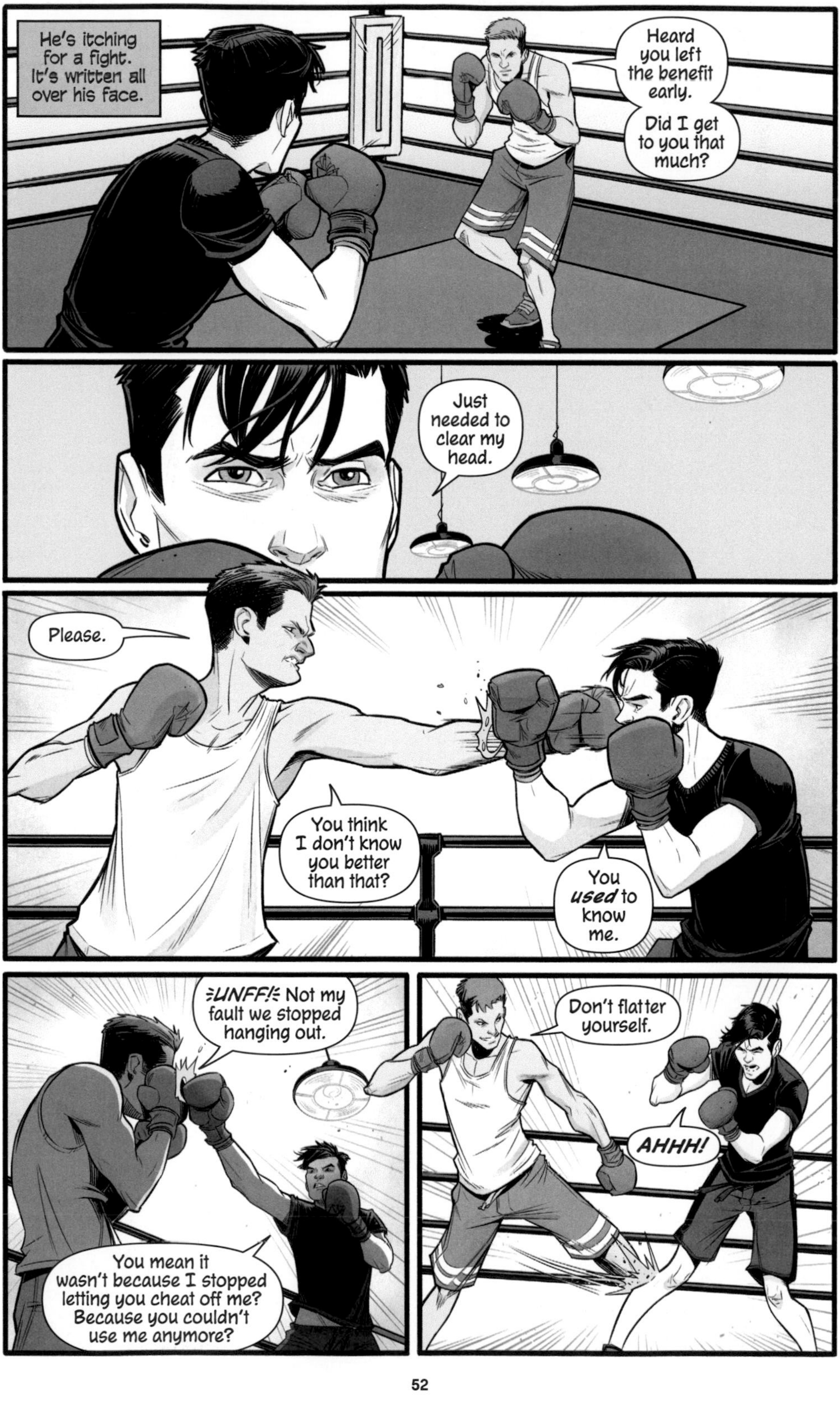
He's itching for a fight. It's written all over his face.
Heard you left the benefit early.
Did I get to you that much?
Just needed to clear my head.
Please.
You think I don't know you better than that?
You *used* to know me.
UNFF! Not my fault we stopped hanging out.
You mean it wasn't because I stopped letting you cheat off me? Because you couldn't use me anymore?
Don't flatter yourself.
AHHH!

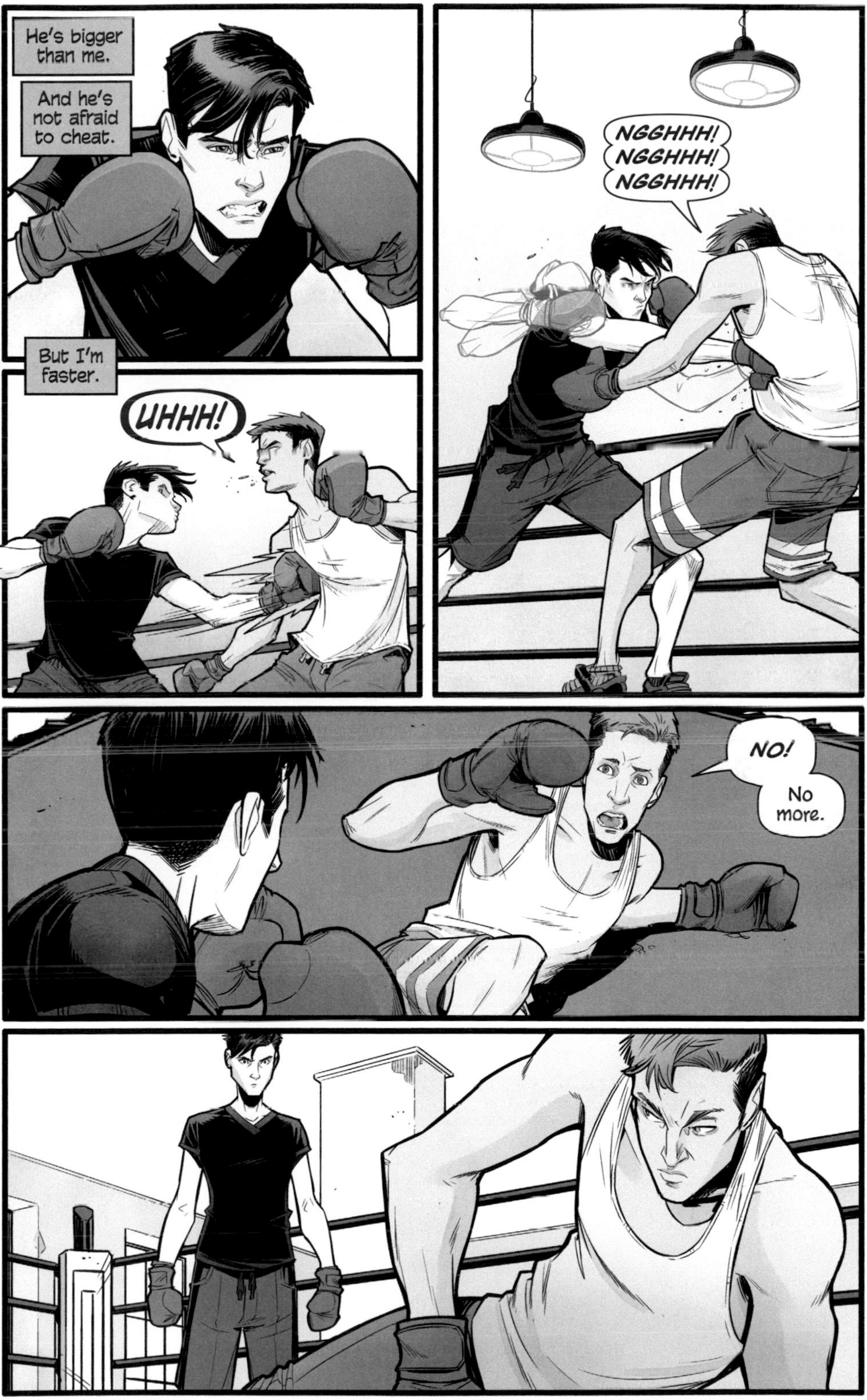
He's bigger than me.
And he's not afraid to cheat.
But I'm faster.
UHHH!
NGGHHH! NGGHHH! NGGHHH!
NO!
No more.

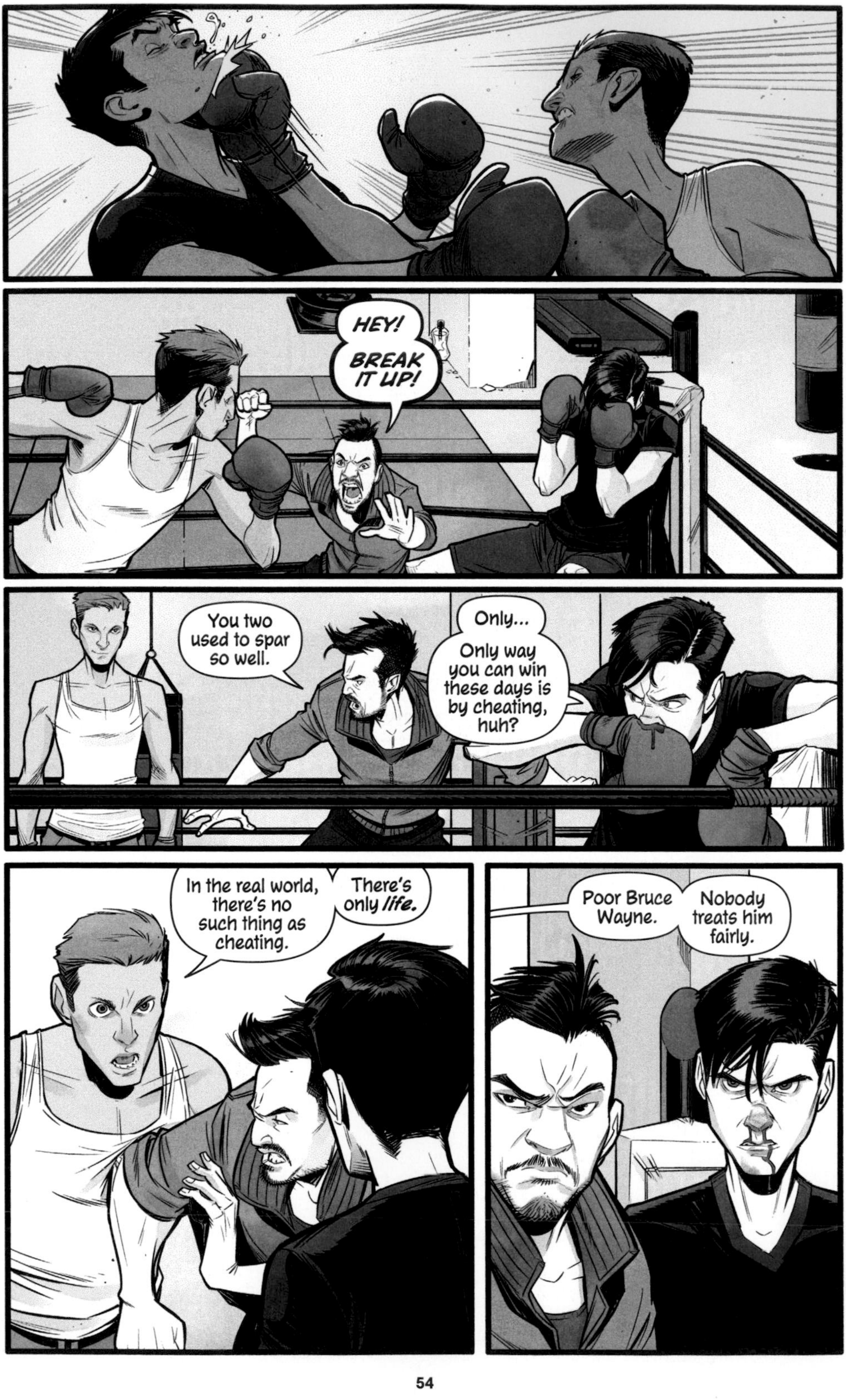
HEY!
BREAK IT UP!
You two used to spar so well.
Only...
Only way you can win these days is by cheating, huh?
In the real world, there's no such thing as cheating.
There's only *life.*
Poor Bruce Wayne.
Nobody treats him fairly.

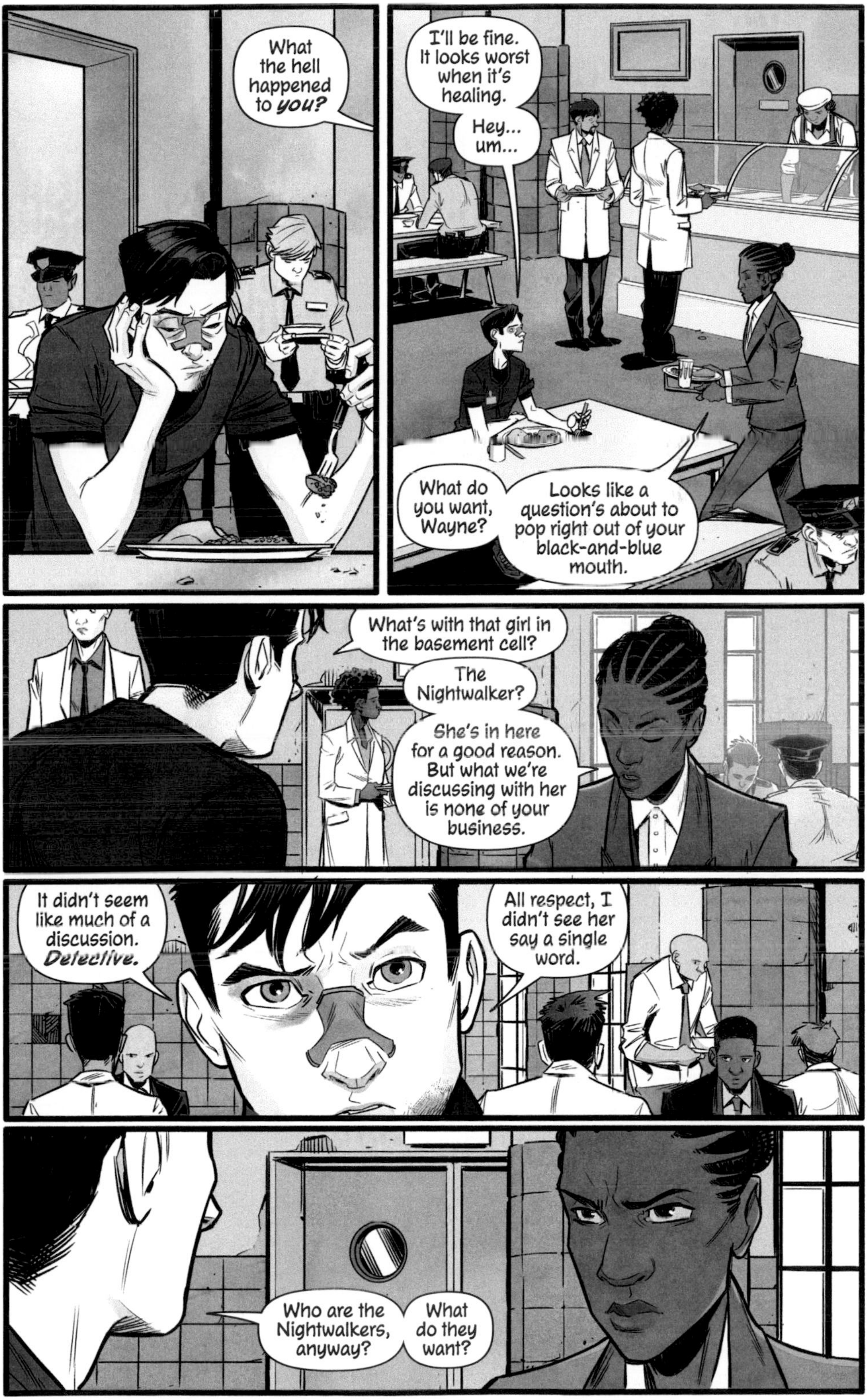

What the hell happened to *you?*
I'll be fine. It looks worst when it's healing.
Hey... um...
What do you want, Wayne?
Looks like a question's about to pop right out of your black-and-blue mouth.
What's with that girl in the basement cell?
The Nightwalker?
She's in here for a good reason. But what we're discussing with her is none of your business.
It didn't seem like much of a discussion. *Detective.*
All respect, I didn't see her say a single word.
Who are the Nightwalkers, anyway?
What do they want?

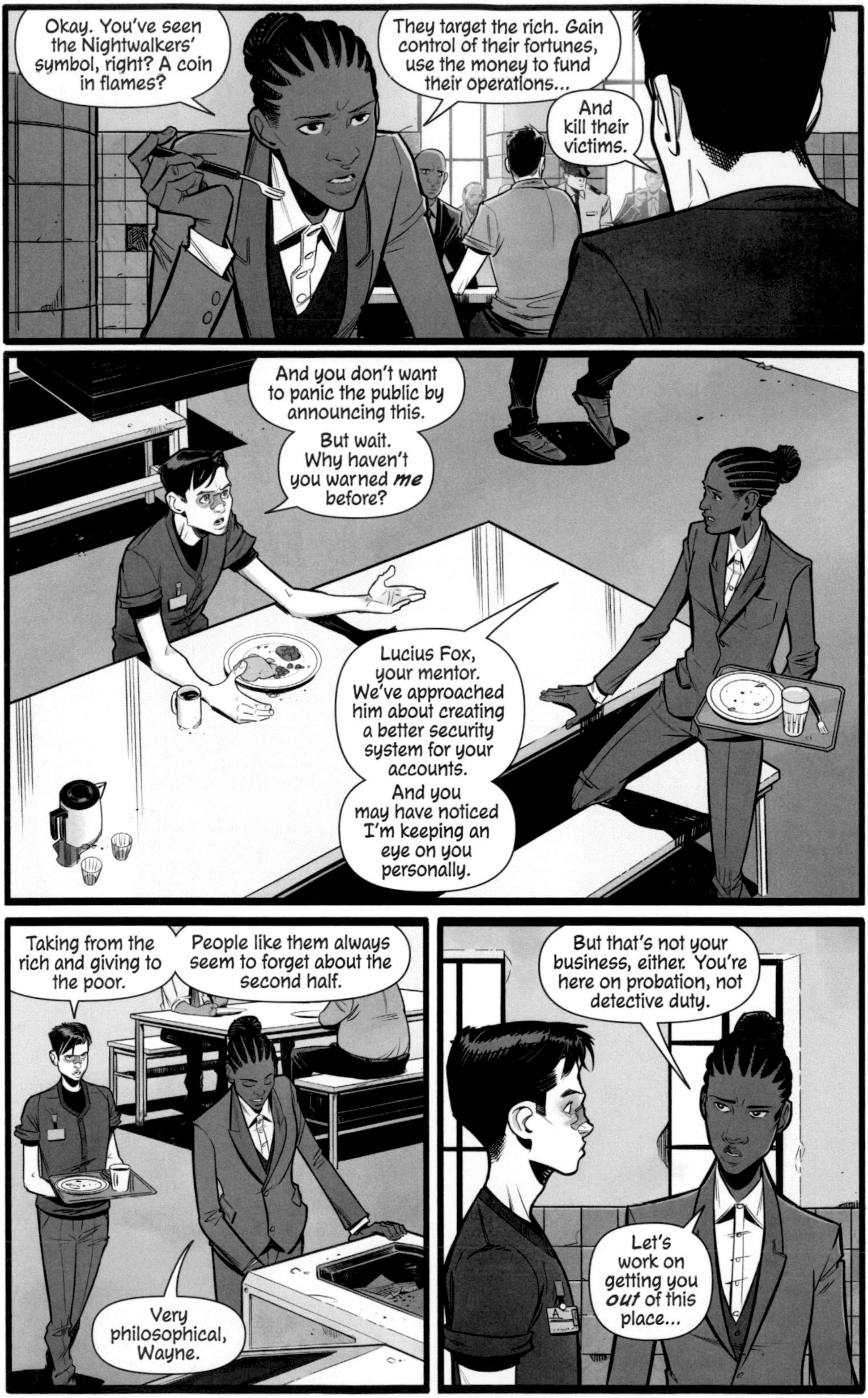
Okay. You've seen the Nightwalkers' symbol, right? A coin in flames?
They target the rich. Gain control of their fortunes, use the money to fund their operations...
And kill their victims.
And you don't want to panic the public by announcing this.
But wait. Why haven't you warned *me* before?
Lucius Fox, your mentor. We've approached him about creating a better security system for your accounts.
And you may have noticed I'm keeping an eye on you personally.
Taking from the rich and giving to the poor.
People like them always seem to forget about the second half.
Very philosophical, Wayne.
But that's not your business, either. You're here on probation, not detective duty.
Let's work on getting you *out* of this place...

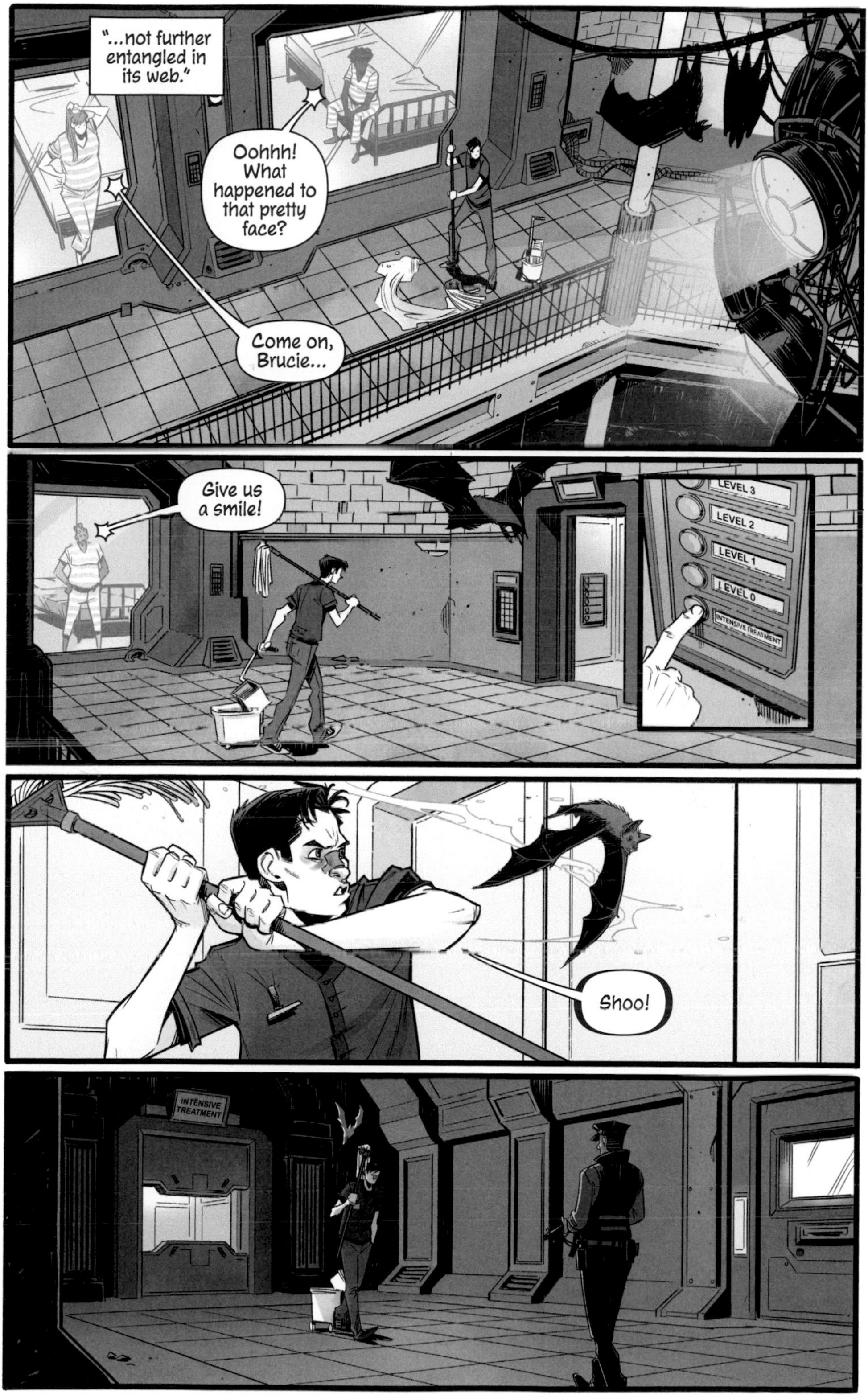
"...not further entangled in its web."
Oohhh! What happened to that pretty face?
Come on, Brucie...
Give us a smile!
LEVEL 3
LEVEL 2
LEVEL 1
LEVEL 0
INTENSIVE TREATMENT
Shoo!
INTENSIVE TREATMENT

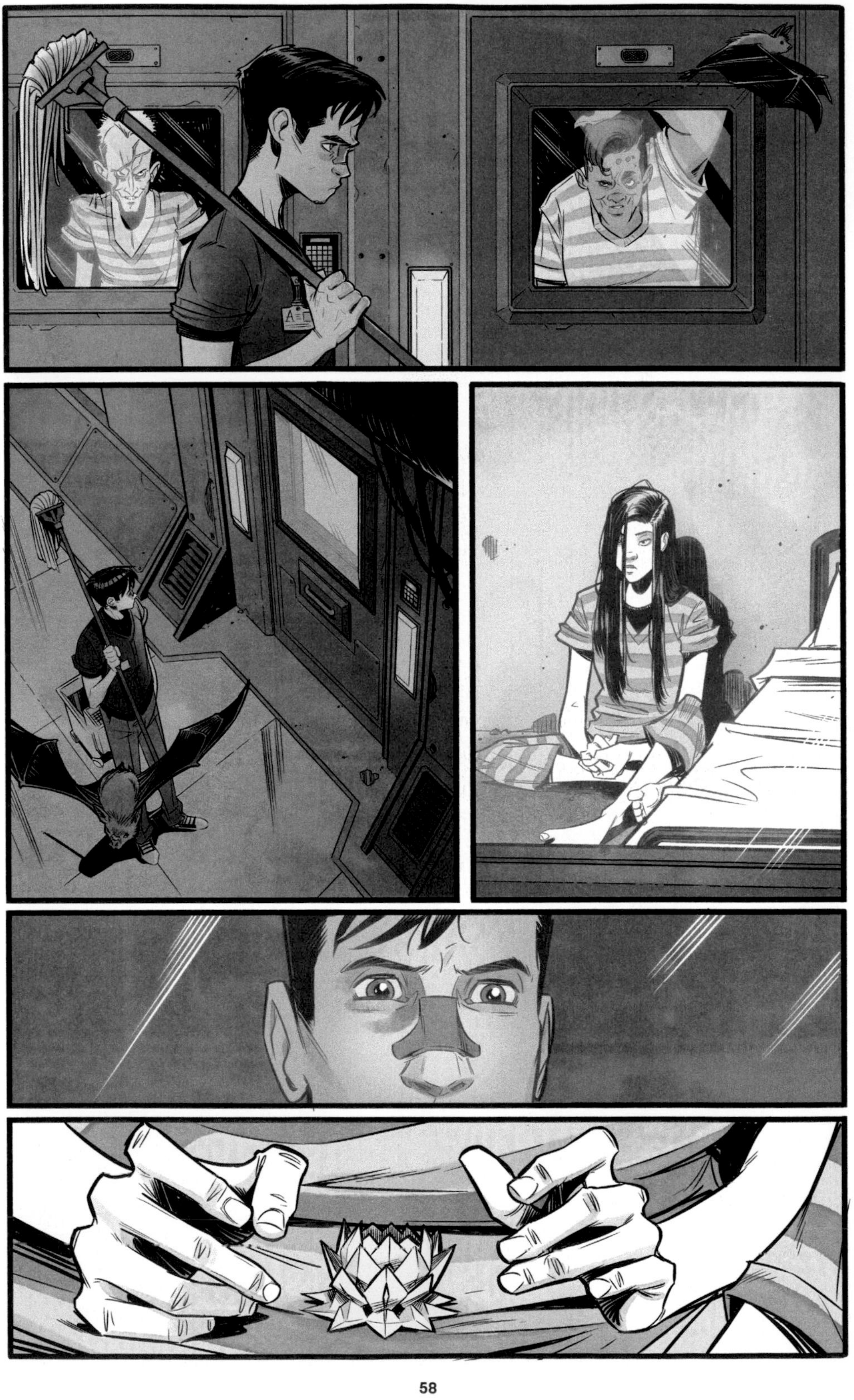

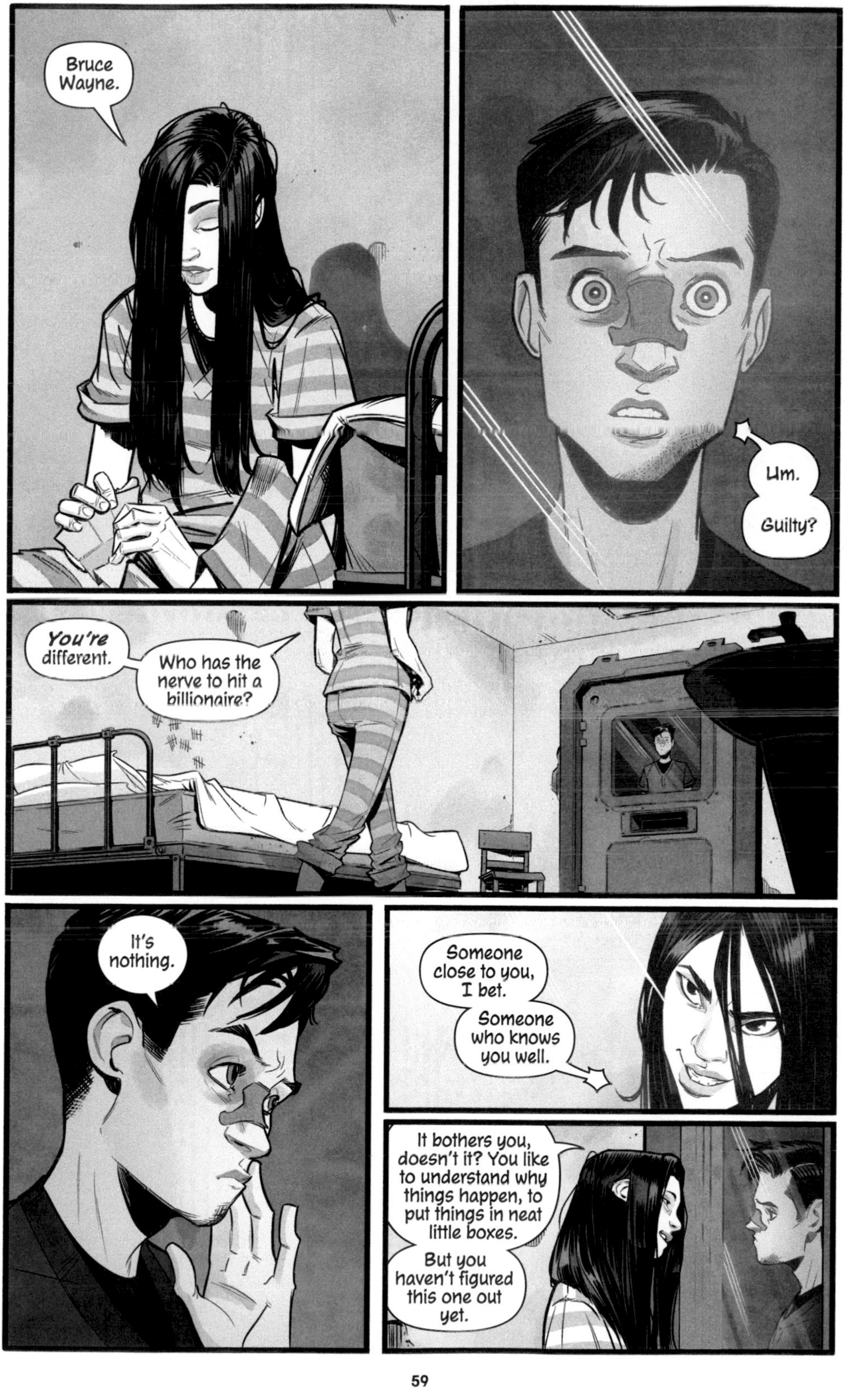

Bruce Wayne.
Um.
Guilty?
You're different.
Who has the nerve to hit a billionaire?
It's nothing.
Someone close to you, I bet.
Someone who knows you well.
It bothers you, doesn't it? You like to understand why things happen, to put things in neat little boxes.
But you haven't figured this one out yet.

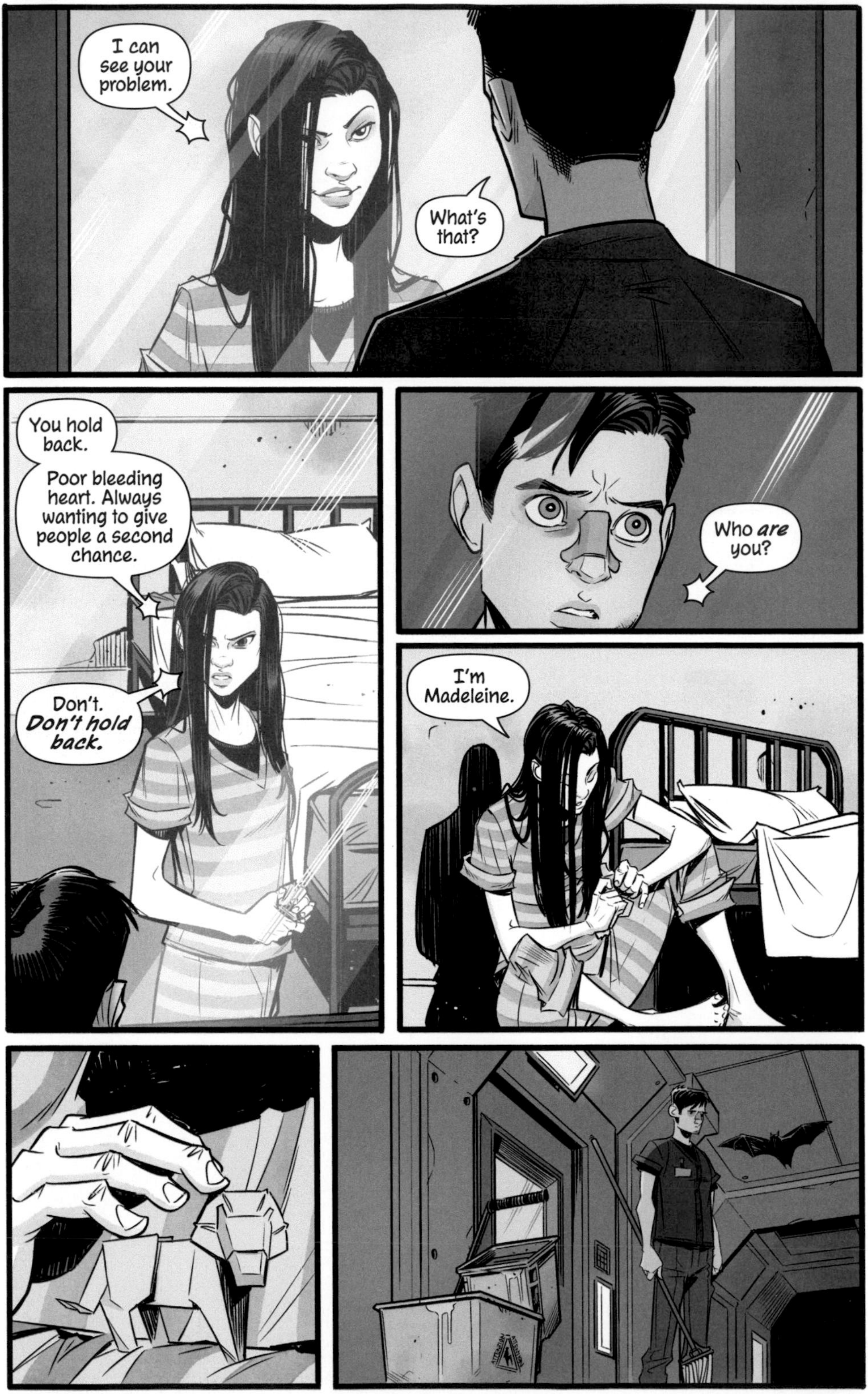
I can see your problem.
What's that?
You hold back.
Poor bleeding heart. Always wanting to give people a second chance.
Don't. **Don't hold back.**
Who *are* you?
I'm Madeleine.

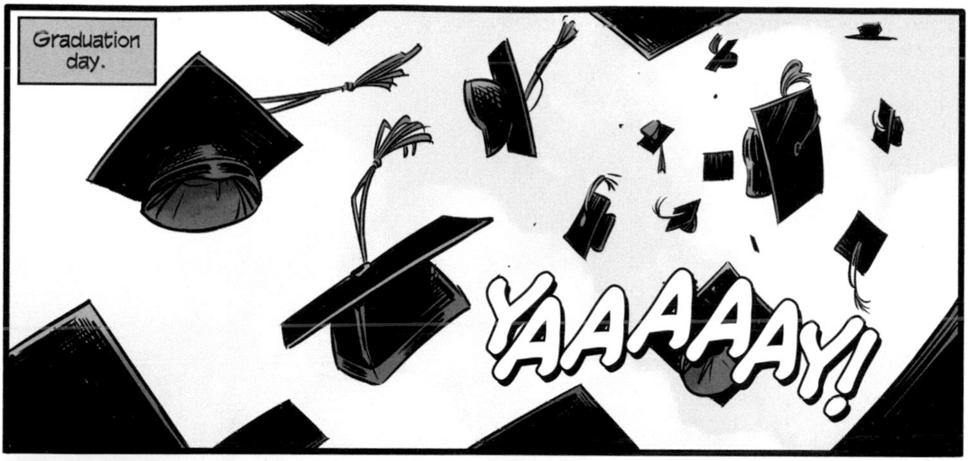
Graduation day.
YAAAAAY!

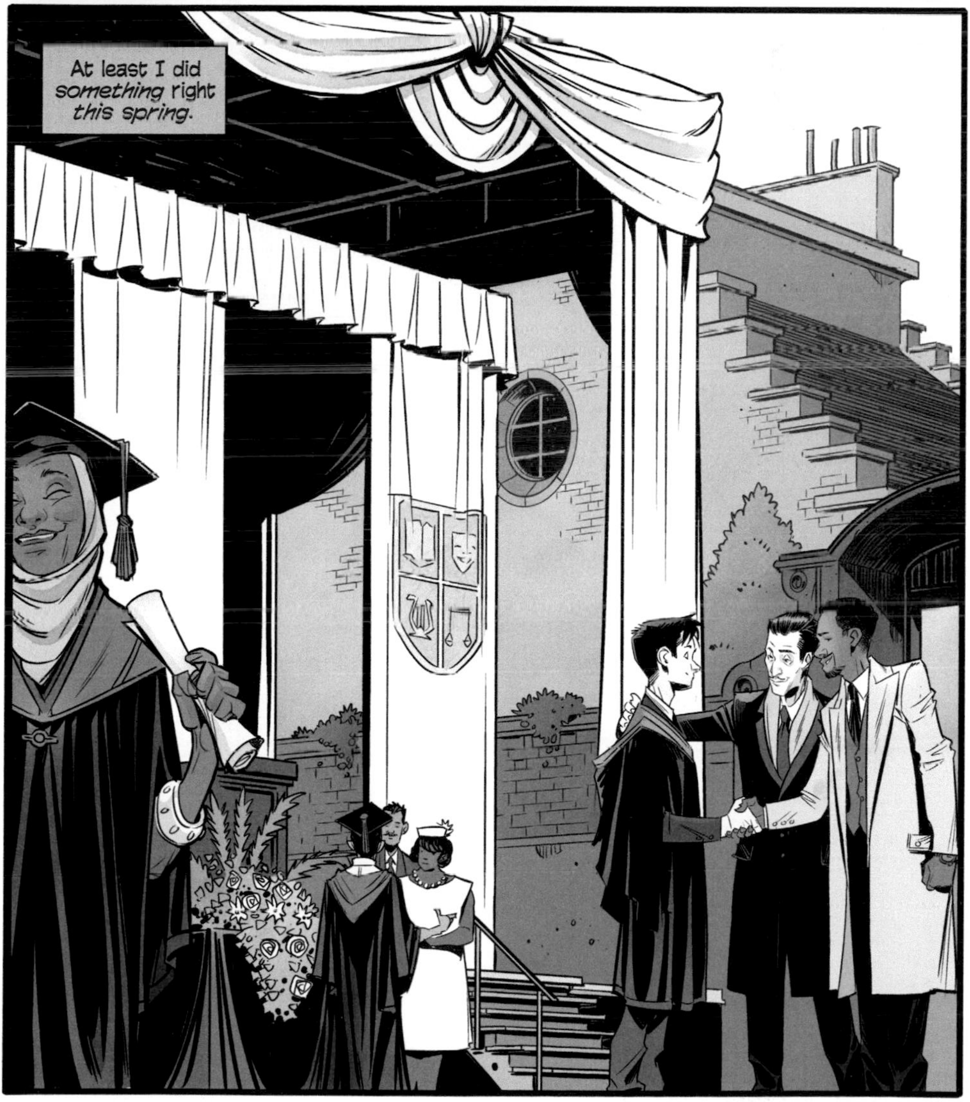
At least I did *something* right *this spring*.

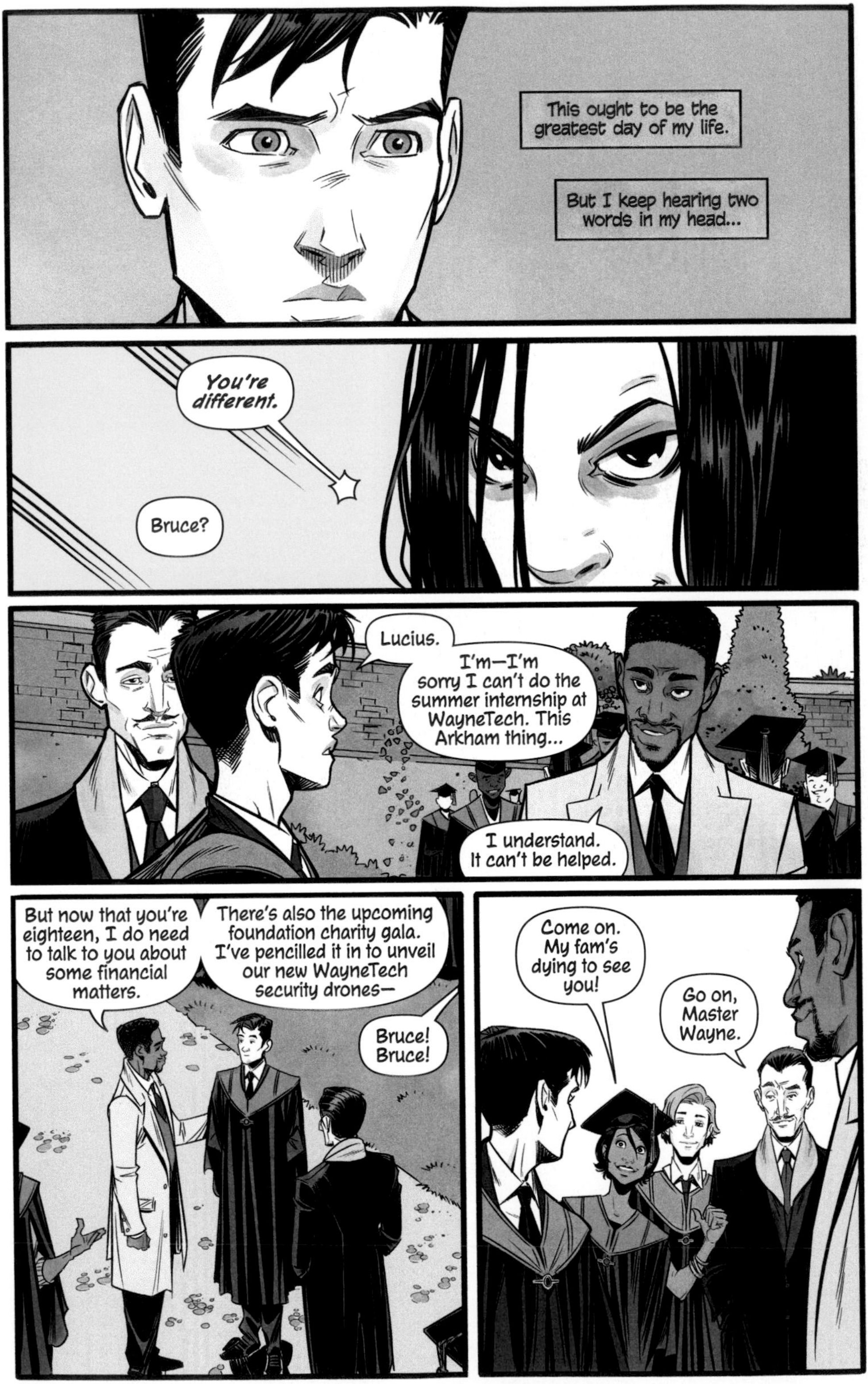
This ought to be the greatest day of my life.
But I keep hearing two words in my head...
You're different.
Bruce?
Lucius.
I'm—I'm sorry I can't do the summer internship at WayneTech. This Arkham thing...
I understand. It can't be helped.
But now that you're eighteen, I do need to talk to you about some financial matters.
There's also the upcoming foundation charity gala. I've pencilled it in to unveil our new WayneTech security drones—
Bruce! Bruce!
Come on. My fam's dying to see you!
Go on, Master Wayne.

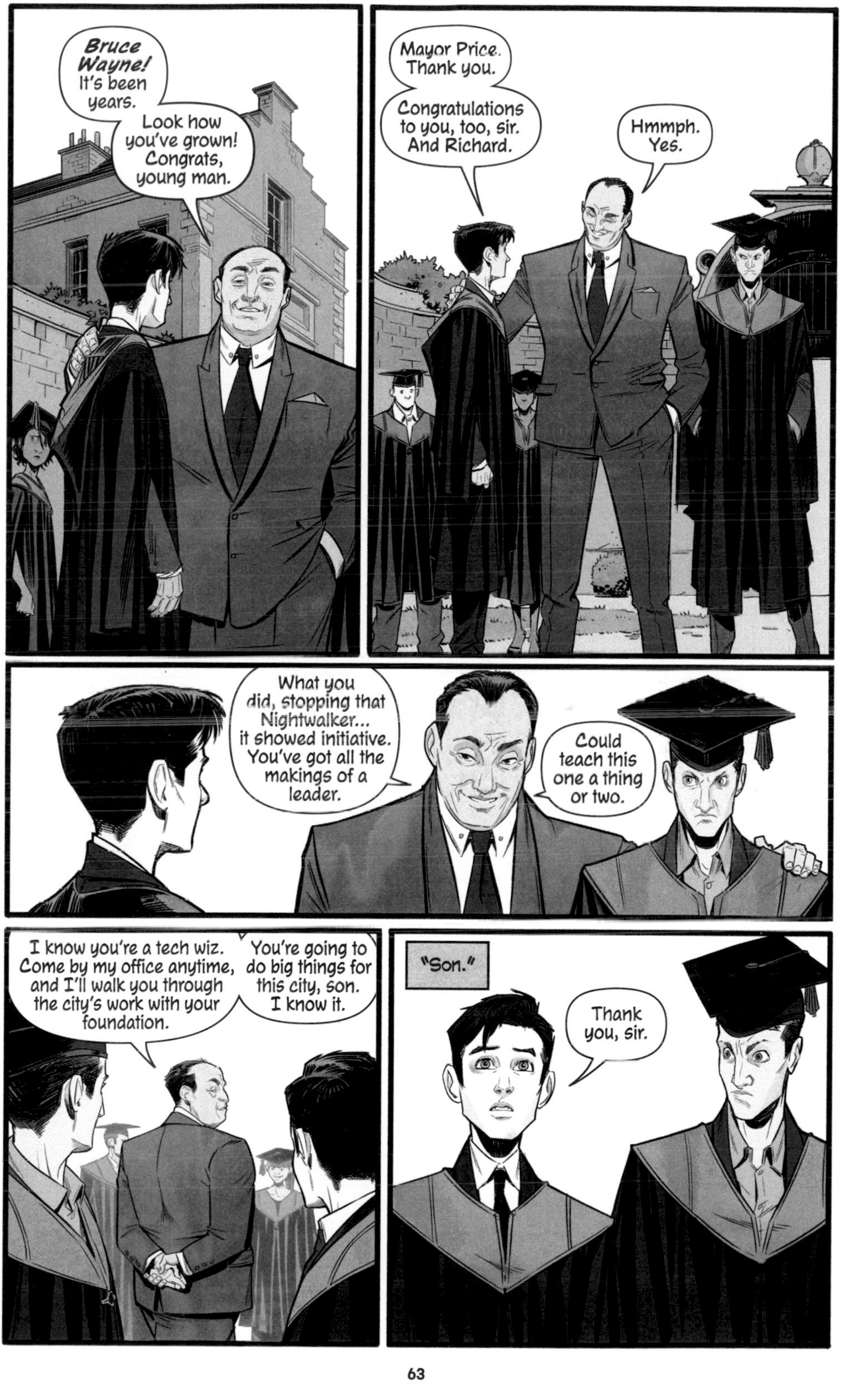
Bruce Wayne! It's been years.
Look how you've grown! Congrats, young man.
Mayor Price. Thank you.
Congratulations to you, too, sir. And Richard.
Hmmph. Yes.
What you did, stopping that Nightwalker... it showed initiative. You've got all the makings of a leader.
Could teach this one a thing or two.
I know you're a tech wiz. Come by my office anytime, and I'll walk you through the city's work with your foundation.
You're going to do big things for this city, son. I know it.
"Son."
Thank you, sir.

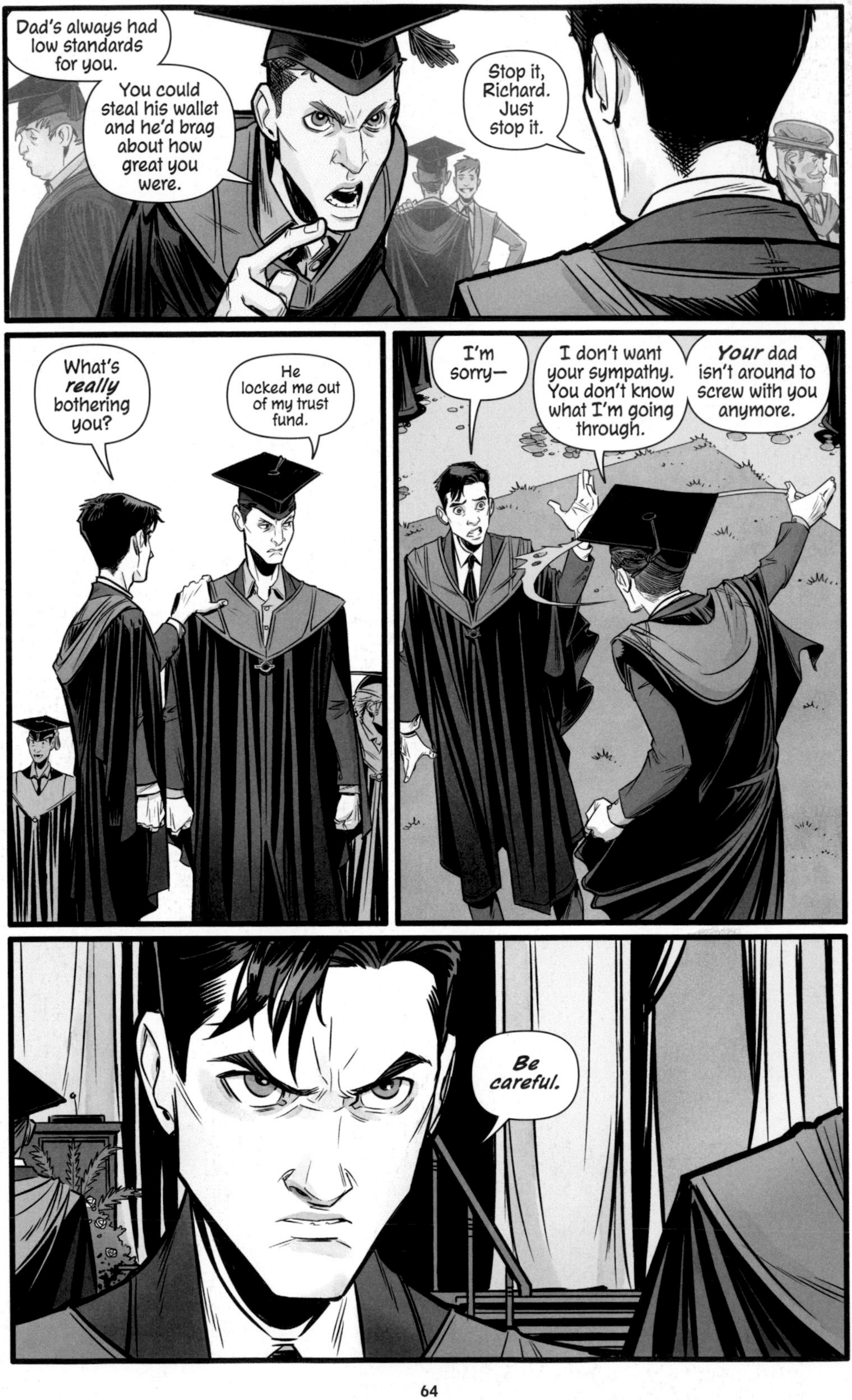

Dad's always had low standards for you.
You could steal his wallet and he'd brag about how great you were.
Stop it, Richard. Just stop it.
What's *really* bothering you?
He locked me out of my trust fund.
I'm sorry—
I don't want your sympathy. You don't know what I'm going through.
Your dad isn't around to screw with you anymore.
Be careful.

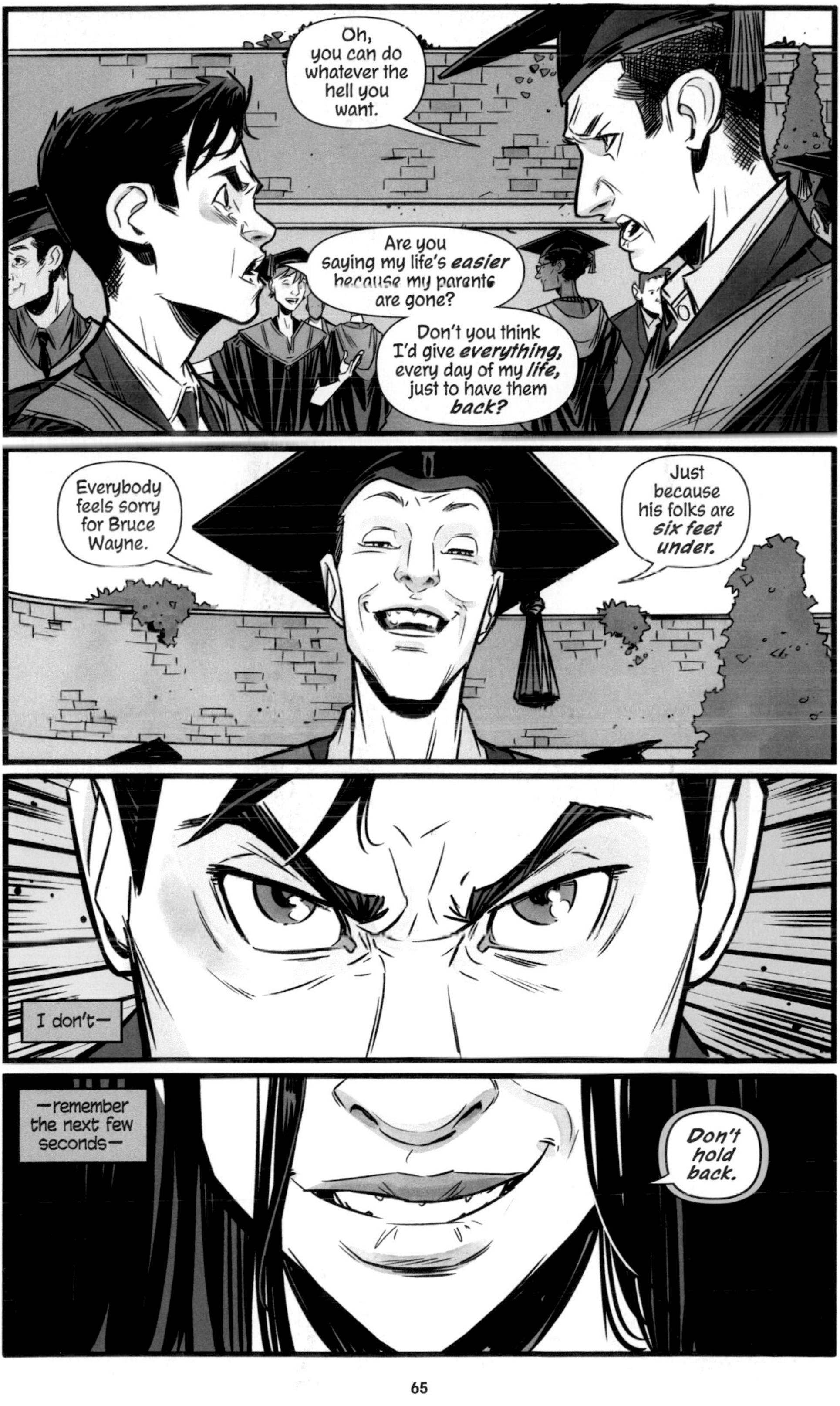
Oh, you can do whatever the hell you want.
Are you saying my life's *easier* because my parents are gone?
Don't you think I'd give *everything*, every day of my *life*, just to have them *back?*
Everybody feels sorry for Bruce Wayne.
Just because his folks are *six feet under.*
I don't—
—remember the next few seconds—
Don't hold back.

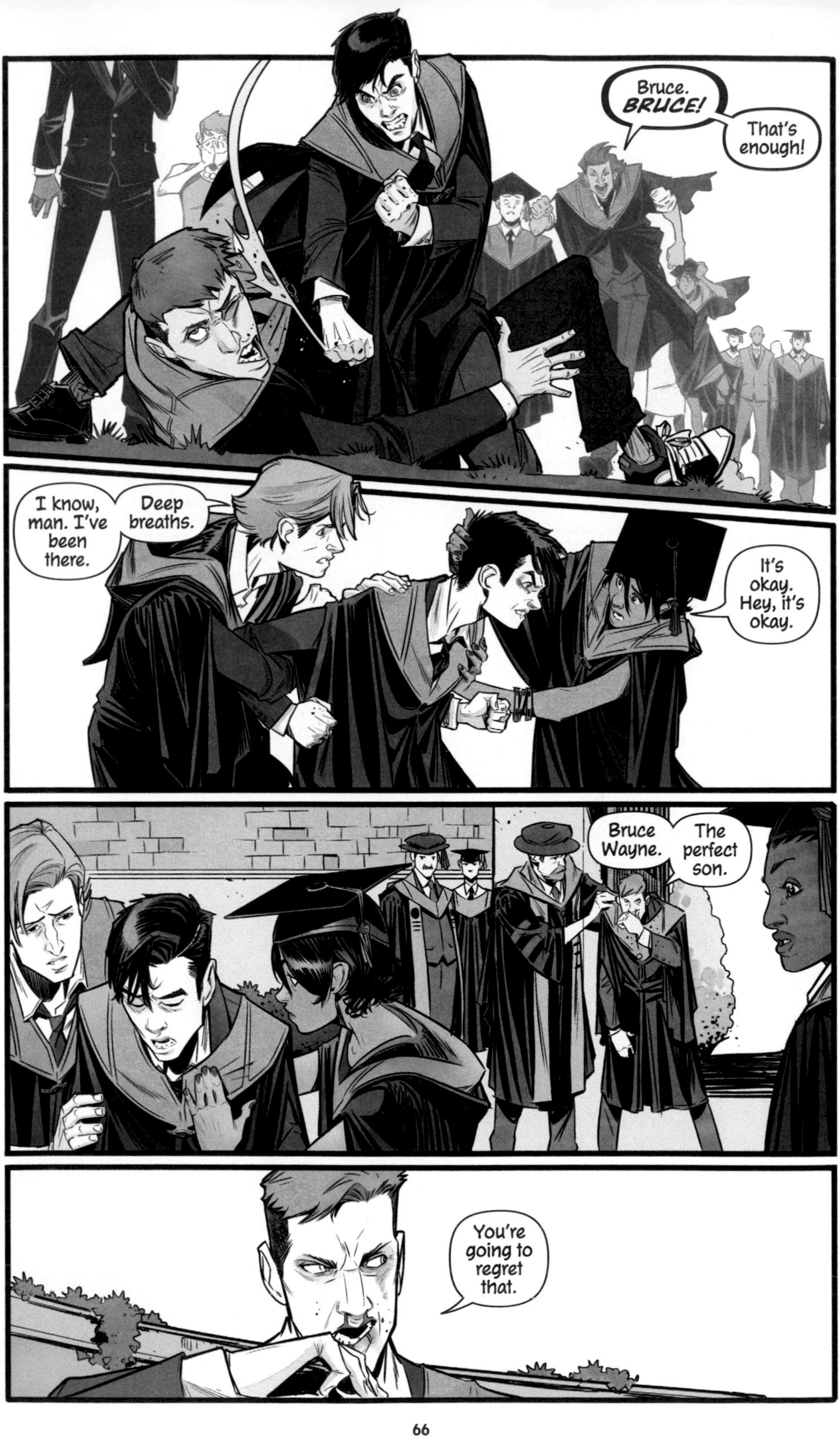
Bruce. BRUCE!
That's enough!
I know, man. I've been there.
Deep breaths.
It's okay. Hey, it's okay.
Bruce Wayne.
The perfect son.
You're going to regret that.

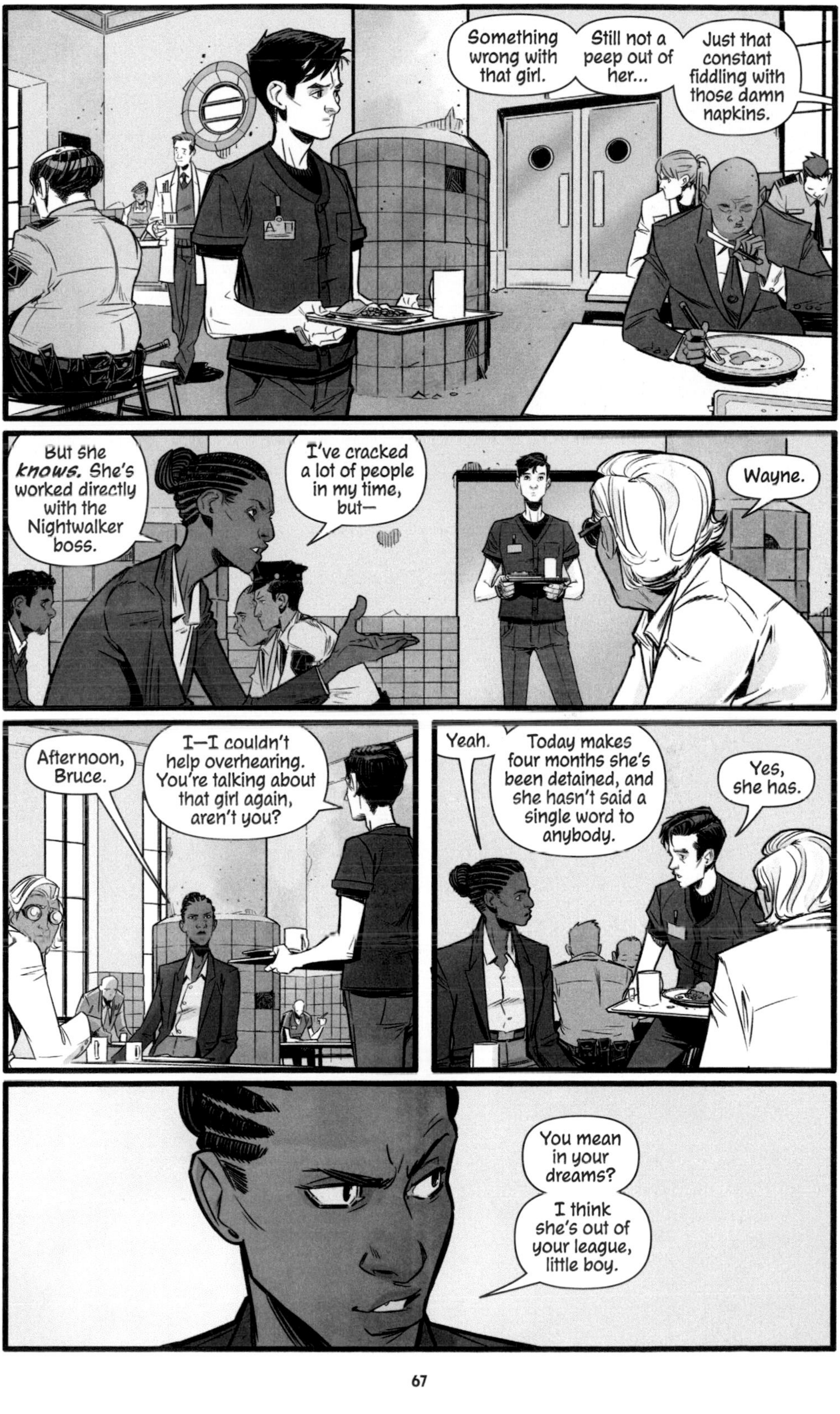
Something wrong with that girl.
Still not a peep out of her...
Just that constant fiddling with those damn napkins.
But she *knows.* She's worked directly with the Nightwalker boss.
I've cracked a lot of people in my time, but—
Wayne.
Afternoon, Bruce.
I—I couldn't help overhearing. You're talking about that girl again, aren't you?
Yeah.
Today makes four months she's been detained, and she hasn't said a single word to anybody.
Yes, she has.
You mean in your dreams?
I think she's out of your league, little boy.

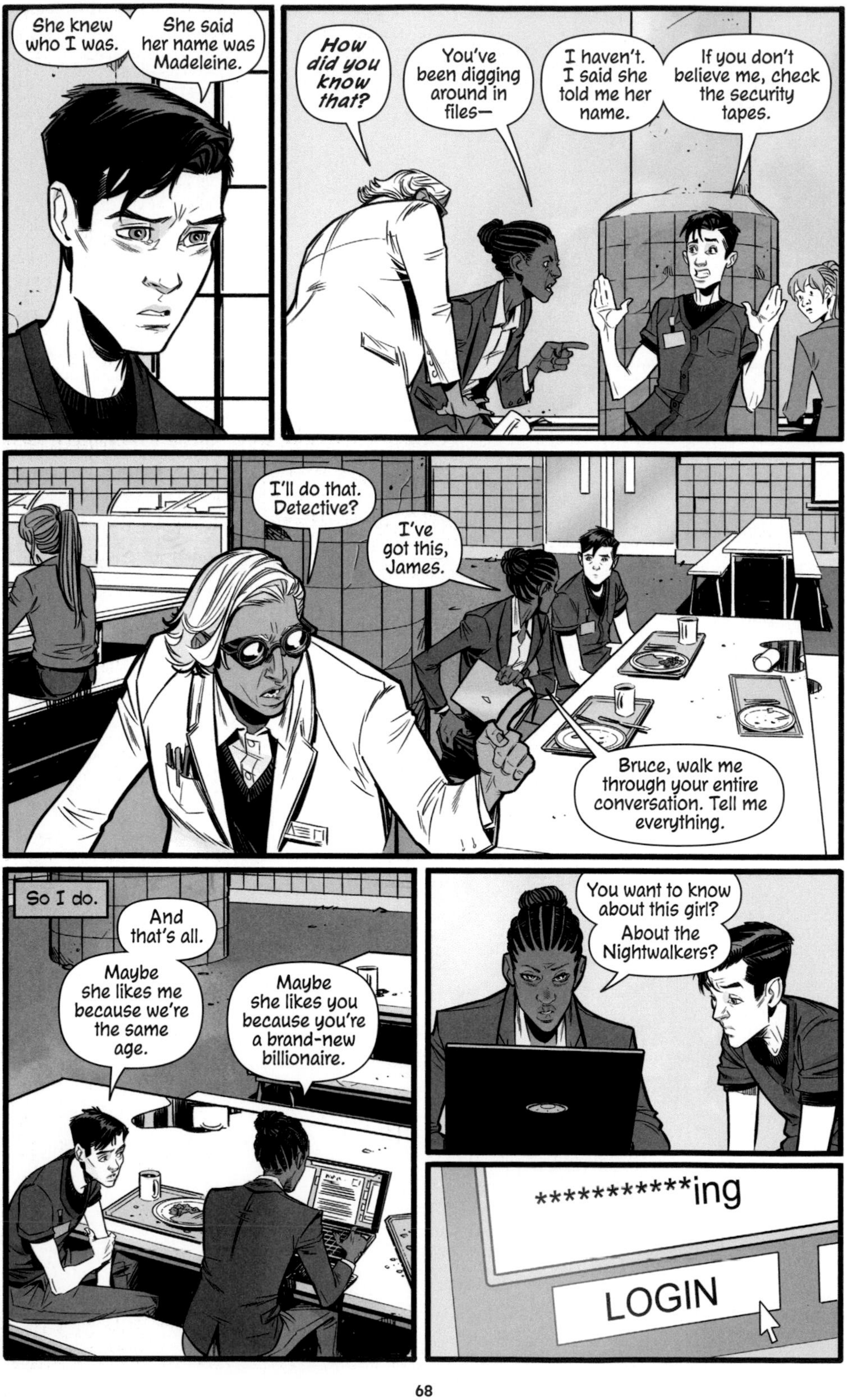
She knew who I was.
She said her name was Madeleine.
How did you know that?
You've been digging around in files—
I haven't. I said she told me her name.
If you don't believe me, check the security tapes.
I'll do that. Detective?
I've got this, James.
Bruce, walk me through your entire conversation. Tell me everything.
So I do.
And that's all.
Maybe she likes me because we're the same age.
Maybe she likes you because you're a brand-new billionaire.
You want to know about this girl?
About the Nightwalkers?
***********ing
LOGIN

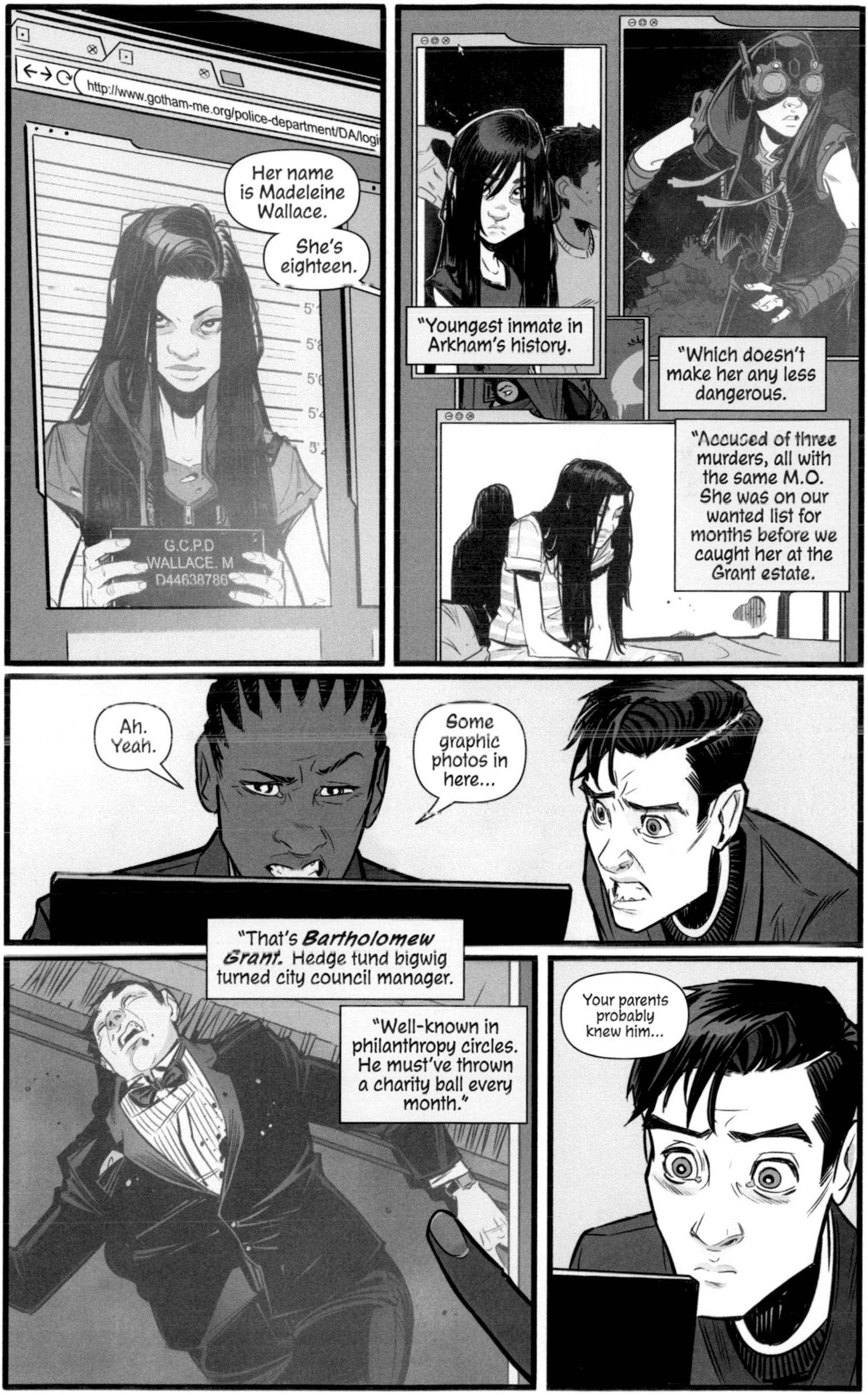
http://www.gotham-me.org/police-department/DA/logi
Her name is Madeleine Wallace.
She's eighteen.
G.C.P.D WALLACE. M D44638786
"Youngest inmate in Arkham's history.
"Which doesn't make her any less dangerous.
"Accused of three murders, all with the same M.O. She was on our wanted list for months before we caught her at the Grant estate.
Ah. Yeah.
Some graphic photos in here...
"That's ***Bartholomew Grant.*** Hedge fund bigwig turned city council manager.
"Well-known in philanthropy circles. He must've thrown a charity ball every month."
Your parents probably knew him...

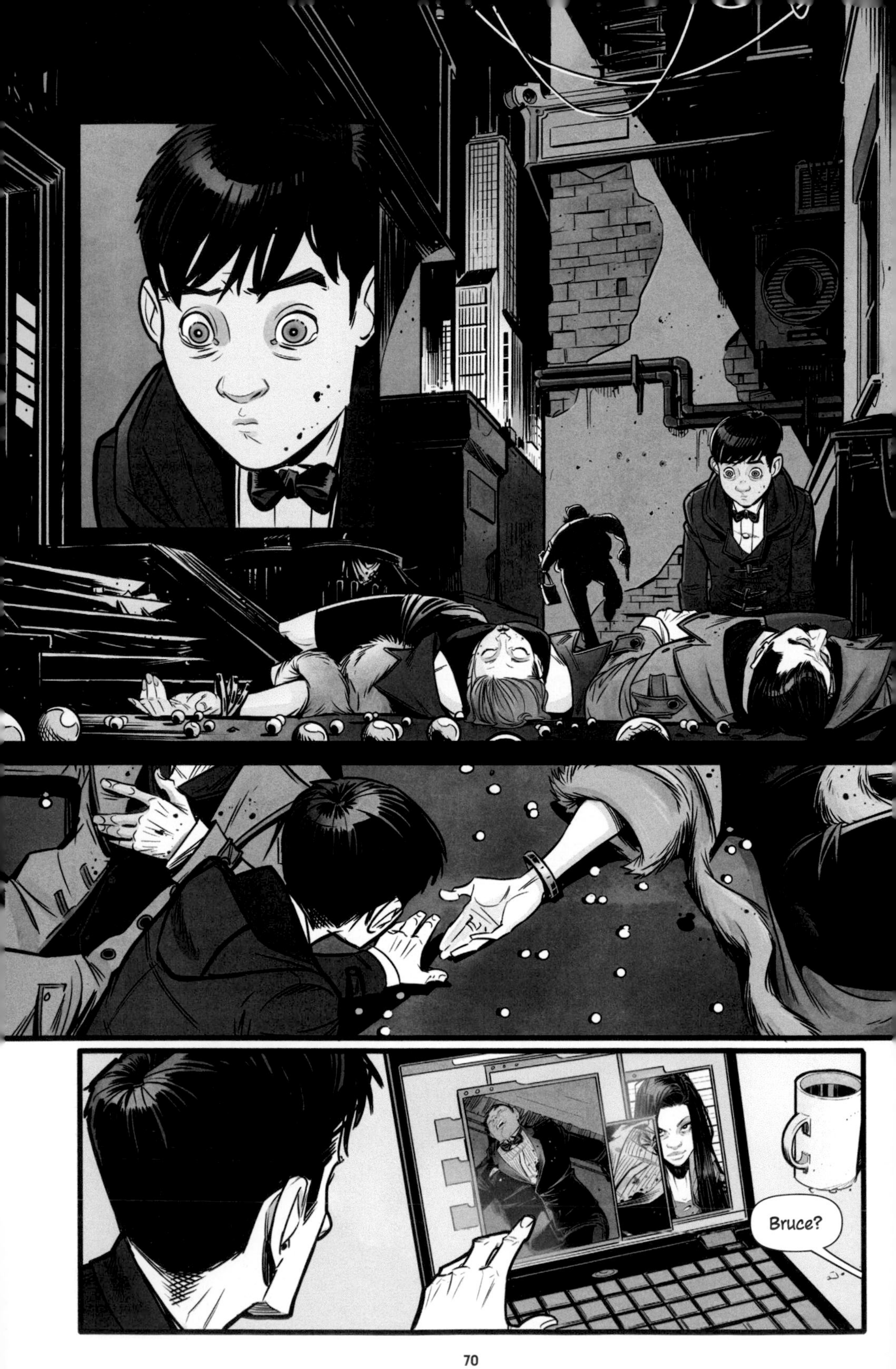
Bruce?

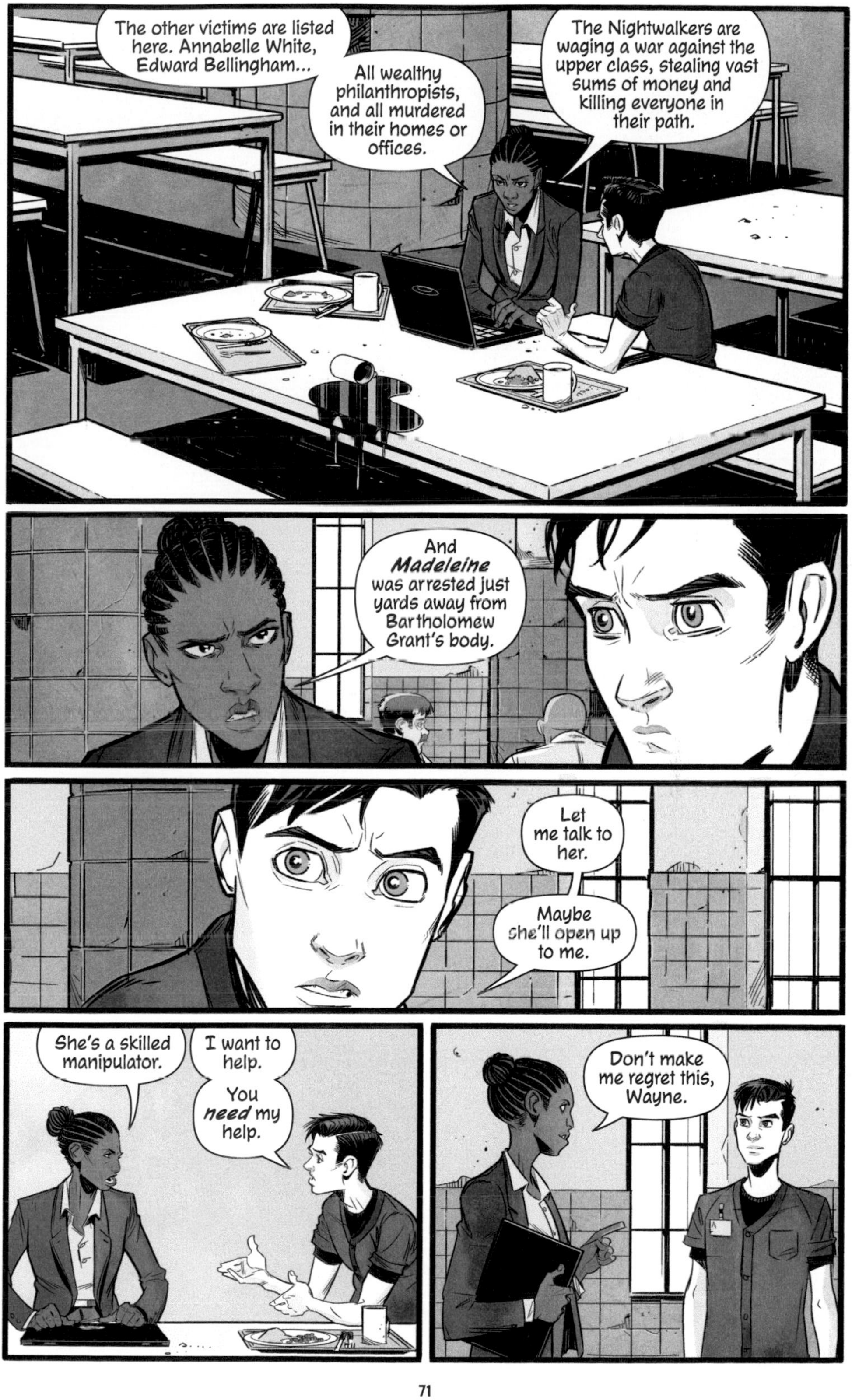
The other victims are listed here. Annabelle White, Edward Bellingham...
All wealthy philanthropists, and all murdered in their homes or offices.
The Nightwalkers are waging a war against the upper class, stealing vast sums of money and killing everyone in their path.
And *Madeleine* was arrested just yards away from Bartholomew Grant's body.
Let me talk to her.
Maybe she'll open up to me.
She's a skilled manipulator.
I want to help.
You *need* my help.
Don't make me regret this, Wayne.

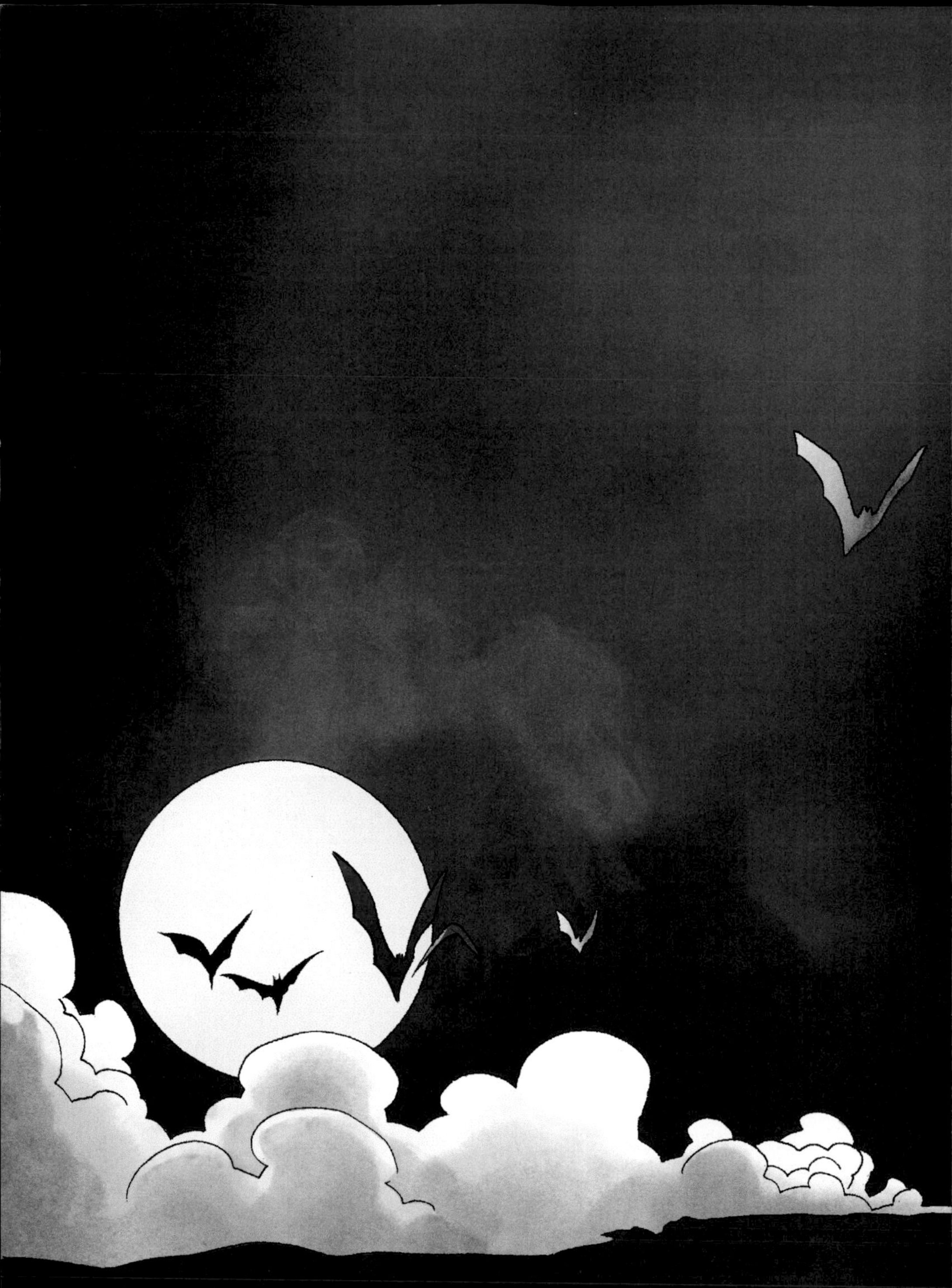

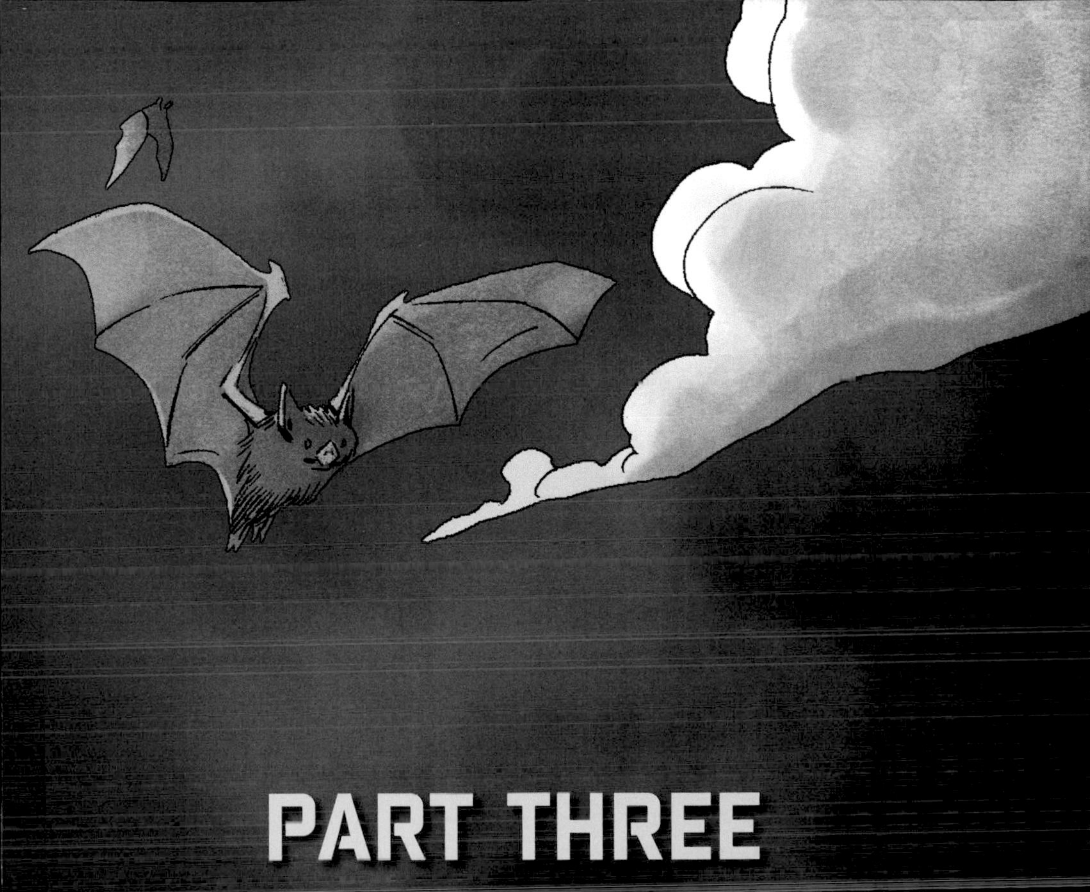

PART THREE

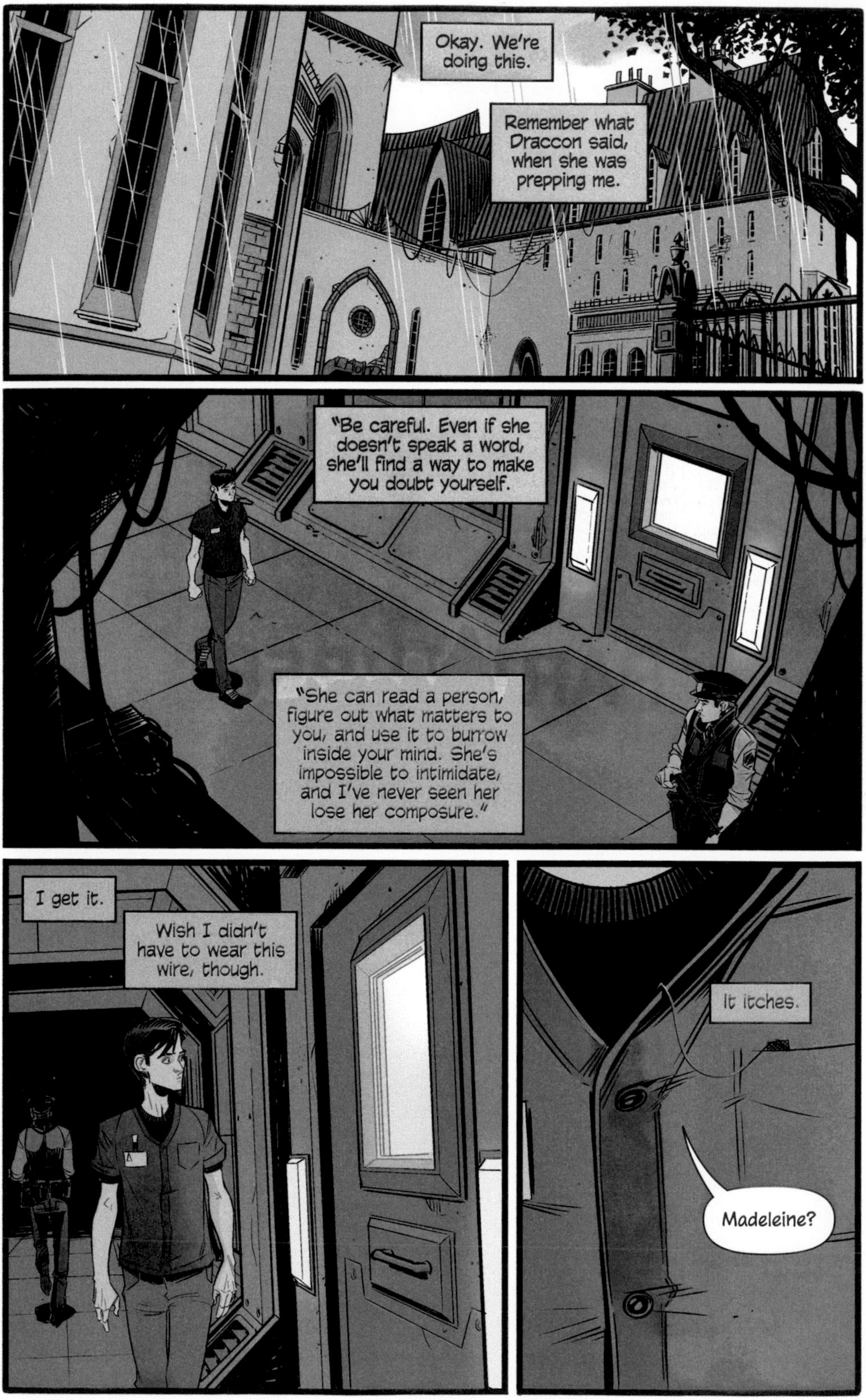
Okay. We're doing this.
Remember what Draccon said, when she was prepping me.
"Be careful. Even if she doesn't speak a word, she'll find a way to make you doubt yourself.
"She can read a person, figure out what matters to you, and use it to burrow inside your mind. She's impossible to intimidate, and I've never seen her lose her composure."
I get it.
Wish I didn't have to wear this wire, though.
It itches.
Madeleine?

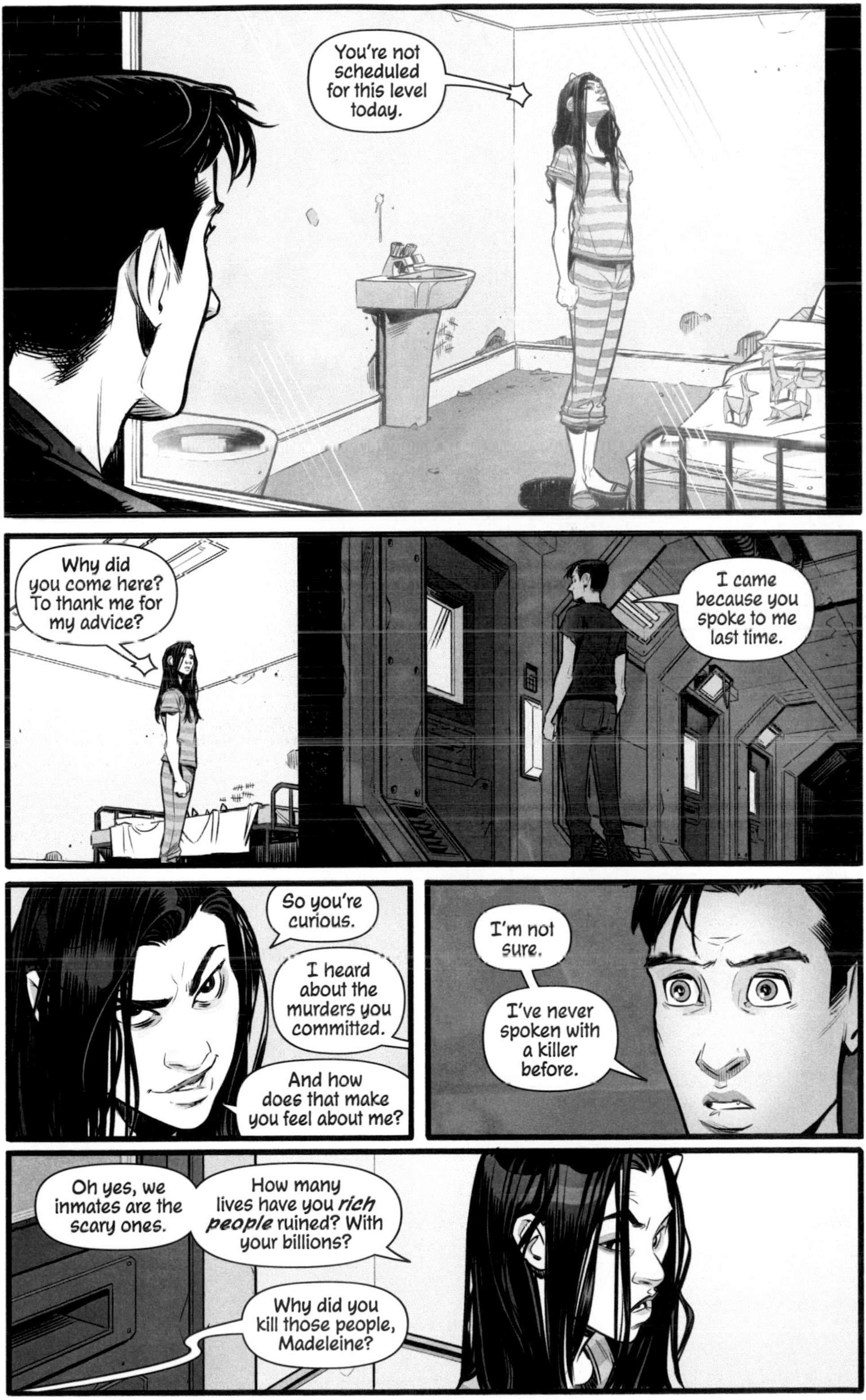
You're not scheduled for this level today.
Why did you come here? To thank me for my advice?
I came because you spoke to me last time.
So you're curious.
I heard about the murders you committed.
And how does that make you feel about me?
I'm not sure.
I've never spoken with a killer before.
Oh yes, we inmates are the scary ones.
How many lives have you *rich people* ruined? With your billions?
Why did you kill those people, Madeleine?

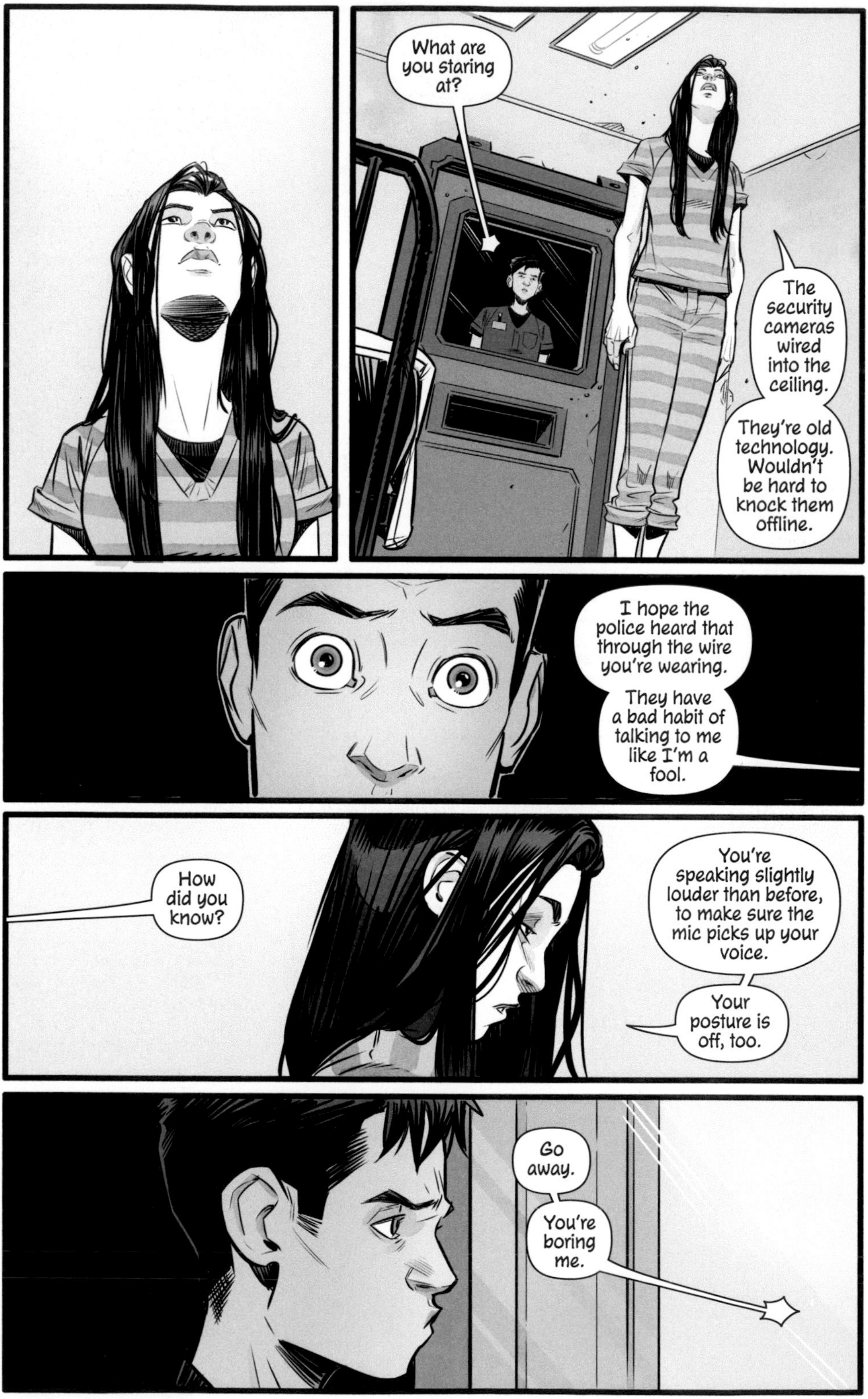
What are you staring at?
The security cameras wired into the ceiling.
They're old technology. Wouldn't be hard to knock them offline.
I hope the police heard that through the wire you're wearing.
They have a bad habit of talking to me like I'm a fool.
How did you know?
You're speaking slightly louder than before, to make sure the mic picks up your voice.
Your posture is off, too.
Go away.
You're boring me.

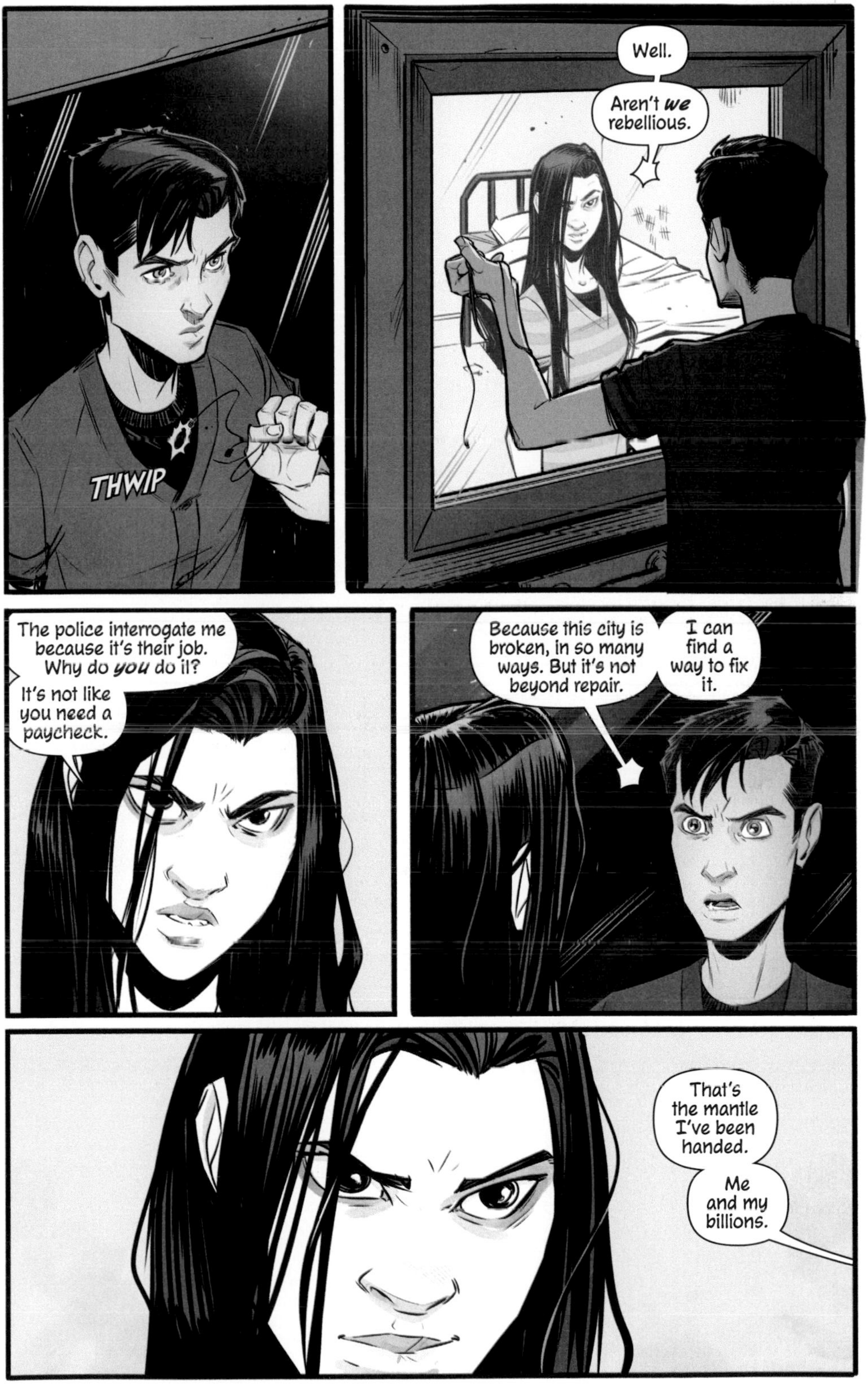
THWIP
Well.
Aren't *we* rebellious.
The police interrogate me because it's their job. Why do *you* do it?
It's not like you need a paycheck.
Because this city is broken, in so many ways. But it's not beyond repair.
I can find a way to fix it.
That's the mantle I've been handed.
Me and my billions.

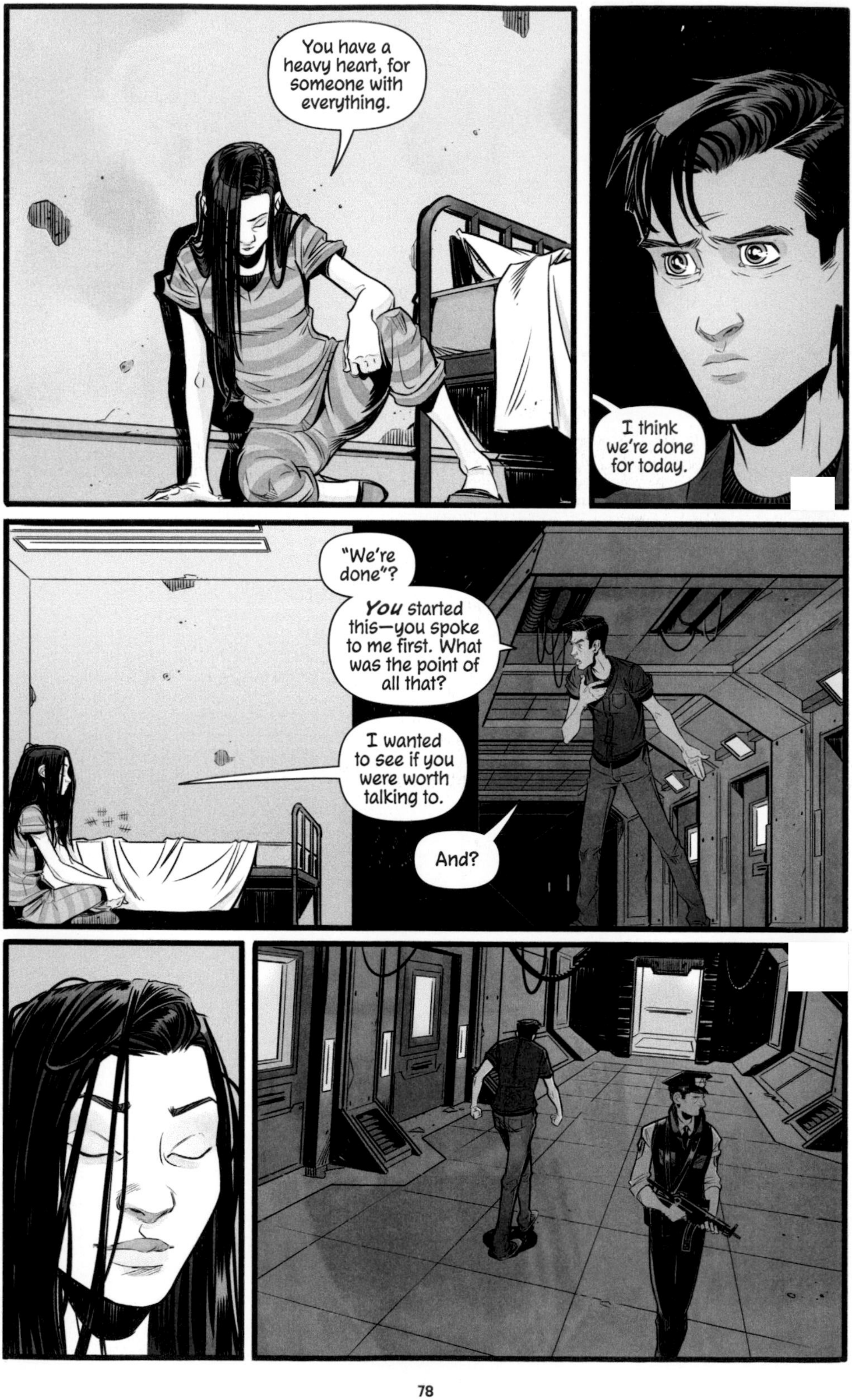
You have a heavy heart, for someone with everything.
I think we're done for today.
"We're done"?
You started this—you spoke to me first. What was the point of all that?
I wanted to see if you were worth talking to.
And?

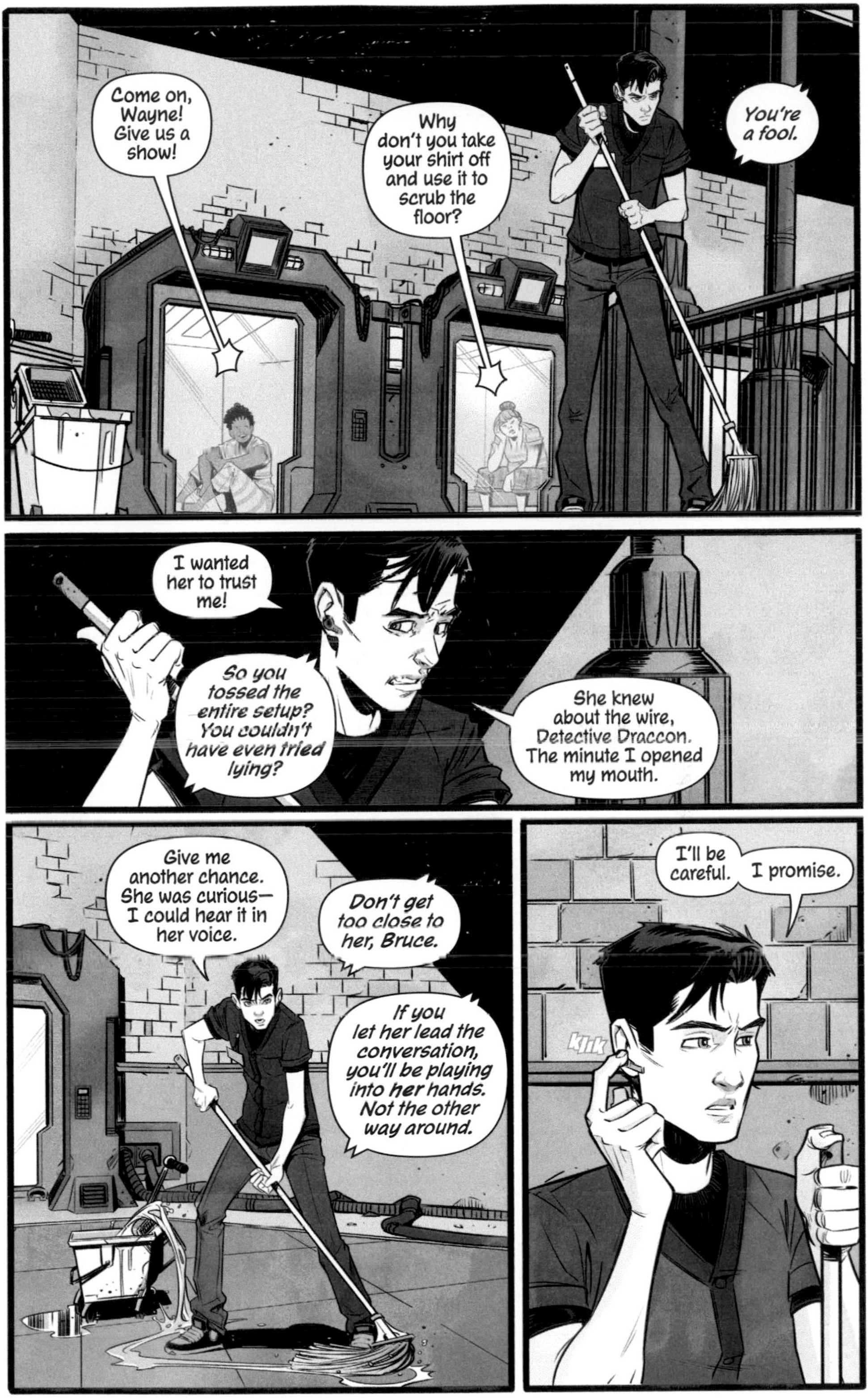
Come on, Wayne! Give us a show!
Why don't you take your shirt off and use it to scrub the floor?
You're a fool.
I wanted her to trust me!
So you tossed the entire setup? You couldn't have even tried lying?
She knew about the wire, Detective Draccon. The minute I opened my mouth.
Give me another chance. She was curious—I could hear it in her voice.
Don't get too close to her, Bruce.
If you let her lead the conversation, you'll be playing into her hands. Not the other way around.
KLIK
I'll be careful.
I promise.

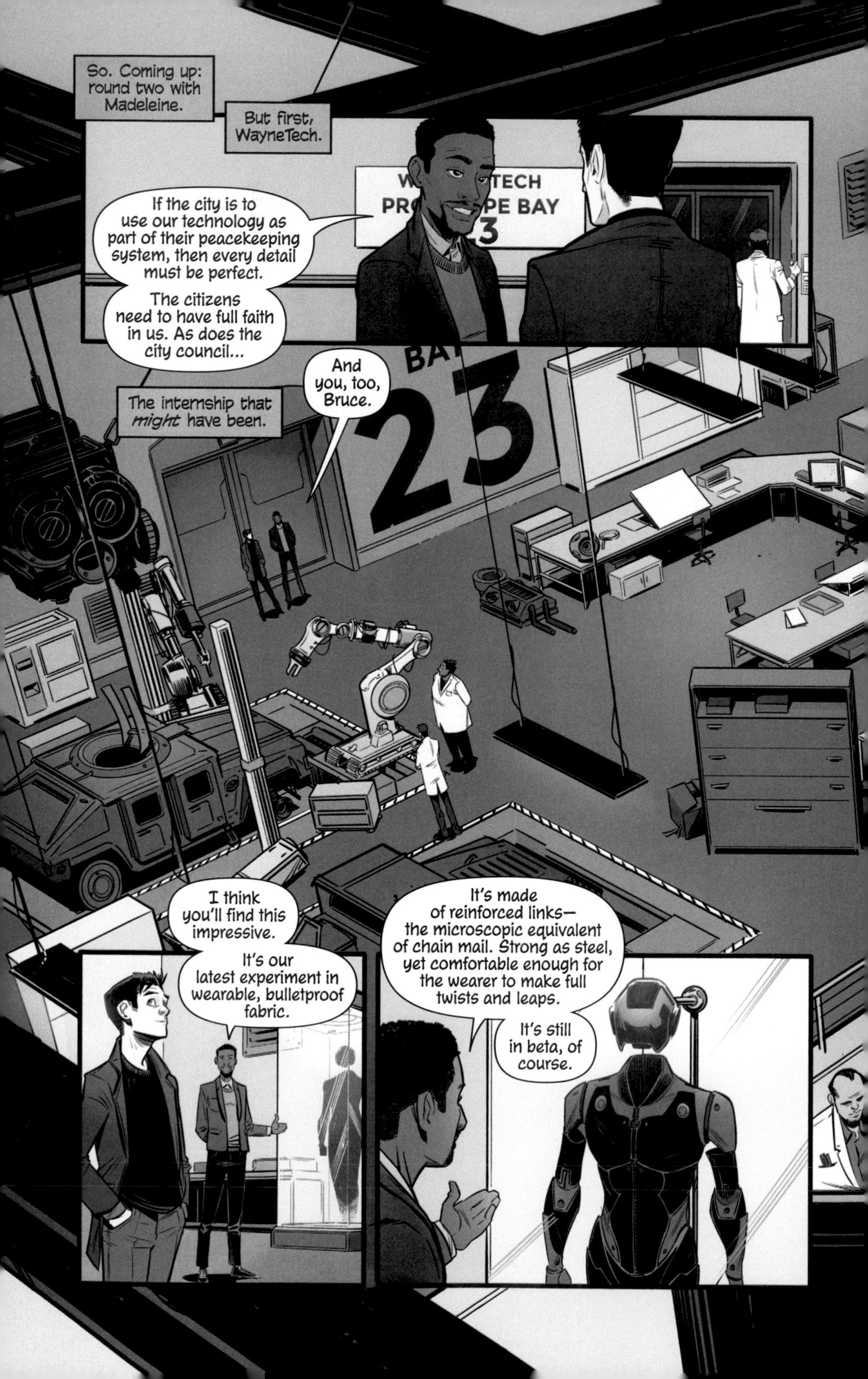
So. Coming up: round two with Madeleine.
But first, WayneTech.
W TECH PRO PE BAY 3
If the city is to use our technology as part of their peacekeeping system, then every detail must be perfect.
The citizens need to have full faith in us. As does the city council...
And you, too, Bruce.
The internship that *might* have been.
BA 23
I think you'll find this impressive.
It's our latest experiment in wearable, bulletproof fabric.
It's made of reinforced links— the microscopic equivalent of chain mail. Strong as steel, yet comfortable enough for the wearer to make full twists and leaps.
It's still in beta, of course.

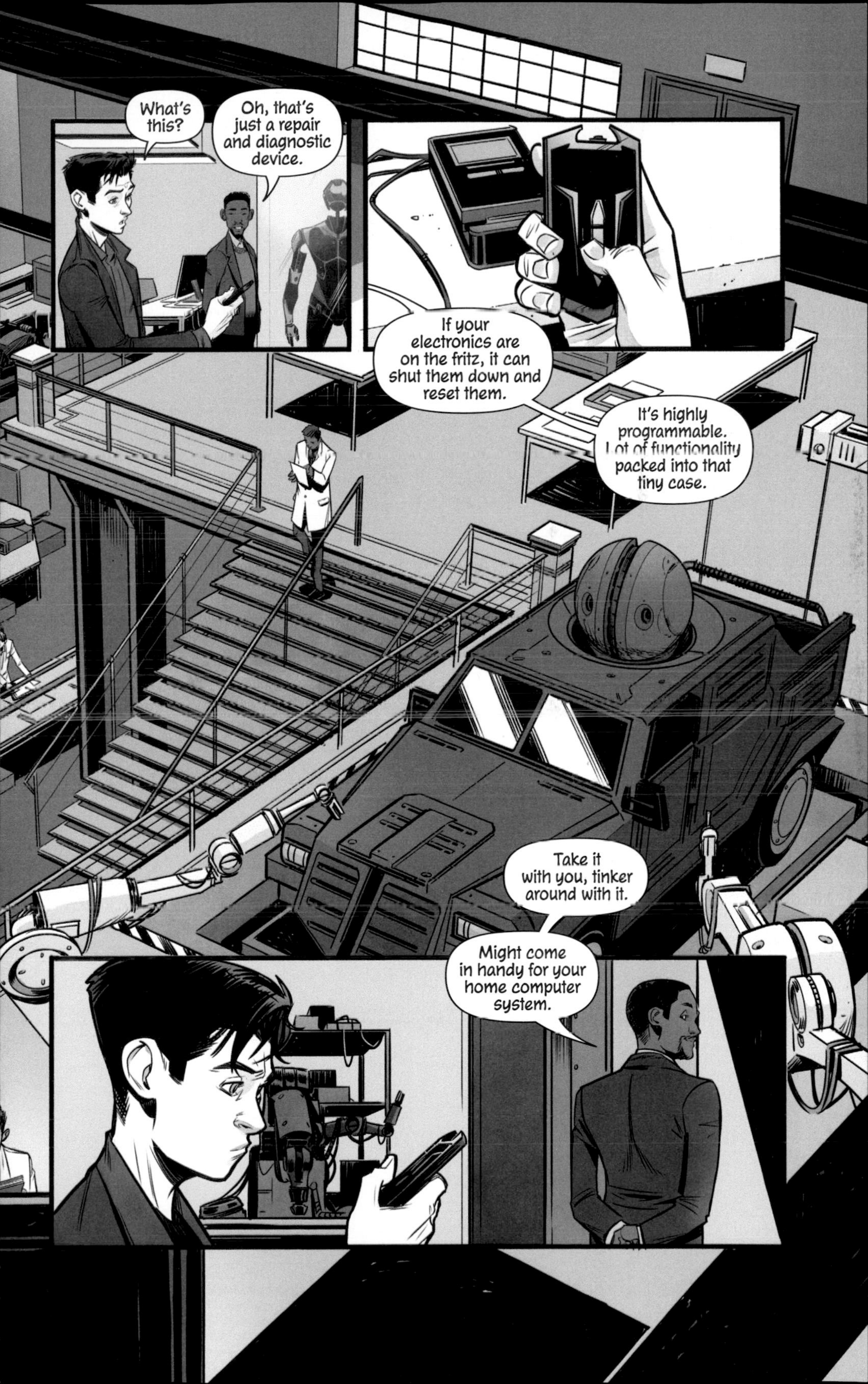
What's this?
Oh, that's just a repair and diagnostic device.
If your electronics are on the fritz, it can shut them down and reset them.
It's highly programmable. Lot of functionality packed into that tiny case.
Take it with you, tinker around with it.
Might come in handy for your home computer system.

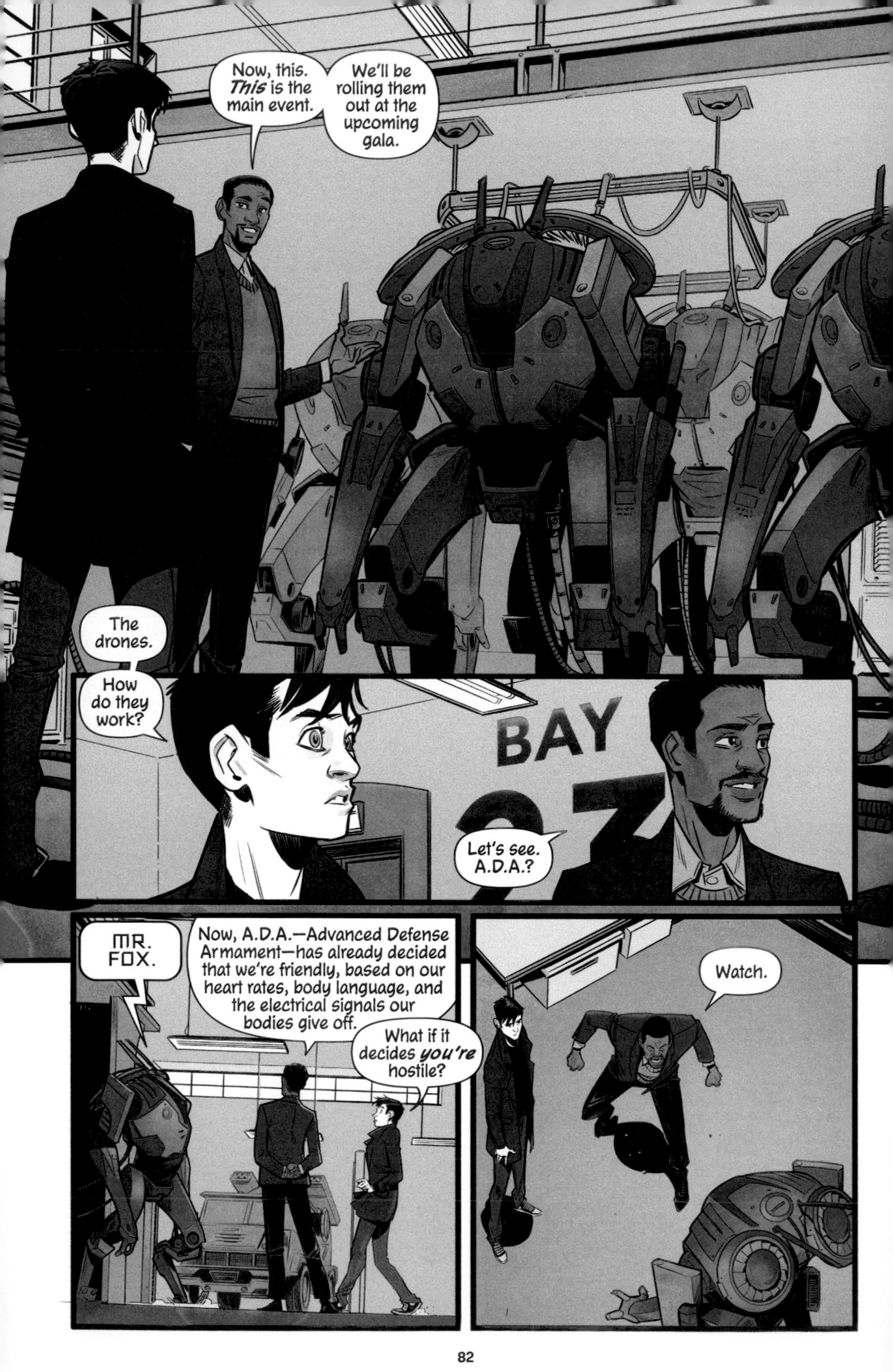
Now, this. *This* is the main event.
We'll be rolling them out at the upcoming gala.
The drones.
How do they work?
BAY
Let's see. A.D.A.?
MR. FOX.
Now, A.D.A.—Advanced Defense Armament—has already decided that we're friendly, based on our heart rates, body language, and the electrical signals our bodies give off.
What if it decides *you're* hostile?
Watch.

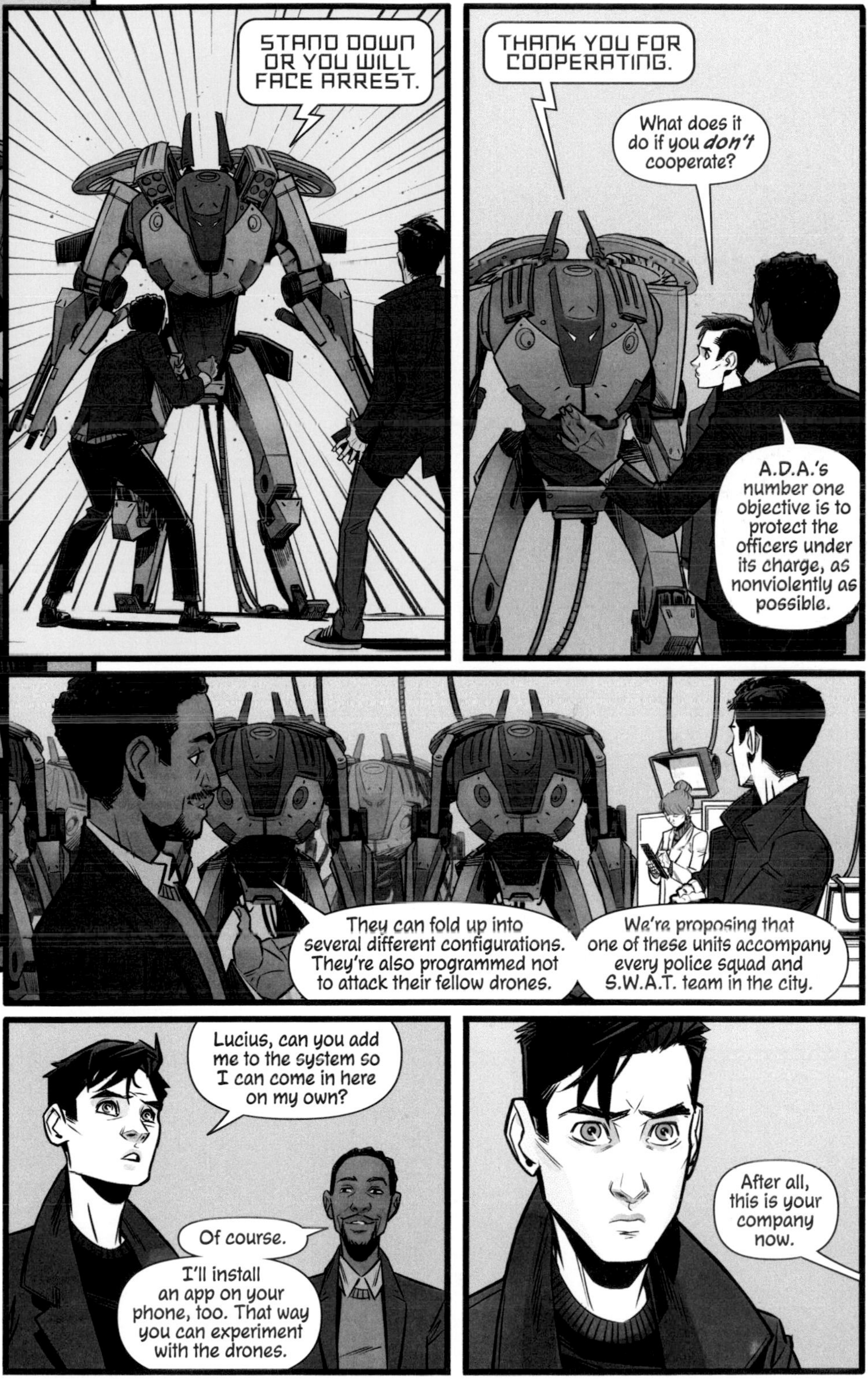
STAND DOWN OR YOU WILL FACE ARREST.
THANK YOU FOR COOPERATING.
What does it do if you *don't* cooperate?
A.D.A.'s number one objective is to protect the officers under its charge, as nonviolently as possible.
They can fold up into several different configurations. They're also programmed not to attack their fellow drones.
We're proposing that one of these units accompany every police squad and S.W.A.T. team in the city.
Lucius, can you add me to the system so I can come in here on my own?
Of course.
I'll install an app on your phone, too. That way you can experiment with the drones.
After all, this is your company now.

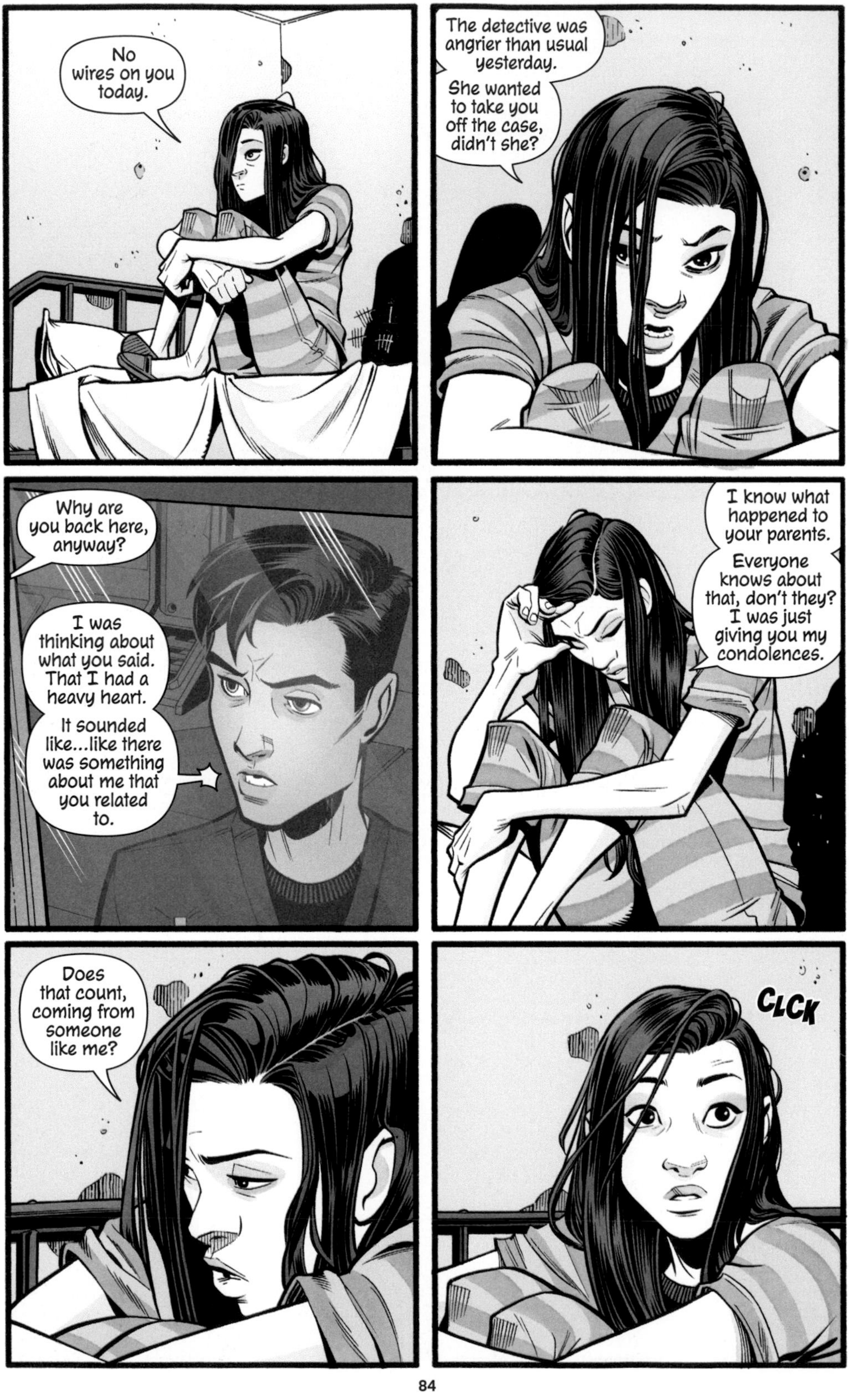

No wires on you today.
The detective was angrier than usual yesterday.
She wanted to take you off the case, didn't she?
Why are you back here, anyway?
I was thinking about what you said. That I had a heavy heart.
It sounded like...like there was something about me that you related to.
I know what happened to your parents.
Everyone knows about that, don't they? I was just giving you my condolences.
Does that count, coming from someone like me?
CLCK

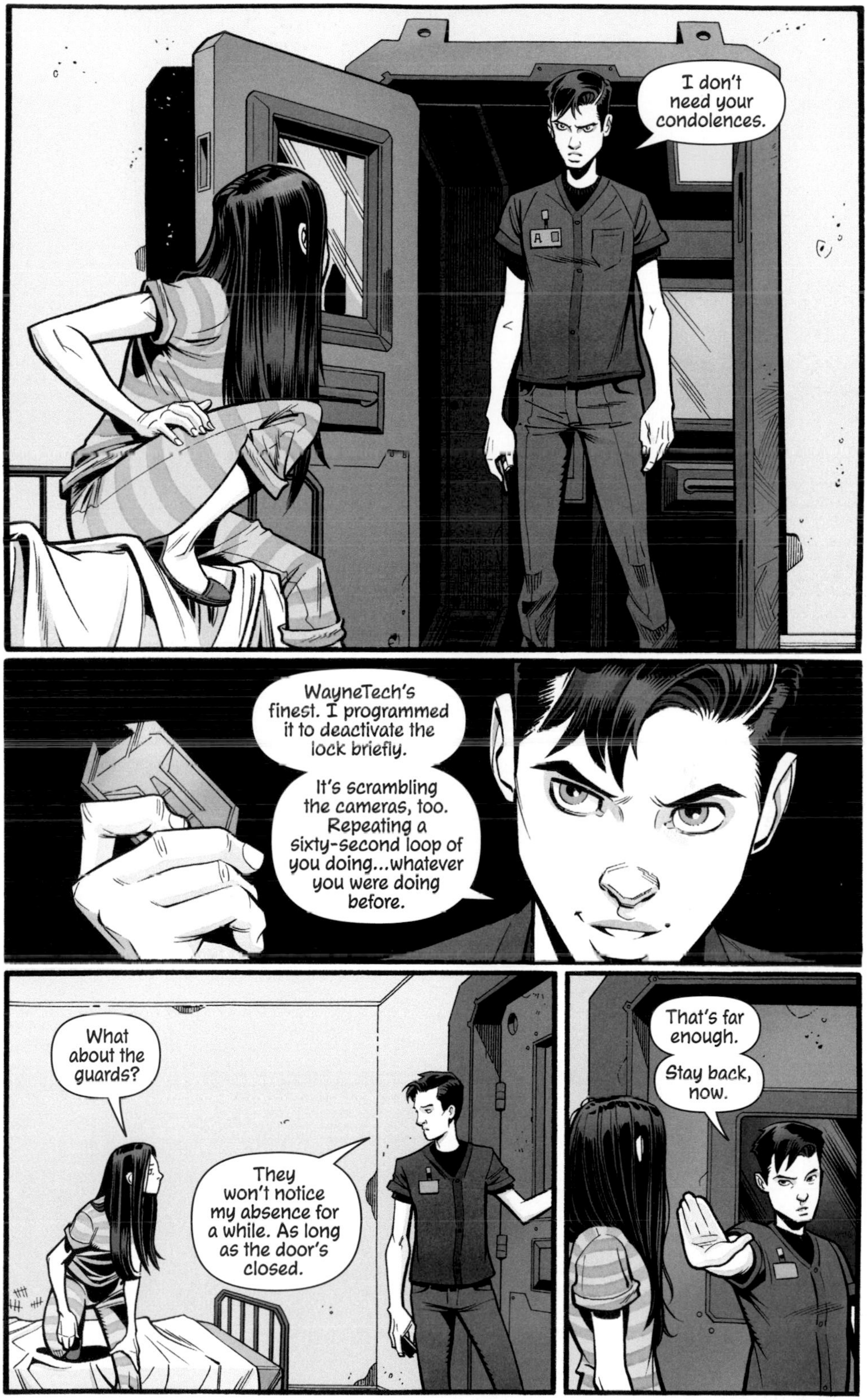
I don't need your condolences.
WayneTech's finest. I programmed it to deactivate the lock briefly.
It's scrambling the cameras, too. Repeating a sixty-second loop of you doing...whatever you were doing before.
What about the guards?
They won't notice my absence for a while. As long as the door's closed.
That's far enough.
Stay back, now.

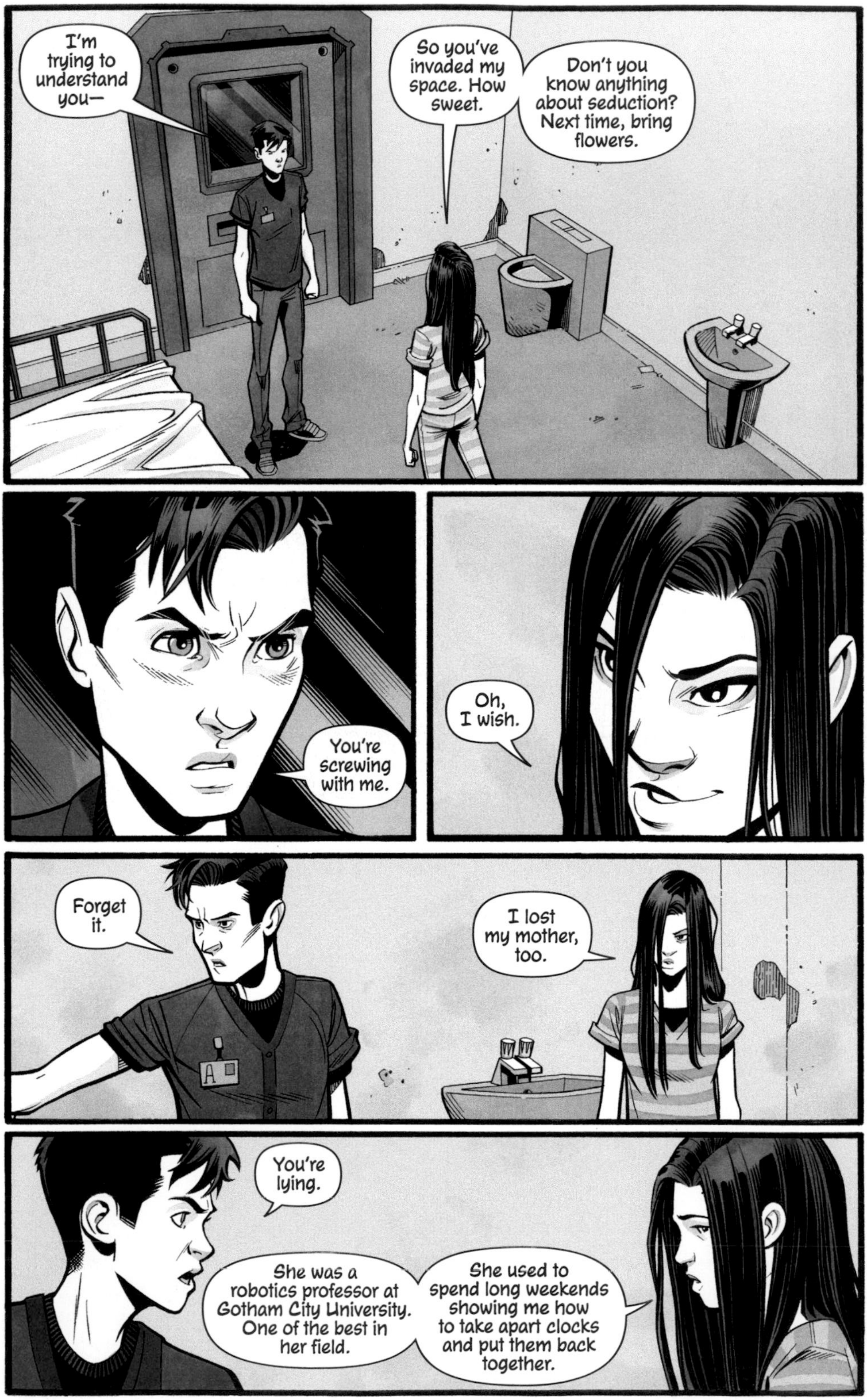
I'm trying to understand you—
So you've invaded my space. How sweet.
Don't you know anything about seduction? Next time, bring flowers.
You're screwing with me.
Oh, I wish.
Forget it.
I lost my mother, too.
You're lying.
She was a robotics professor at Gotham City University. One of the best in her field.
She used to spend long weekends showing me how to take apart clocks and put them back together.

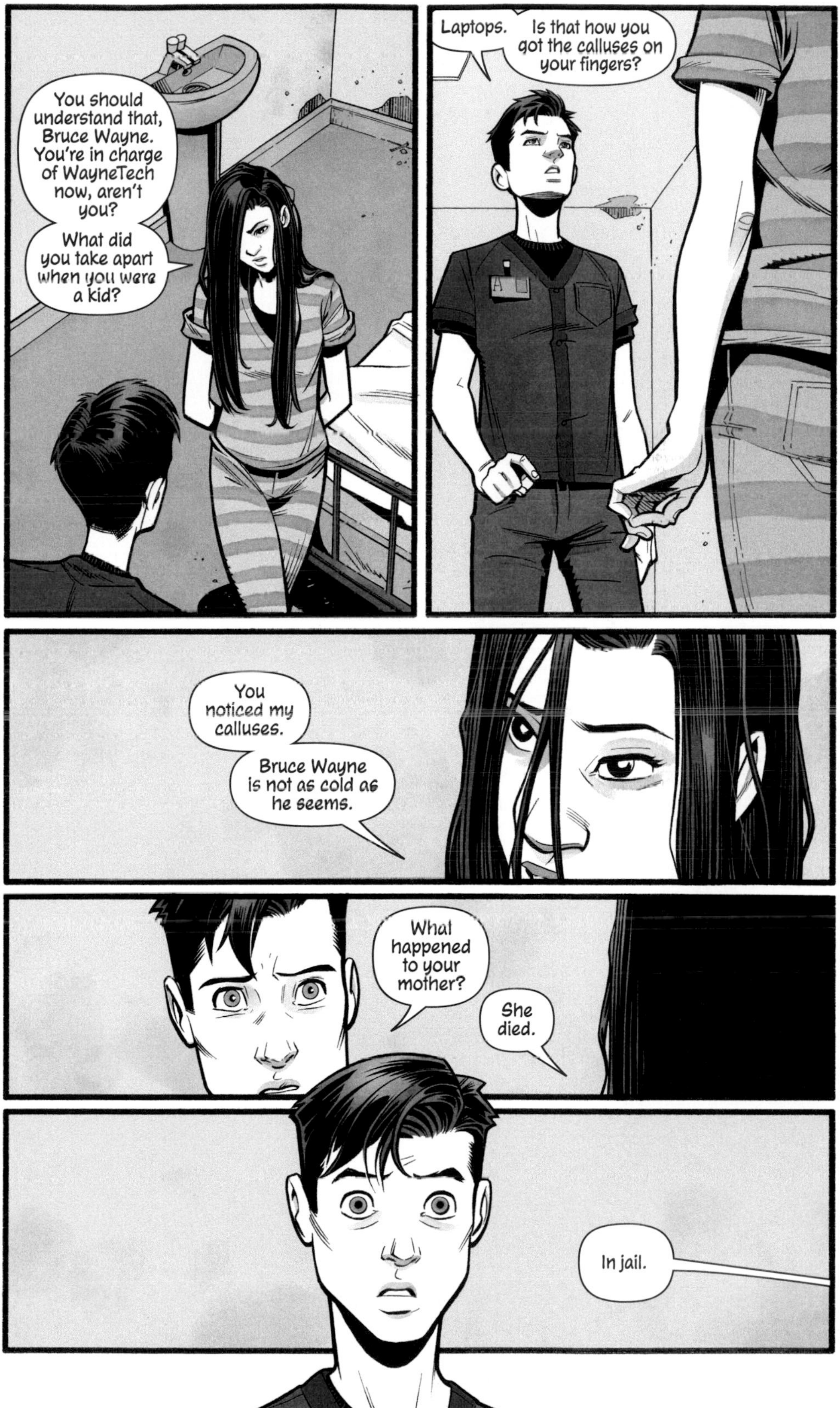
You should understand that, Bruce Wayne. You're in charge of WayneTech now, aren't you?
What did you take apart when you were a kid?
Laptops.
Is that how you got the calluses on your fingers?
You noticed my calluses.
Bruce Wayne is not as cold as he seems.
What happened to your mother?
She died.
In jail.

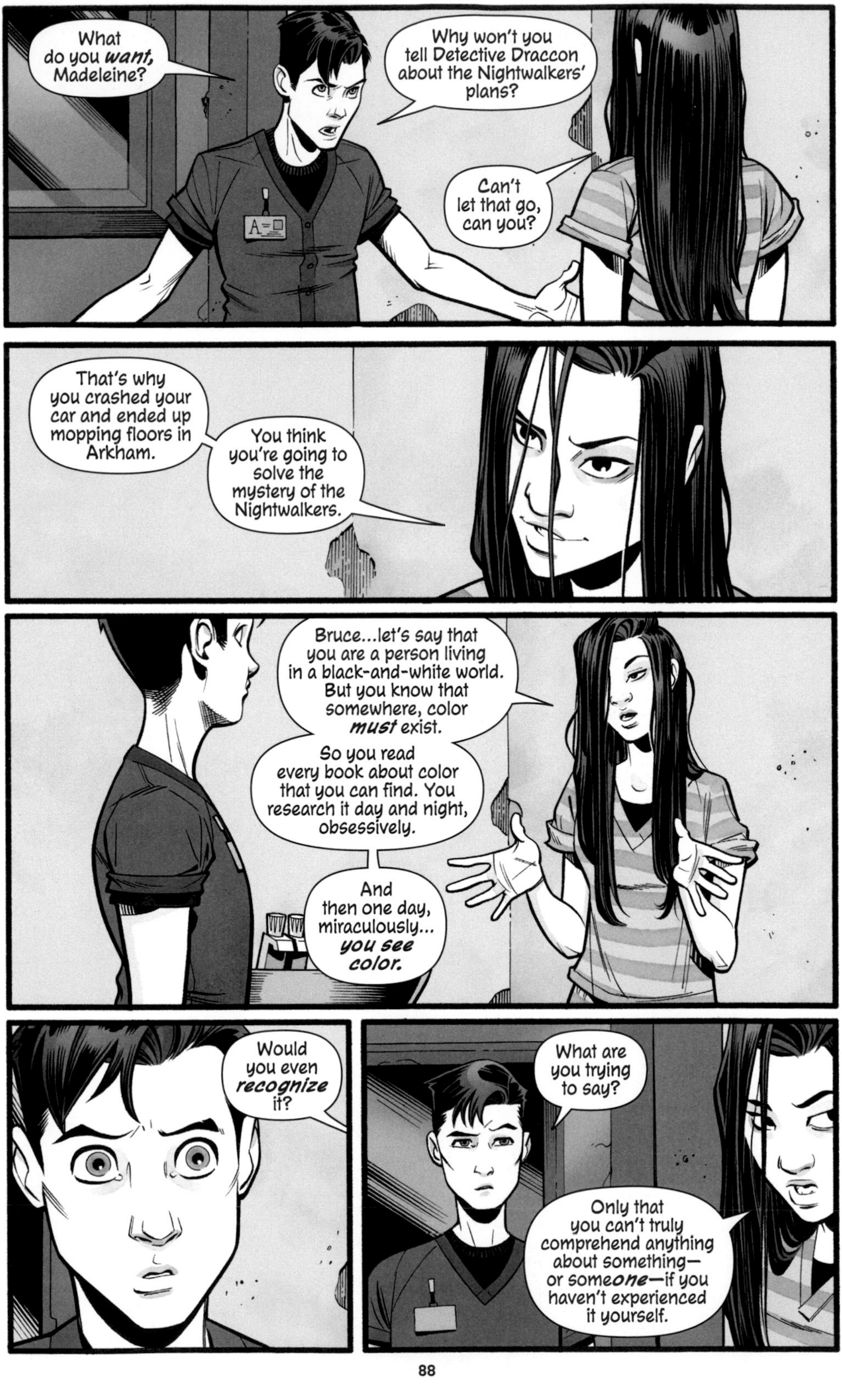

What do you *want,* Madeleine?
Why won't you tell Detective Draccon about the Nightwalkers' plans?
Can't let that go, can you?
That's why you crashed your car and ended up mopping floors in Arkham.
You think you're going to solve the mystery of the Nightwalkers.
Bruce...let's say that you are a person living in a black-and-white world. But you know that somewhere, color *must* exist.
So you read every book about color that you can find. You research it day and night, obsessively.
And then one day, miraculously... ***you see color.***
Would you even ***recognize*** it?
What are you trying to say?
Only that you can't truly comprehend anything about something— or some***one***—if you haven't experienced it yourself.

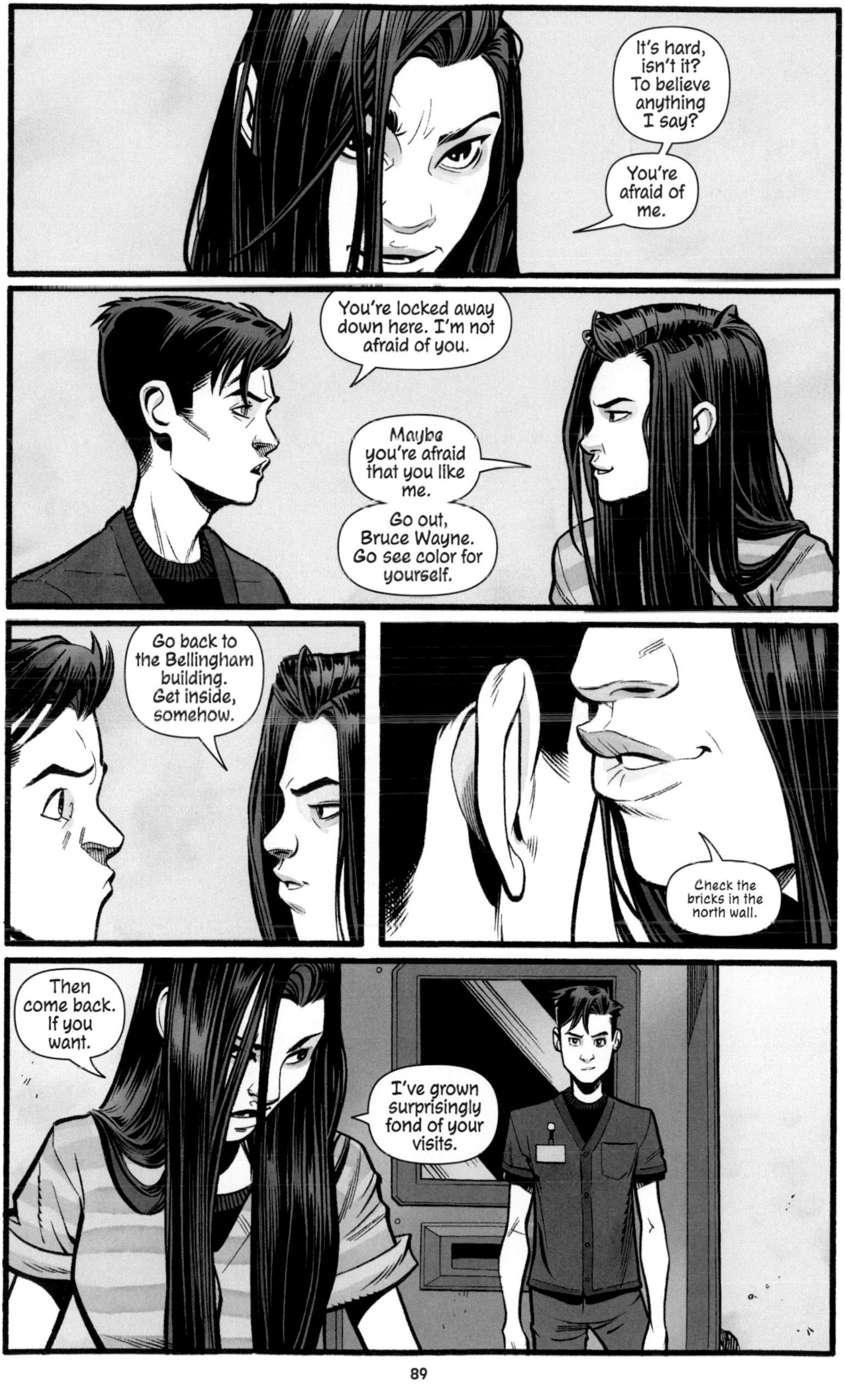
It's hard, isn't it? To believe anything I say?
You're afraid of me.
You're locked away down here. I'm not afraid of you.
Maybe you're afraid that you like me.
Go out, Bruce Wayne. Go see color for yourself.
Go back to the Bellingham building. Get inside, somehow.
Check the bricks in the north wall.
Then come back. If you want.
I've grown surprisingly fond of your visits.

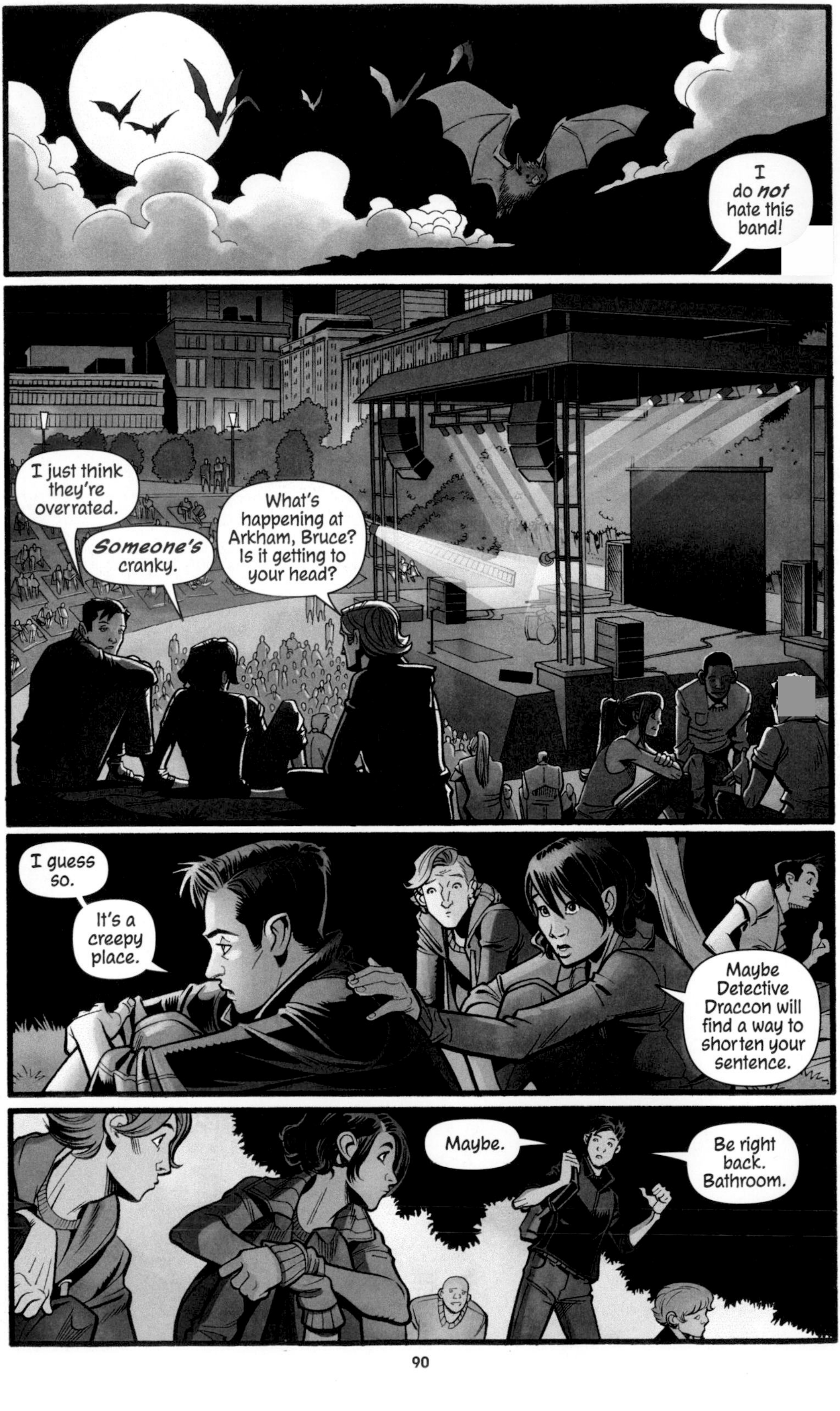
I do *not* hate this band!
I just think they're overrated.
Someone's cranky.
What's happening at Arkham, Bruce? Is it getting to your head?
I guess so.
It's a creepy place.
Maybe Detective Draccon will find a way to shorten your sentence.
Maybe.
Be right back. Bathroom.

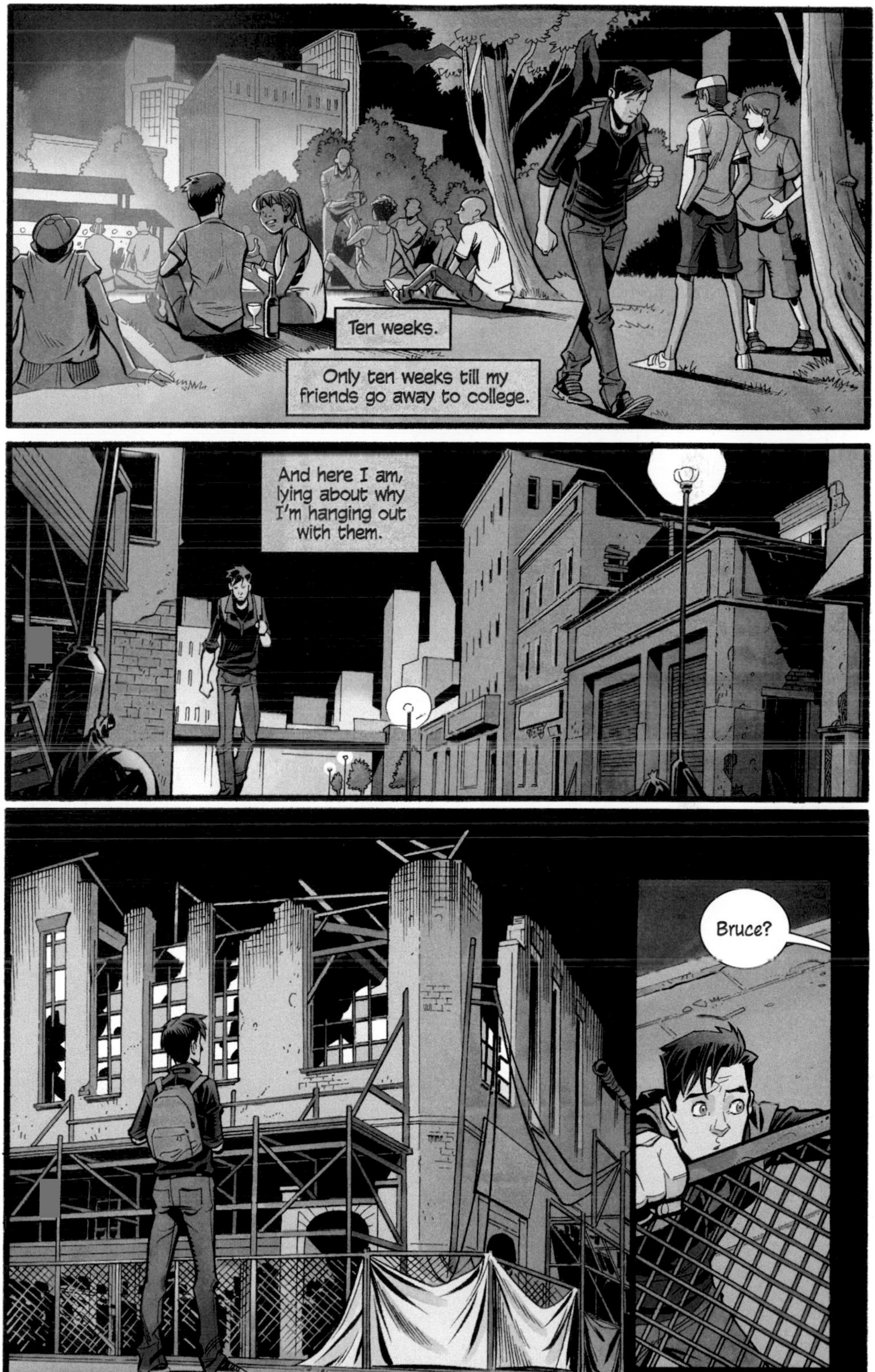
Ten weeks.
Only ten weeks till my friends go away to college.
And here I am, lying about why I'm hanging out with them.
Bruce?

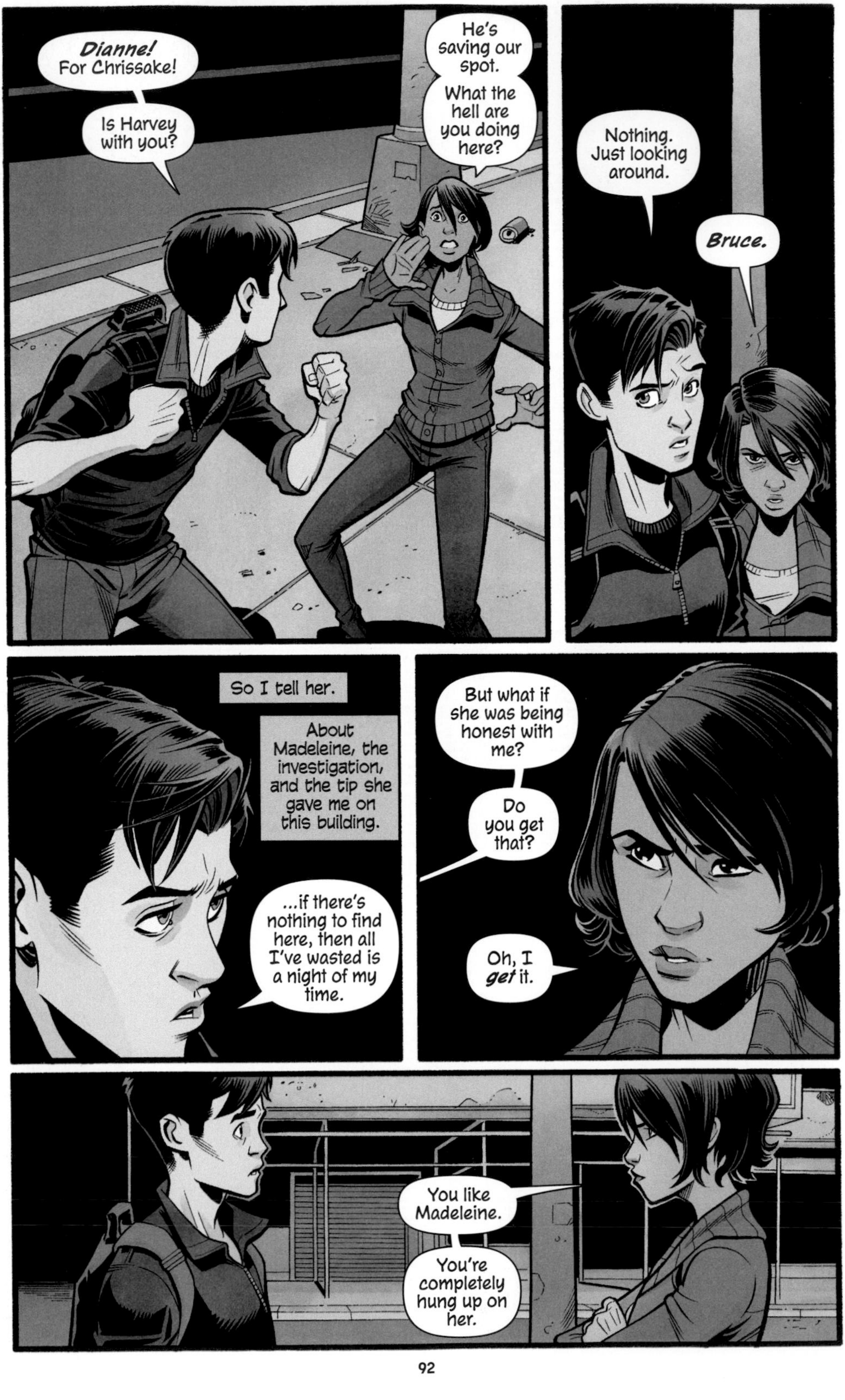

Dianne! For Chrissake!
Is Harvey with you?
He's saving our spot.
What the hell are you doing here?
Nothing. Just looking around.
Bruce.
So I tell her.
About Madeleine, the investigation, and the tip she gave me on this building.
...if there's nothing to find here, then all I've wasted is a night of my time.
But what if she was being honest with me?
Do you get that?
Oh, I *get* it.
You like Madeleine.
You're completely hung up on her.

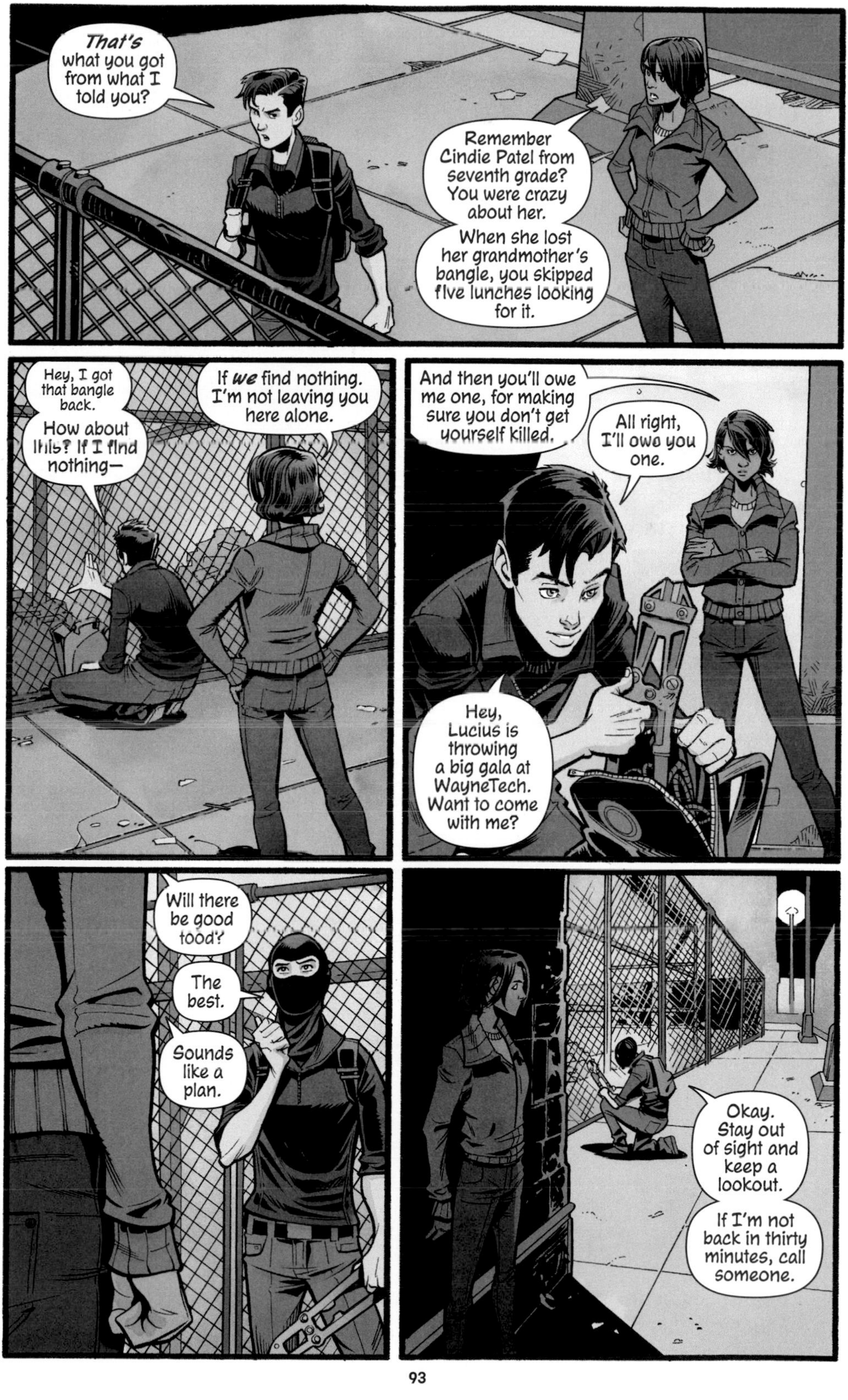
That's what you got from what I told you?
Remember Cindie Patel from seventh grade? You were crazy about her.
When she lost her grandmother's bangle, you skipped five lunches looking for it.
Hey, I got that bangle back.
How about this? If I find nothing—
If *we* find nothing. I'm not leaving you here alone.
And then you'll owe me one, for making sure you don't get yourself killed.
All right, I'll owe you one.
Hey, Lucius is throwing a big gala at WayneTech. Want to come with me?
Will there be good food?
The best.
Sounds like a plan.
Okay. Stay out of sight and keep a lookout.
If I'm not back in thirty minutes, call someone.

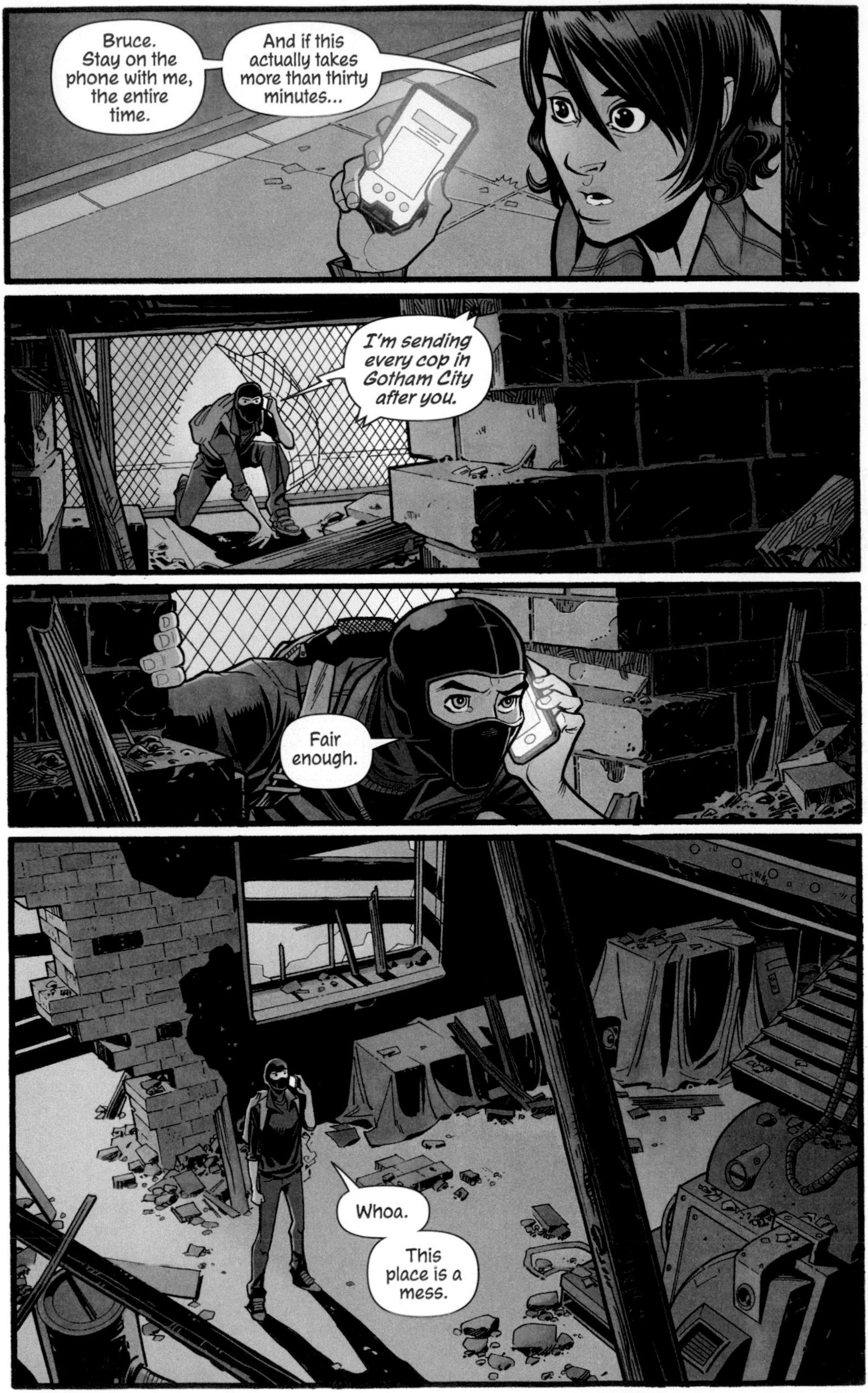
Bruce. Stay on the phone with me, the entire time.
And if this actually takes more than thirty minutes...
I'm sending every cop in Gotham City after you.
Fair enough.
Whoa.
This place is a mess.

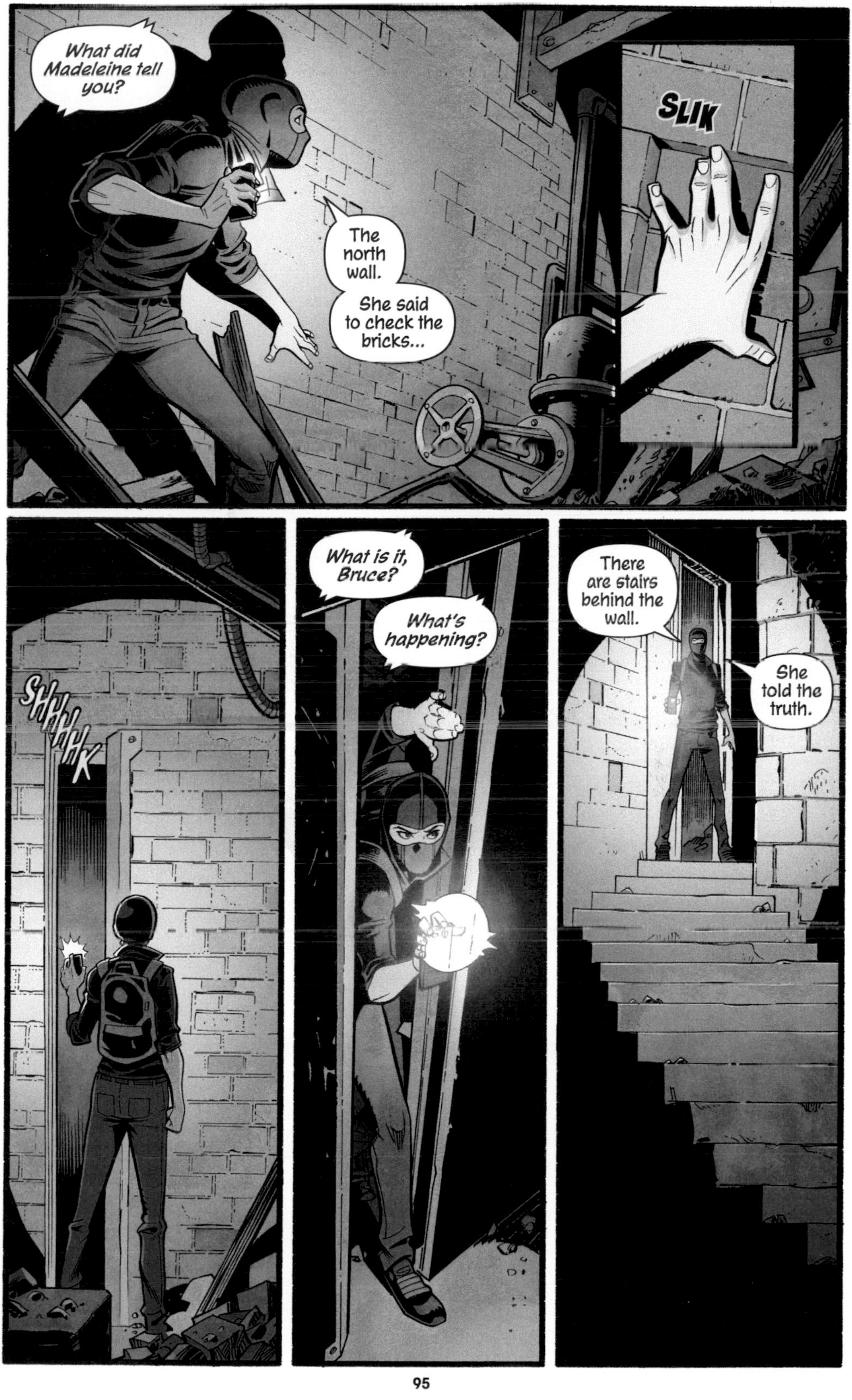
What did Madeleine tell you?
The north wall.
She said to check the bricks...
SLIK
SHHHHK
What is it, Bruce?
What's happening?
There are stairs behind the wall.
She told the truth.

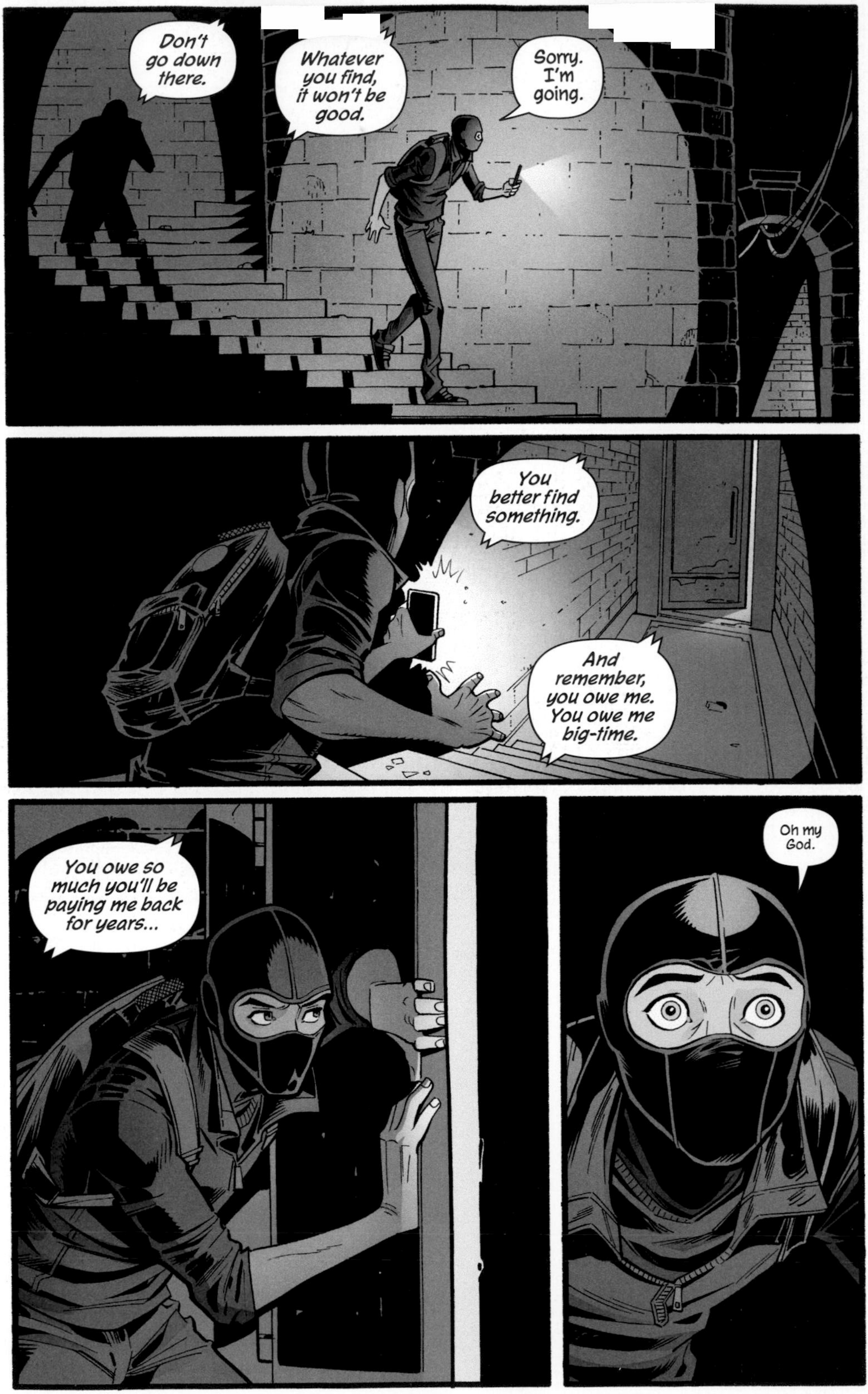
Don't go down there.
Whatever you find, it won't be good.
Sorry. I'm going.
You better find something.
And remember, you owe me. You owe me big-time.
You owe so much you'll be paying me back for years...
Oh my God.

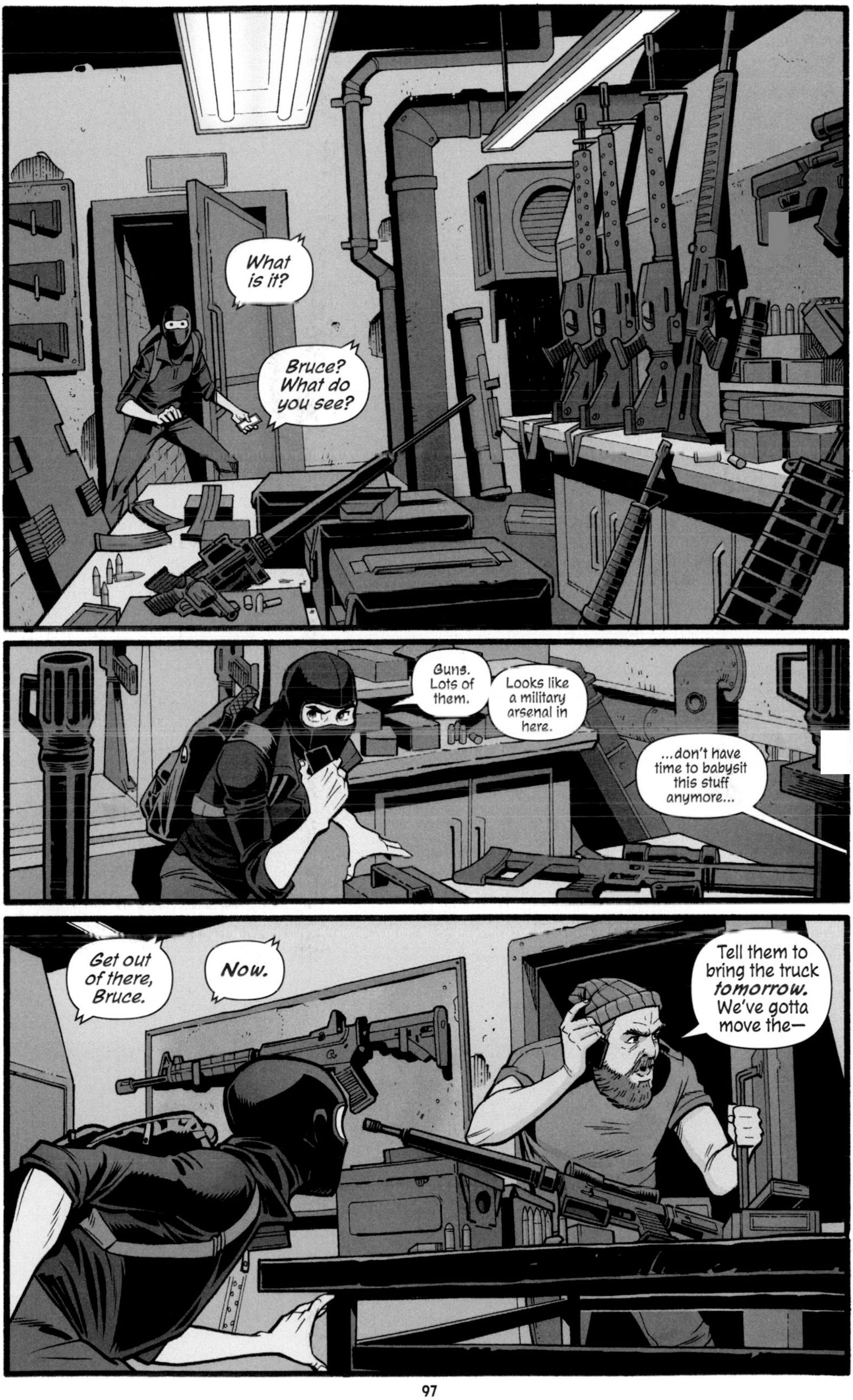
What is it?
Bruce? What do you see?
Guns. Lots of them.
Looks like a military arsenal in here.
...don't have time to babysit this stuff anymore...
Get out of there, Bruce.
Now.
Tell them to bring the truck *tomorrow.* We've gotta move the—

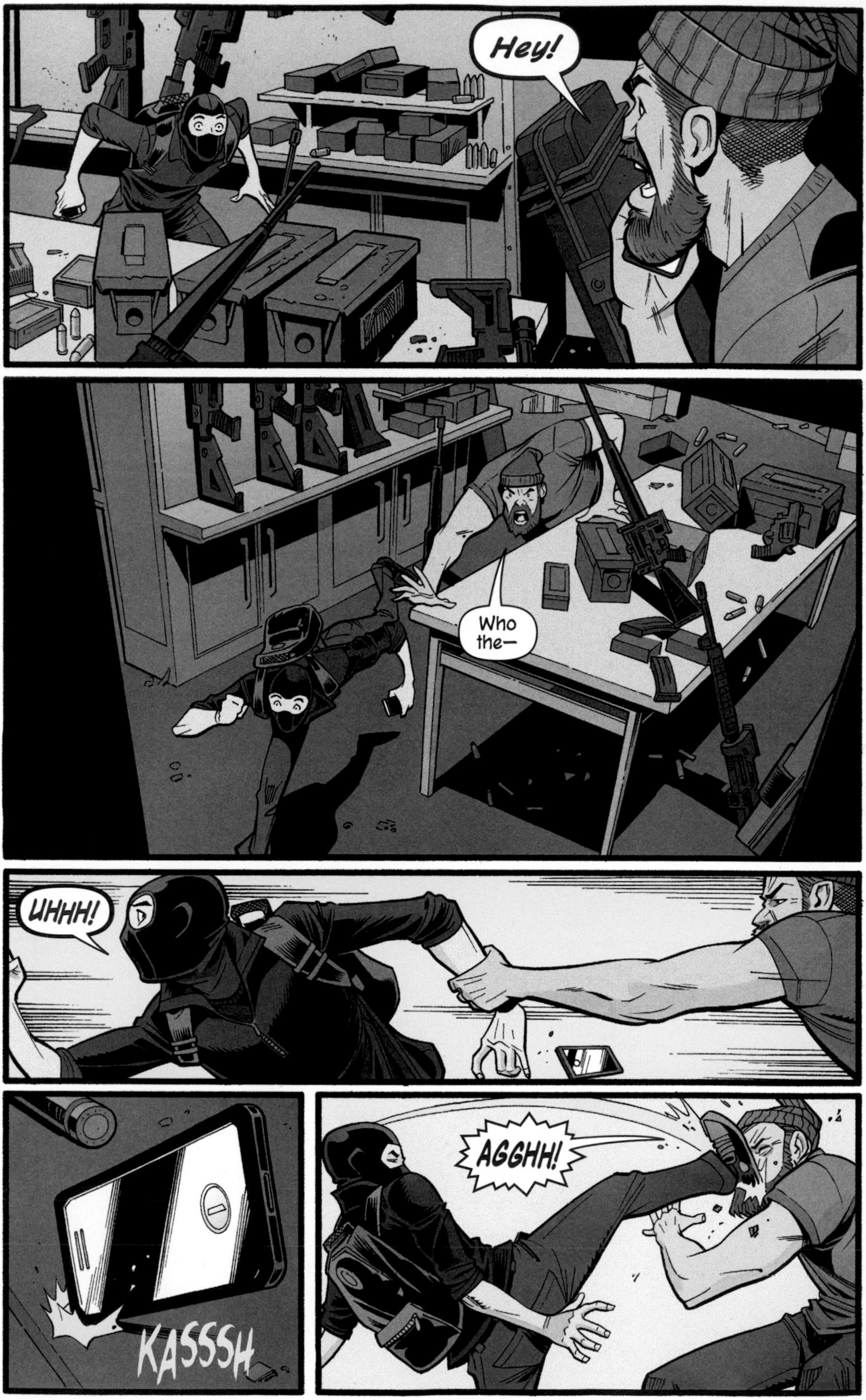
Hey!
Who the—
UHHH!
KASSSH
AGGHH!

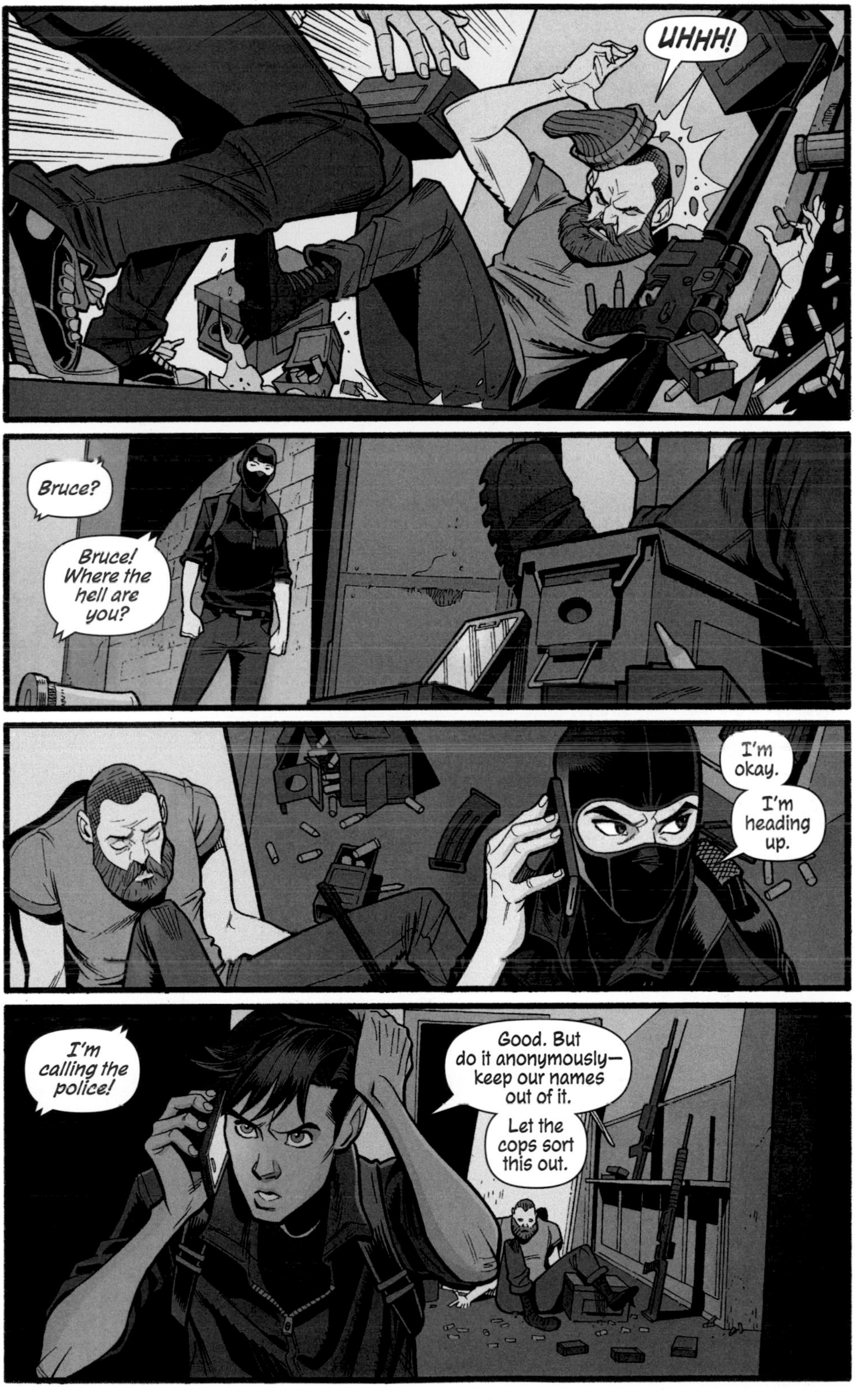
UHHH!
Bruce?
Bruce! Where the hell are you?
I'm okay.
I'm heading up.
I'm calling the police!
Good. But do it anonymously—keep our names out of it.
Let the cops sort this out.

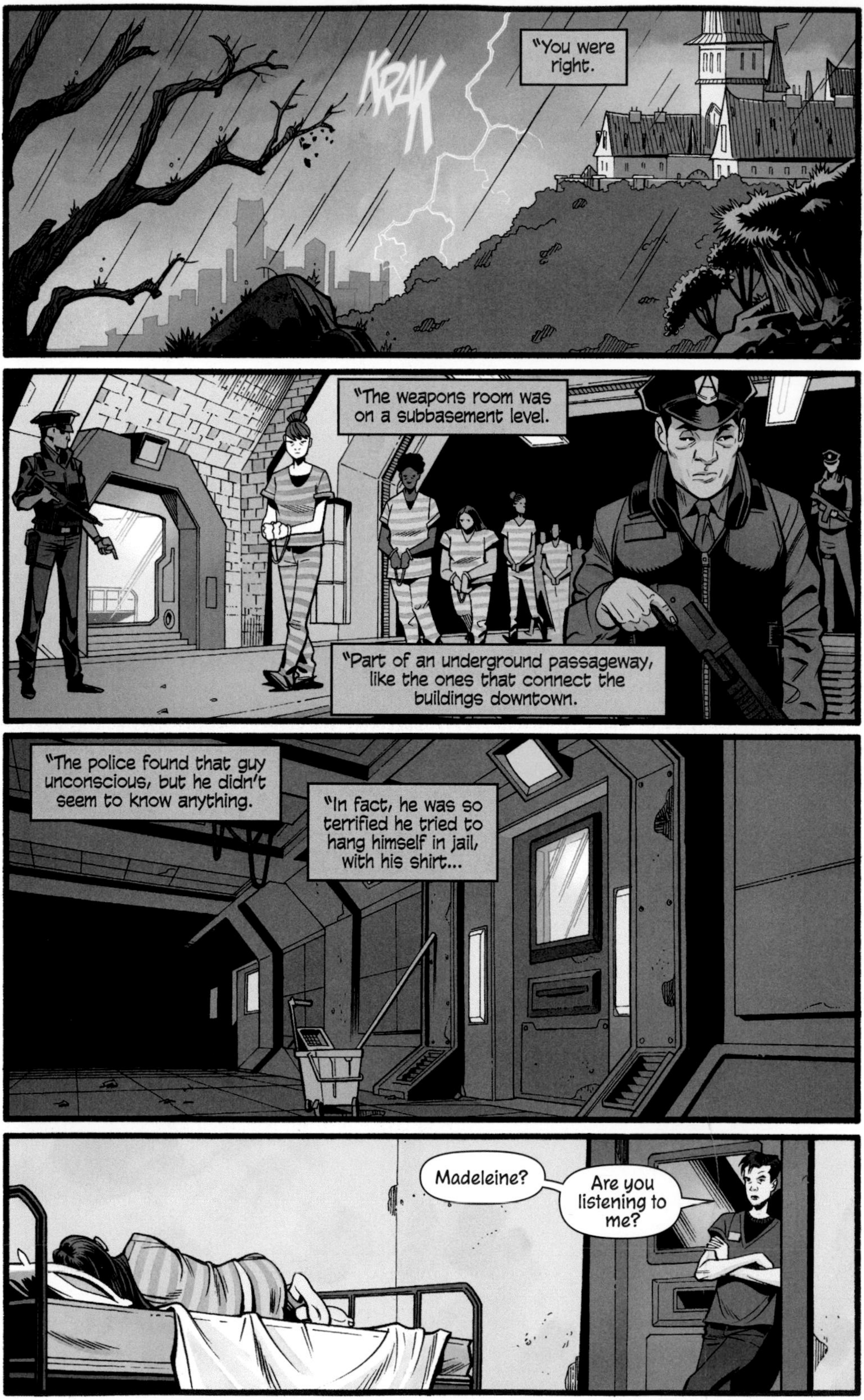
KRAK
"You were right.
"The weapons room was on a subbasement level.
"Part of an underground passageway, like the ones that connect the buildings downtown.
"The police found that guy unconscious, but he didn't seem to know anything.
"In fact, he was so terrified he tried to hang himself in jail, with his shirt...
Madeleine?
Are you listening to me?

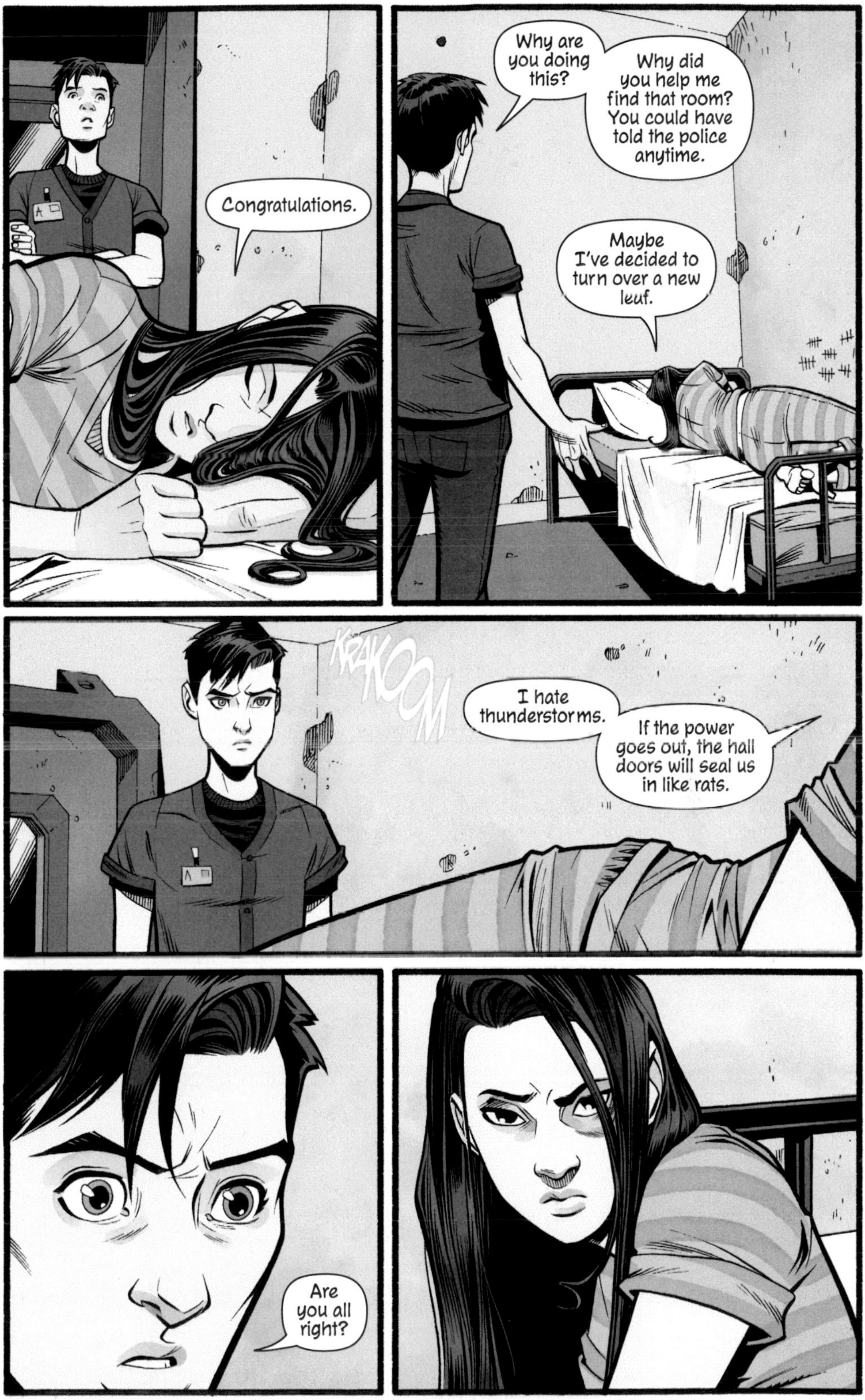
Congratulations.
Why are you doing this?
Why did you help me find that room? You could have told the police anytime.
Maybe I've decided to turn over a new leaf.
KRAKOOM
I hate thunderstorms.
If the power goes out, the hall doors will seal us in like rats.
Are you all right?

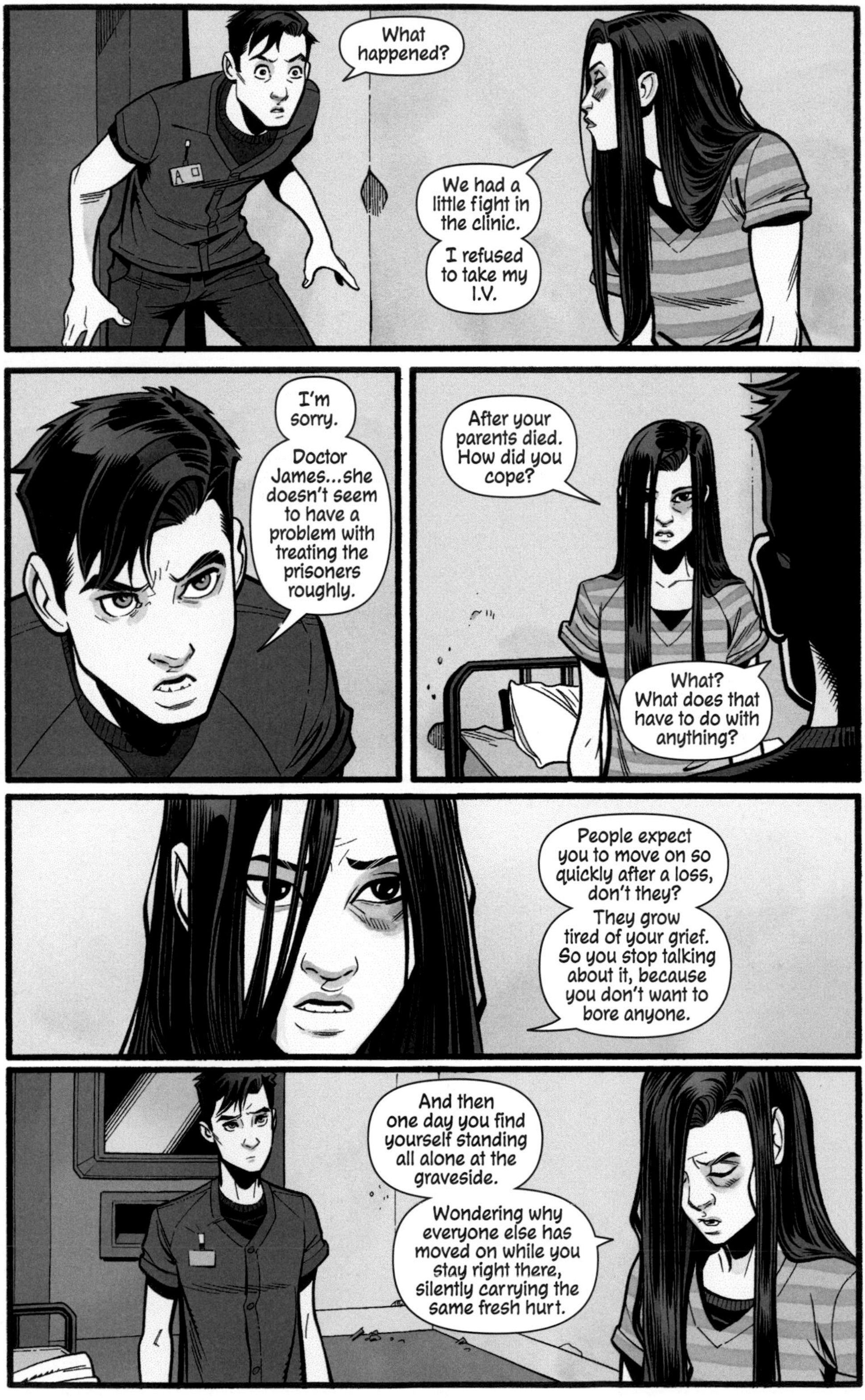
What happened?
We had a little fight in the clinic.
I refused to take my I.V.
I'm sorry.
Doctor James...she doesn't seem to have a problem with treating the prisoners roughly.
After your parents died. How did you cope?
What? What does that have to do with anything?
People expect you to move on so quickly after a loss, don't they?
They grow tired of your grief. So you stop talking about it, because you don't want to bore anyone.
And then one day you find yourself standing all alone at the graveside.
Wondering why everyone else has moved on while you stay right there, silently carrying the same fresh hurt.

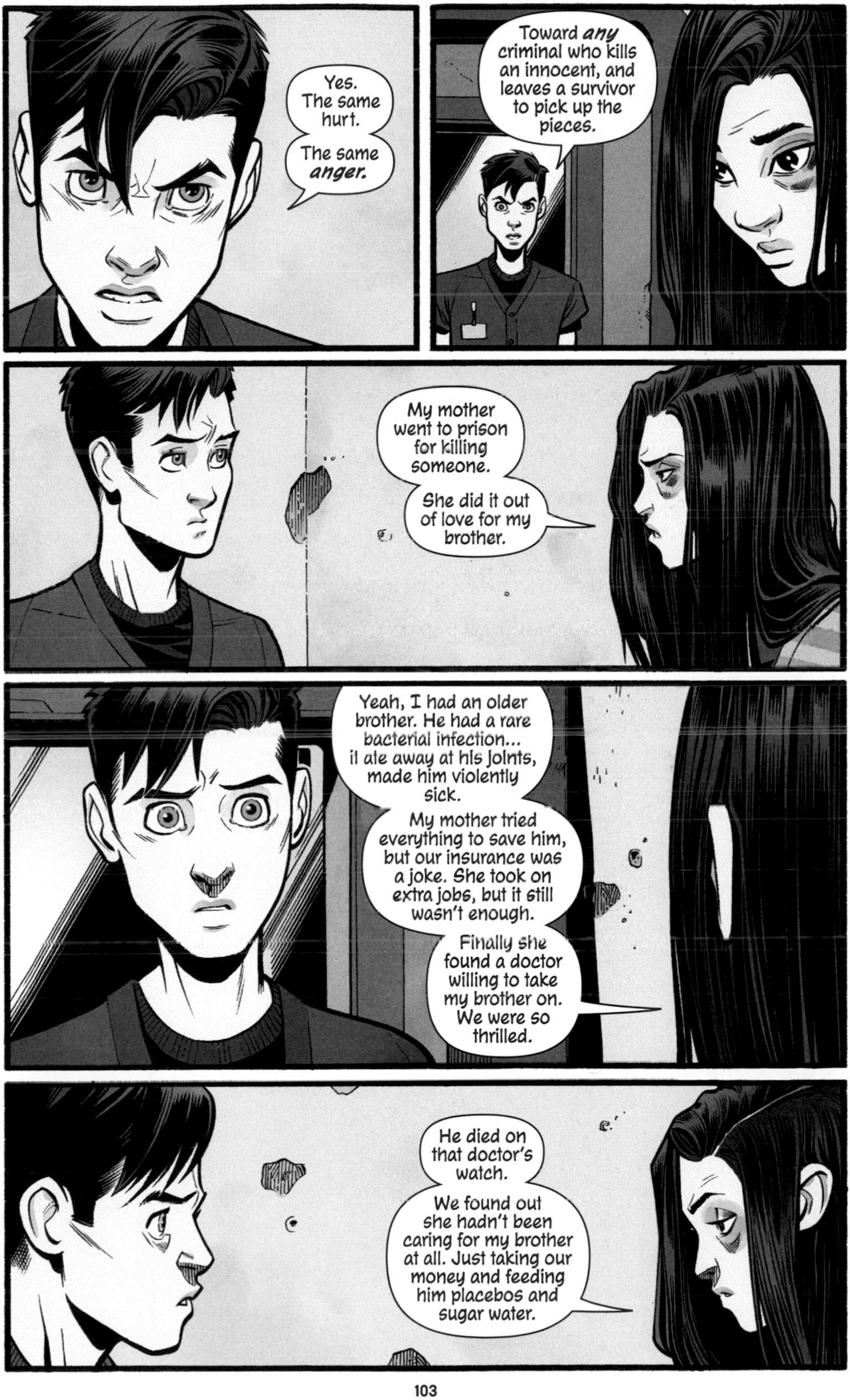
Yes. The same hurt.
The same *anger.*
Toward *any* criminal who kills an innocent, and leaves a survivor to pick up the pieces.
My mother went to prison for killing someone.
She did it out of love for my brother.
Yeah, I had an older brother. He had a rare bacterial infection... it ate away at his joints, made him violently sick.
My mother tried everything to save him, but our insurance was a joke. She took on extra jobs, but it still wasn't enough.
Finally she found a doctor willing to take my brother on. We were so thrilled.
He died on that doctor's watch.
We found out she hadn't been caring for my brother at all. Just taking our money and feeding him placebos and sugar water.

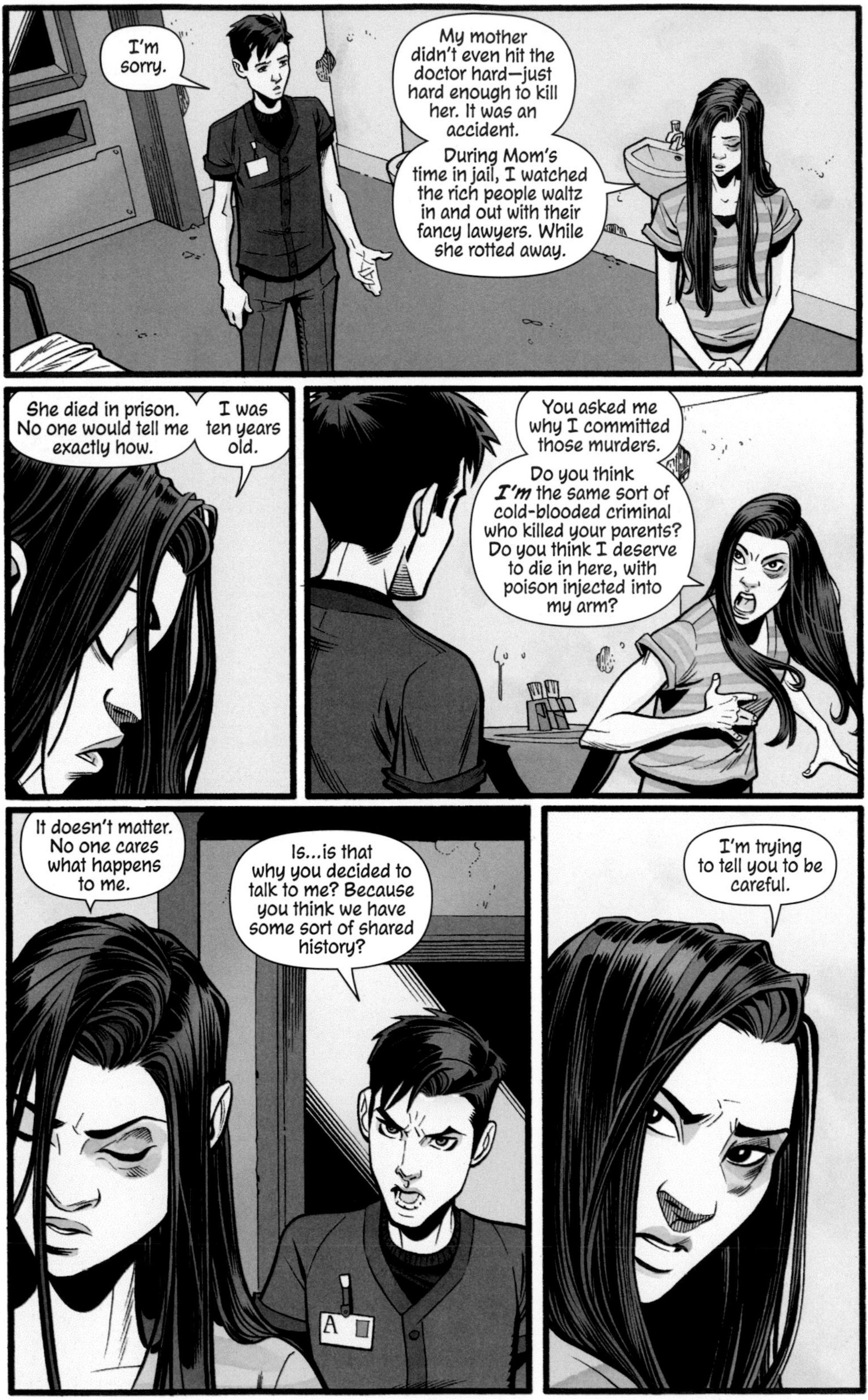
I'm sorry.
My mother didn't even hit the doctor hard—just hard enough to kill her. It was an accident.
During Mom's time in jail, I watched the rich people waltz in and out with their fancy lawyers. While she rotted away.
She died in prison. No one would tell me exactly how.
I was ten years old.
You asked me why I committed those murders.
Do you think *I'm* the same sort of cold-blooded criminal who killed your parents? Do you think I deserve to die in here, with poison injected into my arm?
It doesn't matter. No one cares what happens to me.
Is...is that why you decided to talk to me? Because you think we have some sort of shared history?
I'm trying to tell you to be careful.

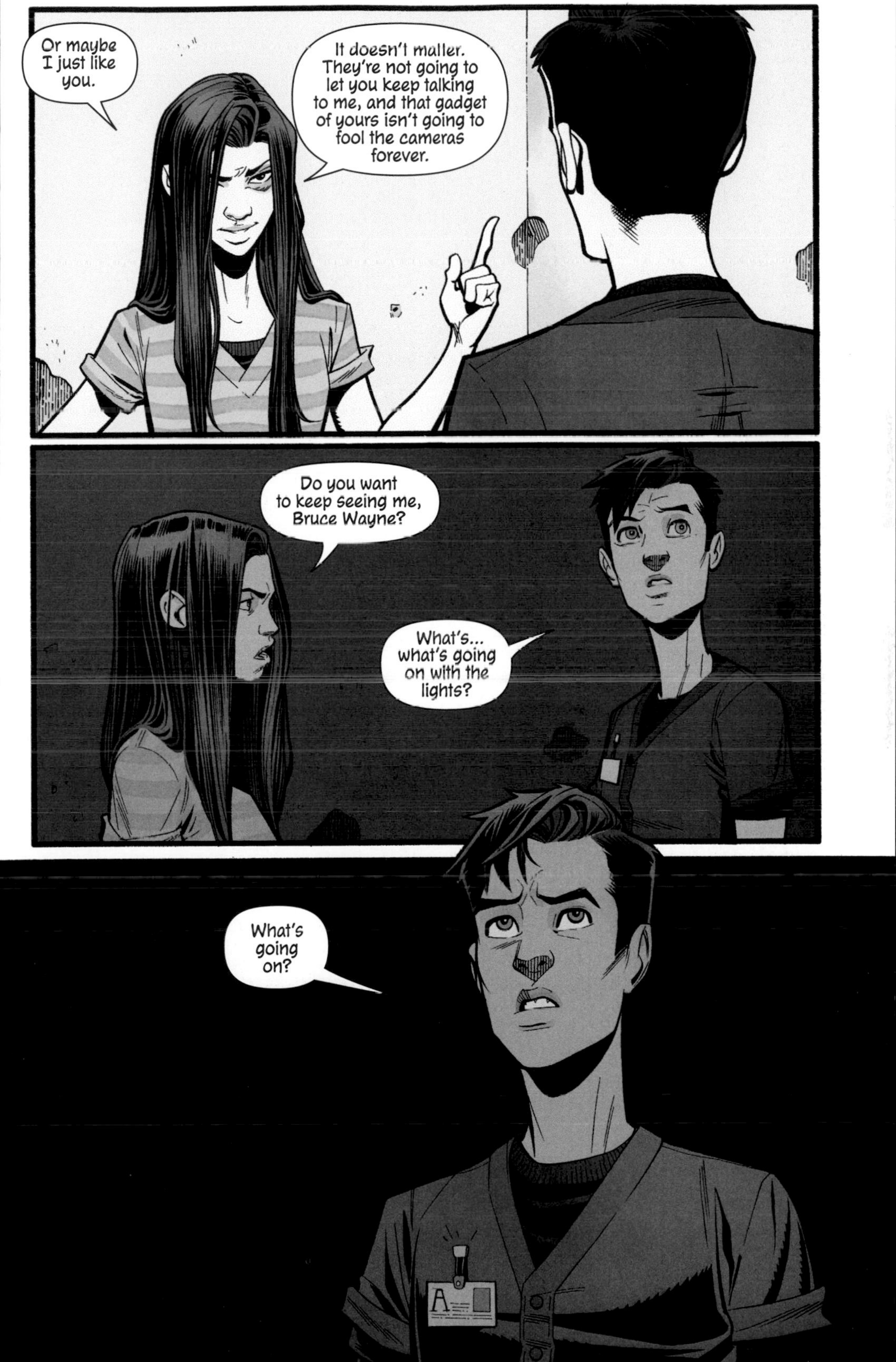
Or maybe I just like you.
It doesn't matter. They're not going to let you keep talking to me, and that gadget of yours isn't going to fool the cameras forever.
Do you want to keep seeing me, Bruce Wayne?
What's... what's going on with the lights?
What's going on?

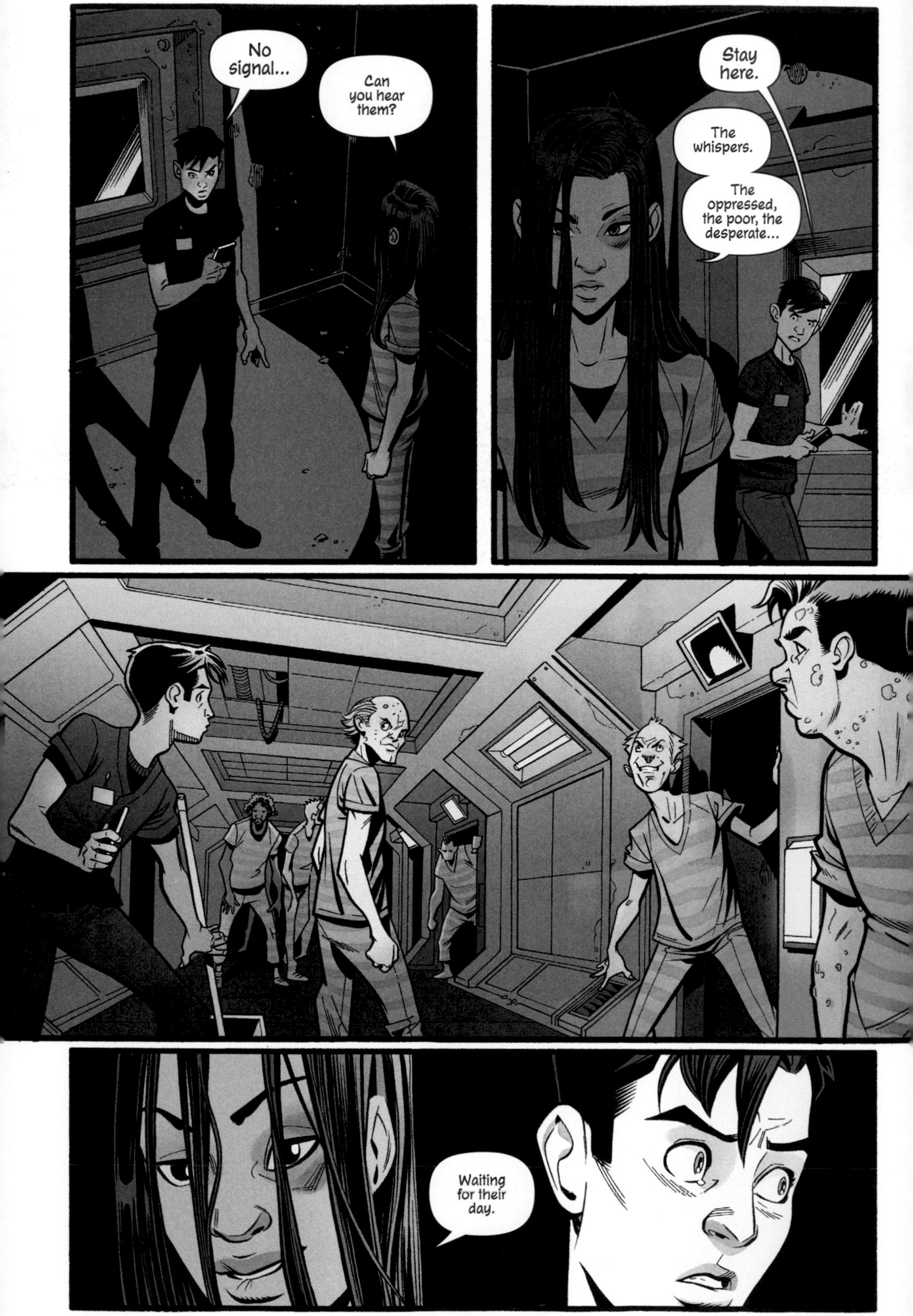
No signal...
Can you hear them?
Stay here.
The whispers.
The oppressed, the poor, the desperate...
Waiting for their day.

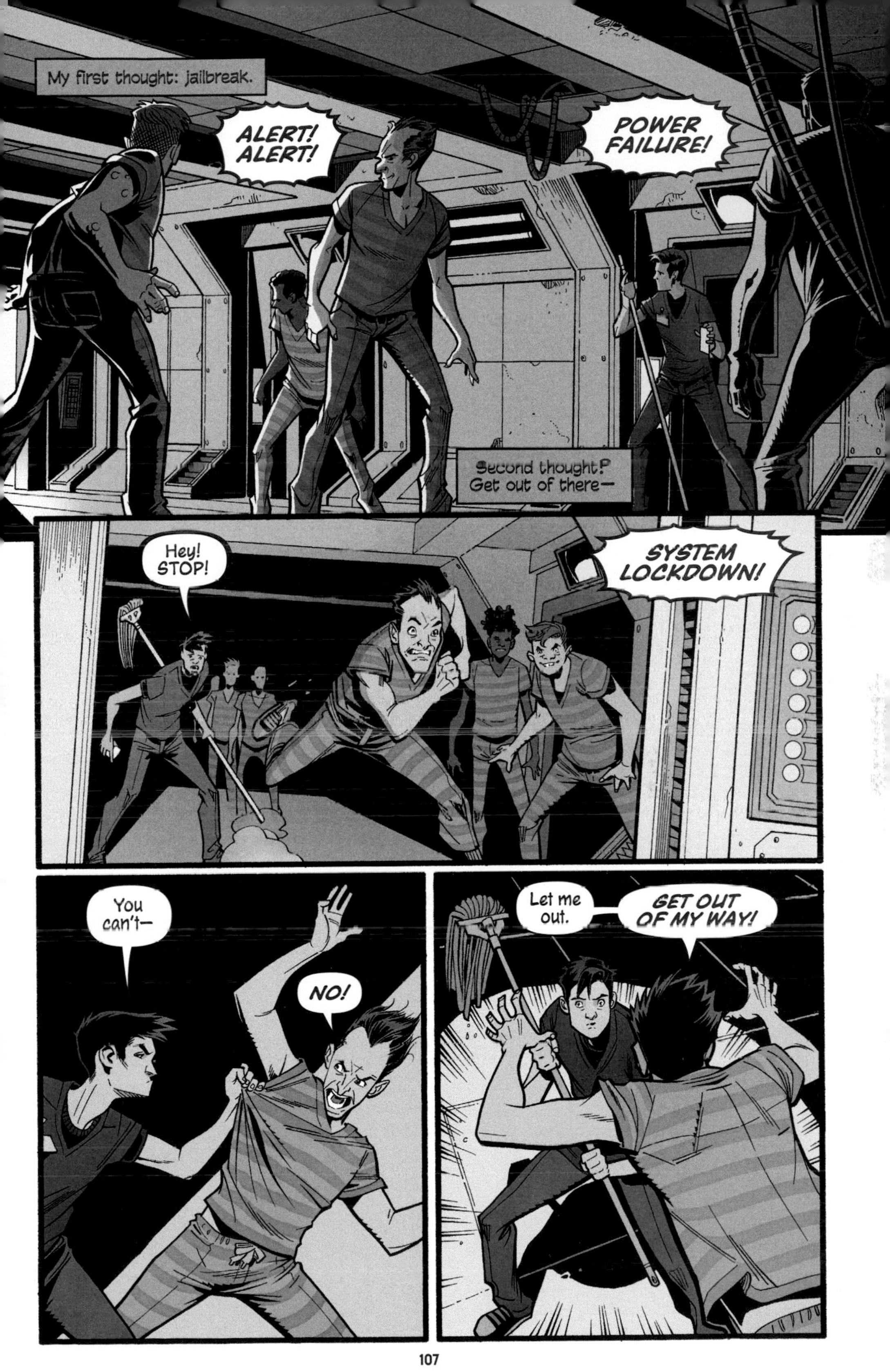
My first thought: jailbreak.
ALERT! ALERT!
POWER FAILURE!
Second thought? Get out of there—
Hey! STOP!
SYSTEM LOCKDOWN!
You can't—
NO!
Let me out.
GET OUT OF MY WAY!

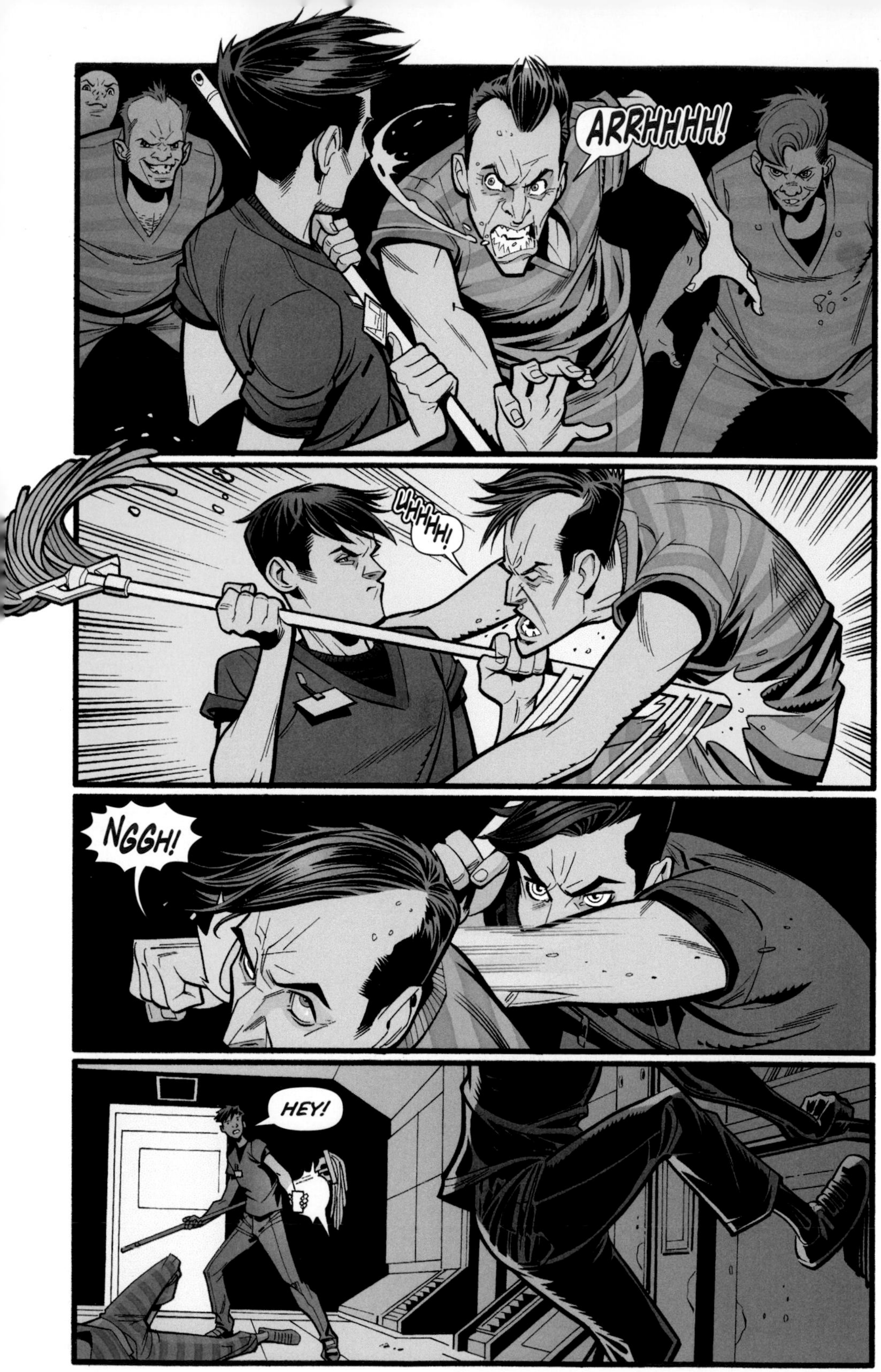
ARRHHHH!
UHHHHH!
NGGH!
HEY!

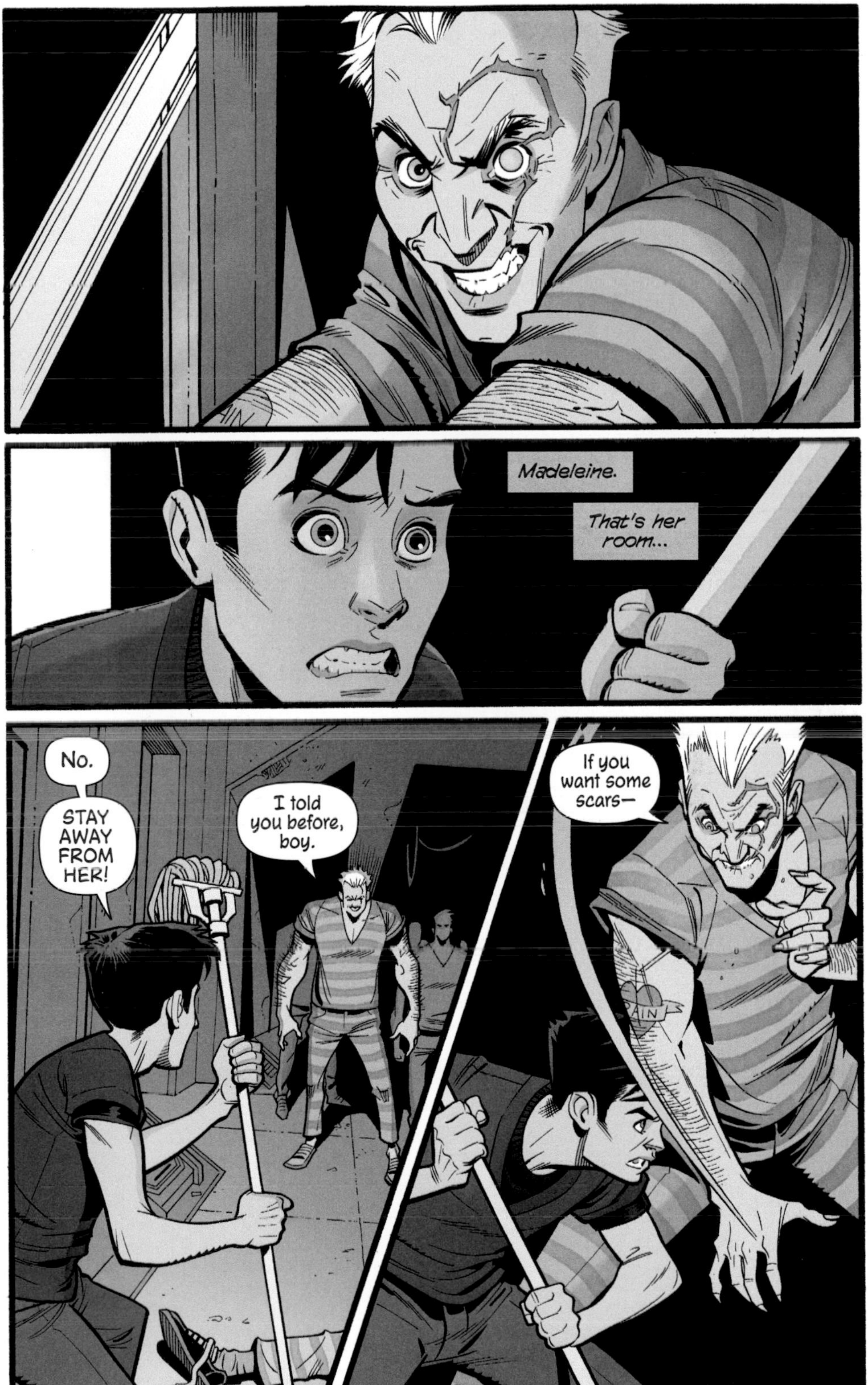
Madeleine.
That's her room...
No.
STAY AWAY FROM HER!
I told you before, boy.
If you want some scars—
PAIN

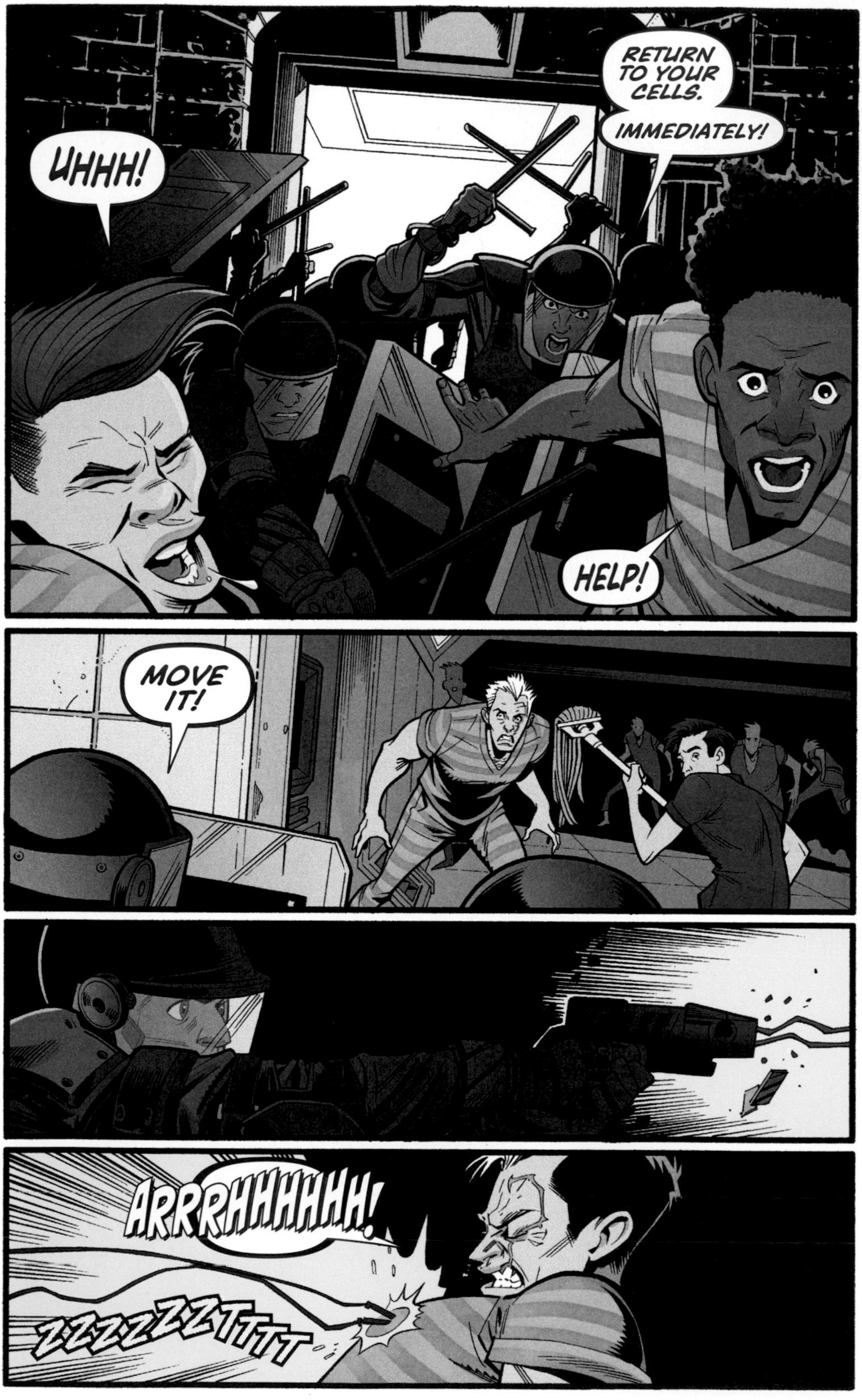
UHHH!
RETURN TO YOUR CELLS.
IMMEDIATELY!
HELP!
MOVE IT!
ARRRHHHHHH!
ZZZZZZZTTTTT

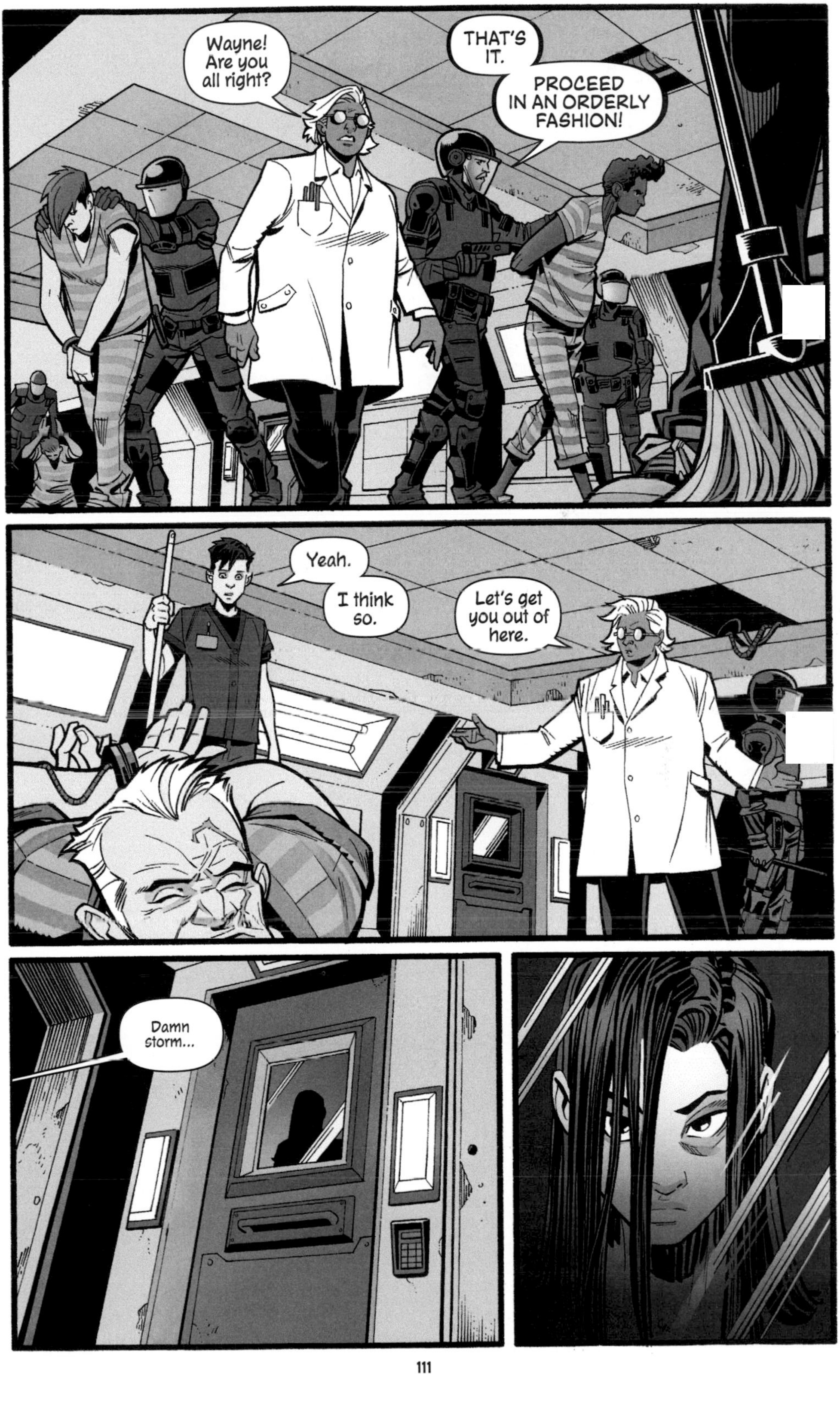
Wayne! Are you all right?
THAT'S IT.
PROCEED IN AN ORDERLY FASHION!
Yeah.
I think so.
Let's get you out of here.
Damn storm...

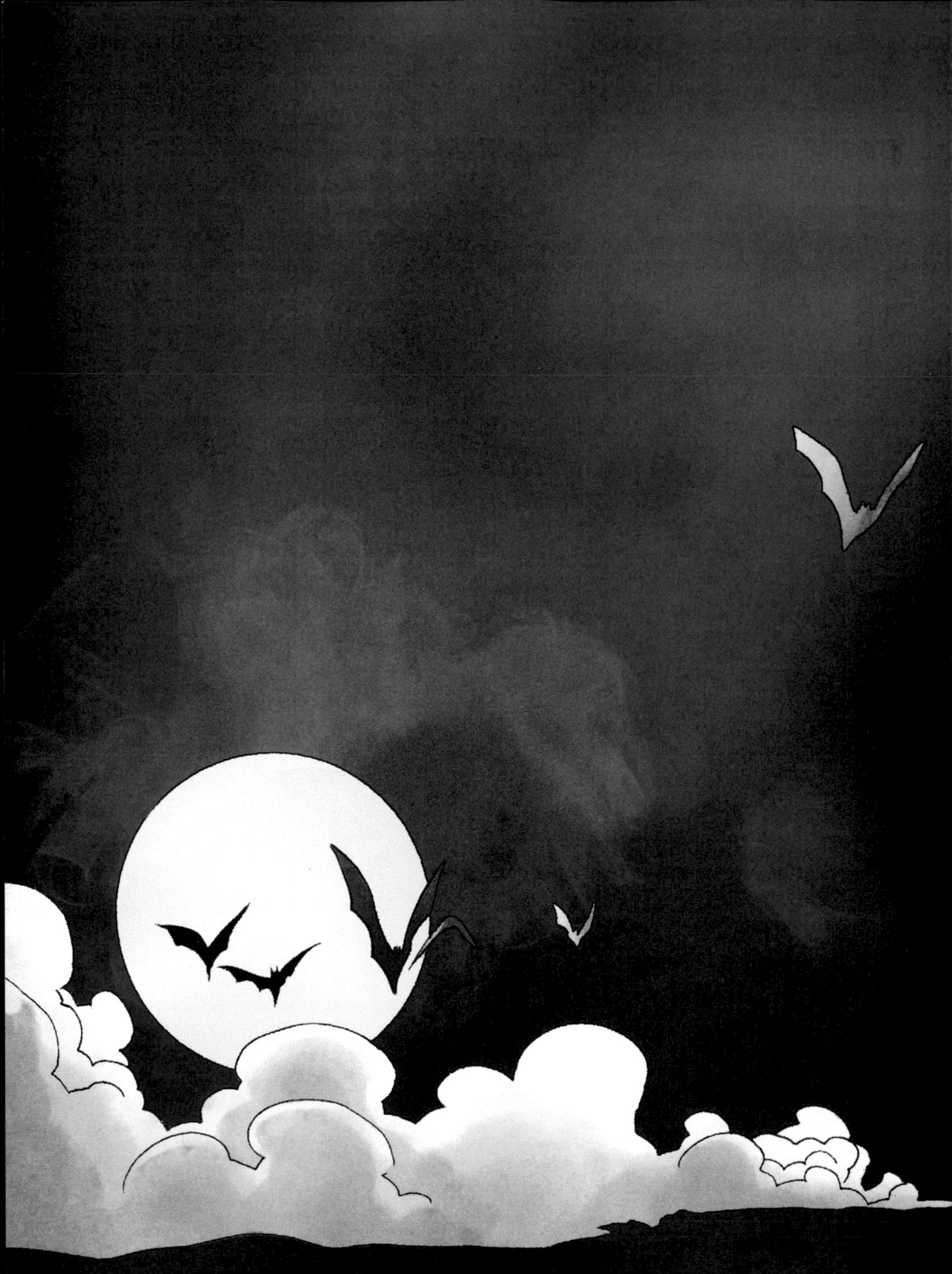

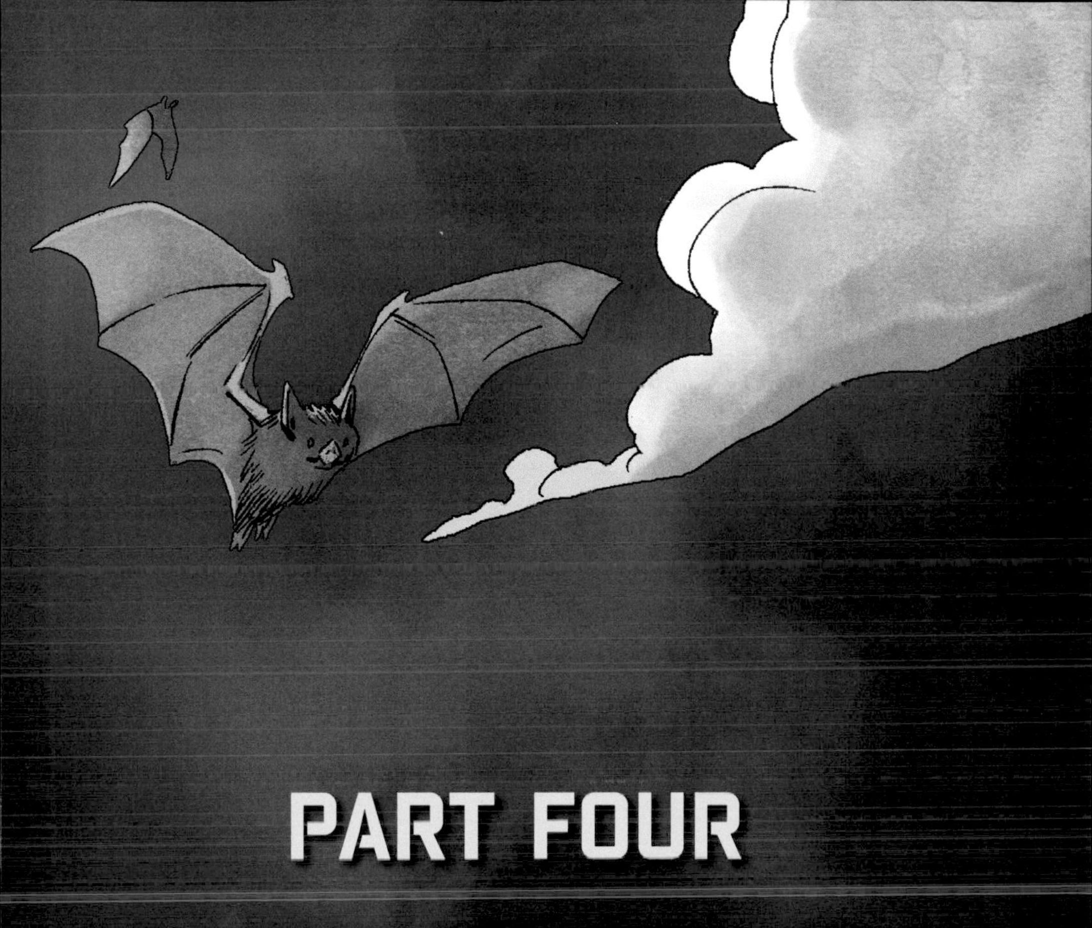

PART FOUR

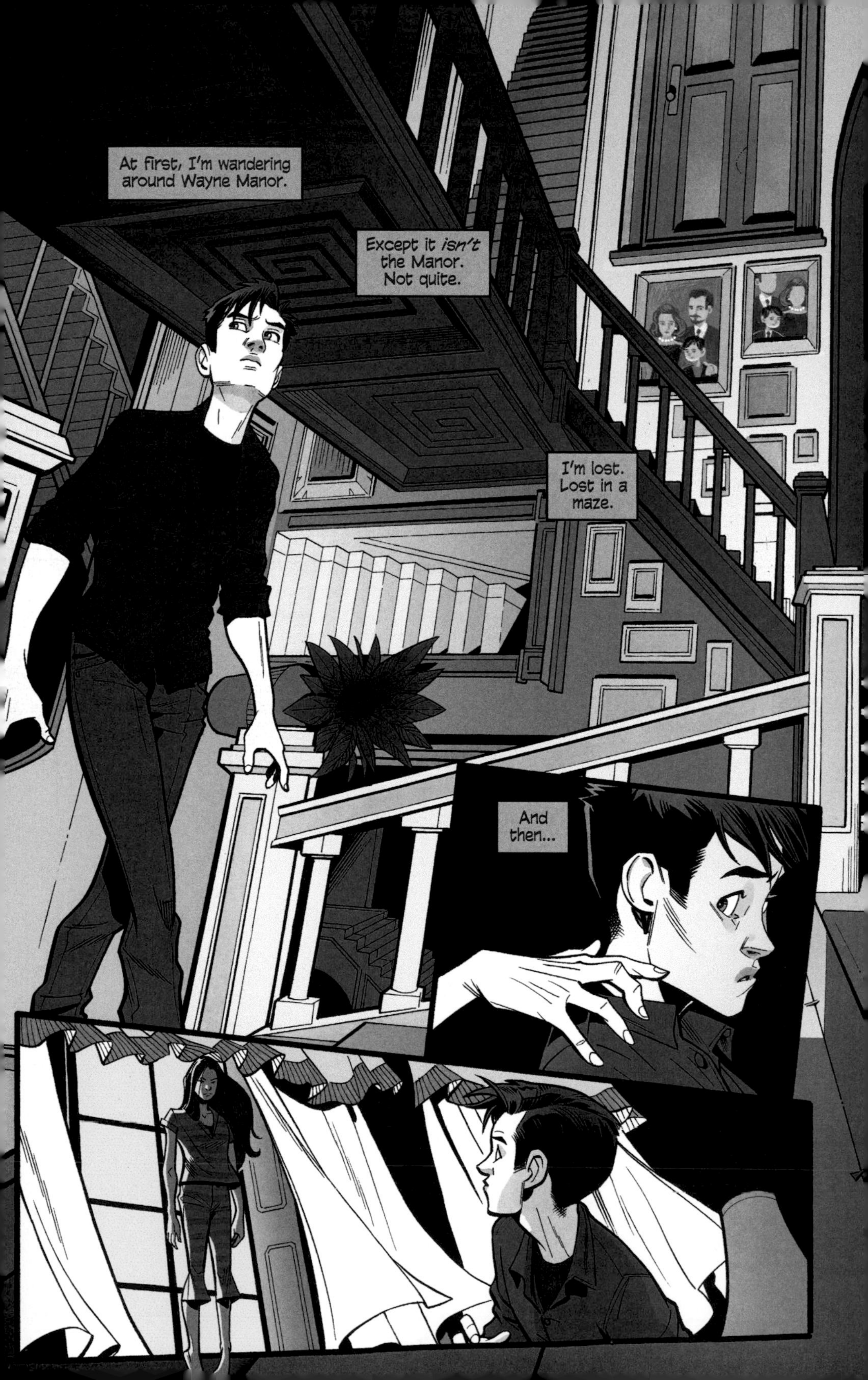
At first, I'm wandering around Wayne Manor.
Except it *isn't* the Manor. Not quite.
I'm lost. Lost in a maze.
And then...

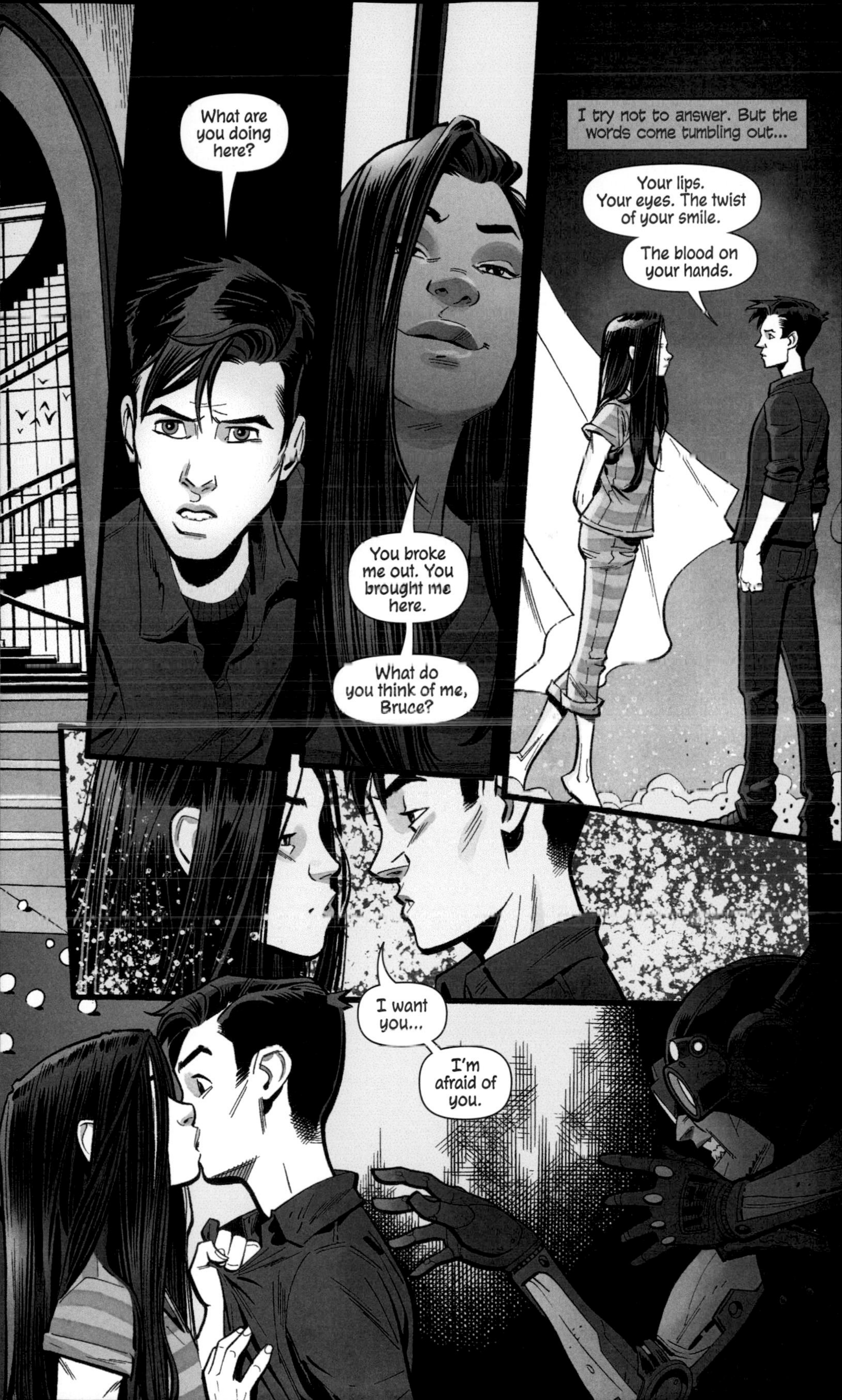
What are you doing here?
You broke me out. You brought me here.
What do you think of me, Bruce?
I try not to answer. But the words come tumbling out...
Your lips. Your eyes. The twist of your smile.
The blood on your hands.
I want you...
I'm afraid of you.

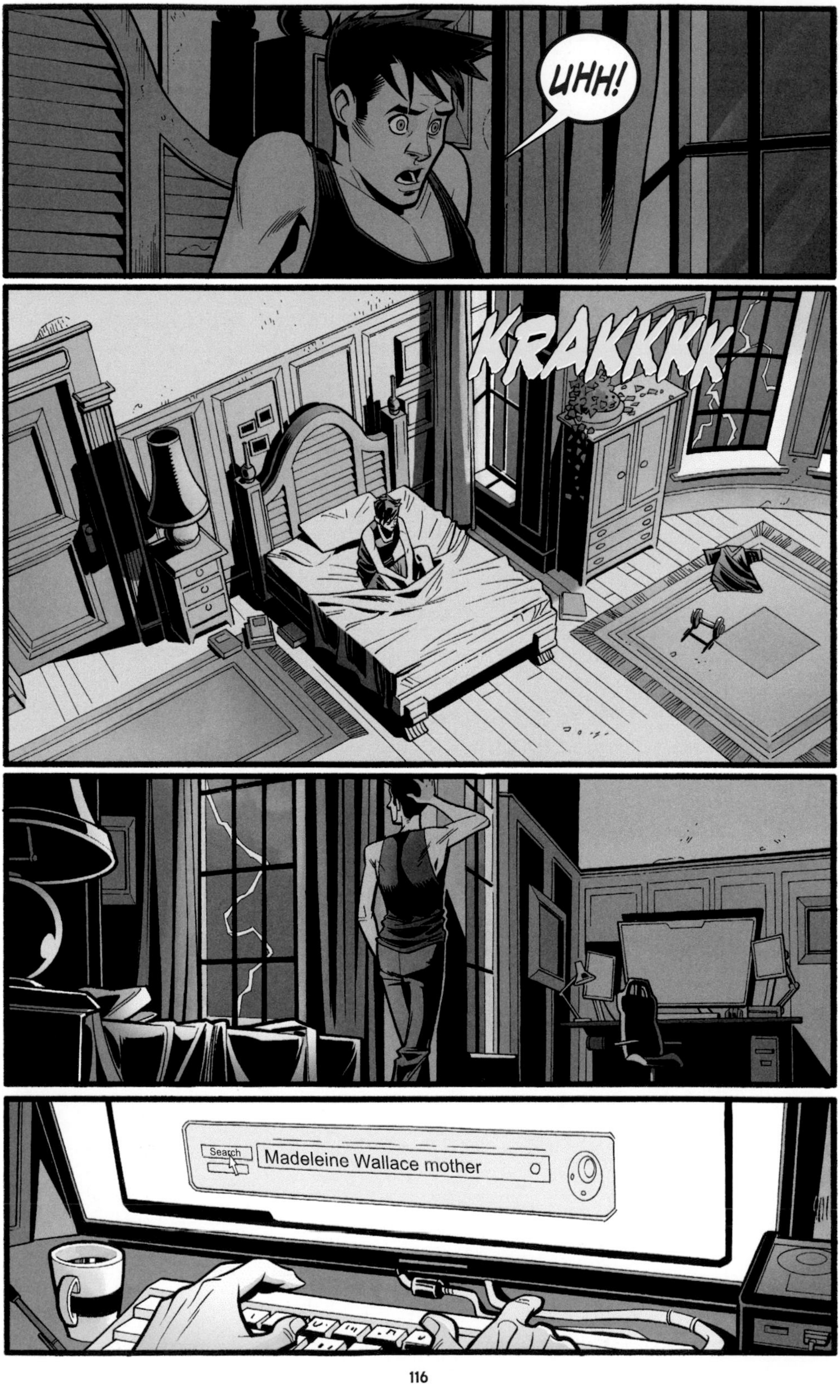
UHH!
KRAKKKK
Search
Madeleine Wallace mother

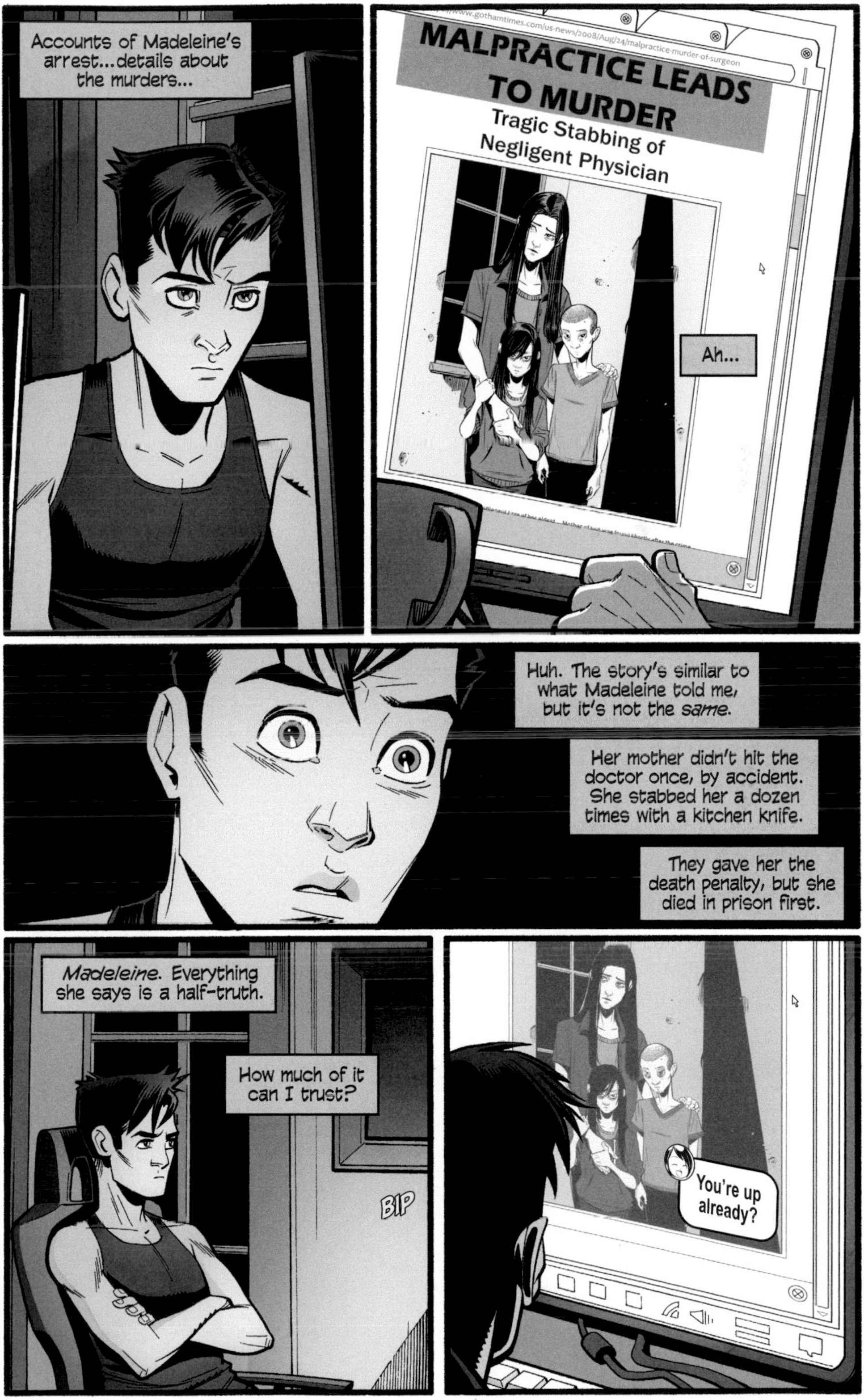
Accounts of Madeleine's arrest...details about the murders...
www.gothamtimes.com/us-news/2008/Aug/24/malpractice-murder-of-surgeon
MALPRACTICE LEADS TO MURDER
Tragic Stabbing of Negligent Physician
Ah...
Huh. The story's similar to what Madeleine told me, but it's not the *same*.
Her mother didn't hit the doctor once, by accident. She stabbed her a dozen times with a kitchen knife.
They gave her the death penalty, but she died in prison first.
Madeleine. Everything she says is a half-truth.
How much of it can I trust?
BIP
You're up already?

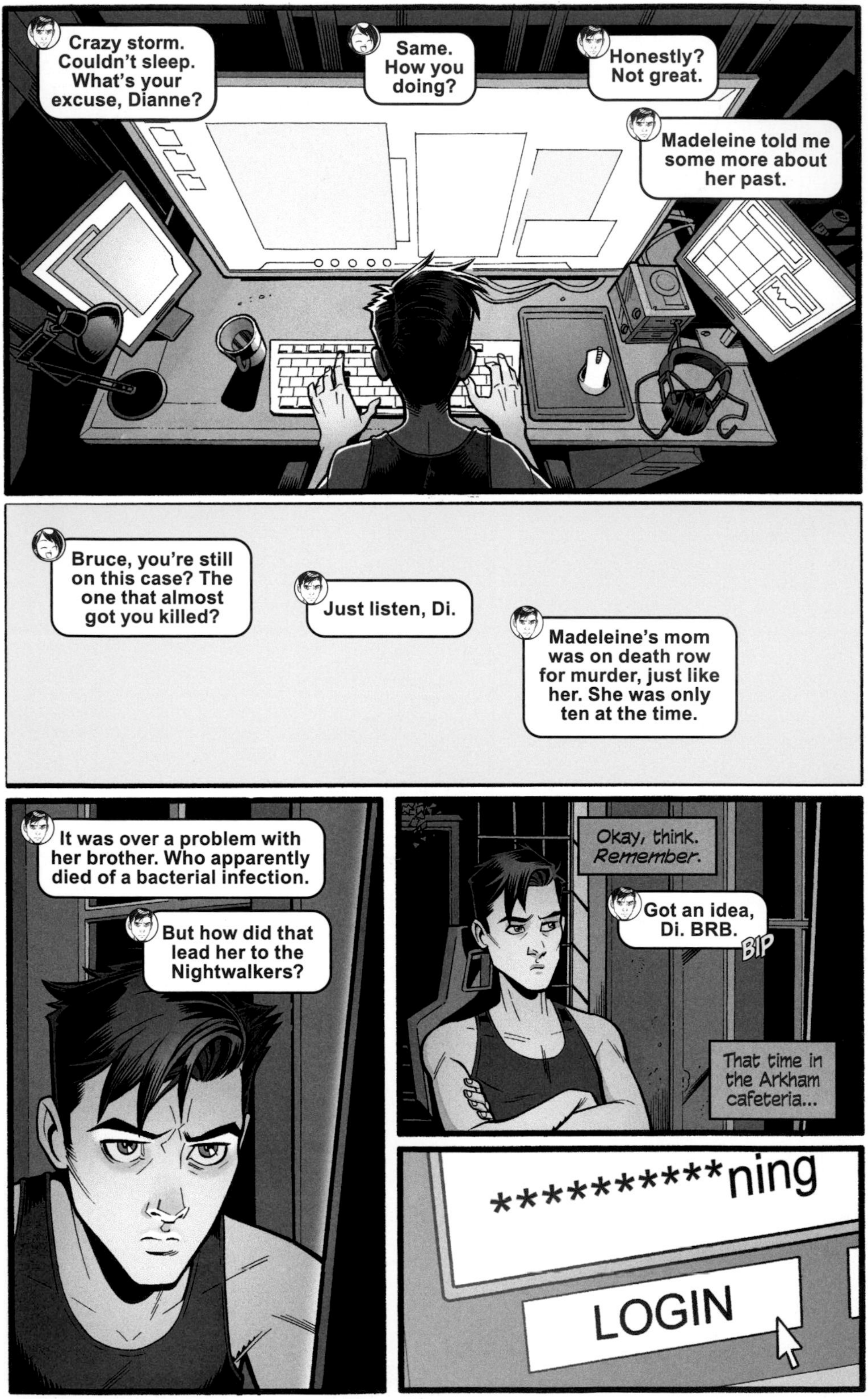
Crazy storm. Couldn't sleep. What's your excuse, Dianne?
Same. How you doing?
Honestly? Not great.
Madeleine told me some more about her past.
Bruce, you're still on this case? The one that almost got you killed?
Just listen, Di.
Madeleine's mom was on death row for murder, just like her. She was only ten at the time.
It was over a problem with her brother. Who apparently died of a bacterial infection.
But how did that lead her to the Nightwalkers?
Okay, think. *Remember*.
Got an idea, Di. BRB.
BIP
That time in the Arkham cafeteria...
**********ning
LOGIN

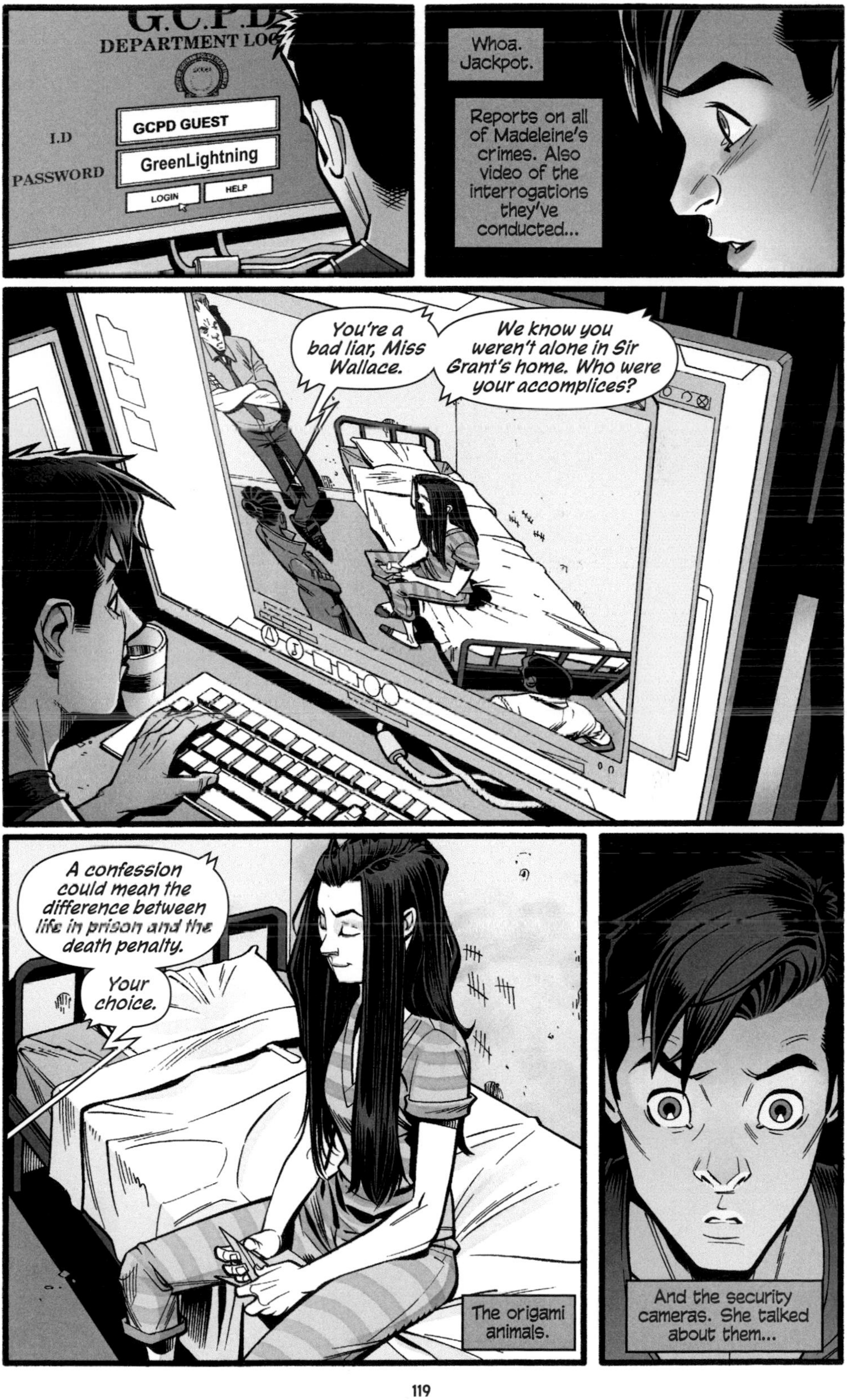
G.C.P.D
DEPARTMENT LOG
I.D
GCPD GUEST
PASSWORD
GreenLightning
LOGIN
HELP
Whoa. Jackpot.
Reports on all of Madeleine's crimes. Also video of the interrogations they've conducted...
You're a bad liar, Miss Wallace.
We know you weren't alone in Sir Grant's home. Who were your accomplices?
A confession could mean the difference between life in prison and the death penalty.
Your choice.
The origami animals.
And the security cameras. She talked about them...

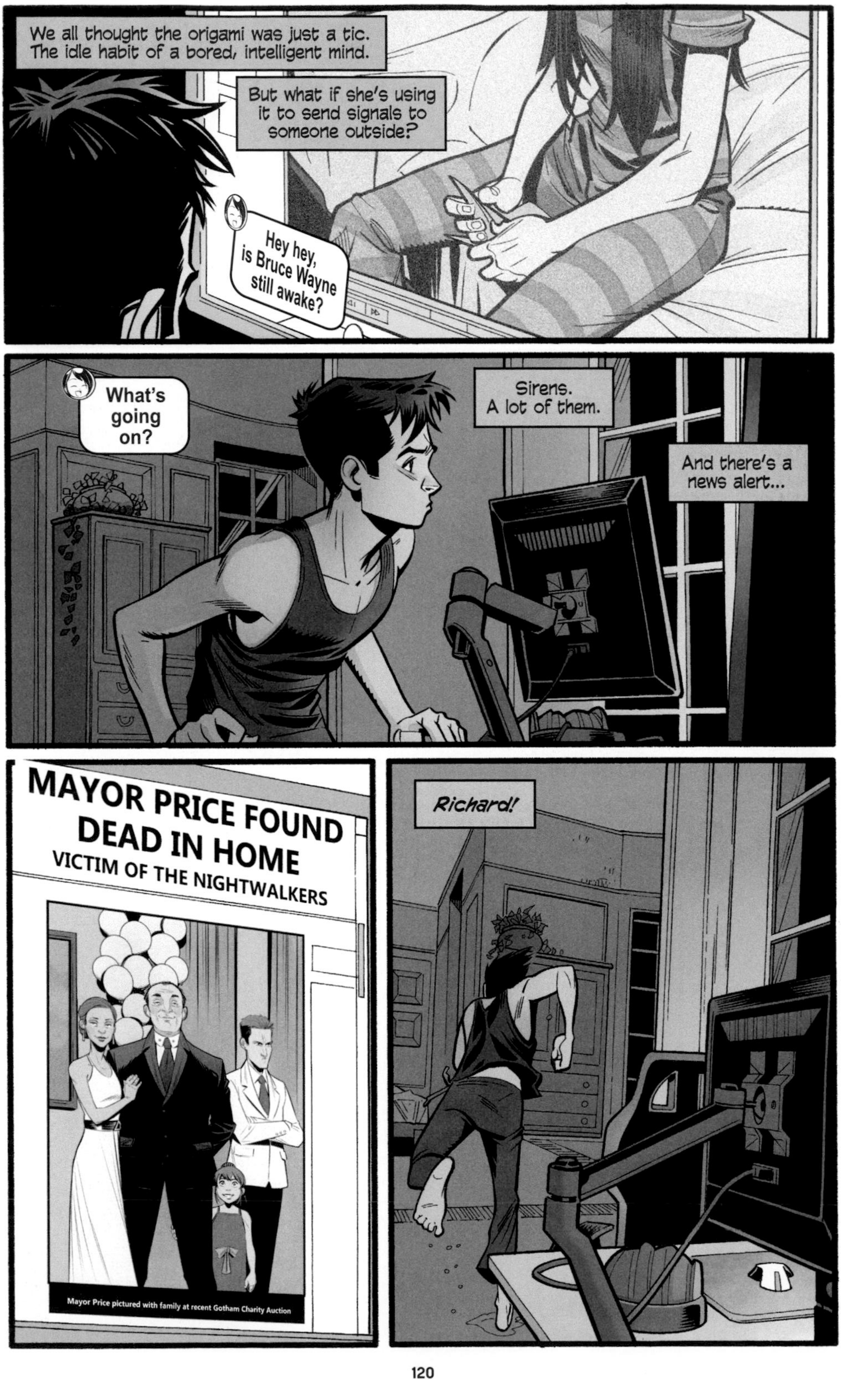
We all thought the origami was just a tic. The idle habit of a bored, intelligent mind.
But what if she's using it to send signals to someone outside?
Hey hey, is Bruce Wayne still awake?
What's going on?
Sirens. A lot of them.
And there's a news alert...
MAYOR PRICE FOUND DEAD IN HOME
VICTIM OF THE NIGHTWALKERS
Mayor Price pictured with family at recent Gotham Charity Auction
Richard!

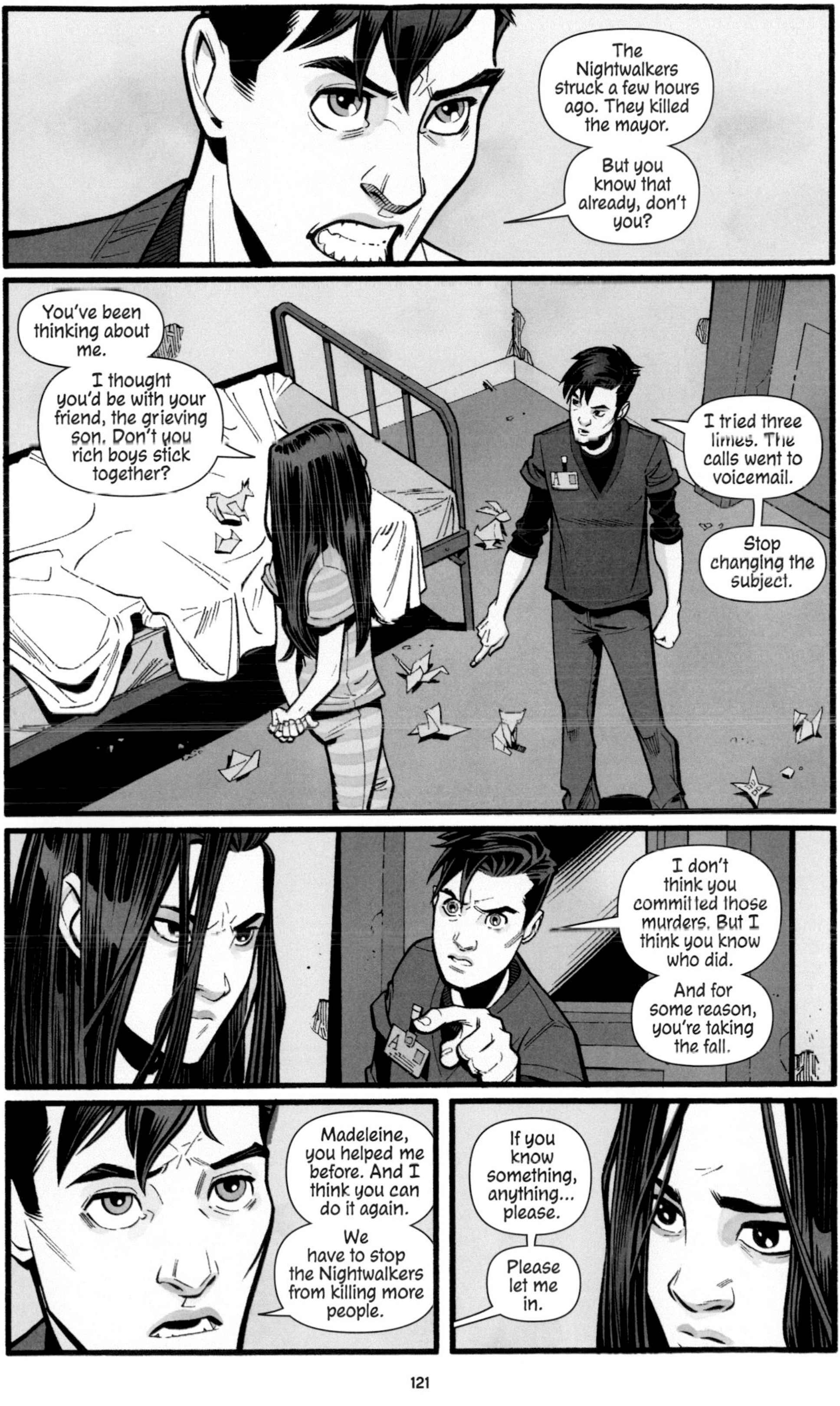
The Nightwalkers struck a few hours ago. They killed the mayor.
But you know that already, don't you?
You've been thinking about me.
I thought you'd be with your friend, the grieving son. Don't you rich boys stick together?
I tried three times. The calls went to voicemail.
Stop changing the subject.
I don't think you committed those murders. But I think you know who did.
And for some reason, you're taking the fall.
Madeleine, you helped me before. And I think you can do it again.
We have to stop the Nightwalkers from killing more people.
If you know something, anything... please.
Please let me in.

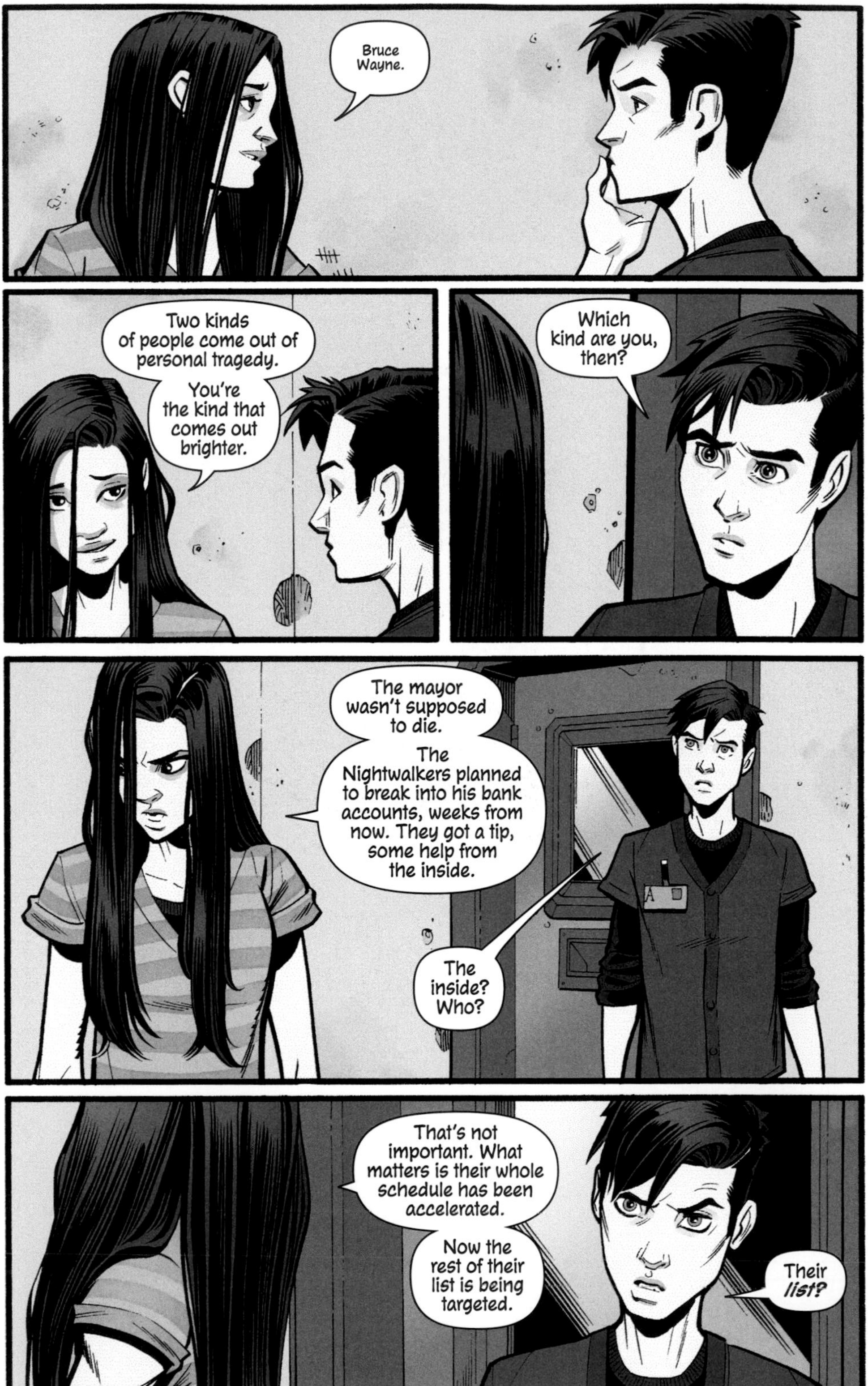
Bruce Wayne.
Two kinds of people come out of personal tragedy.
You're the kind that comes out brighter.
Which kind are you, then?
The mayor wasn't supposed to die.
The Nightwalkers planned to break into his bank accounts, weeks from now. They got a tip, some help from the inside.
The inside? Who?
That's not important. What matters is their whole schedule has been accelerated.
Now the rest of their list is being targeted.
Their *list?*

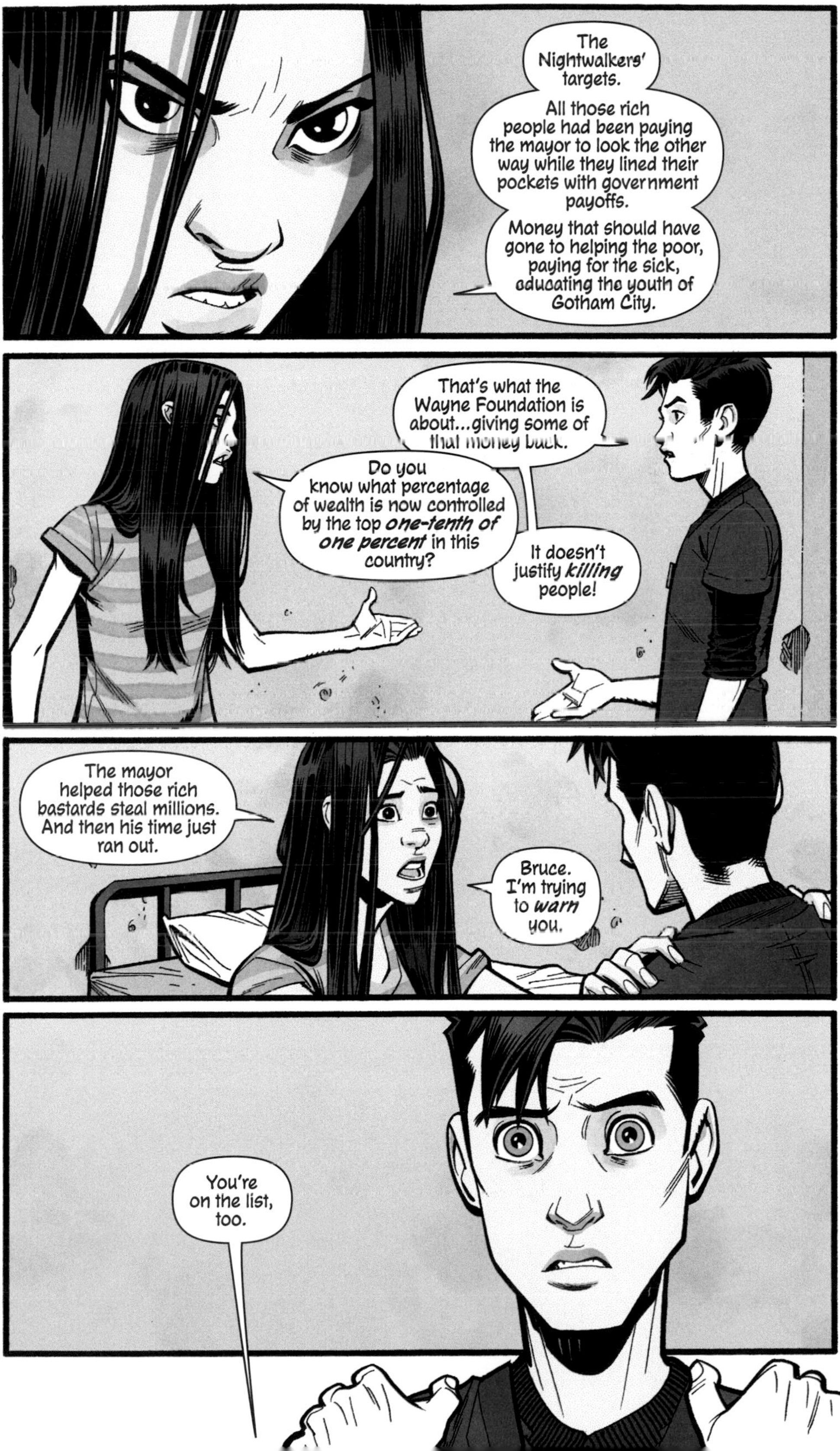

The Nightwalkers' targets.
All those rich people had been paying the mayor to look the other way while they lined their pockets with government payoffs.
Money that should have gone to helping the poor, paying for the sick, educating the youth of Gotham City.
That's what the Wayne Foundation is about...giving some of that money back.
Do you know what percentage of wealth is now controlled by the top *one-tenth of one percent* in this country?
It doesn't justify *killing* people!
The mayor helped those rich bastards steal millions. And then his time just ran out.
Bruce. I'm trying to *warn* you.
You're on the list, too.

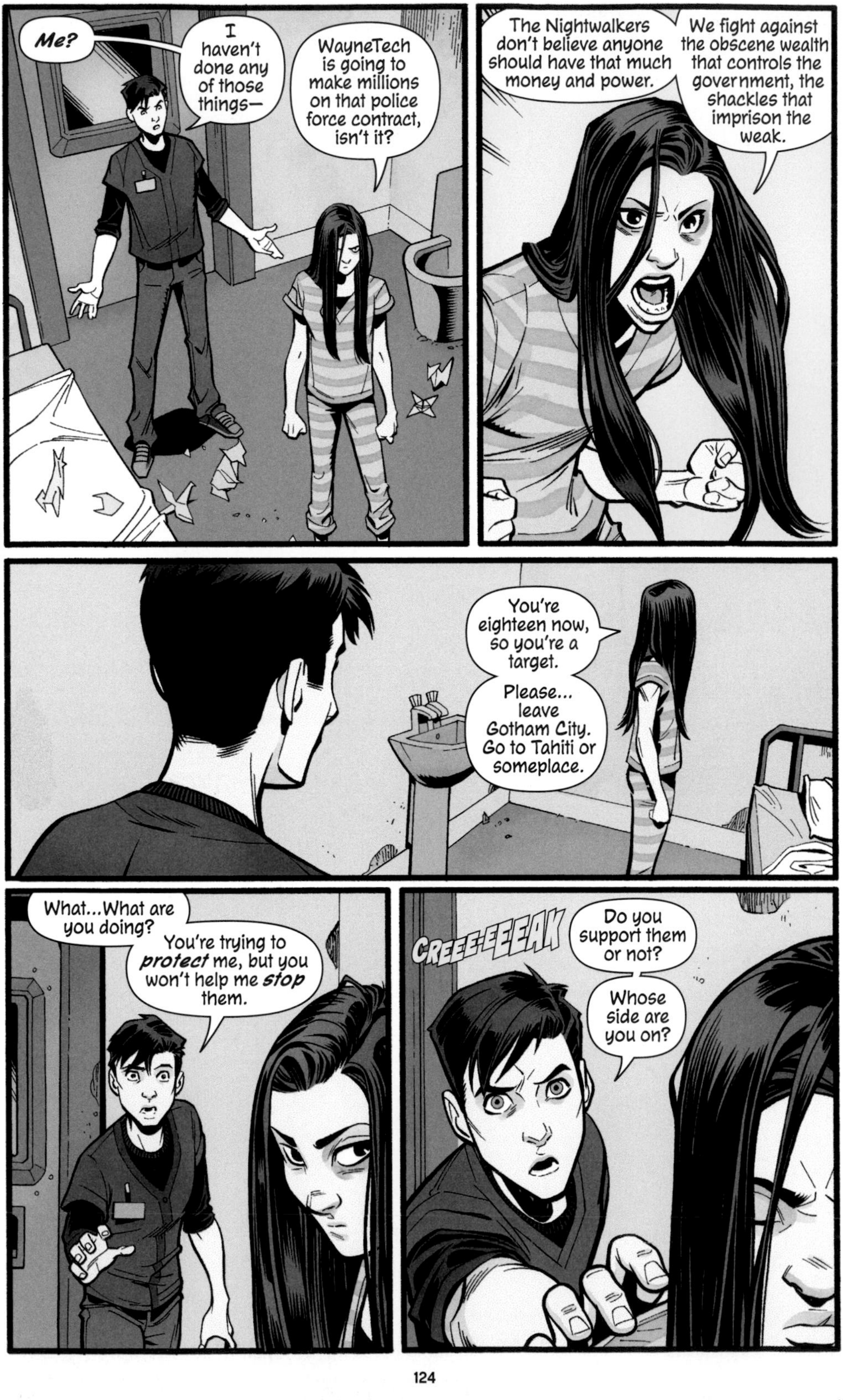
Me?
I haven't done any of those things—
WayneTech is going to make millions on that police force contract, isn't it?
The Nightwalkers don't believe anyone should have that much money and power.
We fight against the obscene wealth that controls the government, the shackles that imprison the weak.
You're eighteen now, so you're a target.
Please... leave Gotham City. Go to Tahiti or someplace.
What...What are you doing?
You're trying to *protect* me, but you won't help me *stop* them.
CREEE-EEEAK
Do you support them or not?
Whose side are you on?

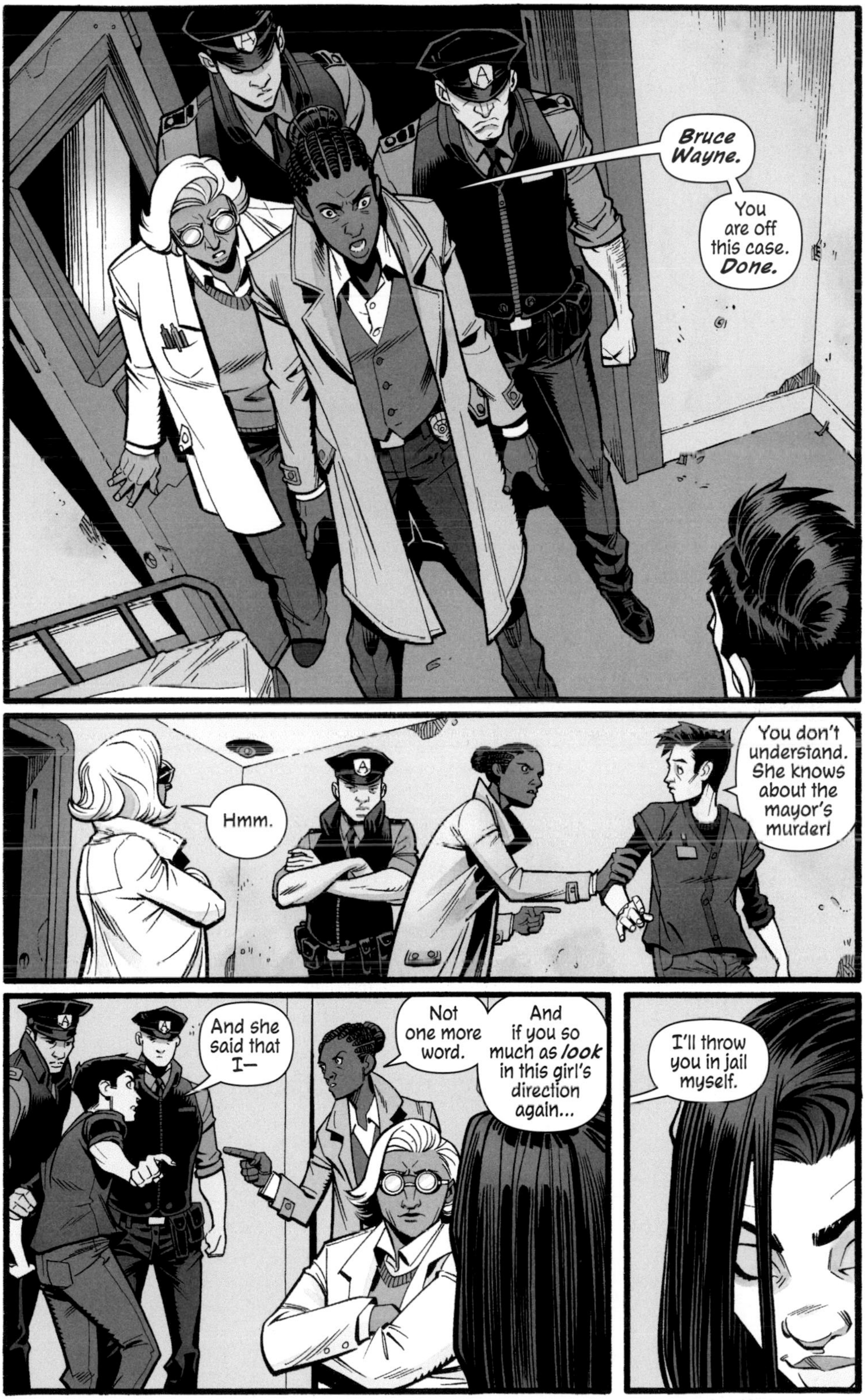
Bruce Wayne.
You are off this case. Done.
Hmm.
You don't understand. She knows about the mayor's murder!
And she said that I—
Not one more word.
And if you so much as look in this girl's direction again...
I'll throw you in jail myself.

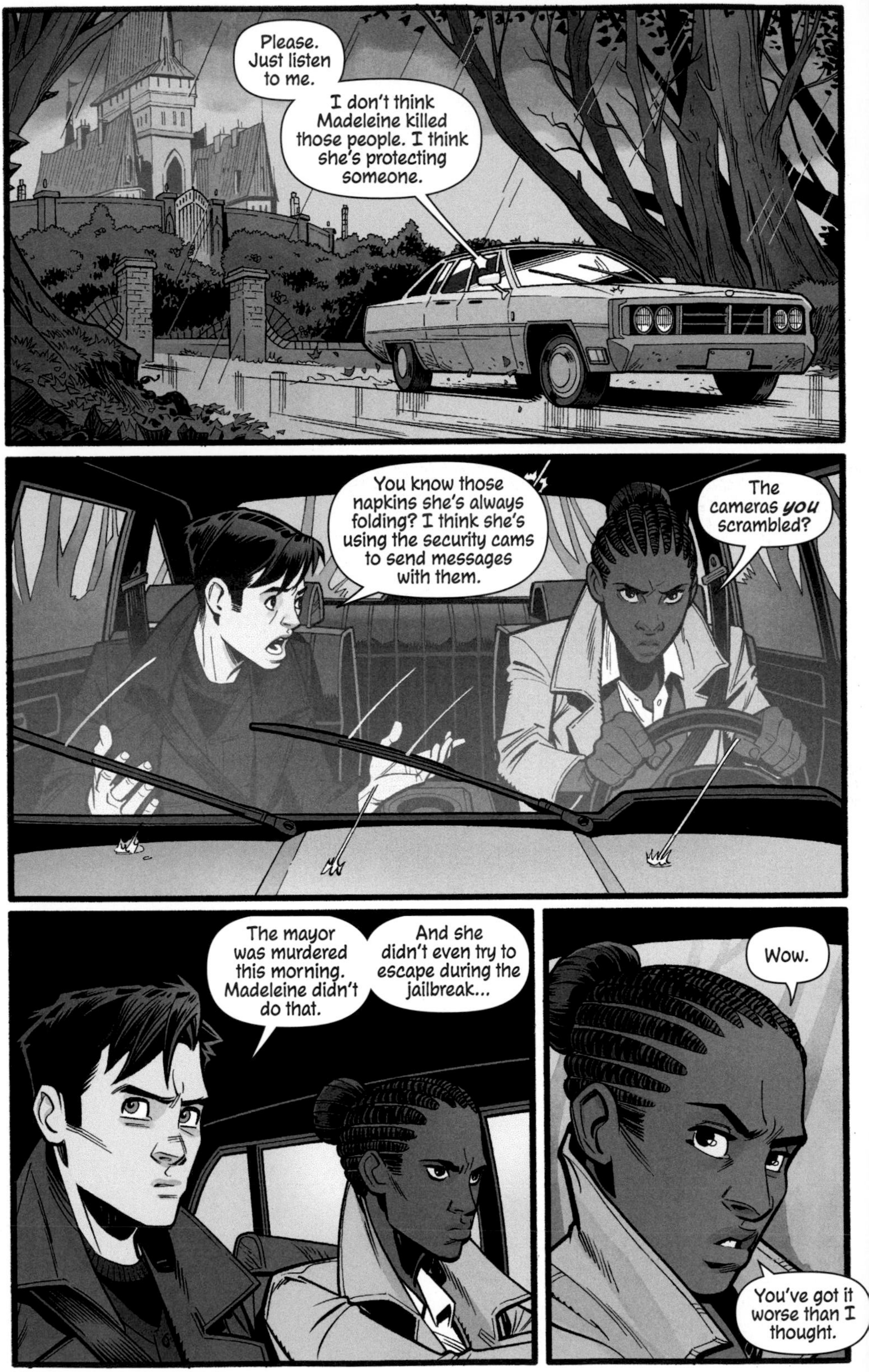
Please. Just listen to me.
I don't think Madeleine killed those people. I think she's protecting someone.
You know those napkins she's always folding? I think she's using the security cams to send messages with them.
The cameras *you* scrambled?
The mayor was murdered this morning. Madeleine didn't do that.
And she didn't even try to escape during the jailbreak...
Wow.
You've got it worse than I thought.

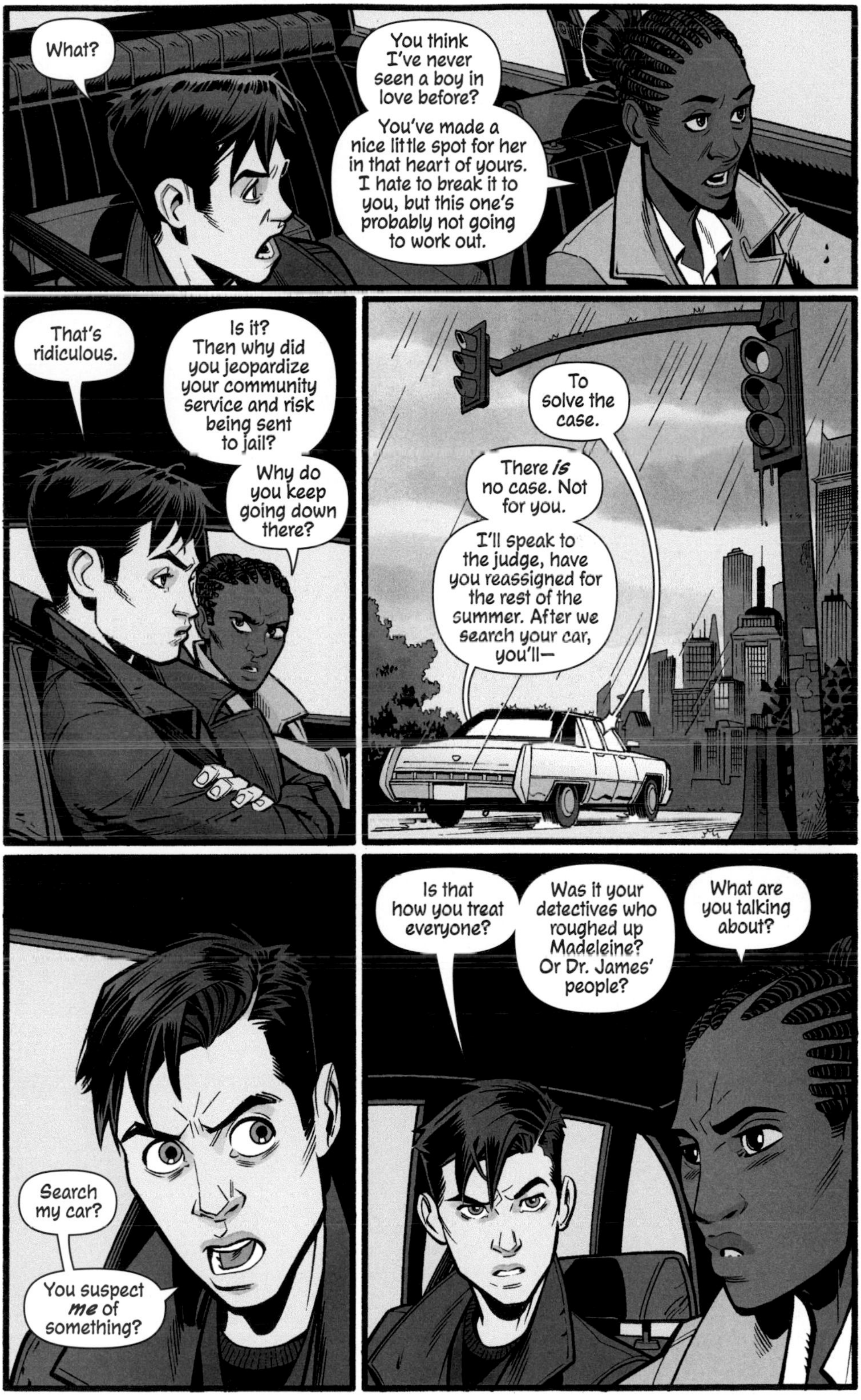
What?
You think I've never seen a boy in love before?
You've made a nice little spot for her in that heart of yours. I hate to break it to you, but this one's probably not going to work out.
That's ridiculous.
Is it? Then why did you jeopardize your community service and risk being sent to jail?
Why do you keep going down there?
To solve the case.
There *is* no case. Not for you.
I'll speak to the judge, have you reassigned for the rest of the summer. After we search your car, you'll—
Search my car?
You suspect *me* of something?
Is that how you treat everyone?
Was it your detectives who roughed up Madeleine? Or Dr. James' people?
What are you talking about?

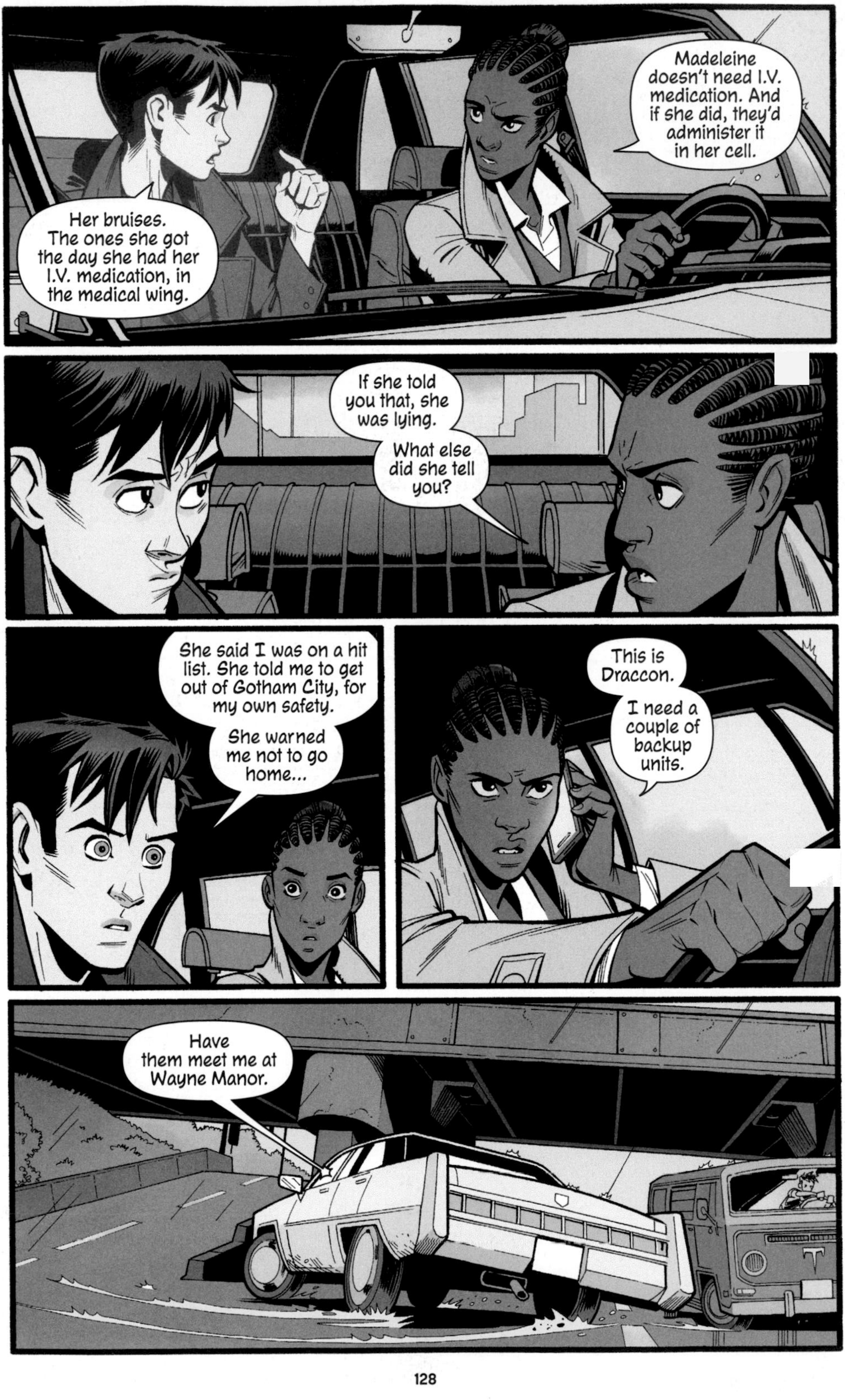
Madeleine doesn't need I.V. medication. And if she did, they'd administer it in her cell.
Her bruises. The ones she got the day she had her I.V. medication, in the medical wing.
If she told you that, she was lying.
What else did she tell you?
She said I was on a hit list. She told me to get out of Gotham City, for my own safety.
She warned me not to go home...
This is Draccon.
I need a couple of backup units.
Have them meet me at Wayne Manor.

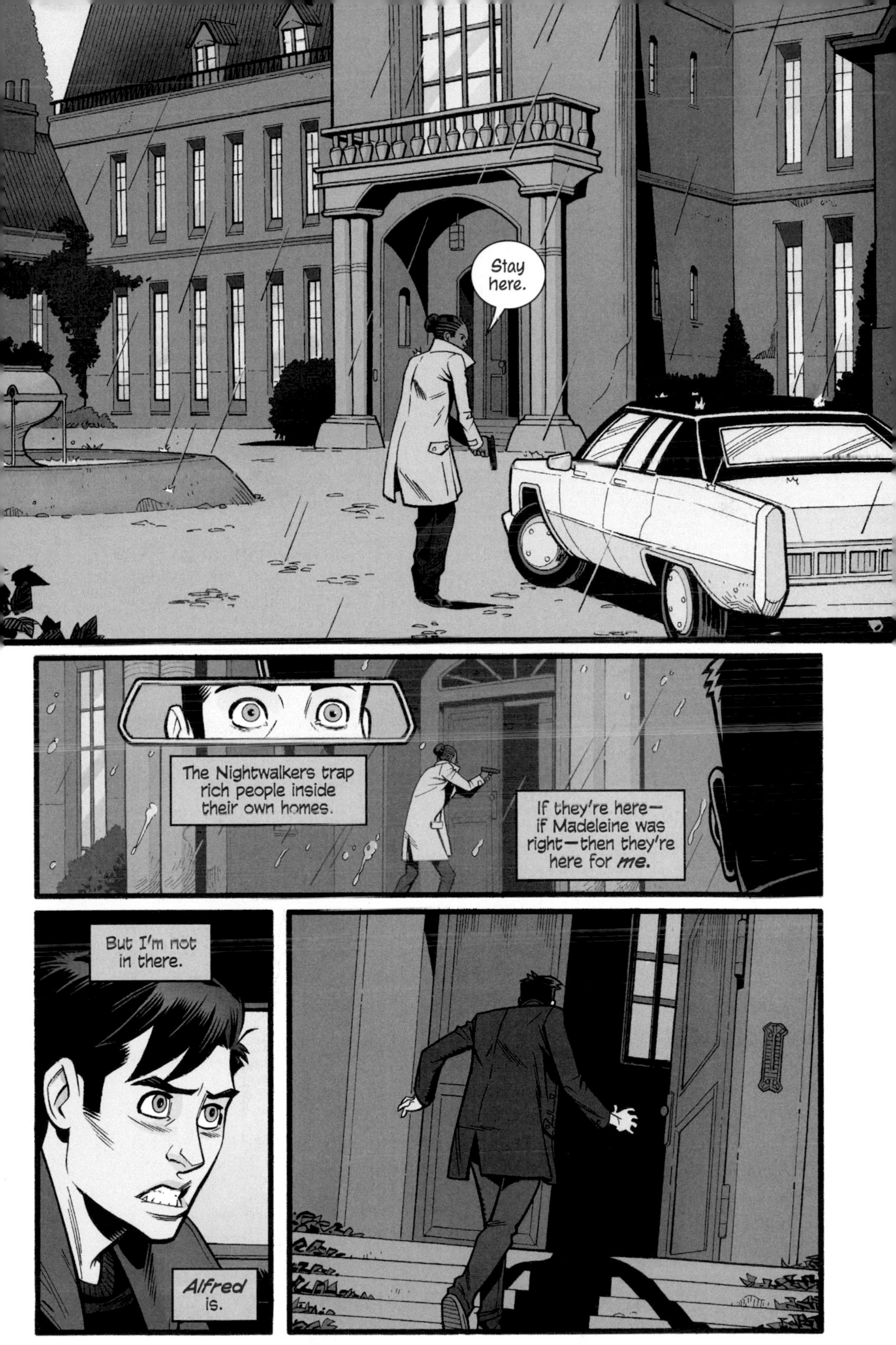
Stay here.
The Nightwalkers trap rich people inside their own homes.
If they're here—if Madeleine was right—then they're here for *me*.
But I'm not in there.
Alfred is.

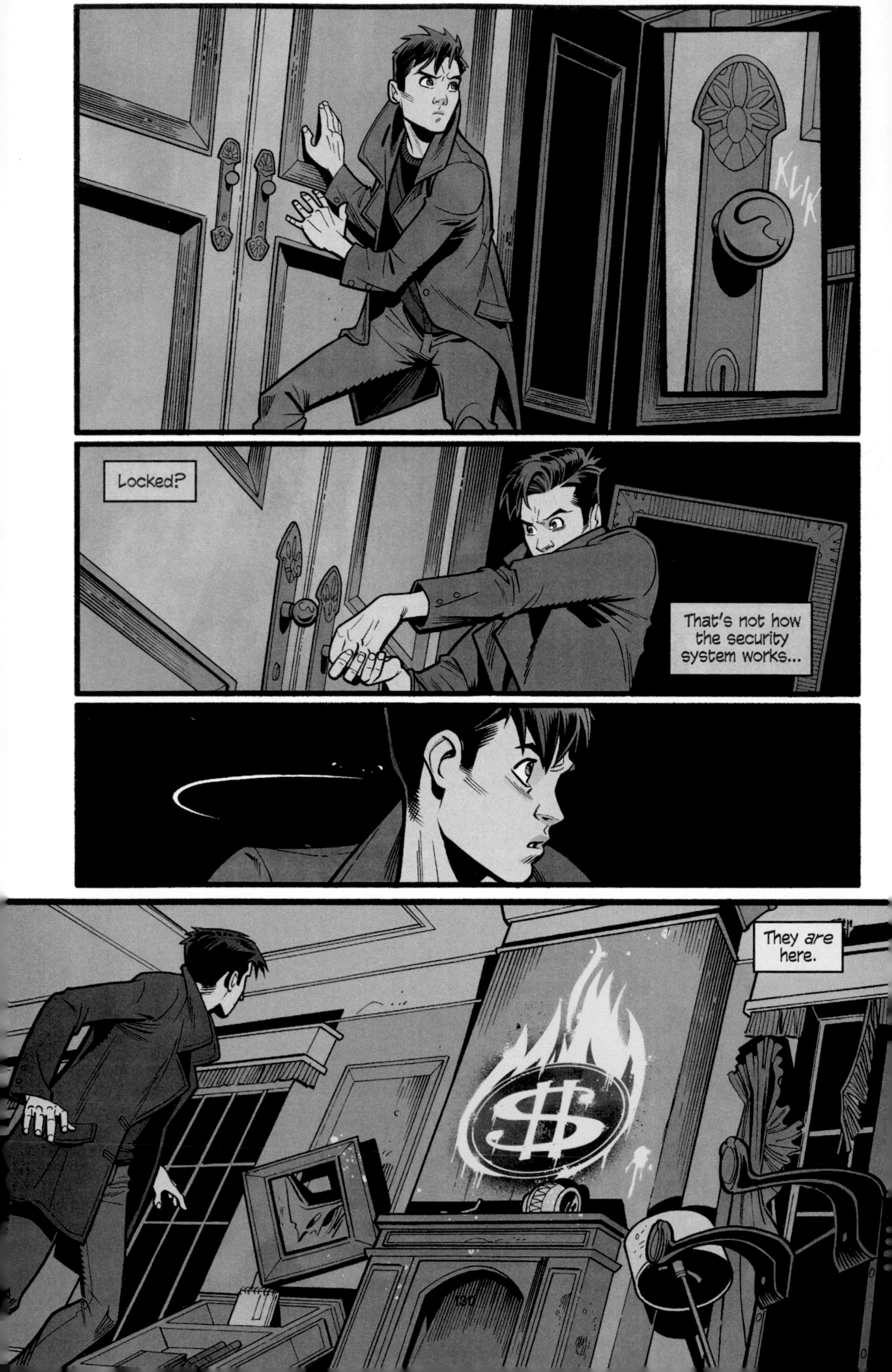
KLIK
Locked?
That's not how the security system works...
They *are* here.

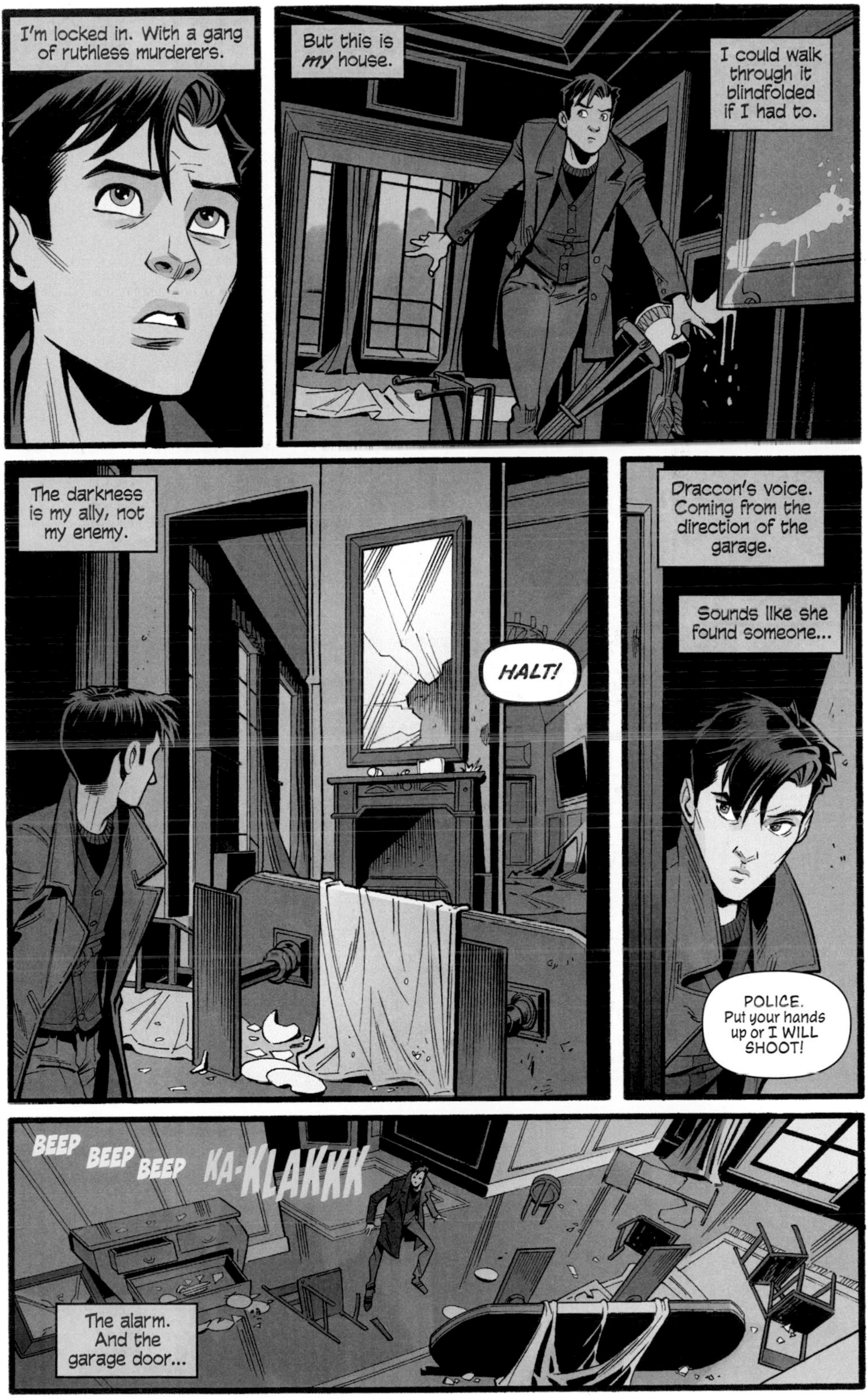

I'm locked in. With a gang of ruthless murderers.
But this is *my* house.
I could walk through it blindfolded if I had to.
The darkness is my ally, not my enemy.
HALT!
Draccon's voice. Coming from the direction of the garage.
Sounds like she found someone...
POLICE. Put your hands up or I WILL SHOOT!
BEEP BEEP BEEP KA-KLAKKK
The alarm. And the garage door...

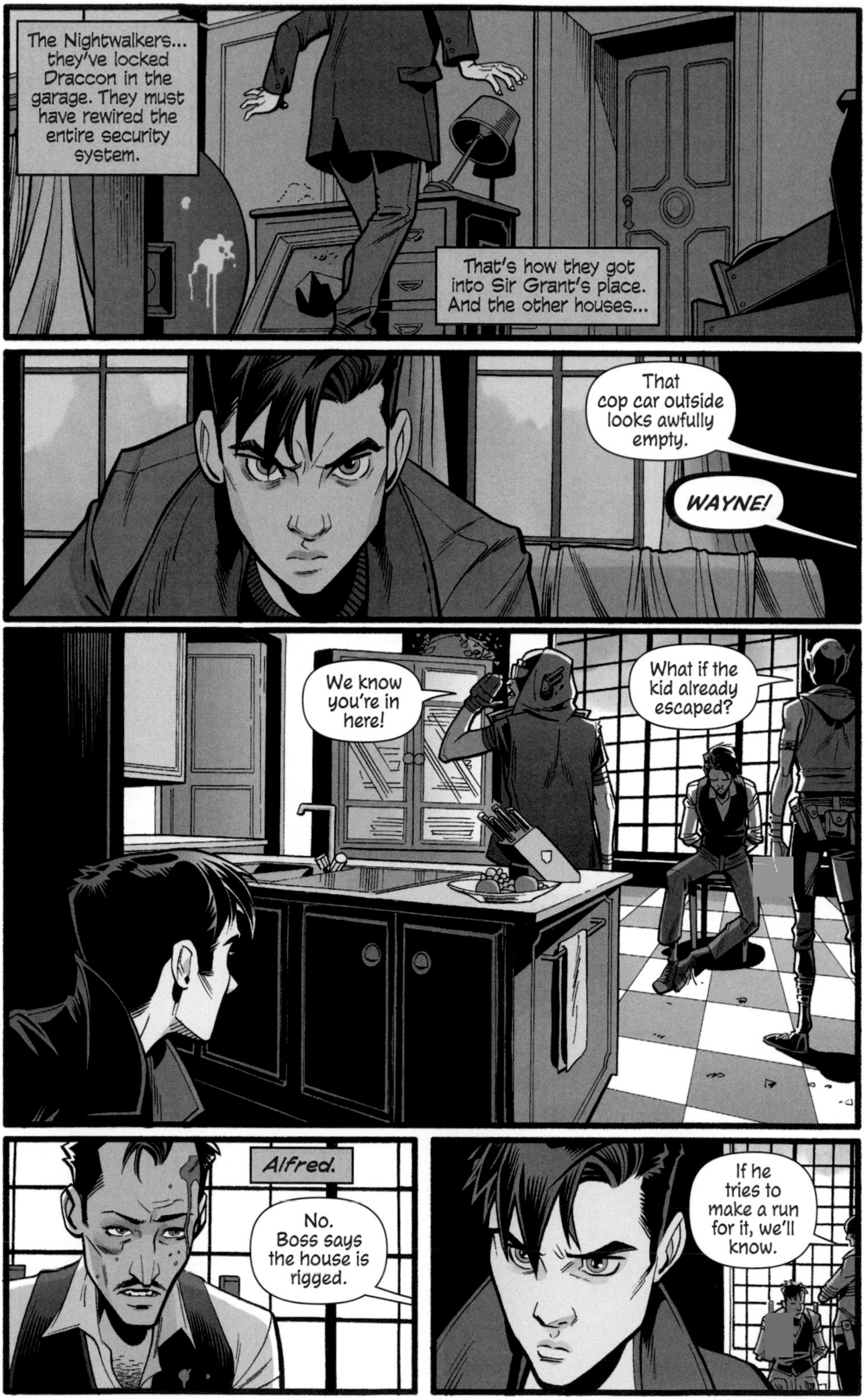

The Nightwalkers... they've locked Draccon in the garage. They must have rewired the entire security system.
That's how they got into Sir Grant's place. And the other houses...
That cop car outside looks awfully empty.
WAYNE!
We know you're in here!
What if the kid already escaped?
Alfred.
No. Boss says the house is rigged.
If he tries to make a run for it, we'll know.

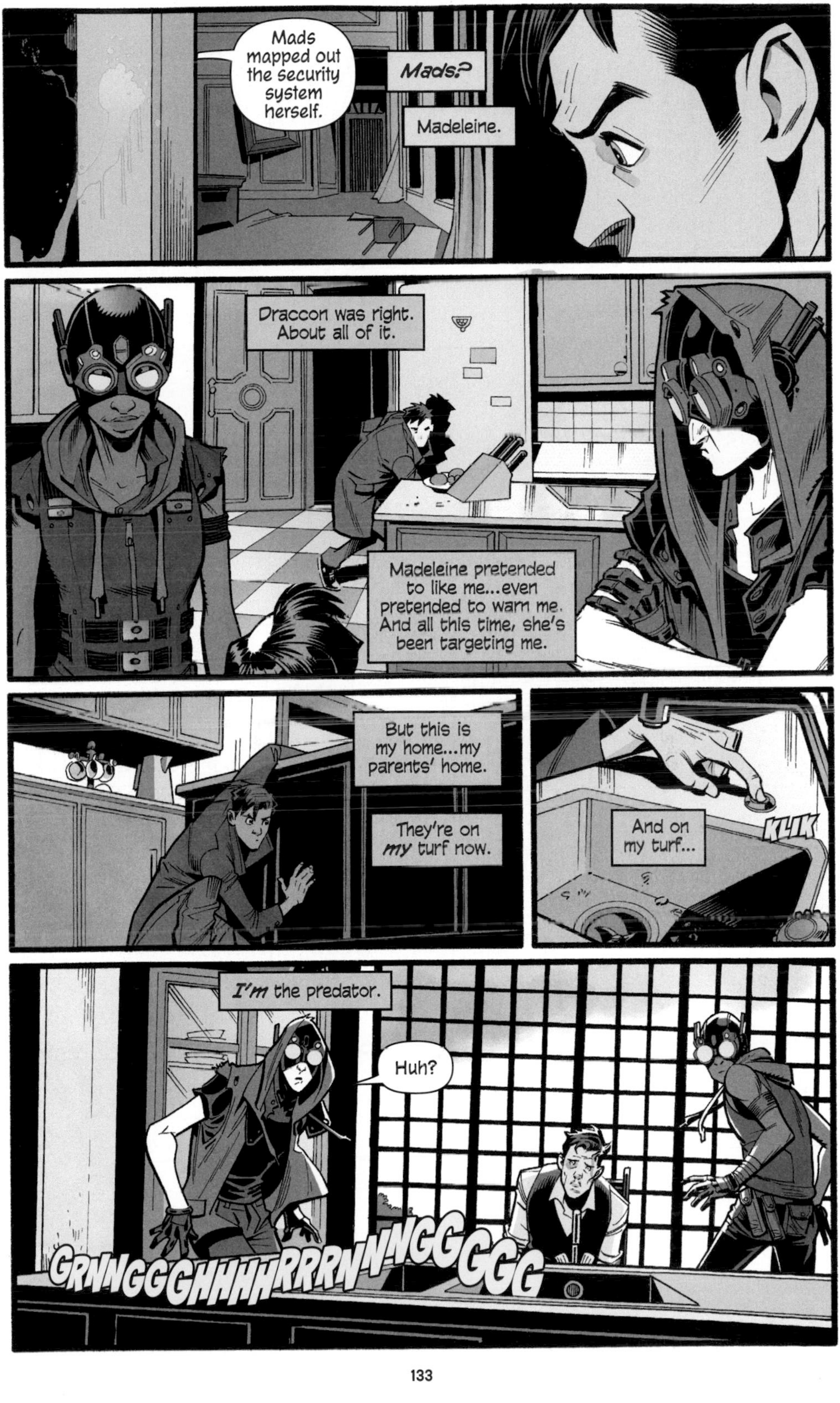

Mads mapped out the security system herself.
Mads?
Madeleine.
Draccon was right. About all of it.
Madeleine pretended to like me...even pretended to warn me. And all this time, she's been targeting me.
But this is my home...my parents' home.
They're on *my* turf now.
And on my turf...
KLIK
I'm the predator.
Huh?
GRNNGGGHHHHRRRNNNGGGGG

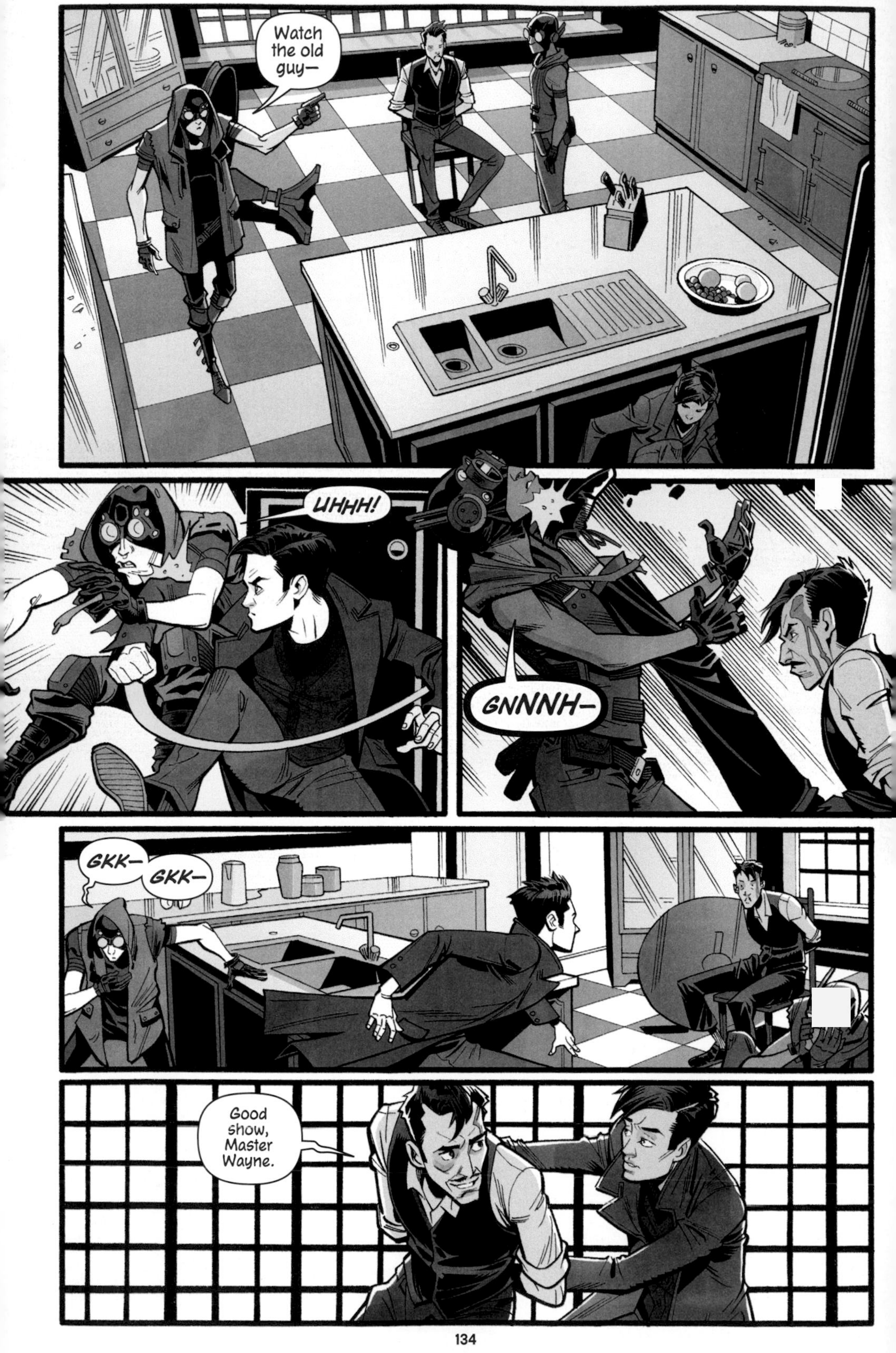
Watch the old guy—
UHHH!
GNNNH-
GKK-
GKK-
Good show, Master Wayne.

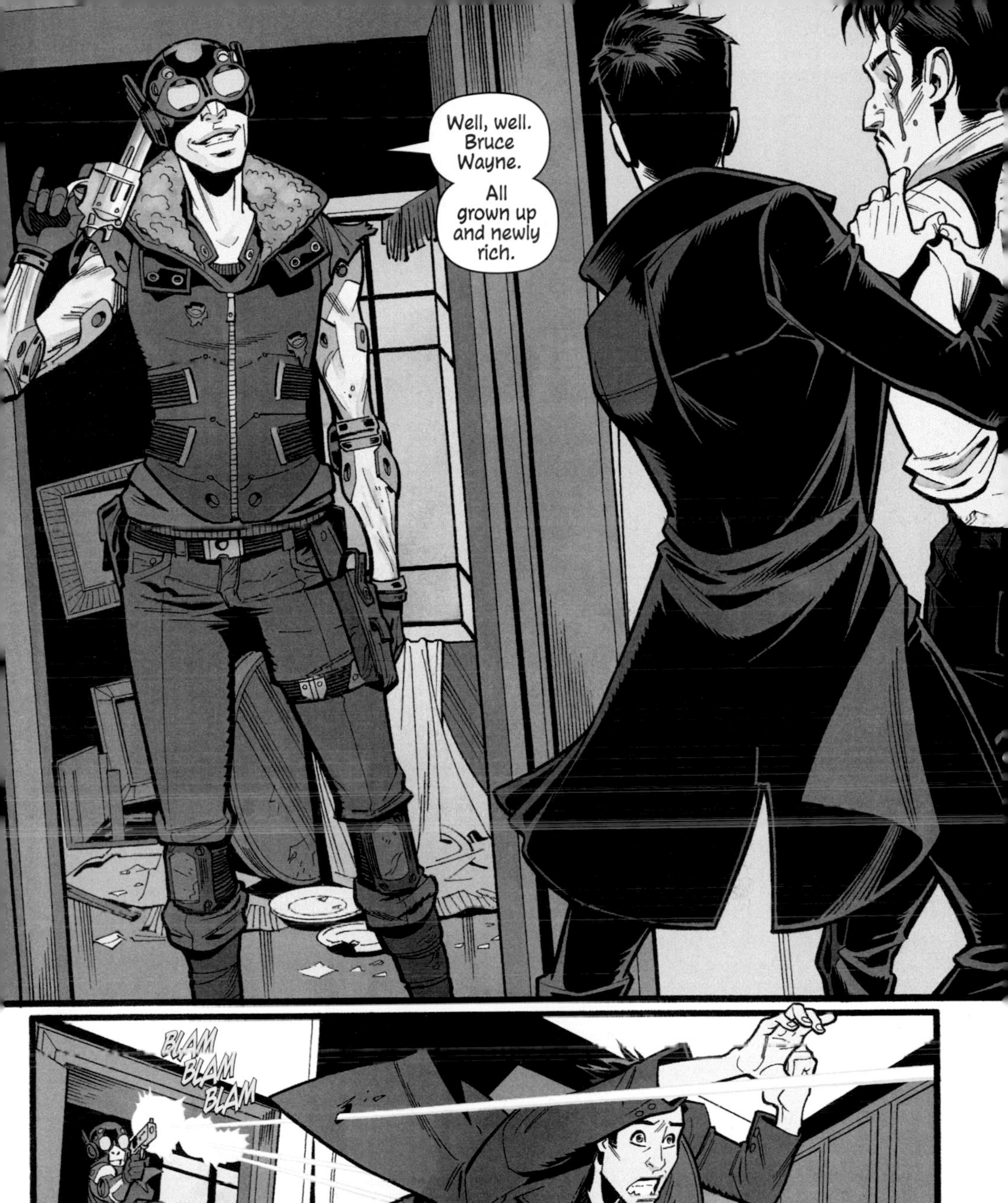
Well, well. Bruce Wayne.
All grown up and newly rich.

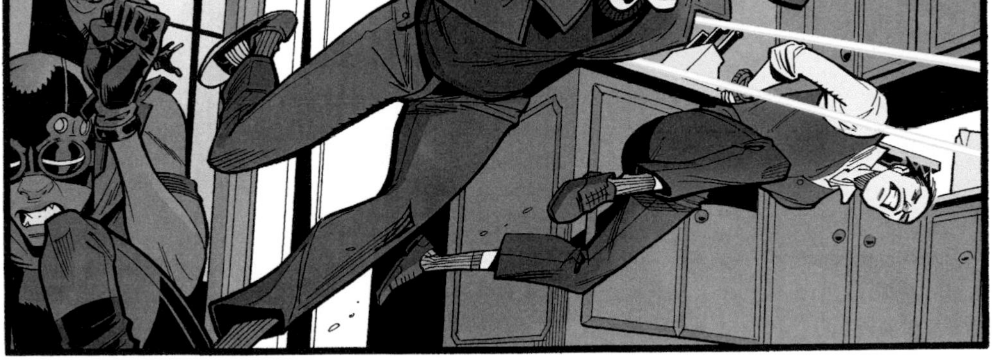
BLAM BLAM BLAM

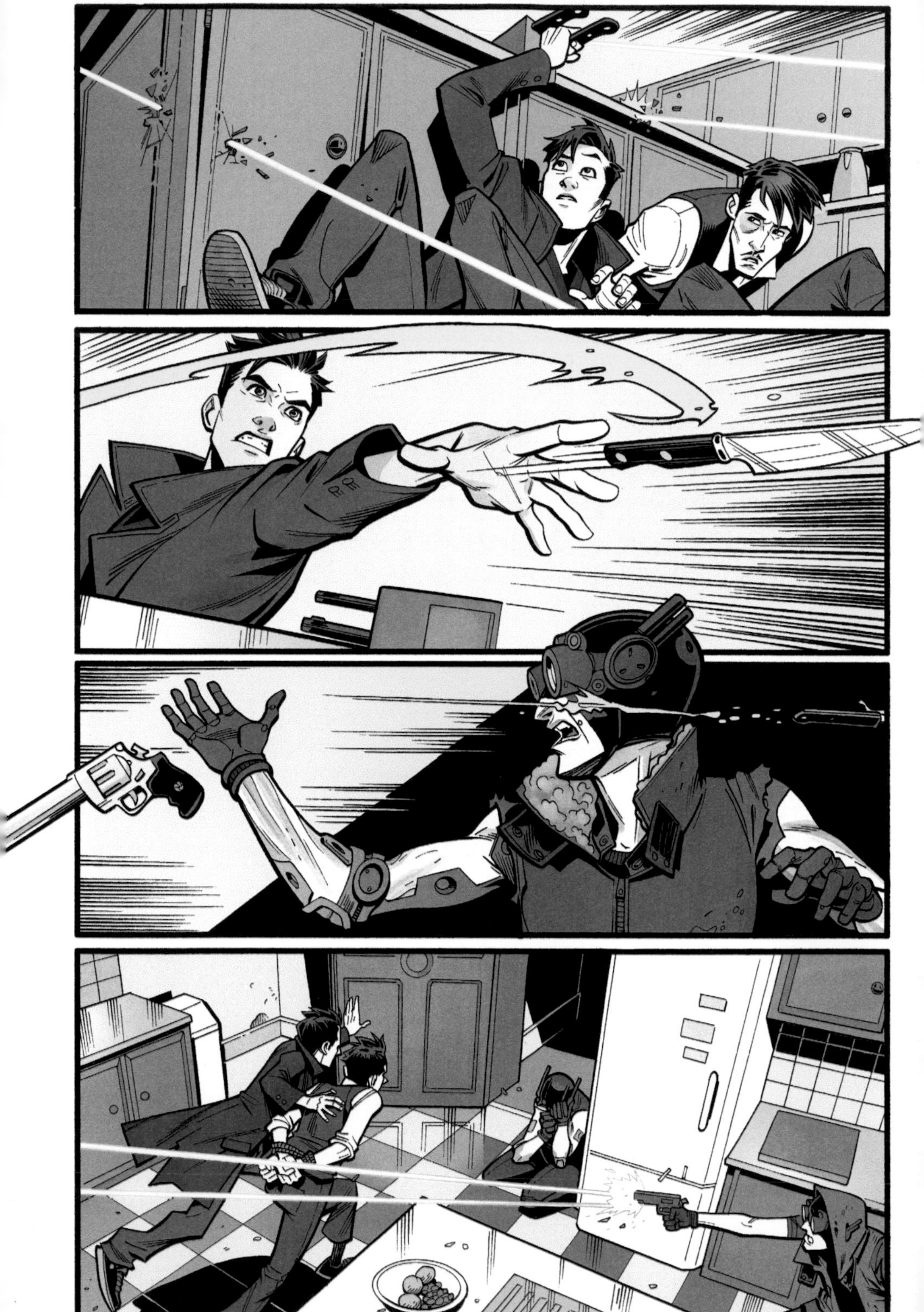

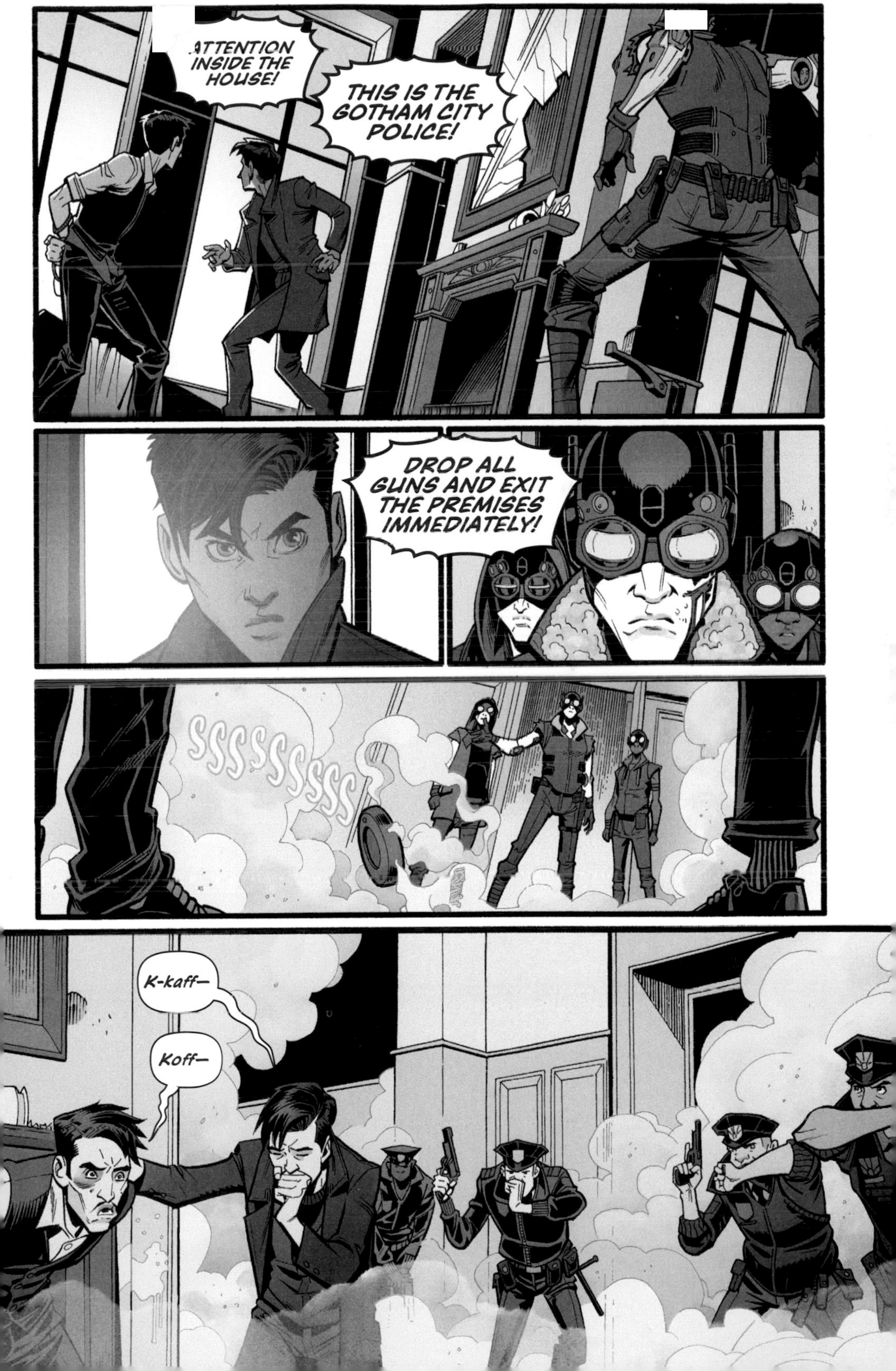
ATTENTION INSIDE THE HOUSE!
THIS IS THE GOTHAM CITY POLICE!
DROP ALL GUNS AND EXIT THE PREMISES IMMEDIATELY!
SSSSSSSSS
K-kaff—
Koff—

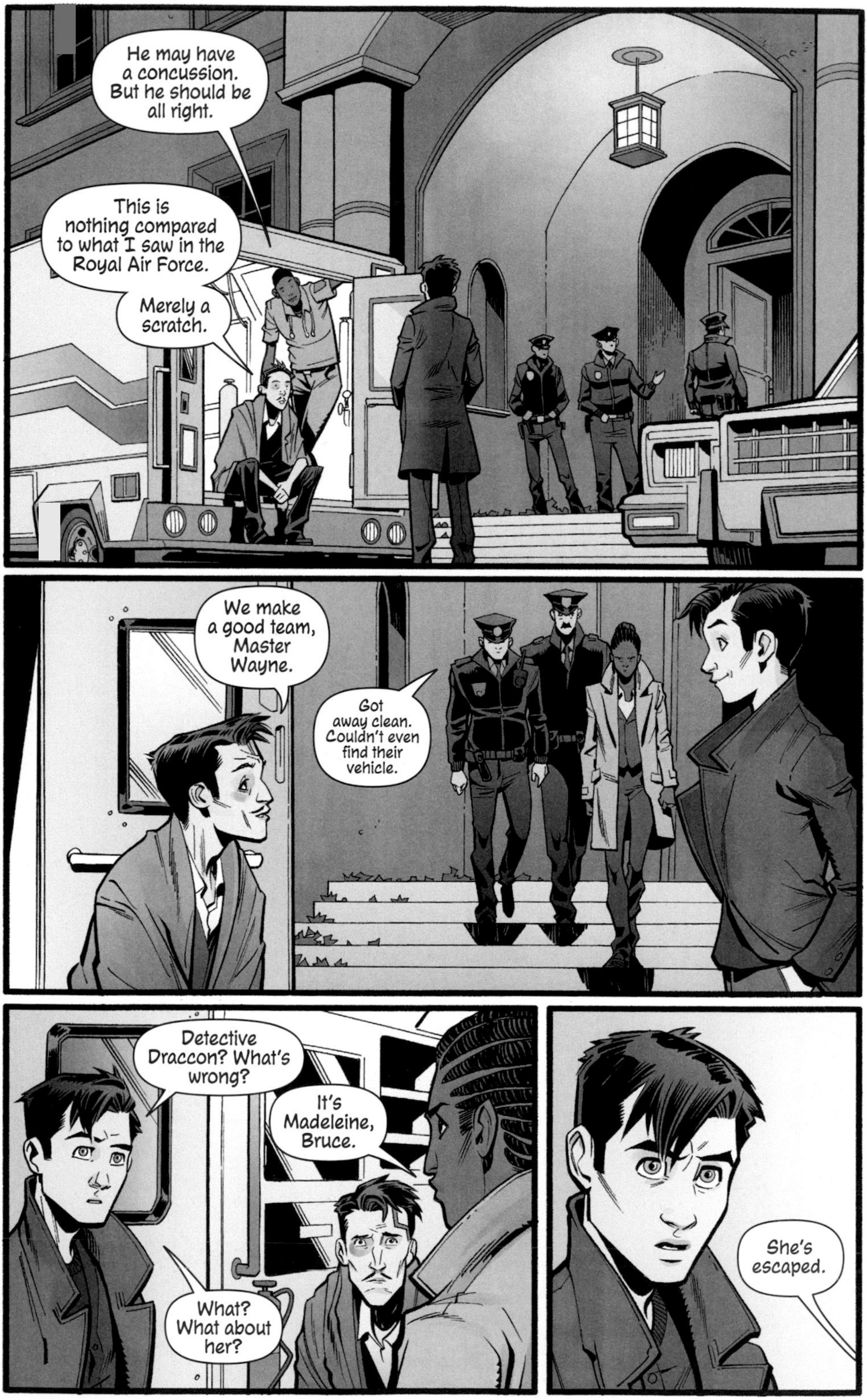
He may have a concussion. But he should be all right.
This is nothing compared to what I saw in the Royal Air Force.
Merely a scratch.
We make a good team, Master Wayne.
Got away clean. Couldn't even find their vehicle.
Detective Draccon? What's wrong?
It's Madeleine, Bruce.
What? What about her?
She's escaped.

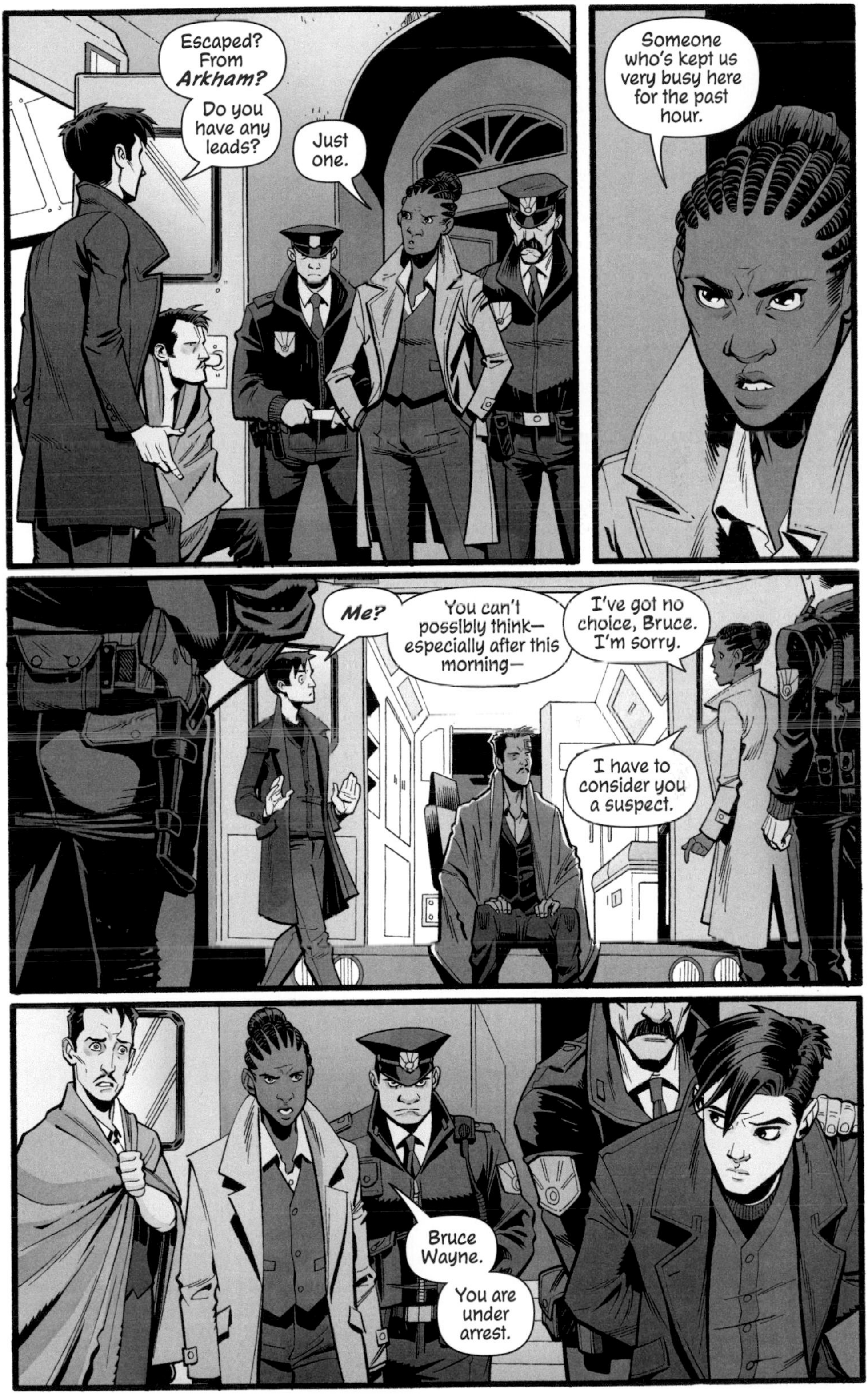
Escaped? From *Arkham?*
Do you have any leads?
Just one.
Someone who's kept us very busy here for the past hour.
Me?
You can't possibly think— especially after this morning—
I've got no choice, Bruce. I'm sorry.
I have to consider you a suspect.
Bruce Wayne.
You are under arrest.

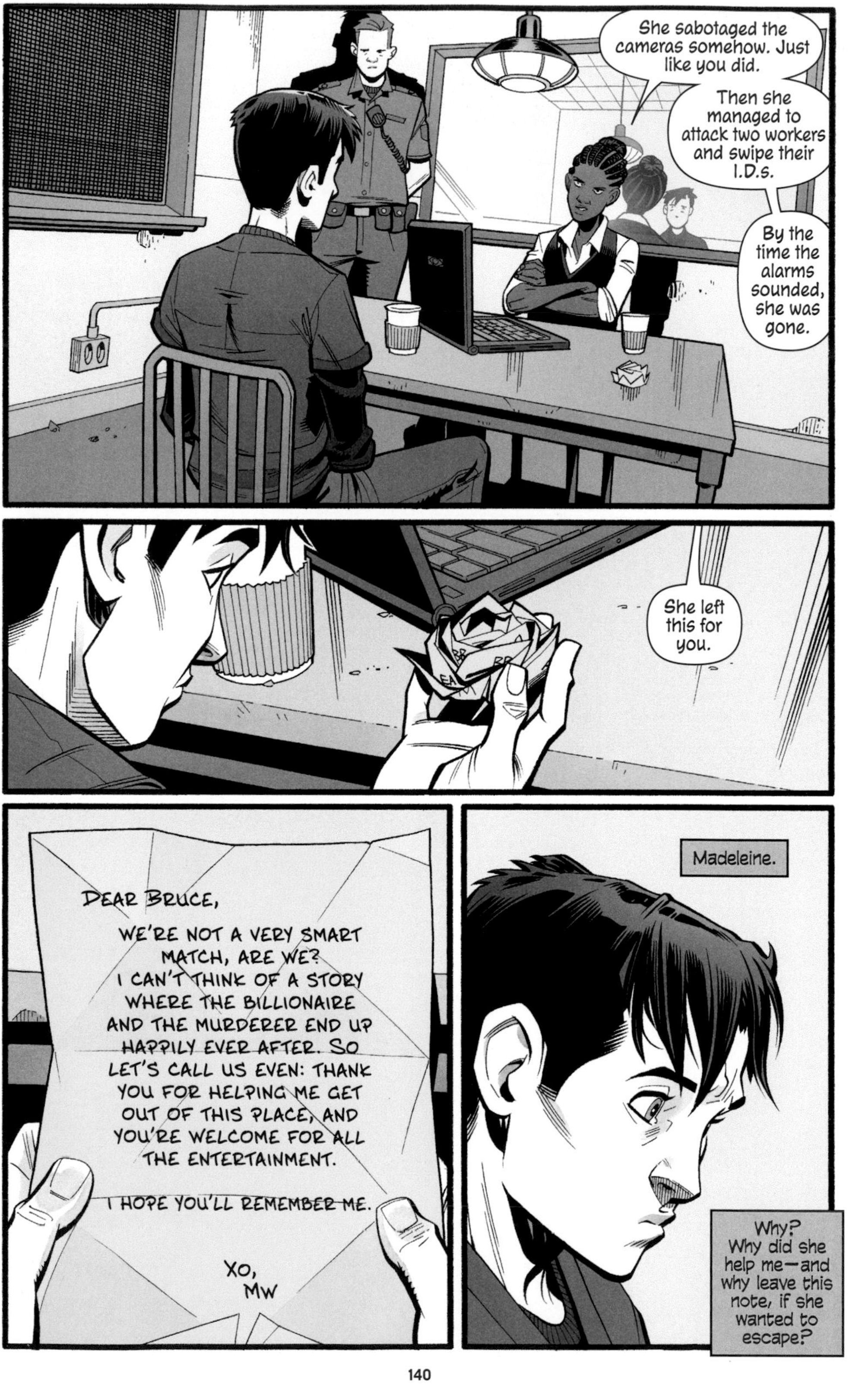
She sabotaged the cameras somehow. Just like you did.
Then she managed to attack two workers and swipe their I.D.s.
By the time the alarms sounded, she was gone.
She left this for you.
DEAR BRUCE,
WE'RE NOT A VERY SMART MATCH, ARE WE? I CAN'T THINK OF A STORY WHERE THE BILLIONAIRE AND THE MURDERER END UP HAPPILY EVER AFTER. SO LET'S CALL US EVEN: THANK YOU FOR HELPING ME GET OUT OF THIS PLACE, AND YOU'RE WELCOME FOR ALL THE ENTERTAINMENT.
I HOPE YOU'LL REMEMBER ME.
XO, MW
Madeleine.
Why? Why did she help me—and why leave this note, if she wanted to escape?

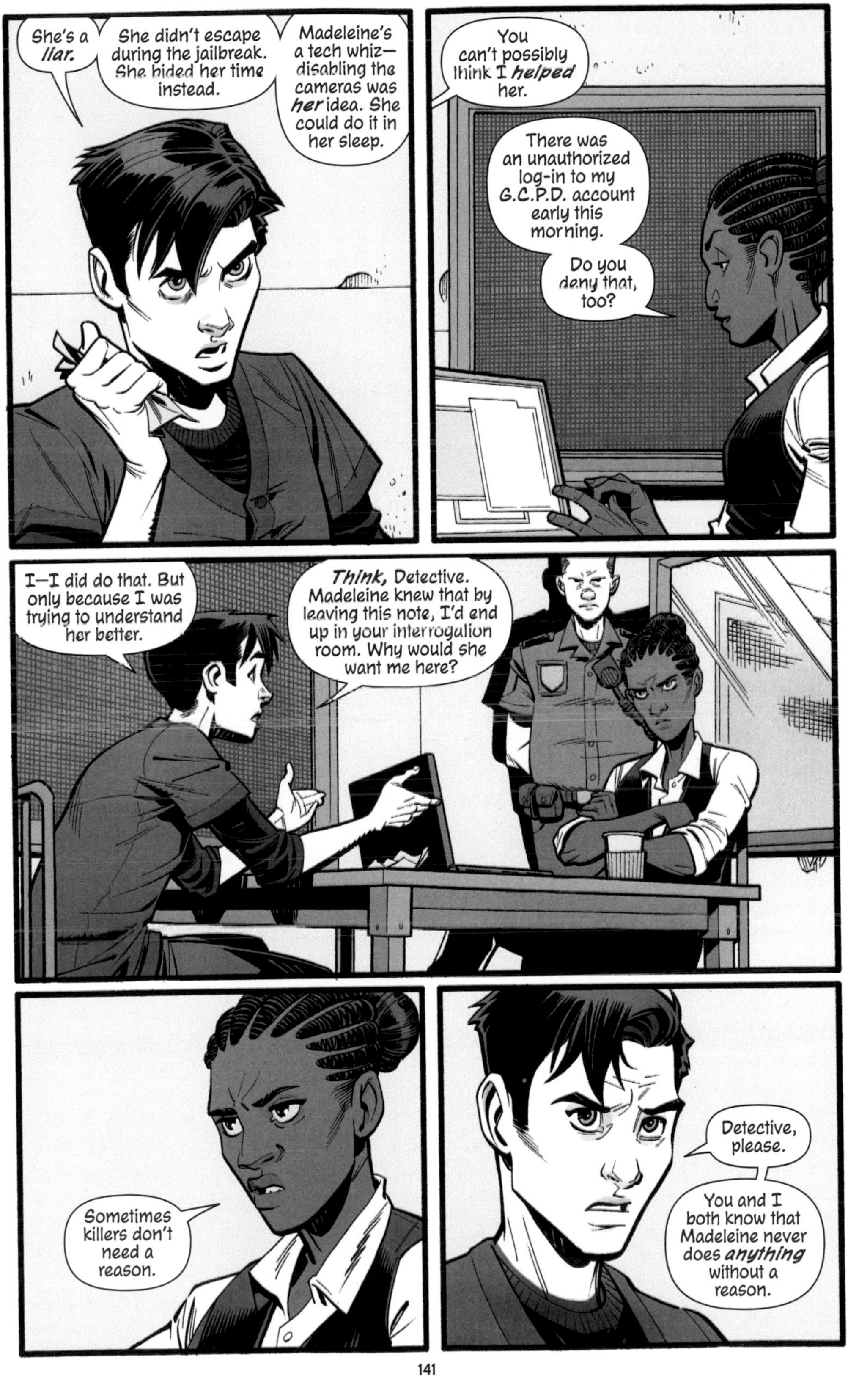
She's a *liar.*
She didn't escape during the jailbreak. She bided her time instead.
Madeleine's a tech whiz—disabling the cameras was *her* idea. She could do it in her sleep.
You can't possibly think I *helped* her.
There was an unauthorized log-in to my G.C.P.D. account early this morning.
Do you deny that, too?
I—I did do that. But only because I was trying to understand her better.
Think, Detective. Madeleine knew that by leaving this note, I'd end up in your interrogation room. Why would she want me here?
Sometimes killers don't need a reason.
Detective, please.
You and I both know that Madeleine never does *anything* without a reason.

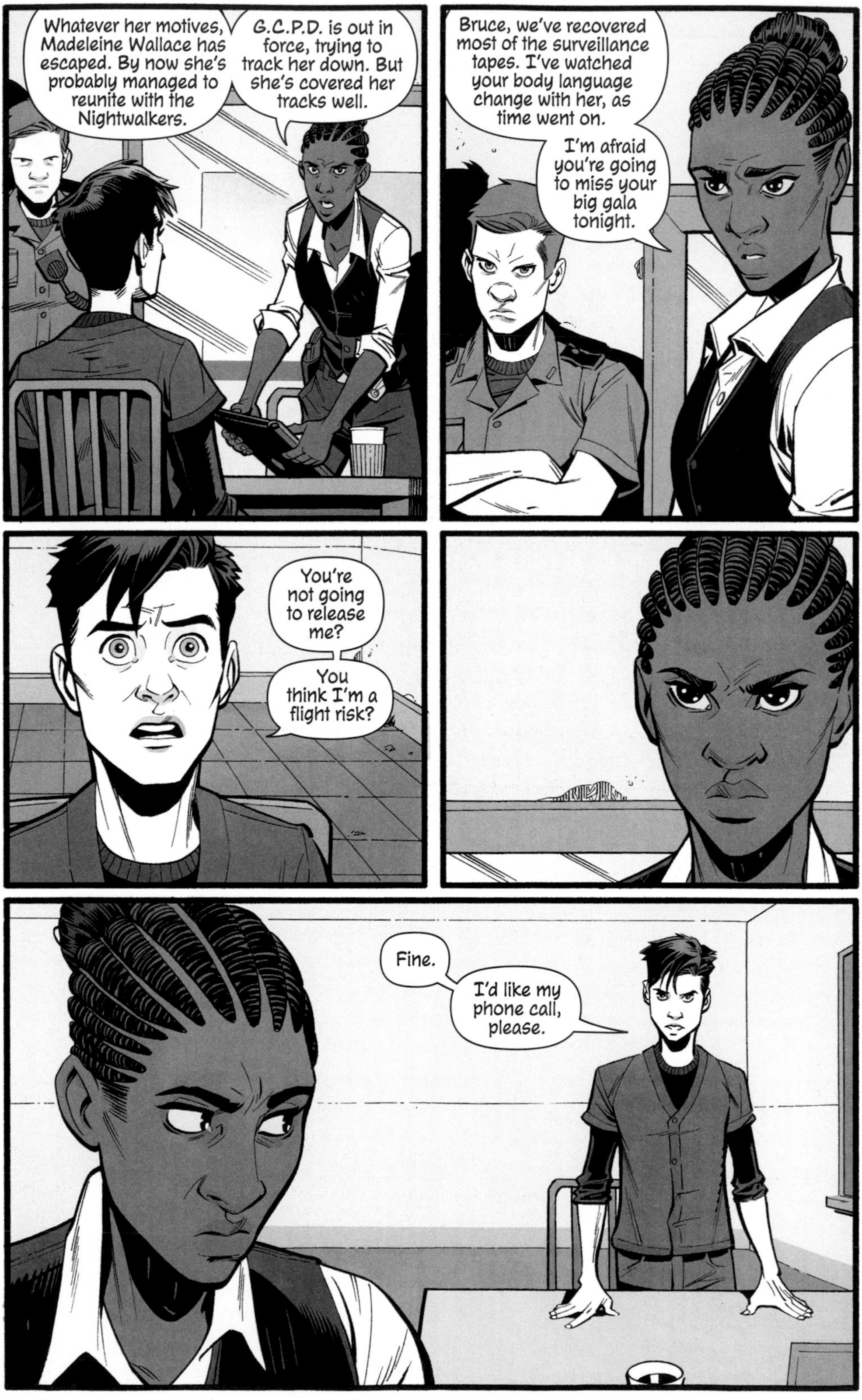
Whatever her motives, Madeleine Wallace has escaped. By now she's probably managed to reunite with the Nightwalkers.
G.C.P.D. is out in force, trying to track her down. But she's covered her tracks well.
Bruce, we've recovered most of the surveillance tapes. I've watched your body language change with her, as time went on.
I'm afraid you're going to miss your big gala tonight.
You're not going to release me?
You think I'm a flight risk?
Fine.
I'd like my phone call, please.

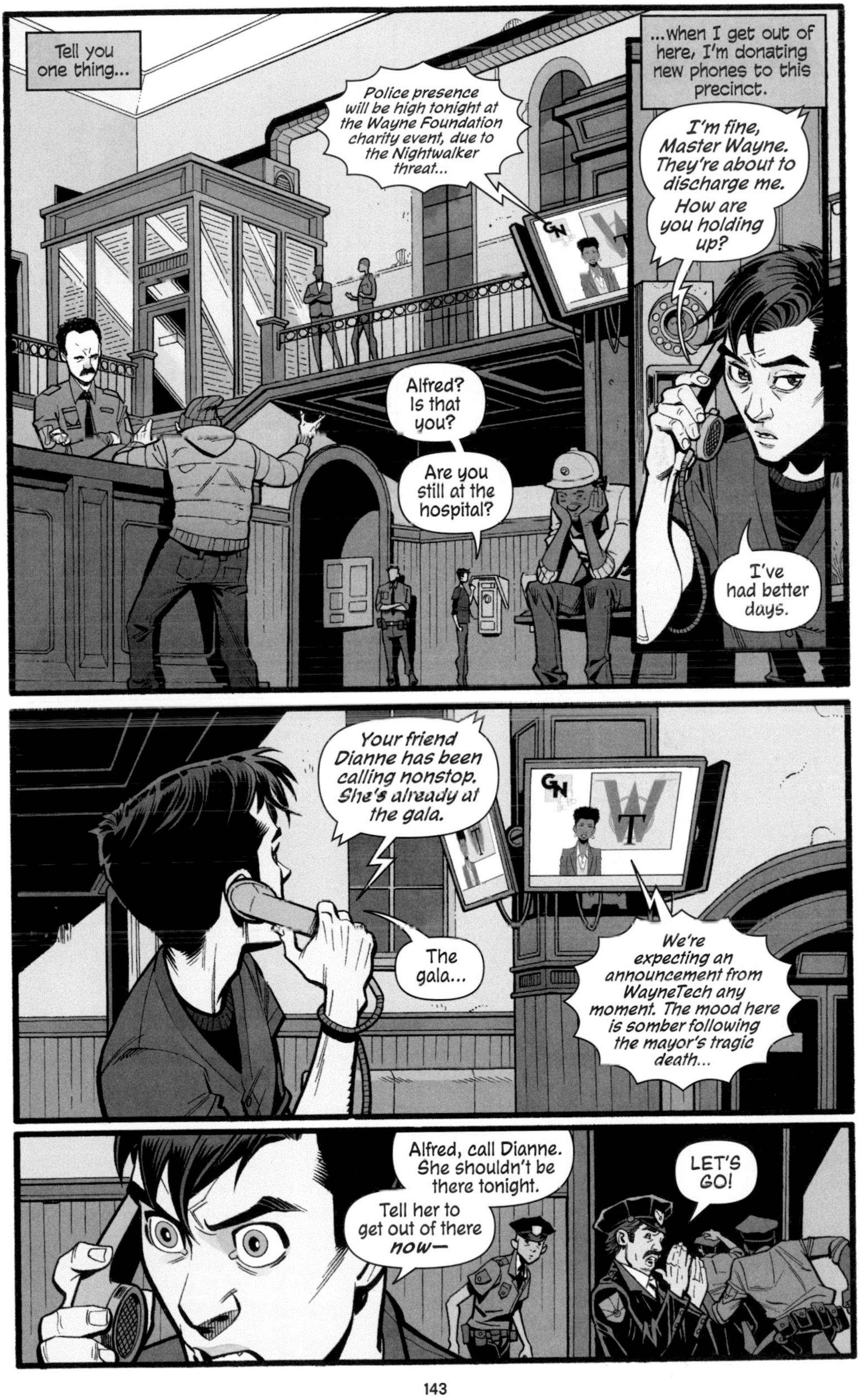
Tell you one thing...
Police presence will be high tonight at the Wayne Foundation charity event, due to the Nightwalker threat...
...when I get out of here, I'm donating new phones to this precinct.
I'm fine, Master Wayne. They're about to discharge me.
How are you holding up?
Alfred? Is that you?
Are you still at the hospital?
I've had better days.
Your friend Dianne has been calling nonstop. She's already at the gala.
The gala...
We're expecting an announcement from WayneTech any moment. The mood here is somber following the mayor's tragic death...
Alfred, call Dianne. She shouldn't be there tonight.
Tell her to get out of there now—
LET'S GO!

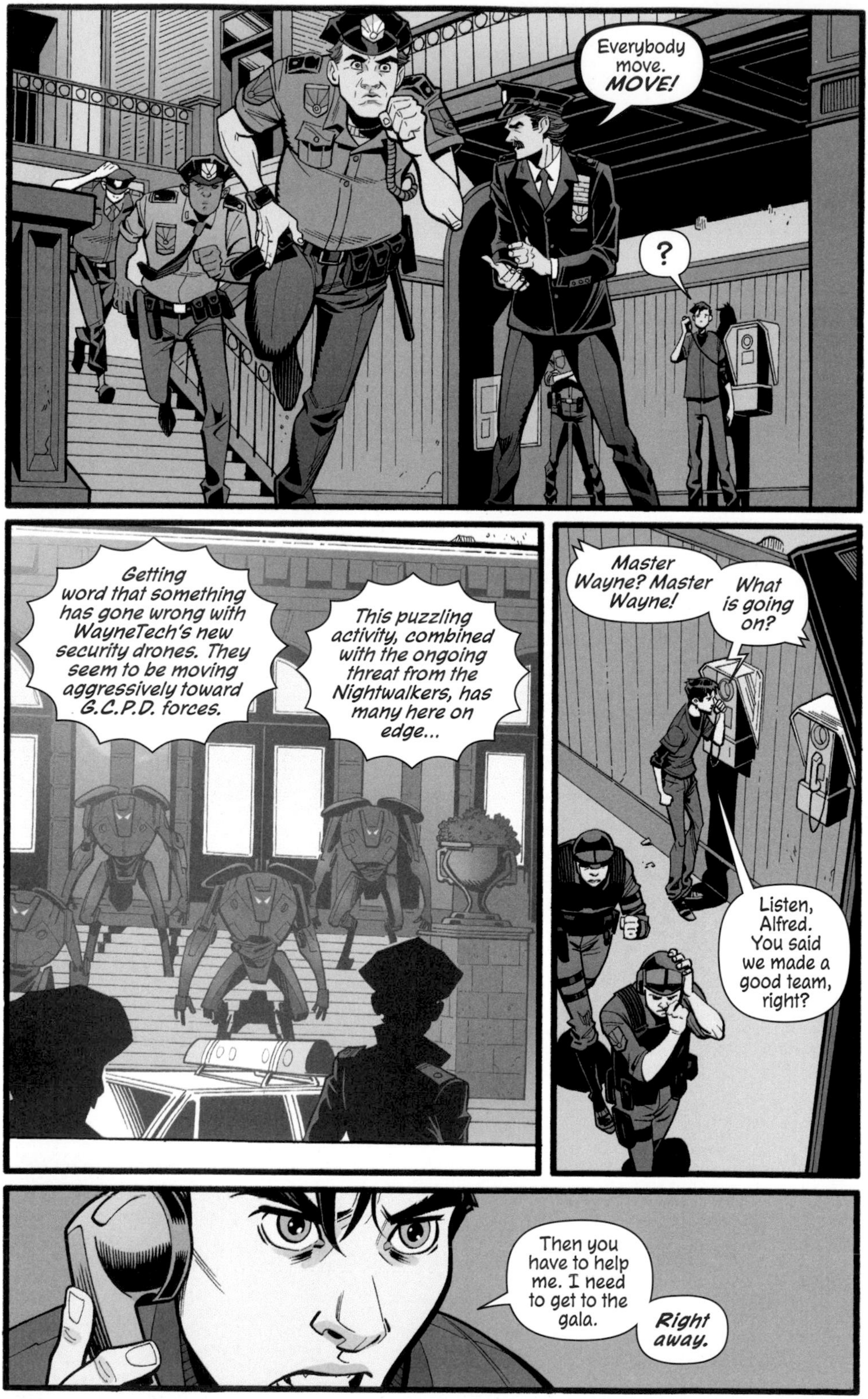
Everybody move. MOVE!
?
Getting word that something has gone wrong with WayneTech's new security drones. They seem to be moving aggressively toward G.C.P.D. forces.
This puzzling activity, combined with the ongoing threat from the Nightwalkers, has many here on edge...
Master Wayne? Master Wayne!
What is going on?
Listen, Alfred. You said we made a good team, right?
Then you have to help me. I need to get to the gala.
Right away.

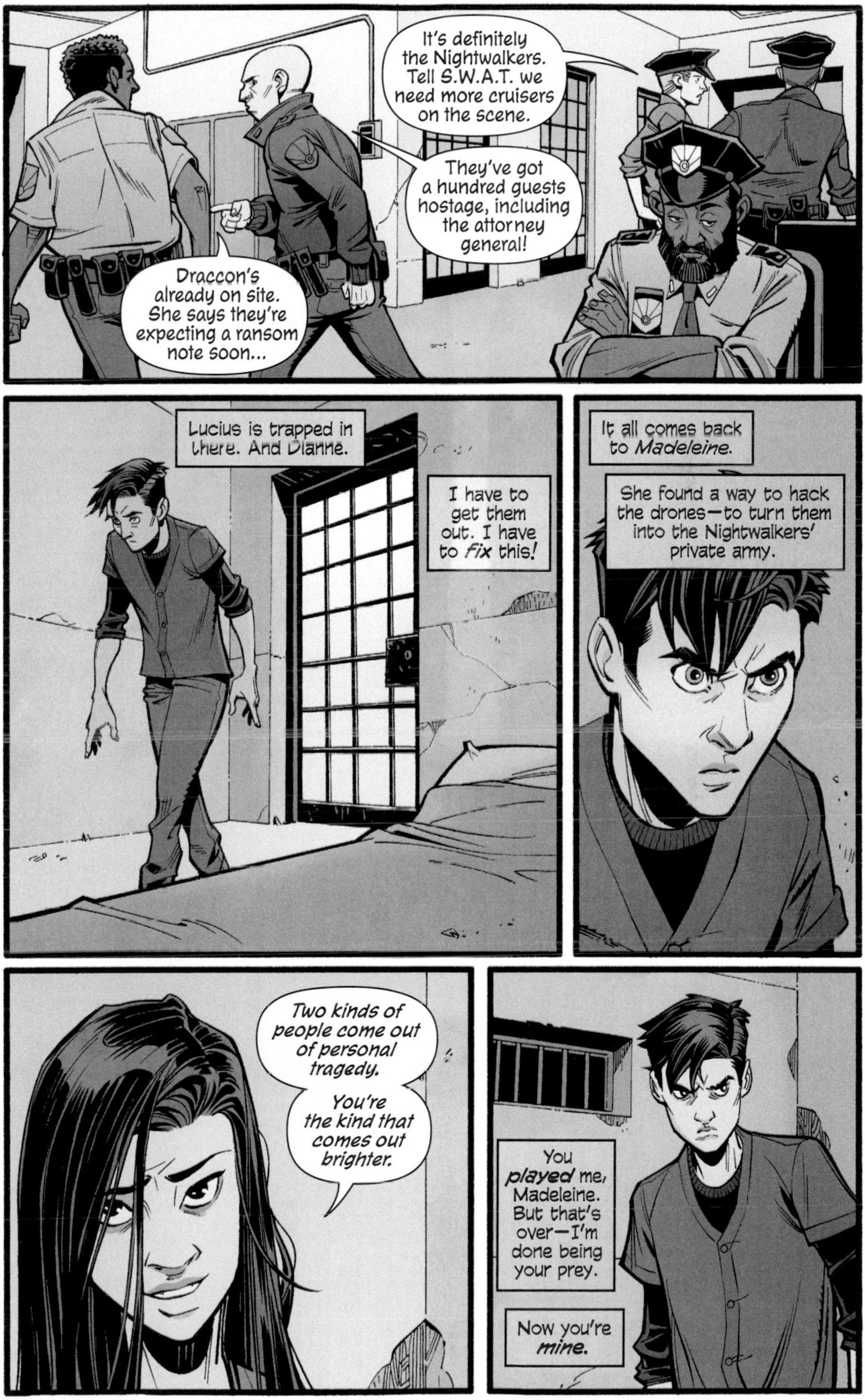
It's definitely the Nightwalkers. Tell S.W.A.T. we need more cruisers on the scene.
They've got a hundred guests hostage, including the attorney general!
Draccon's already on site. She says they're expecting a ransom note soon...
Lucius is trapped in there. And Dianne.
I have to get them out. I have to *fix* this!
It all comes back to *Madeleine*.
She found a way to hack the drones—to turn them into the Nightwalkers' private army.
Two kinds of people come out of personal tragedy.
You're the kind that comes out brighter.
You ***played*** me, Madeleine. But that's over—I'm done being your prey.
Now you're ***mine.***

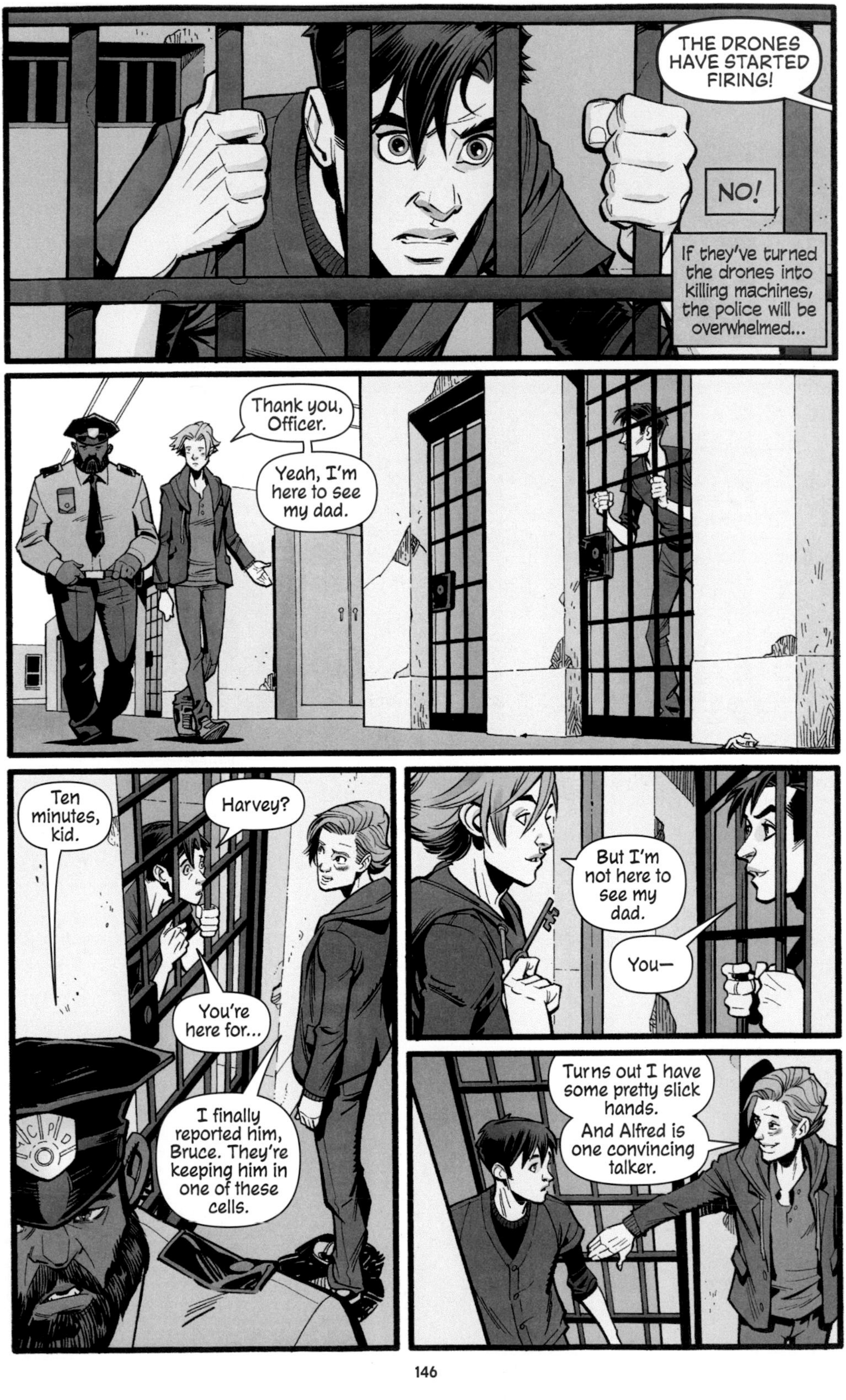
THE DRONES HAVE STARTED FIRING!
NO!
If they've turned the drones into killing machines, the police will be overwhelmed...
Thank you, Officer.
Yeah, I'm here to see my dad.
Ten minutes, kid.
Harvey?
You're here for...
I finally reported him, Bruce. They're keeping him in one of these cells.
But I'm not here to see my dad.
You—
Turns out I have some pretty slick hands.
And Alfred is one convincing talker.

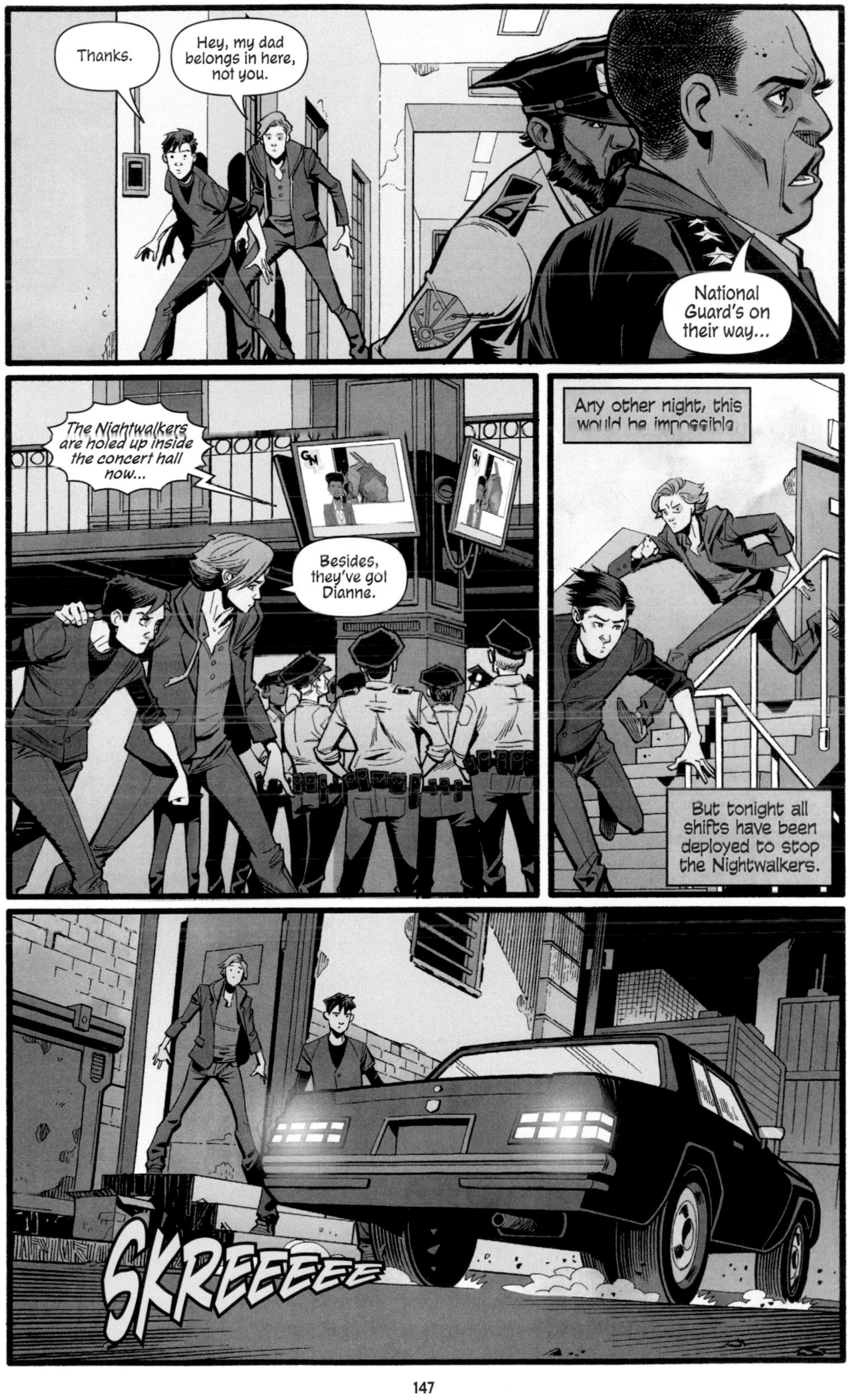

Thanks.
Hey, my dad belongs in here, not you.
National Guard's on their way...
The Nightwalkers are holed up inside the concert hall now...
Besides, they've got Dianne.
Any other night, this would be impossible.
But tonight all shifts have been deployed to stop the Nightwalkers.
SKREEEEEE

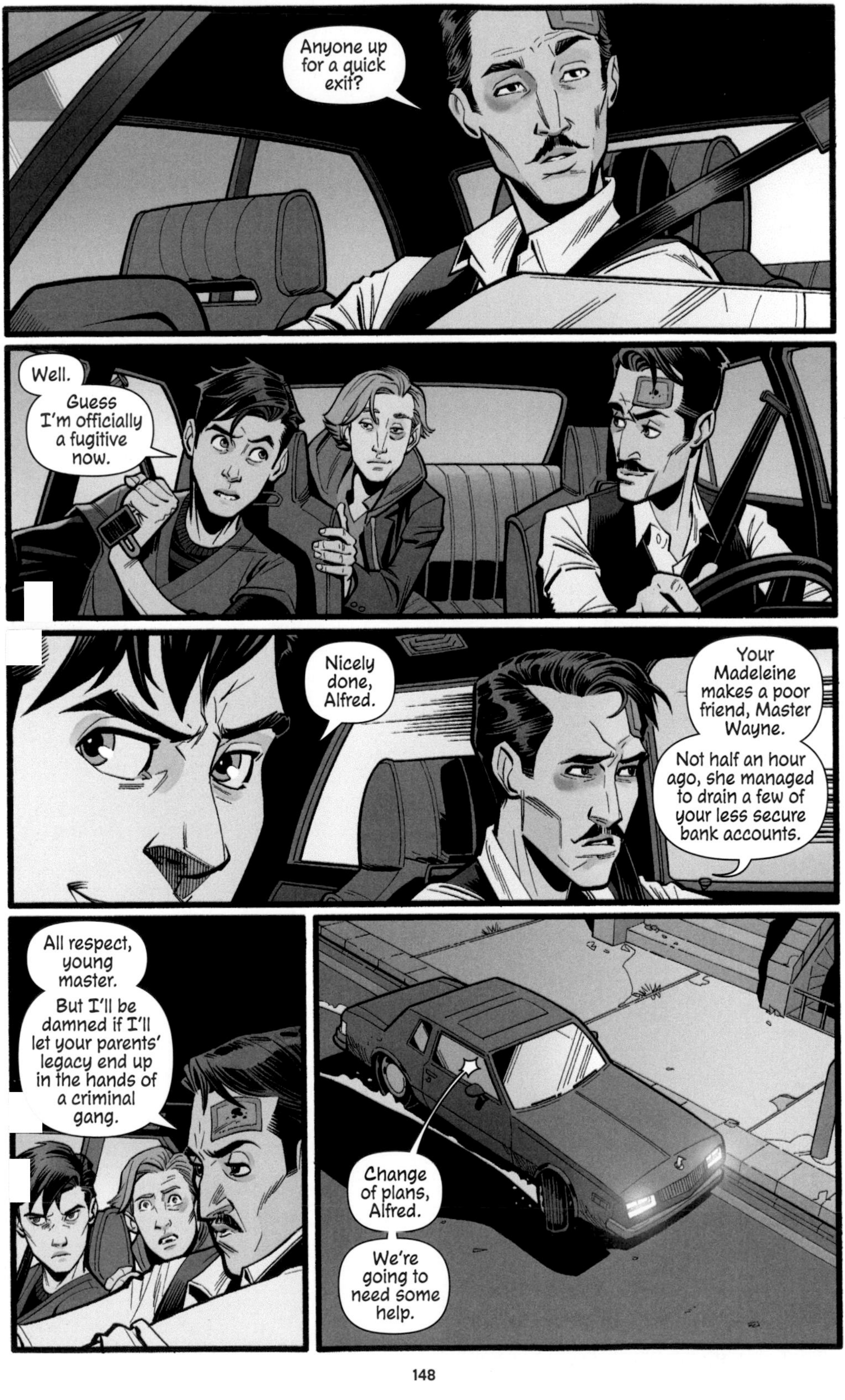
Anyone up for a quick exit?
Well.
Guess I'm officially a fugitive now.
Nicely done, Alfred.
Your Madeleine makes a poor friend, Master Wayne.
Not half an hour ago, she managed to drain a few of your less secure bank accounts.
All respect, young master.
But I'll be damned if I'll let your parents' legacy end up in the hands of a criminal gang.
Change of plans, Alfred.
We're going to need some help.

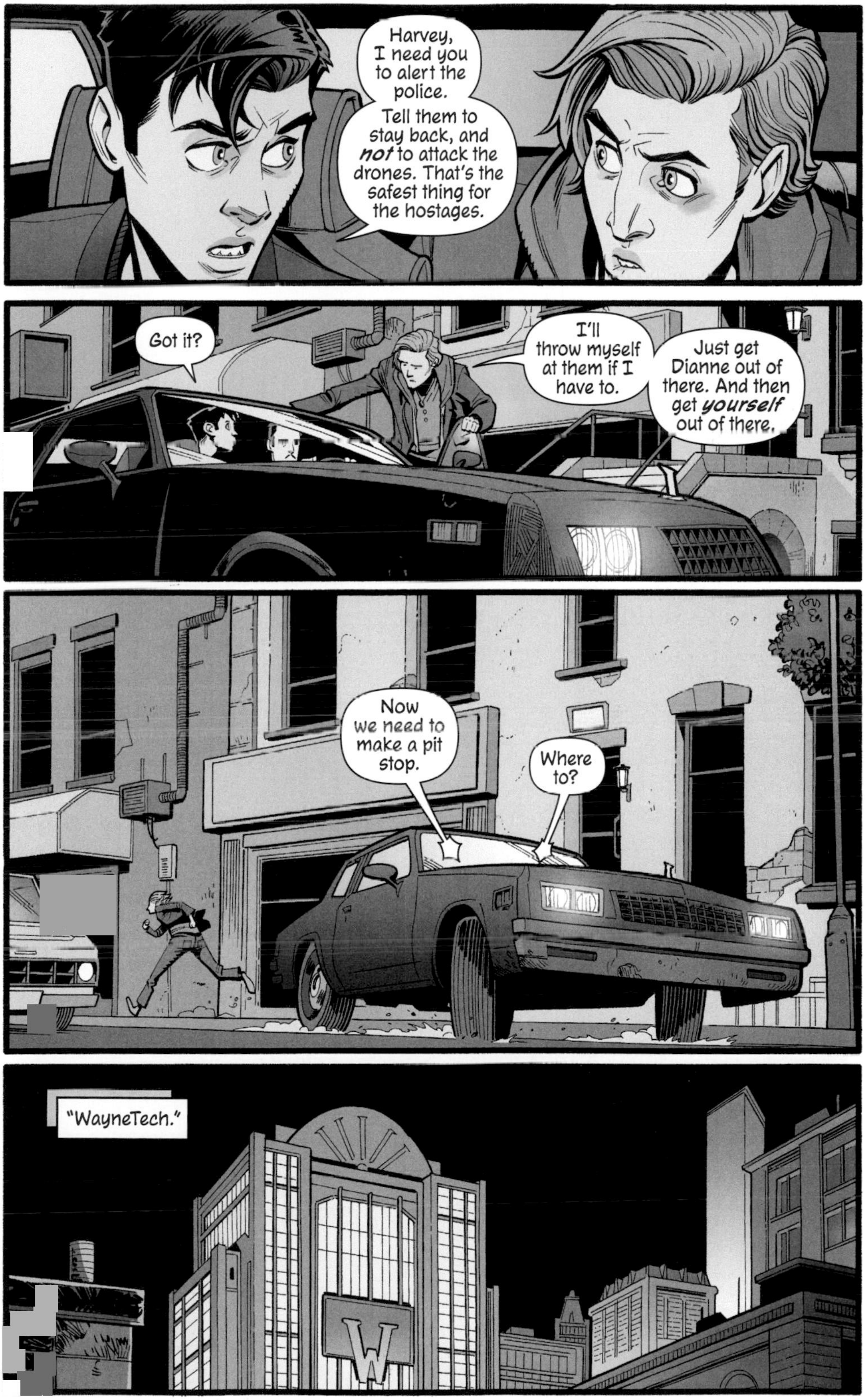
Harvey, I need you to alert the police.
Tell them to stay back, and *not* to attack the drones. That's the safest thing for the hostages.
Got it?
I'll throw myself at them if I have to.
Just get Dianne out of there. And then get *yourself* out of there.
Now we need to make a pit stop.
Where to?
"WayneTech."

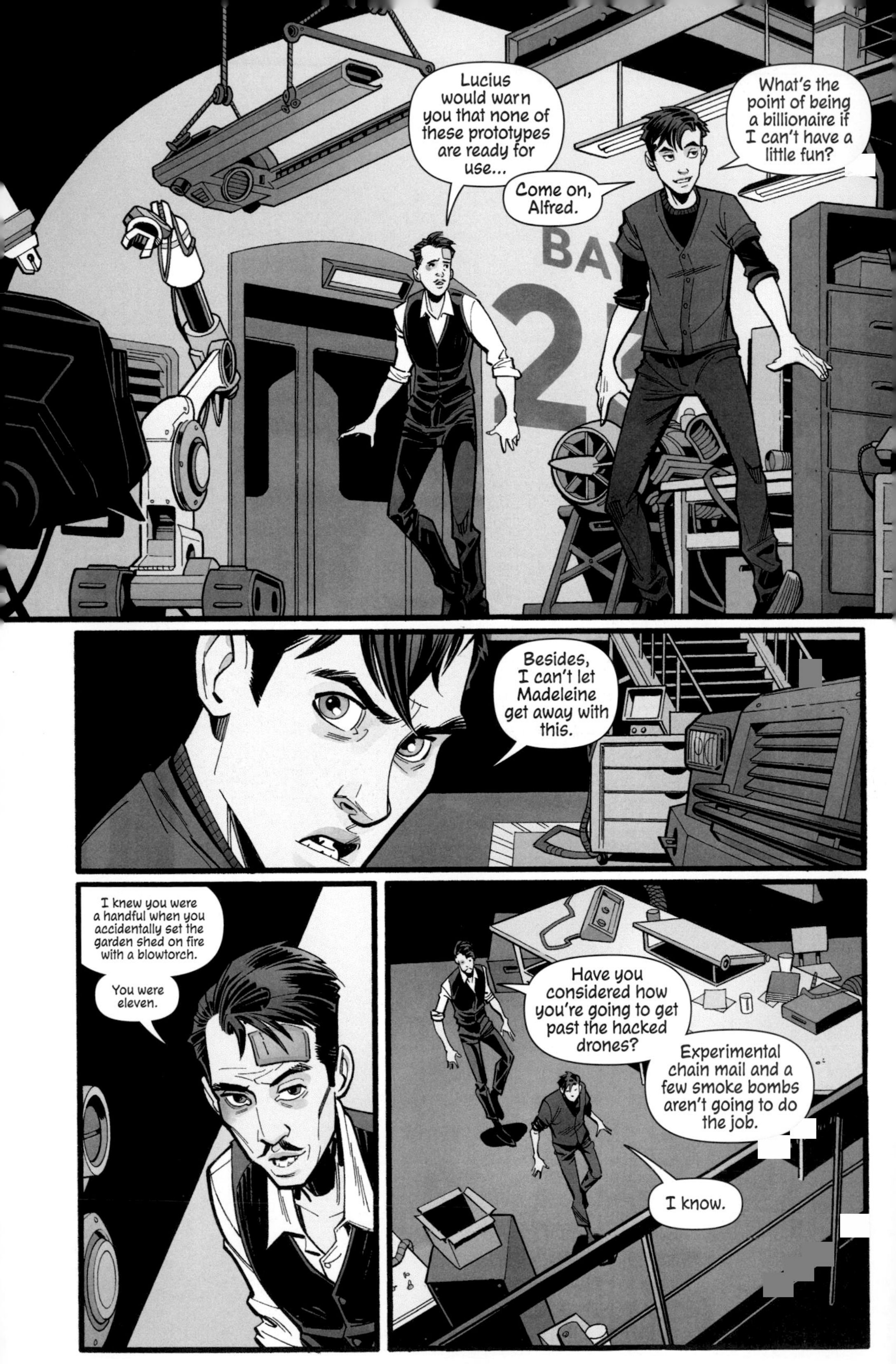

Lucius would warn you that none of these prototypes are ready for use...
What's the point of being a billionaire if I can't have a little fun?
Come on, Alfred.
BAY 2
Besides, I can't let Madeleine get away with this.
I knew you were a handful when you accidentally set the garden shed on fire with a blowtorch.
You were eleven.
Have you considered how you're going to get past the hacked drones?
Experimental chain mail and a few smoke bombs aren't going to do the job.
I know.

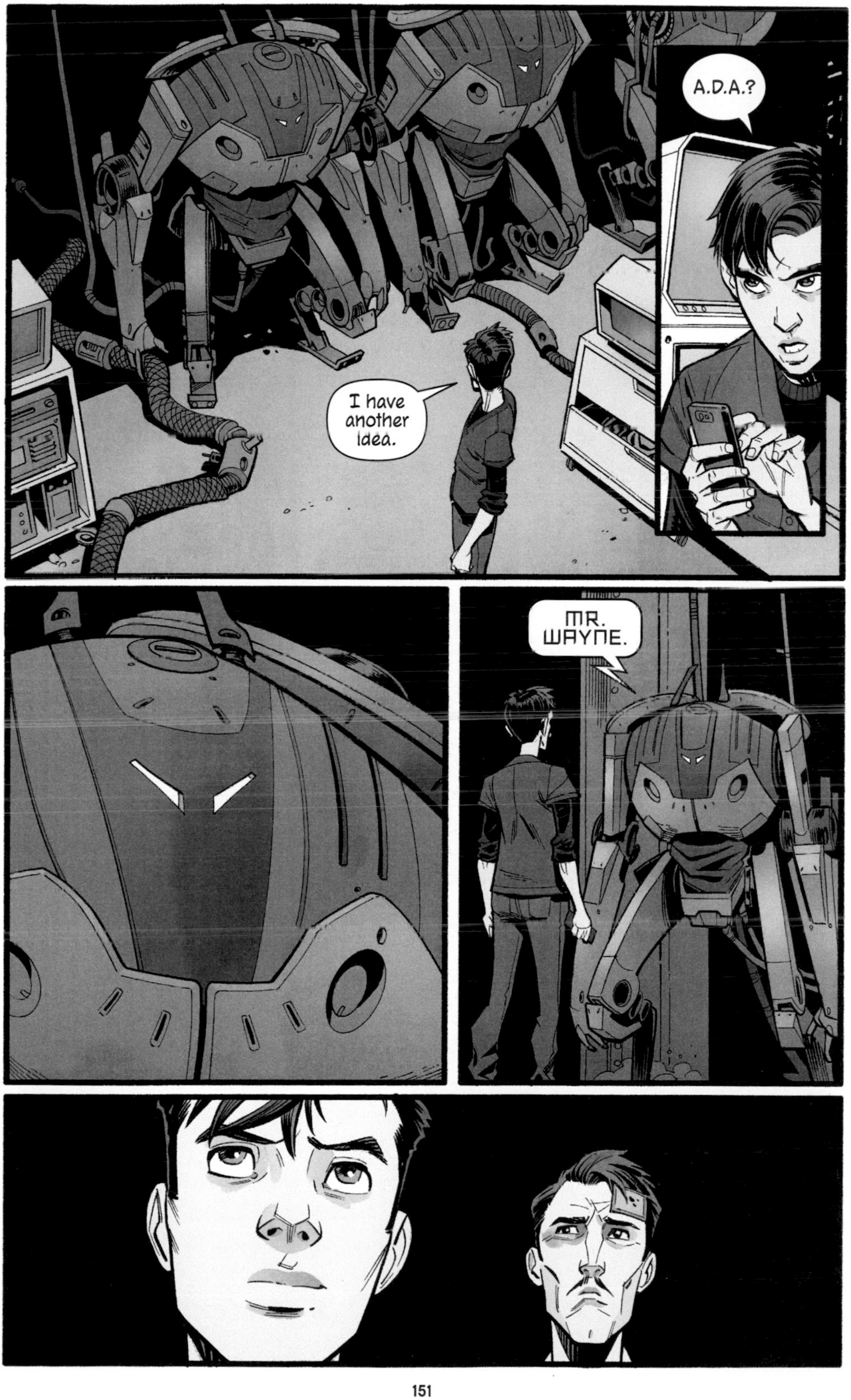
I have another idea.
A.D.A.?
MR. WAYNE.

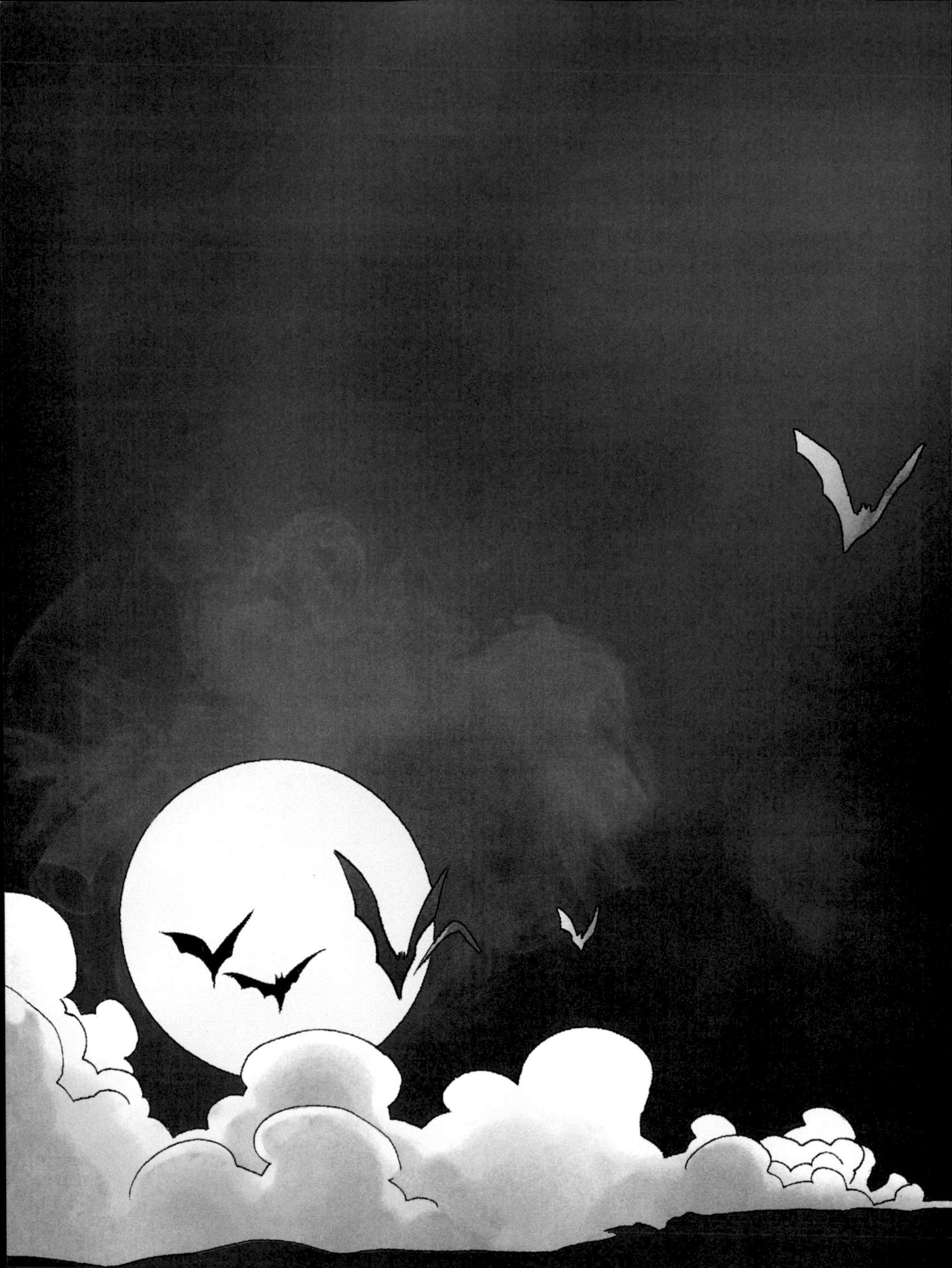

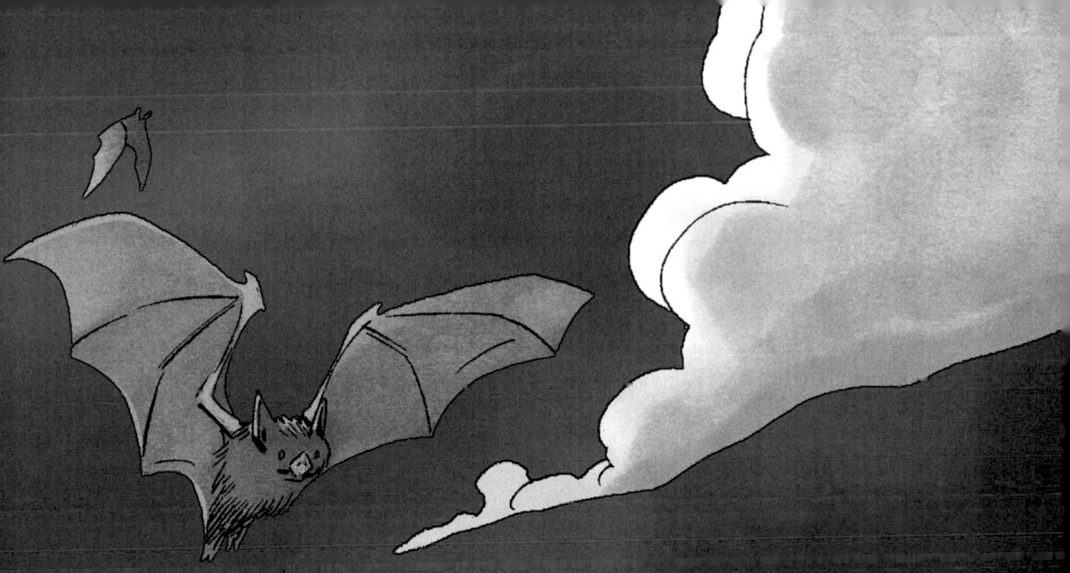

PART FIVE

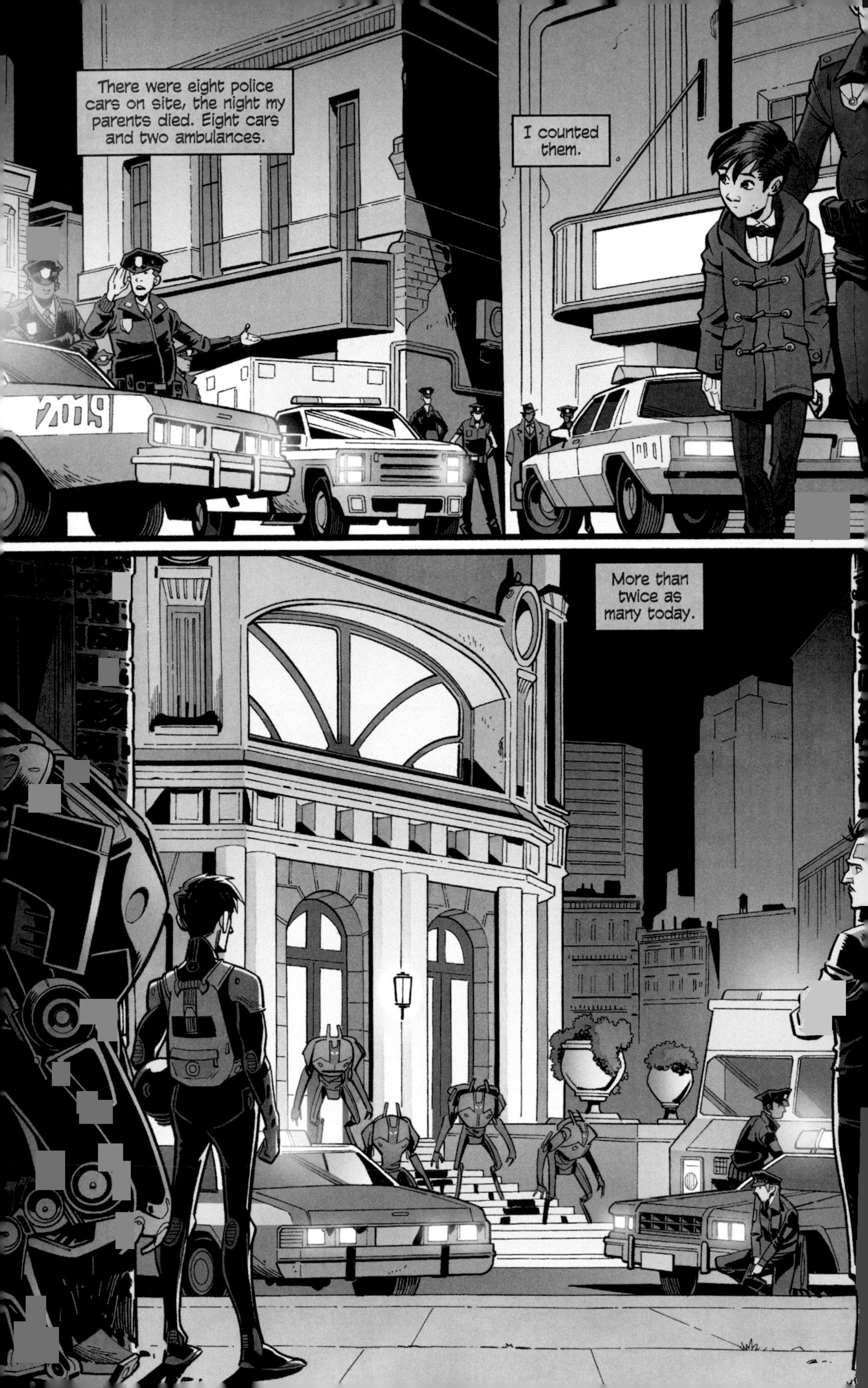
There were eight police cars on site, the night my parents died. Eight cars and two ambulances.
2019
I counted them.
More than twice as many today.

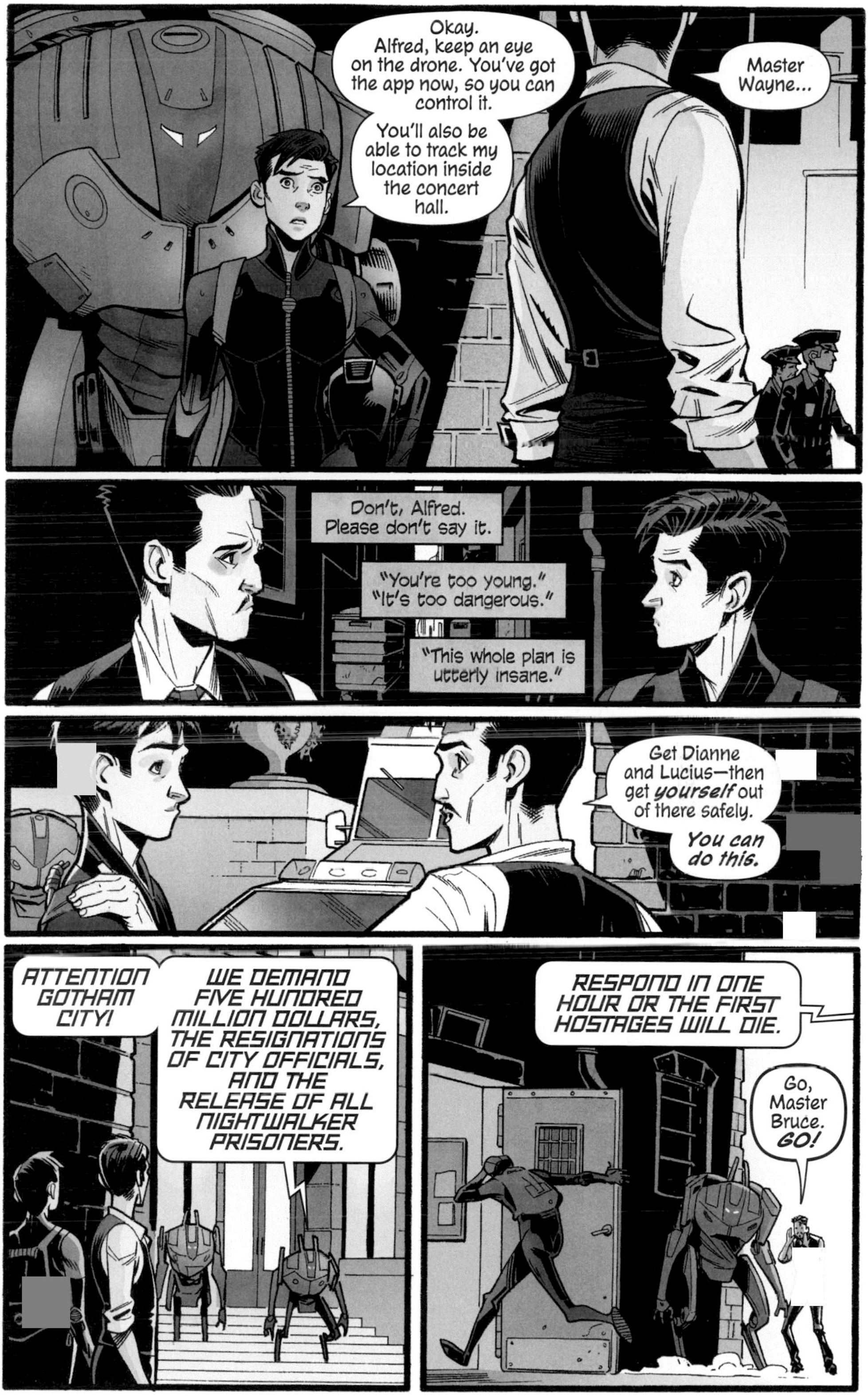
Okay. Alfred, keep an eye on the drone. You've got the app now, so you can control it.
You'll also be able to track my location inside the concert hall.
Master Wayne...
Don't, Alfred. Please don't say it.
"You're too young." "It's too dangerous."
"This whole plan is utterly insane."
Get Dianne and Lucius—then get *yourself* out of there safely.
You can do this.
ATTENTION GOTHAM CITY!
WE DEMAND FIVE HUNDRED MILLION DOLLARS, THE RESIGNATIONS OF CITY OFFICIALS, AND THE RELEASE OF ALL NIGHTWALKER PRISONERS.
RESPOND IN ONE HOUR OR THE FIRST HOSTAGES WILL DIE.
Go, Master Bruce. *GO!*

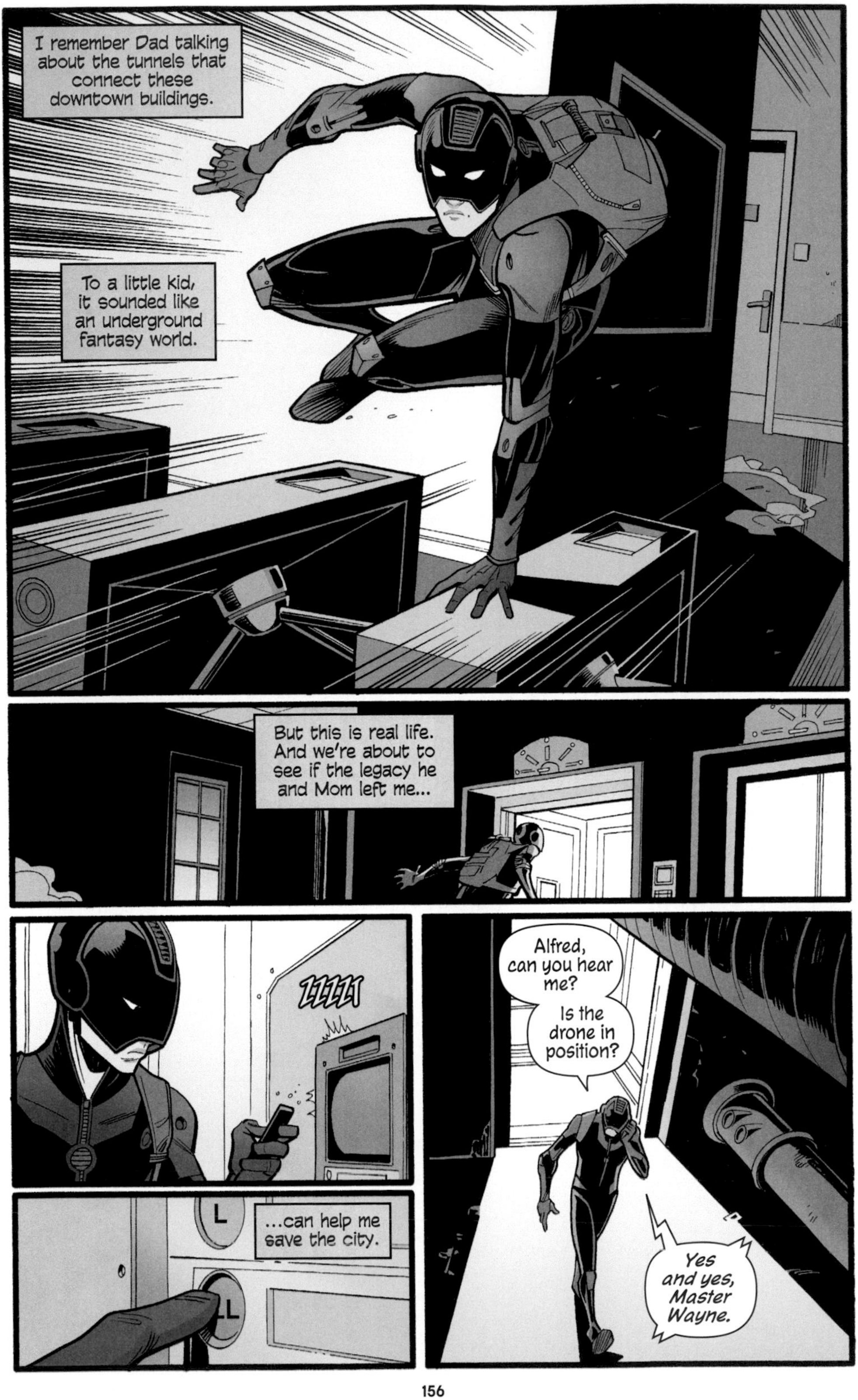
I remember Dad talking about the tunnels that connect these downtown buildings.
To a little kid, it sounded like an underground fantasy world.
But this is real life. And we're about to see if the legacy he and Mom left me...
ZZZZT
L
LL
...can help me save the city.
Alfred, can you hear me?
Is the drone in position?
Yes and yes, Master Wayne.

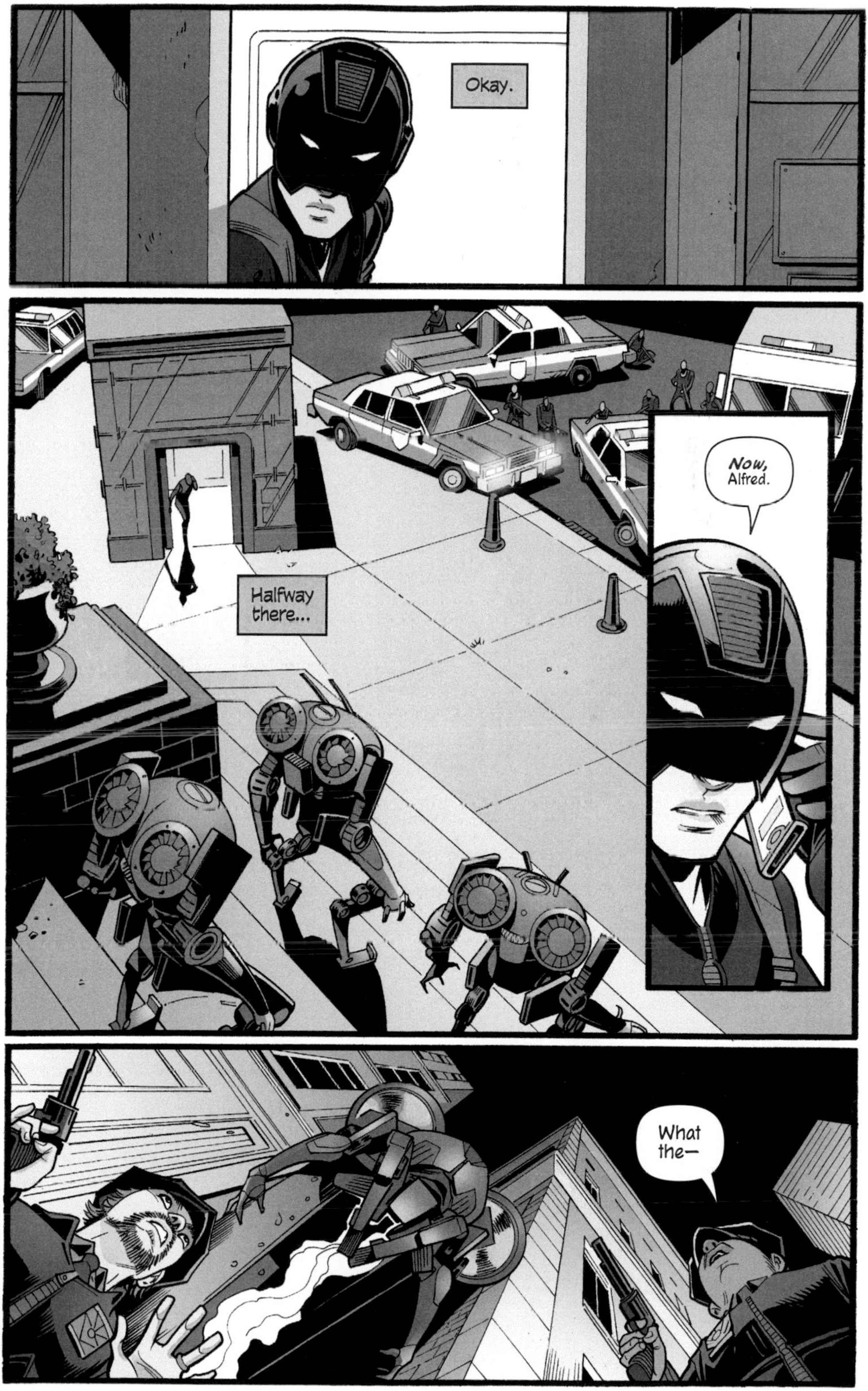
Okay.
Halfway there...
Now, Alfred.
What the—

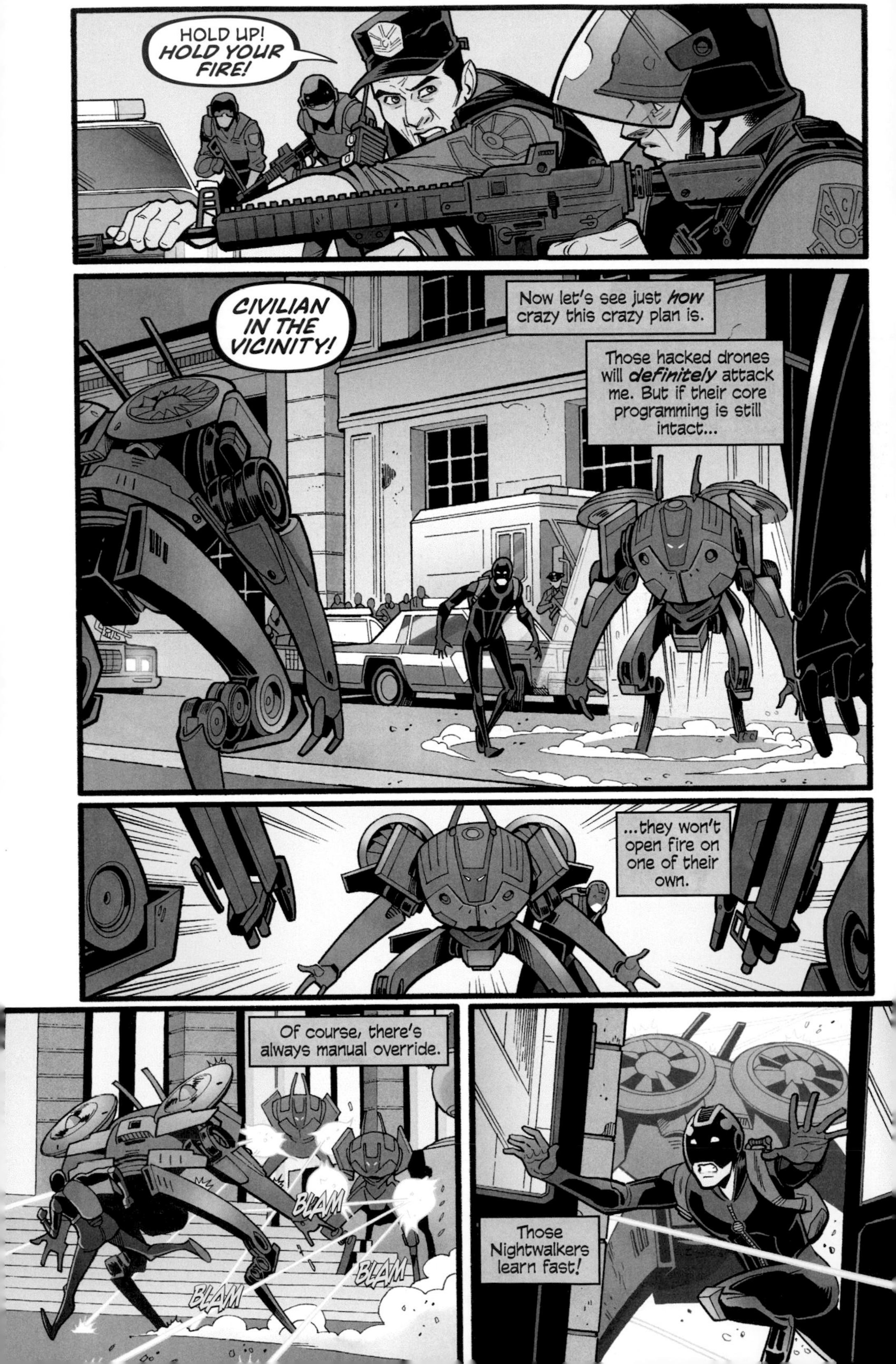
HOLD UP! HOLD YOUR FIRE!
CIVILIAN IN THE VICINITY!
Now let's see just how crazy this crazy plan is.
Those hacked drones will definitely attack me. But if their core programming is still intact...
...they won't open fire on one of their own.
Of course, there's always manual override.
BLAM
BLAM
BLAM
Those Nightwalkers learn fast!

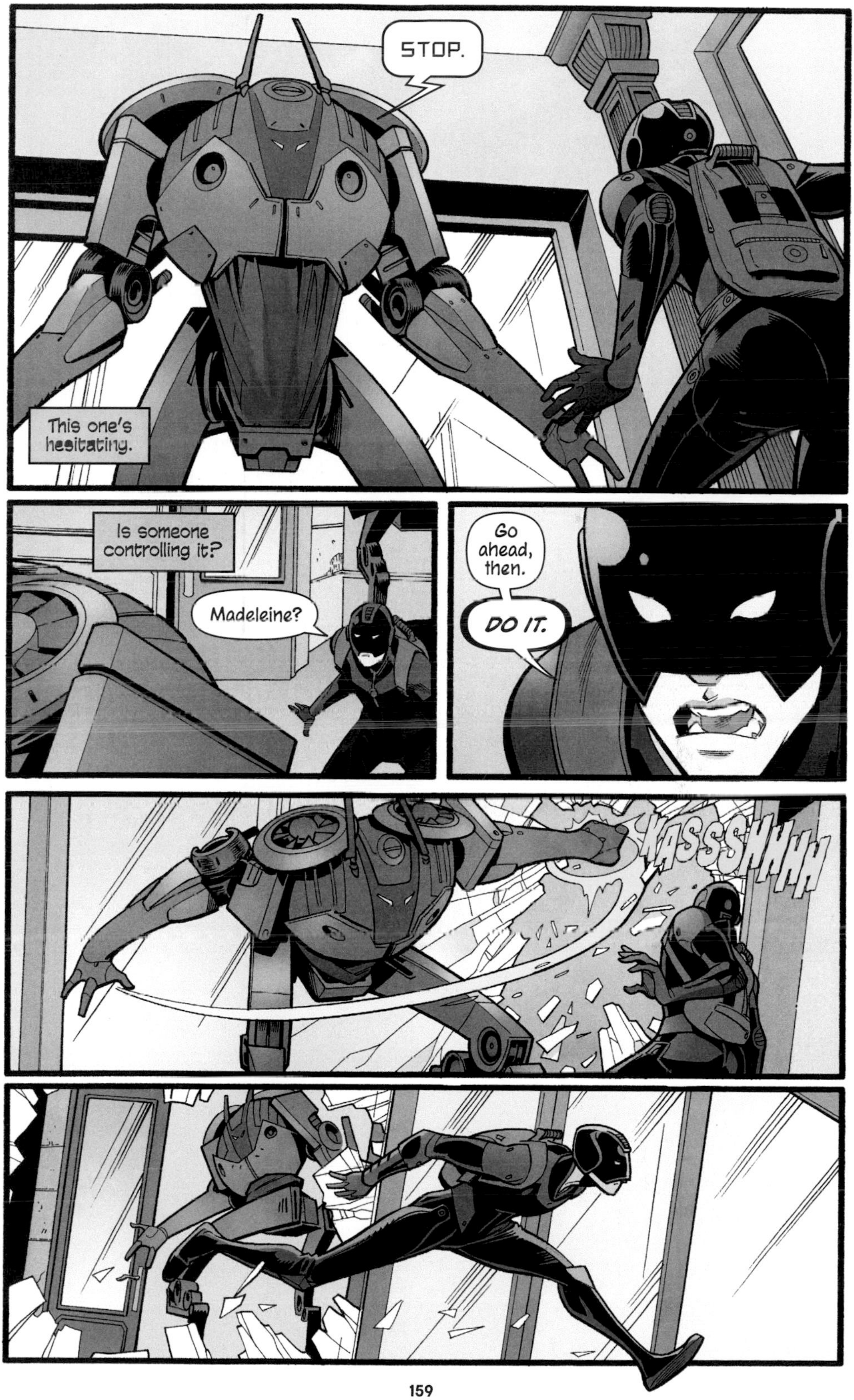
STOP.
This one's hesitating.
Is someone controlling it?
Madeleine?
Go ahead, then.
DO IT.
KASSSHHHH

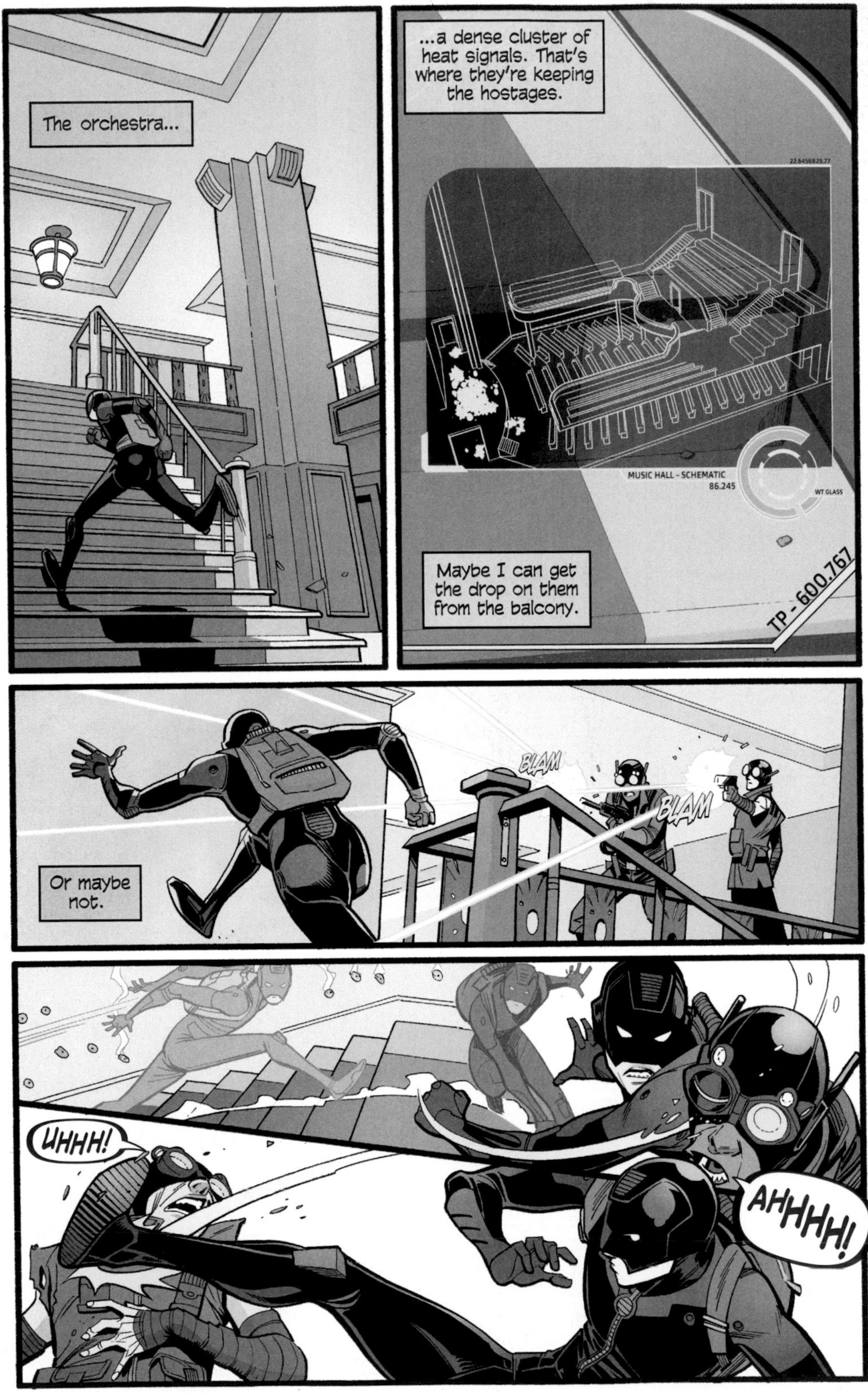
The orchestra...
...a dense cluster of heat signals. That's where they're keeping the hostages.
MUSIC HALL - SCHEMATIC
86.245
WT GLASS
Maybe I can get the drop on them from the balcony.
TP - 600.767
BLAM
BLAM
Or maybe not.
UHHH!
AHHHH!

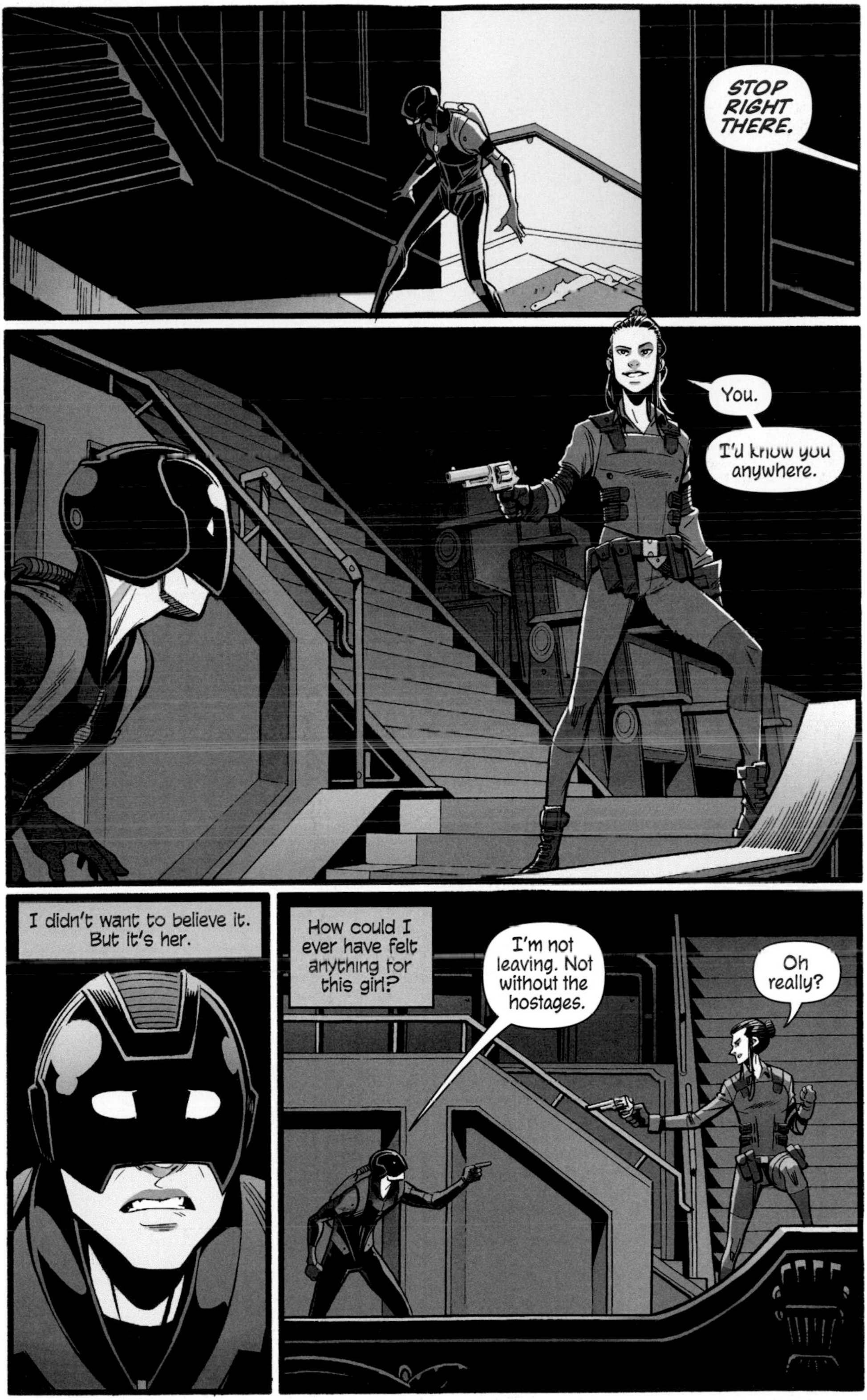
STOP RIGHT THERE.
You.
I'd know you anywhere.
I didn't want to believe it. But it's her.
How could I ever have felt anything for this girl?
I'm not leaving. Not without the hostages.
Oh really?

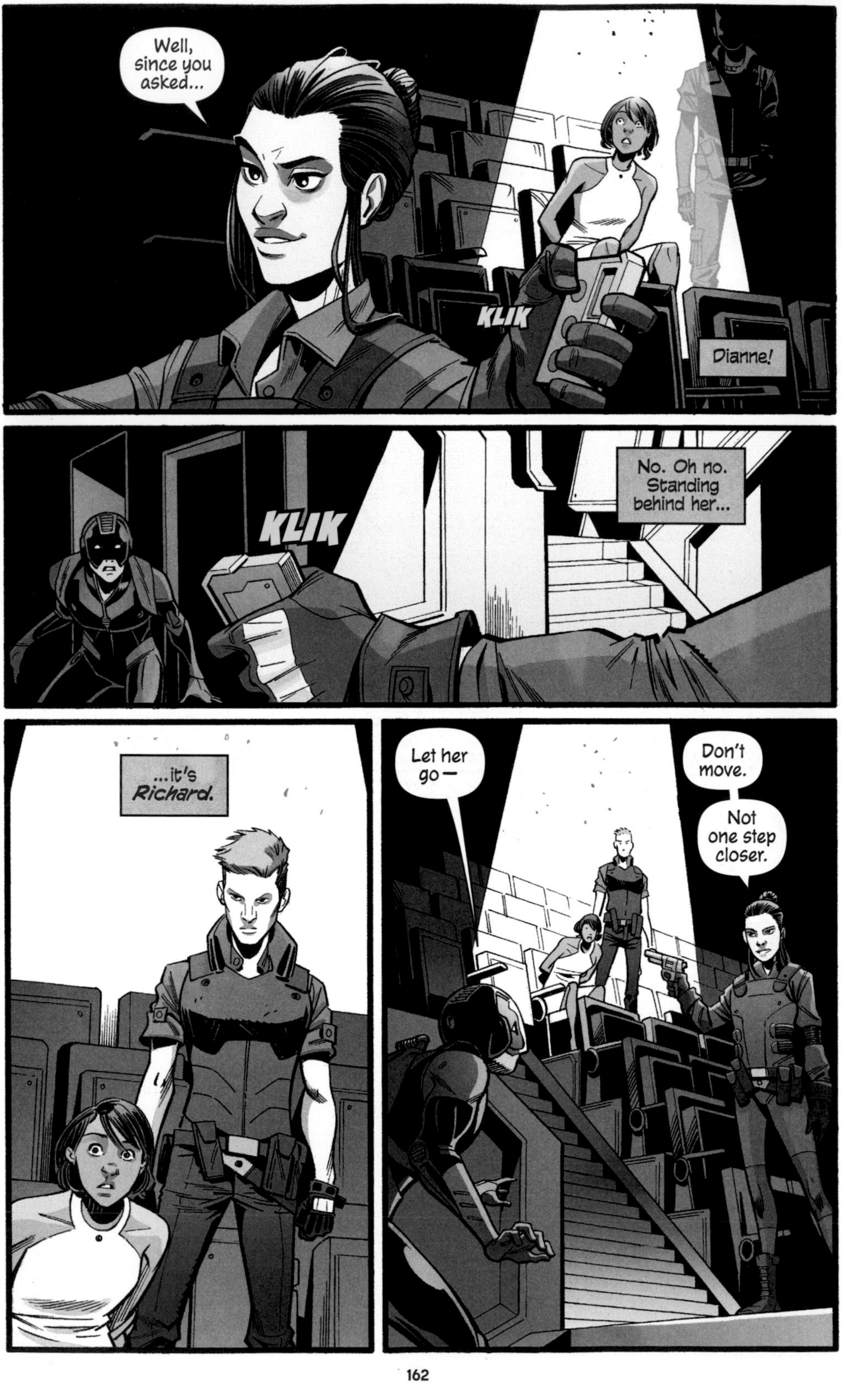
Well, since you asked...
KLIK
Dianne!
No. Oh no. Standing behind her...
KLIK
...it's *Richard.*
Let her go—
Don't move.
Not one step closer.

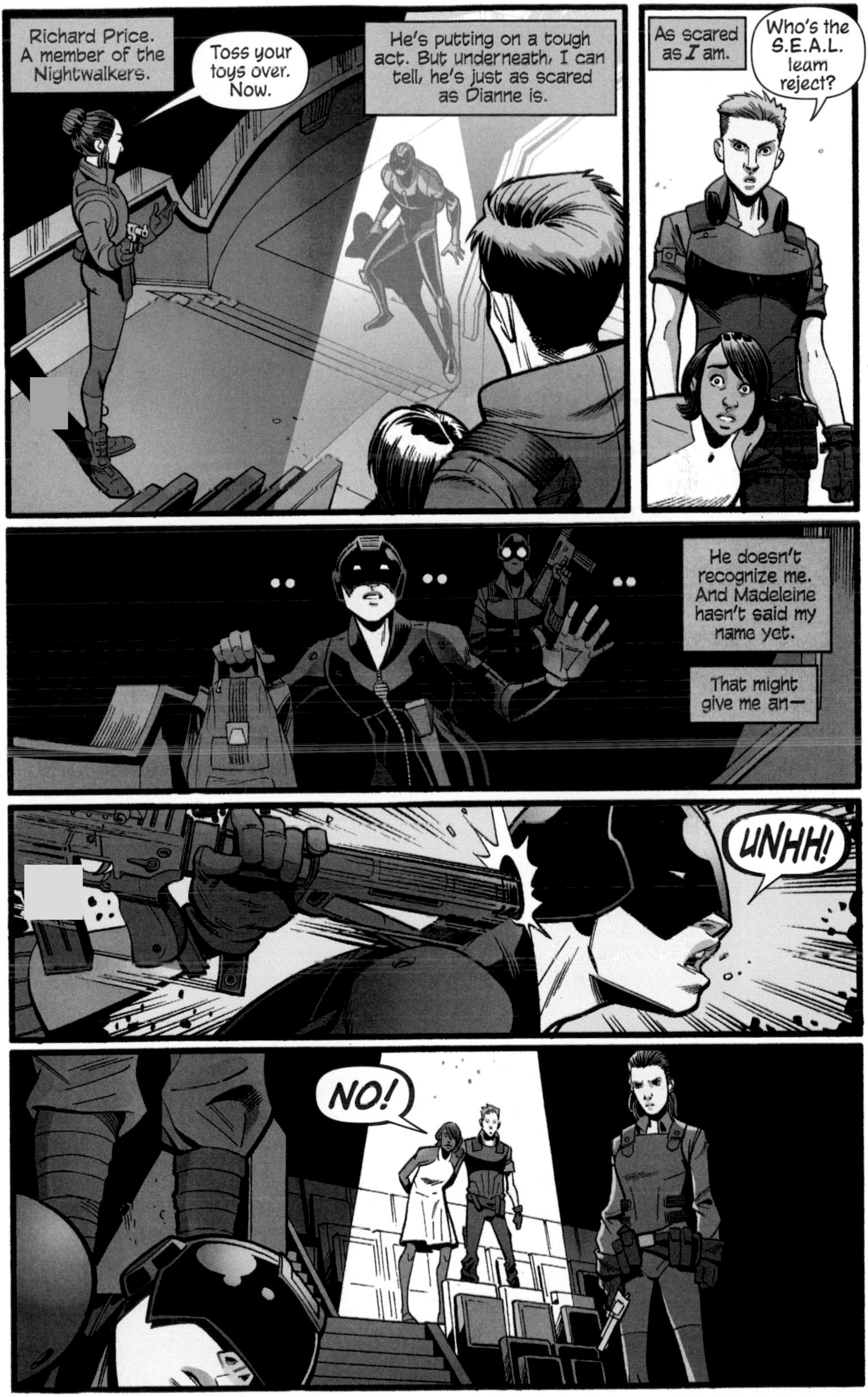
Richard Price. A member of the Nightwalkers.
Toss your toys over. Now.
He's putting on a tough act. But underneath, I can tell, he's just as scared as Dianne is.
As scared as I am.
Who's the S.E.A.L. team reject?
He doesn't recognize me. And Madeleine hasn't said my name yet.
That might give me an—
UNHH!
NO!

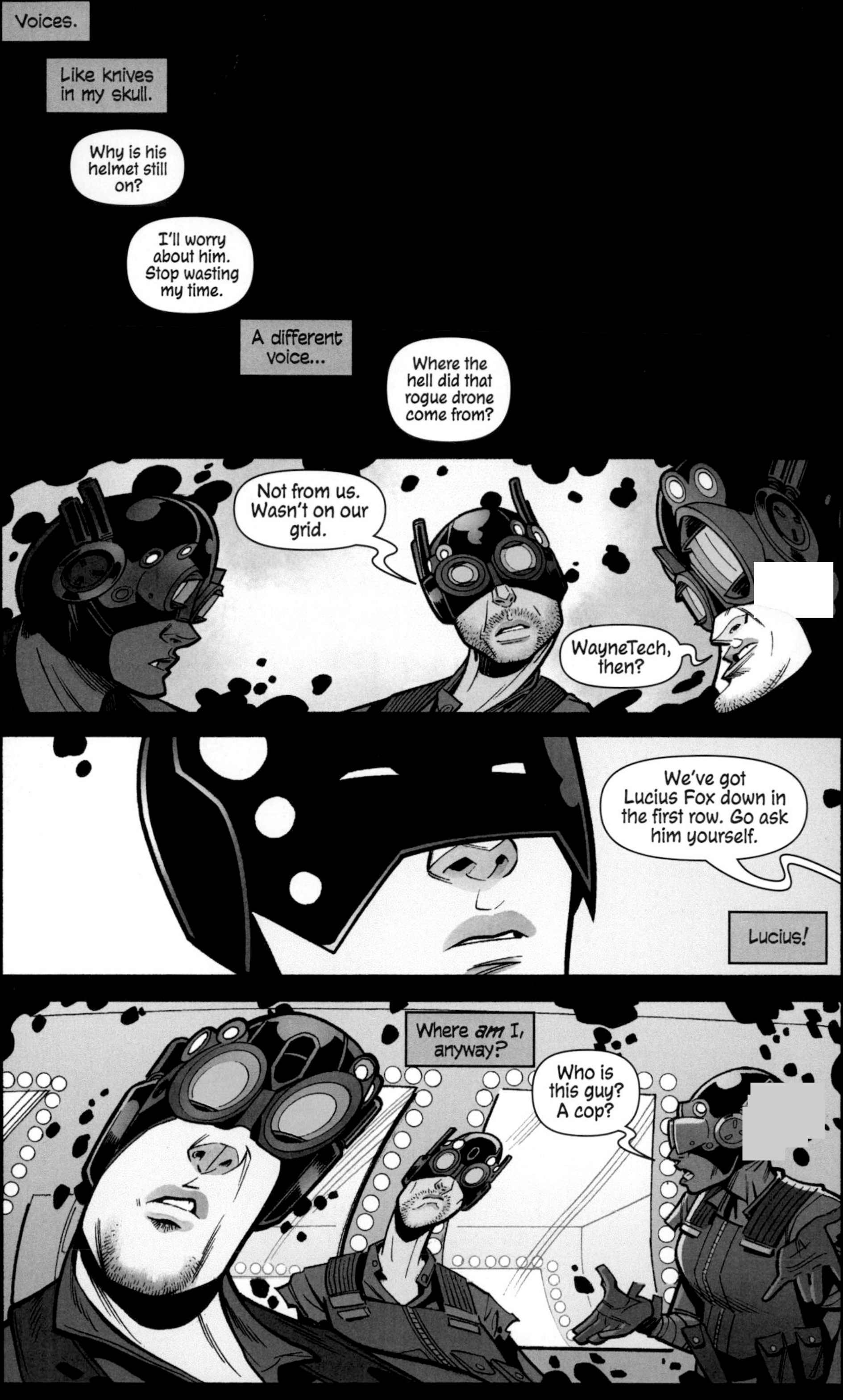

Voices.
Like knives in my skull.
Why is his helmet still on?
I'll worry about him. Stop wasting my time.
A different voice...
Where the hell did that rogue drone come from?
Not from us. Wasn't on our grid.
WayneTech, then?
We've got Lucius Fox down in the first row. Go ask him yourself.
Lucius!
Where *am* I, anyway?
Who is this guy? A cop?

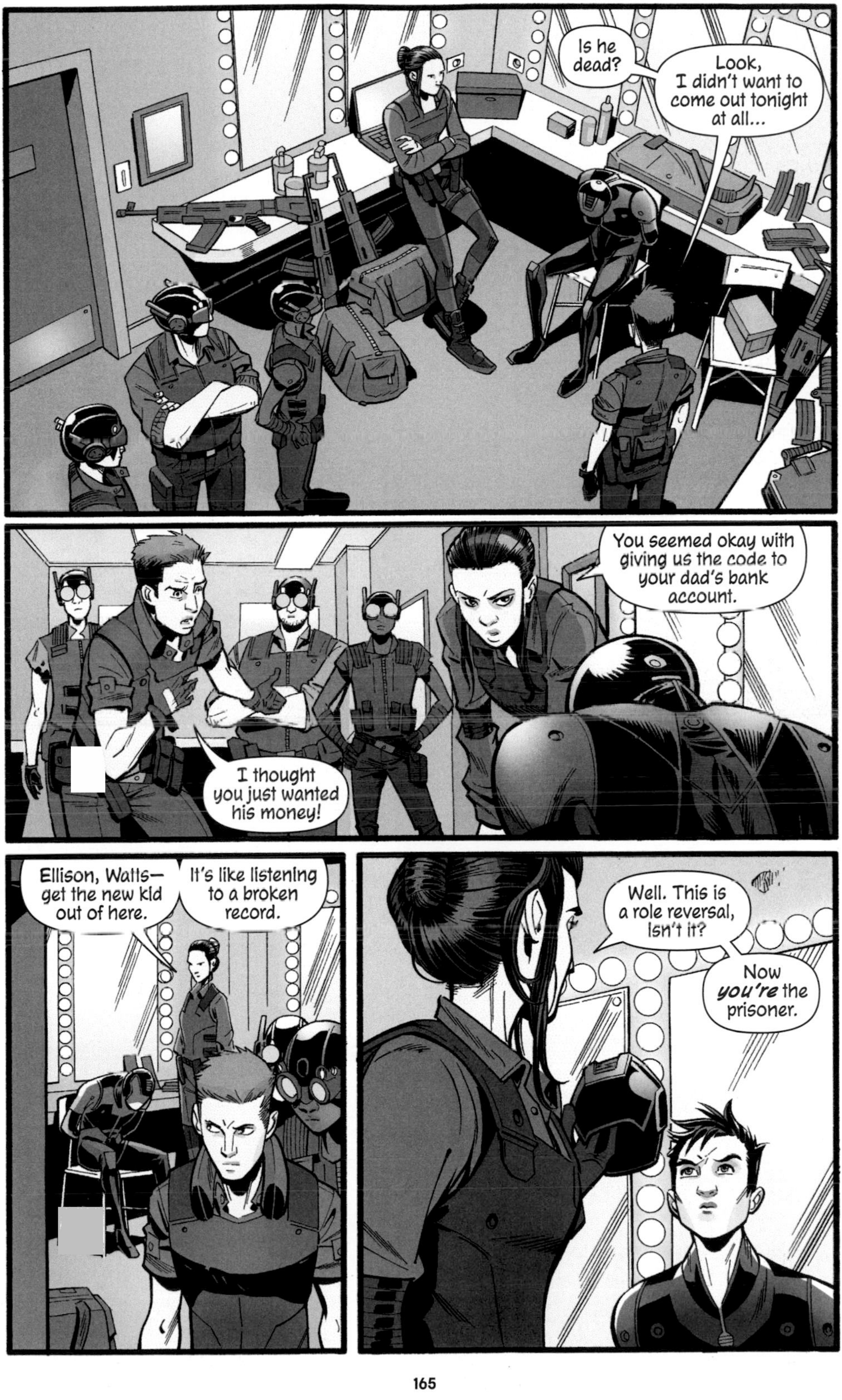
Is he dead?
Look, I didn't want to come out tonight at all...
You seemed okay with giving us the code to your dad's bank account.
I thought you just wanted his money!
Ellison, Watts— get the new kid out of here.
It's like listening to a broken record.
Well. This is a role reversal, isn't it?
Now *you're* the prisoner.

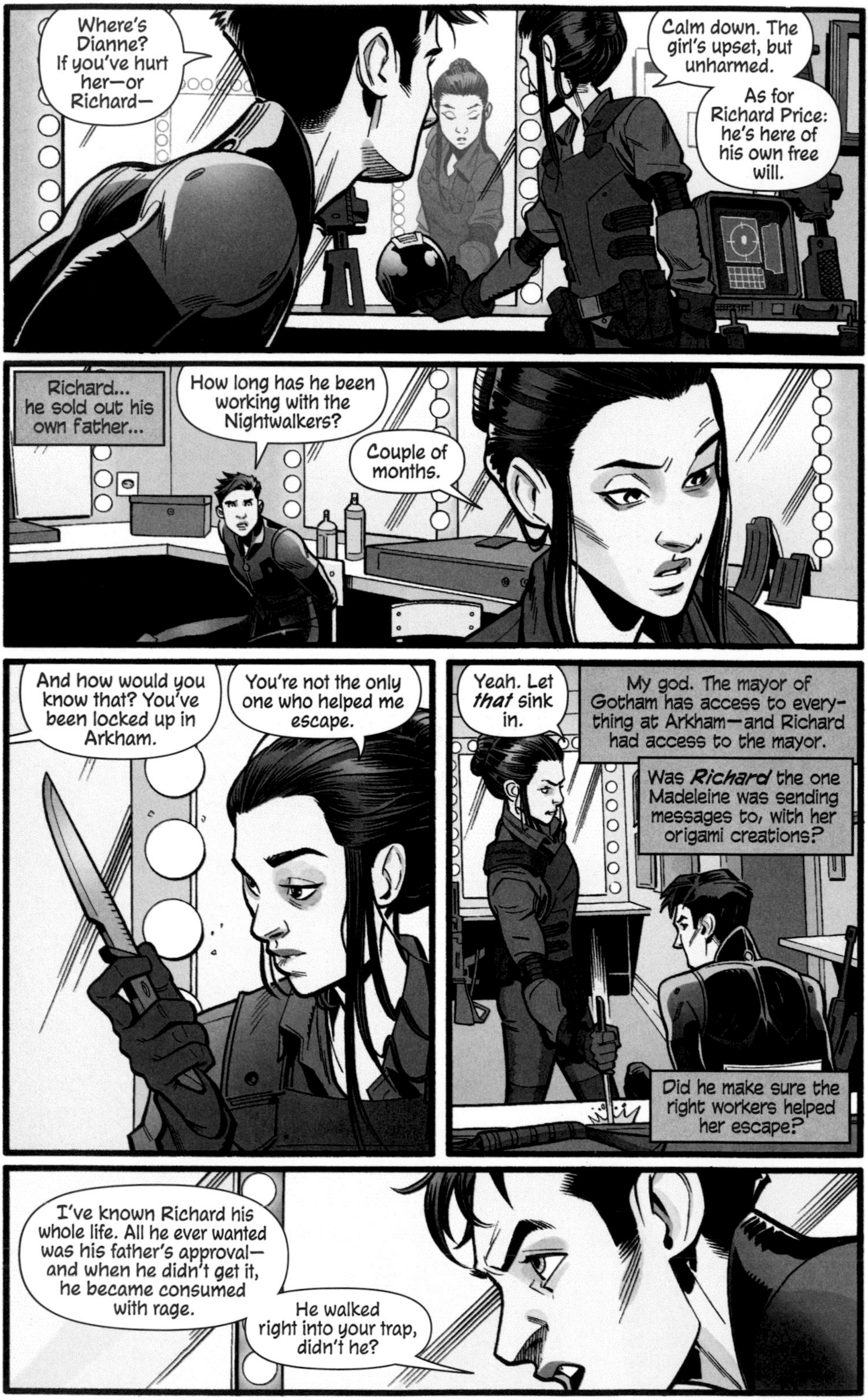
Where's Dianne? If you've hurt her—or Richard—
Calm down. The girl's upset, but unharmed.
As for Richard Price: he's here of his own free will.
Richard... he sold out his own father...
How long has he been working with the Nightwalkers?
Couple of months.
And how would you know that? You've been locked up in Arkham.
You're not the only one who helped me escape.
Yeah. Let *that* sink in.
My god. The mayor of Gotham has access to everything at Arkham—and Richard had access to the mayor.
Was *Richard* the one Madeleine was sending messages to, with her origami creations?
Did he make sure the right workers helped her escape?
I've known Richard his whole life. All he ever wanted was his father's approval—and when he didn't get it, he became consumed with rage.
He walked right into your trap, didn't he?

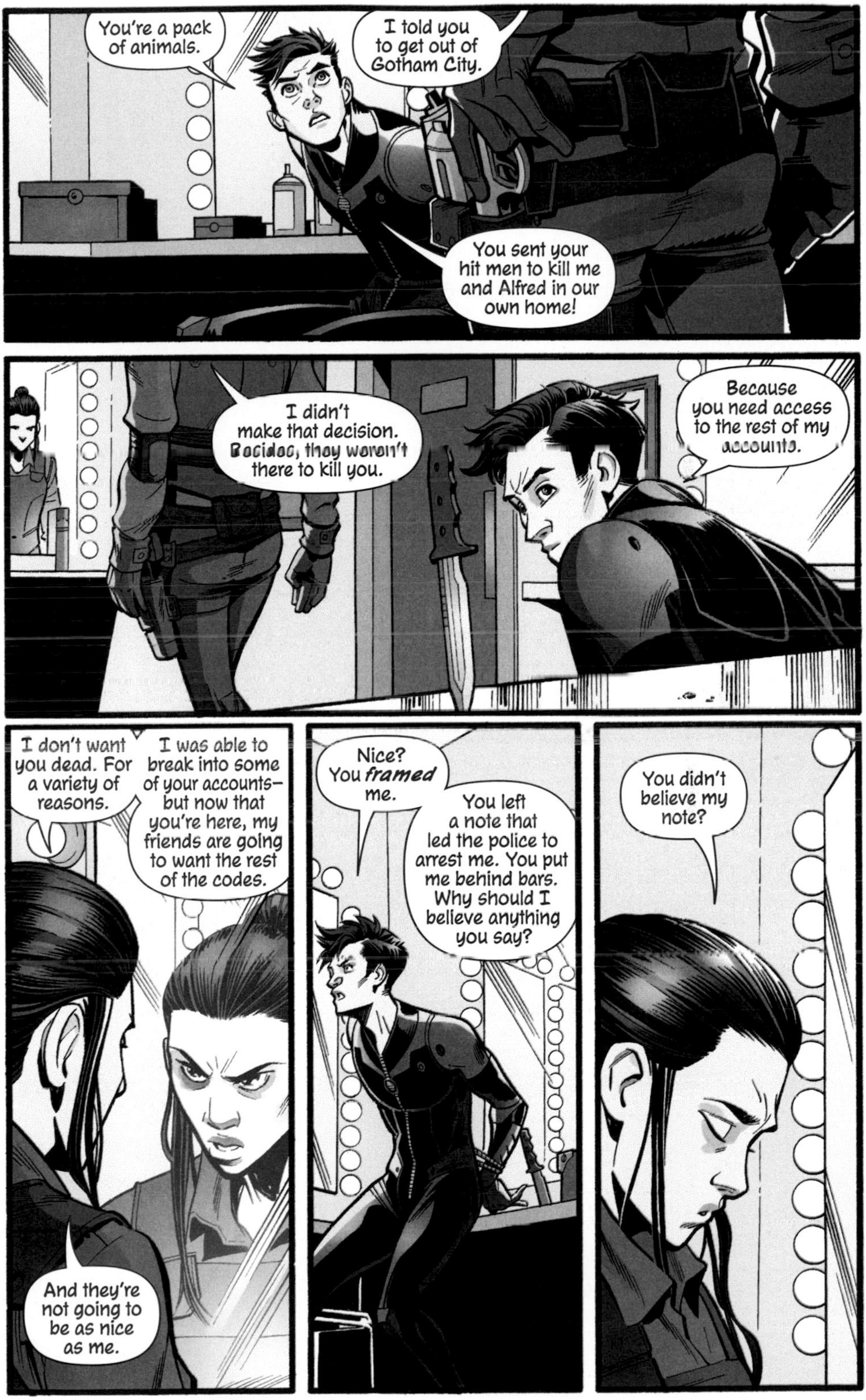
You're a pack of animals.
I told you to get out of Gotham City.
You sent your hit men to kill me and Alfred in our own home!
I didn't make that decision. Besides, they weren't there to kill you.
Because you need access to the rest of my accounts.
I don't want you dead. For a variety of reasons.
I was able to break into some of your accounts—but now that you're here, my friends are going to want the rest of the codes.
And they're not going to be as nice as me.
Nice? You *framed* me.
You left a note that led the police to arrest me. You put me behind bars. Why should I believe anything you say?
You didn't believe my note?

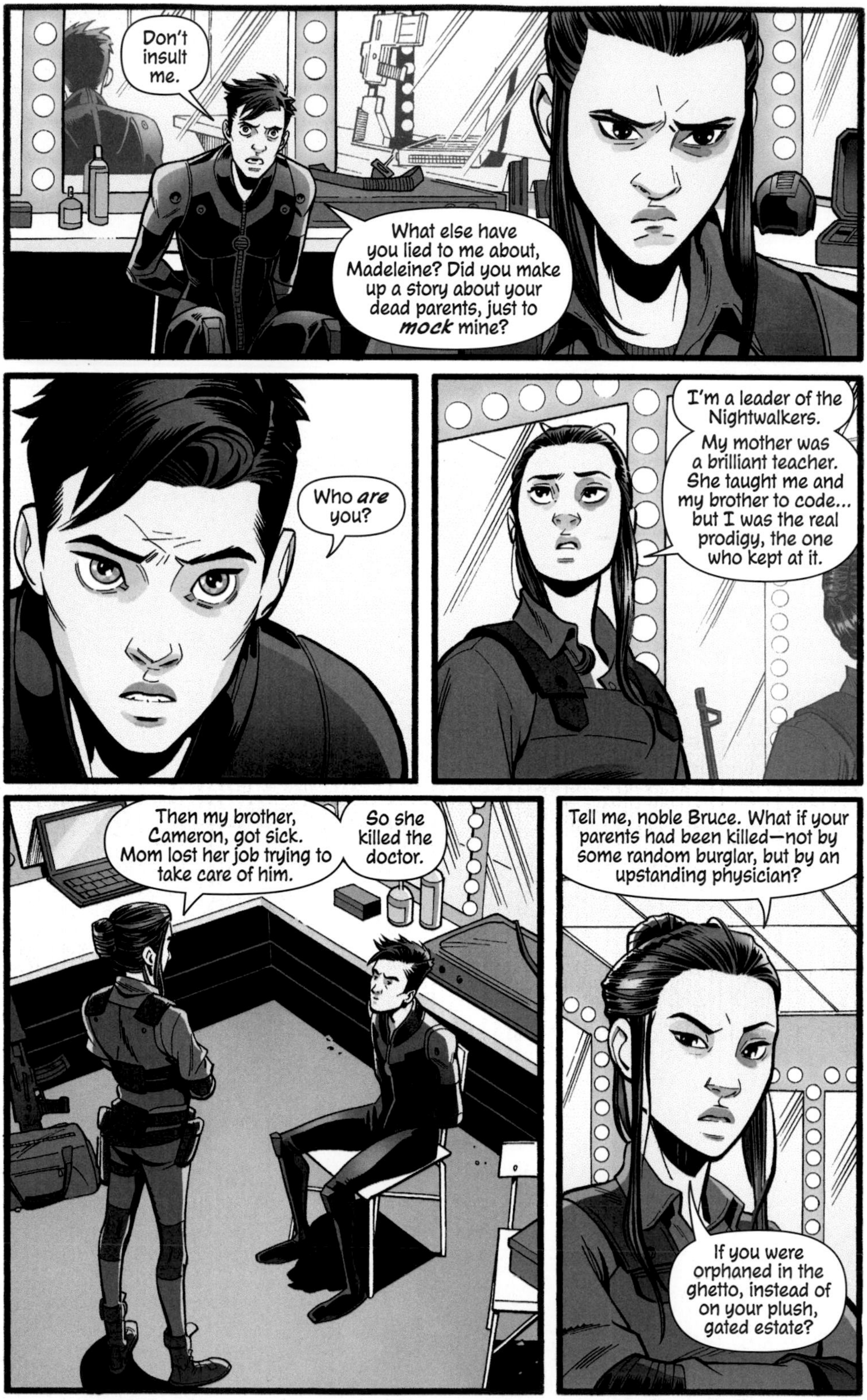
Don't insult me.
What else have you lied to me about, Madeleine? Did you make up a story about your dead parents, just to *mock* mine?
Who *are* you?
I'm a leader of the Nightwalkers.
My mother was a brilliant teacher. She taught me and my brother to code... but I was the real prodigy, the one who kept at it.
Then my brother, Cameron, got sick. Mom lost her job trying to take care of him.
So she killed the doctor.
Tell me, noble Bruce. What if your parents had been killed—not by some random burglar, but by an upstanding physician?
If you were orphaned in the ghetto, instead of on your plush, gated estate?

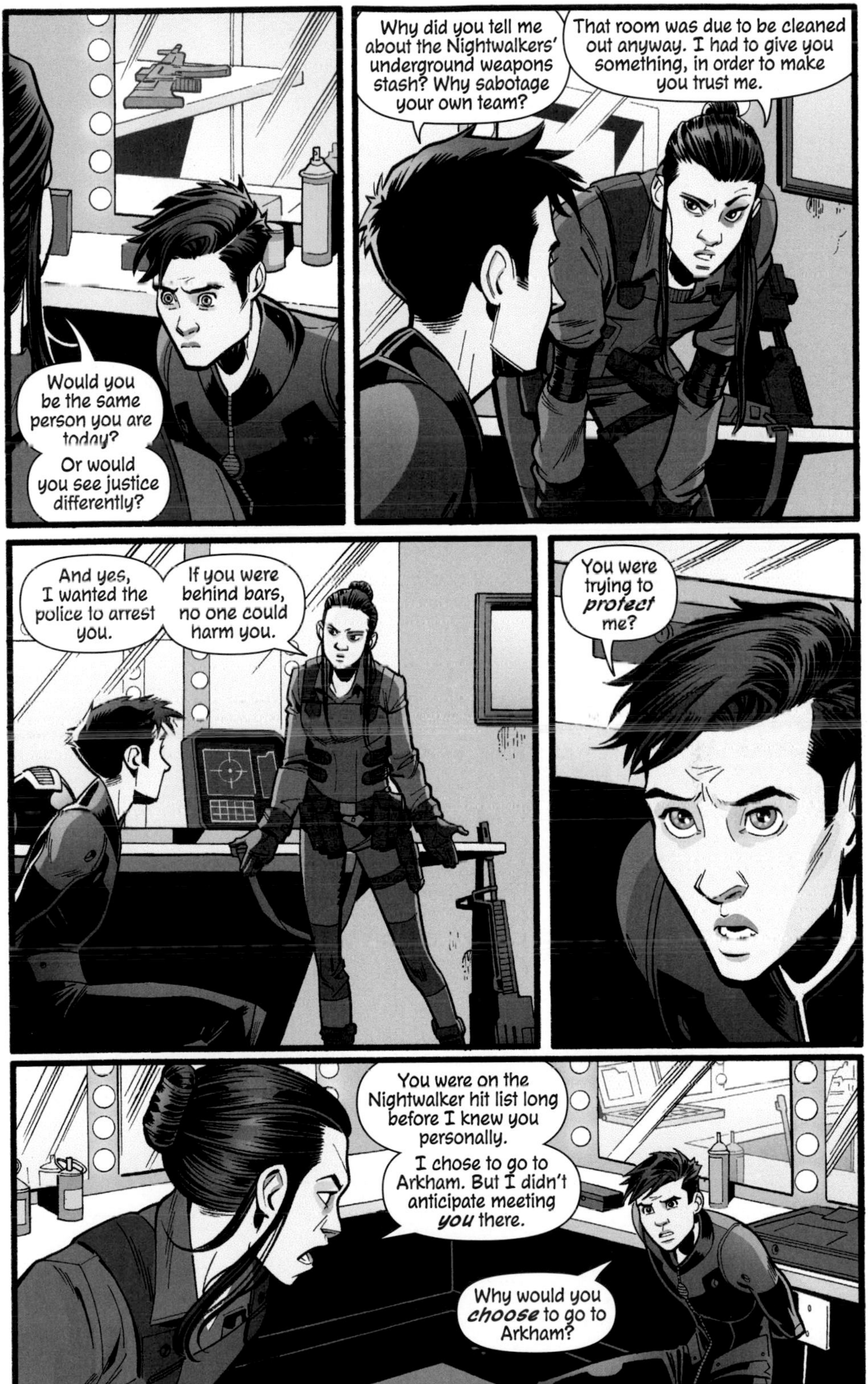
Would you be the same person you are today?
Or would you see justice differently?
Why did you tell me about the Nightwalkers' underground weapons stash? Why sabotage your own team?
That room was due to be cleaned out anyway. I had to give you something, in order to make you trust me.
And yes, I wanted the police to arrest you.
If you were behind bars, no one could harm you.
You were trying to *protect* me?
You were on the Nightwalker hit list long before I knew you personally.
I chose to go to Arkham. But I didn't anticipate meeting *you* there.
Why would you *choose* to go to Arkham?

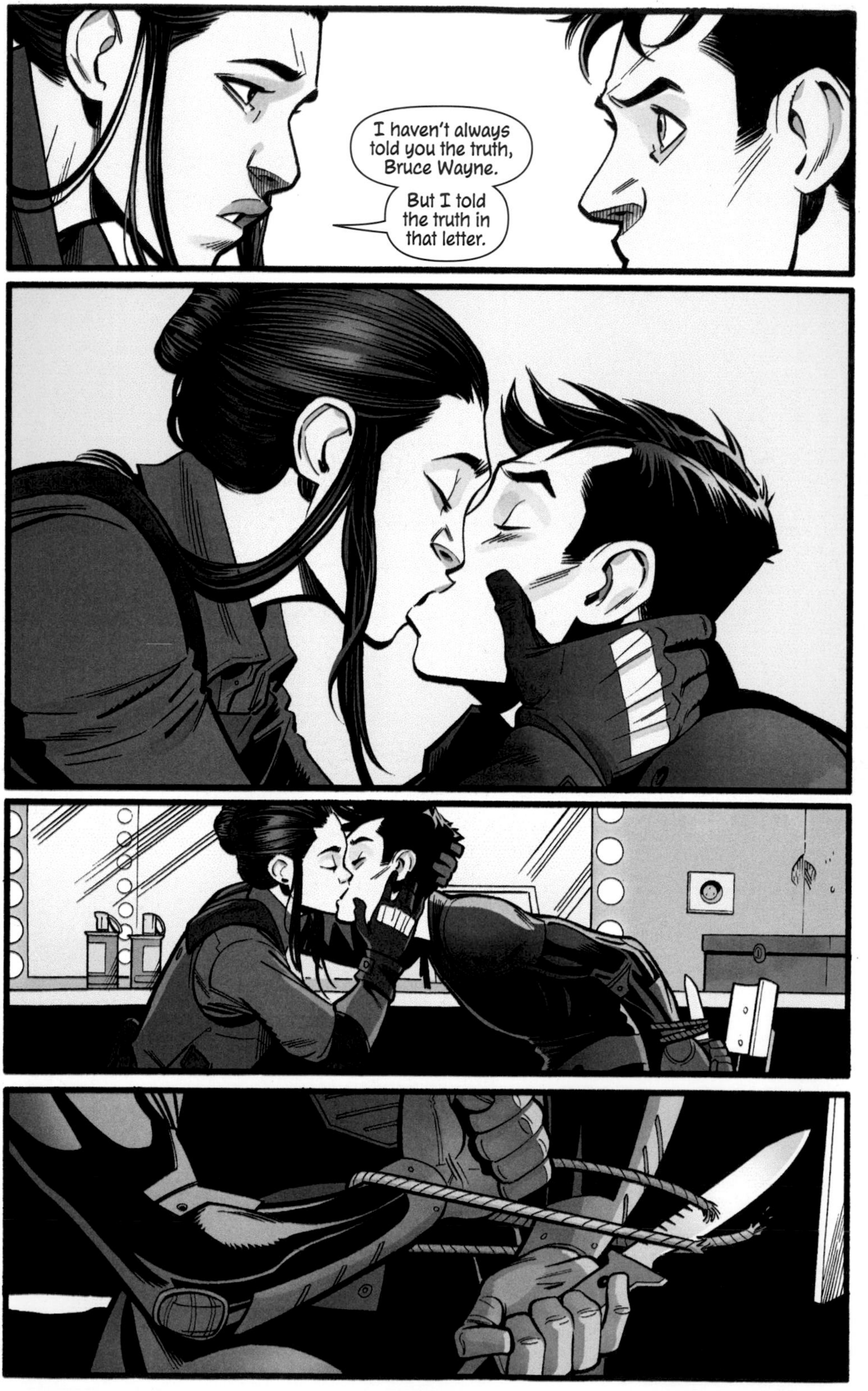
I haven't always told you the truth, Bruce Wayne.
But I told the truth in that letter.

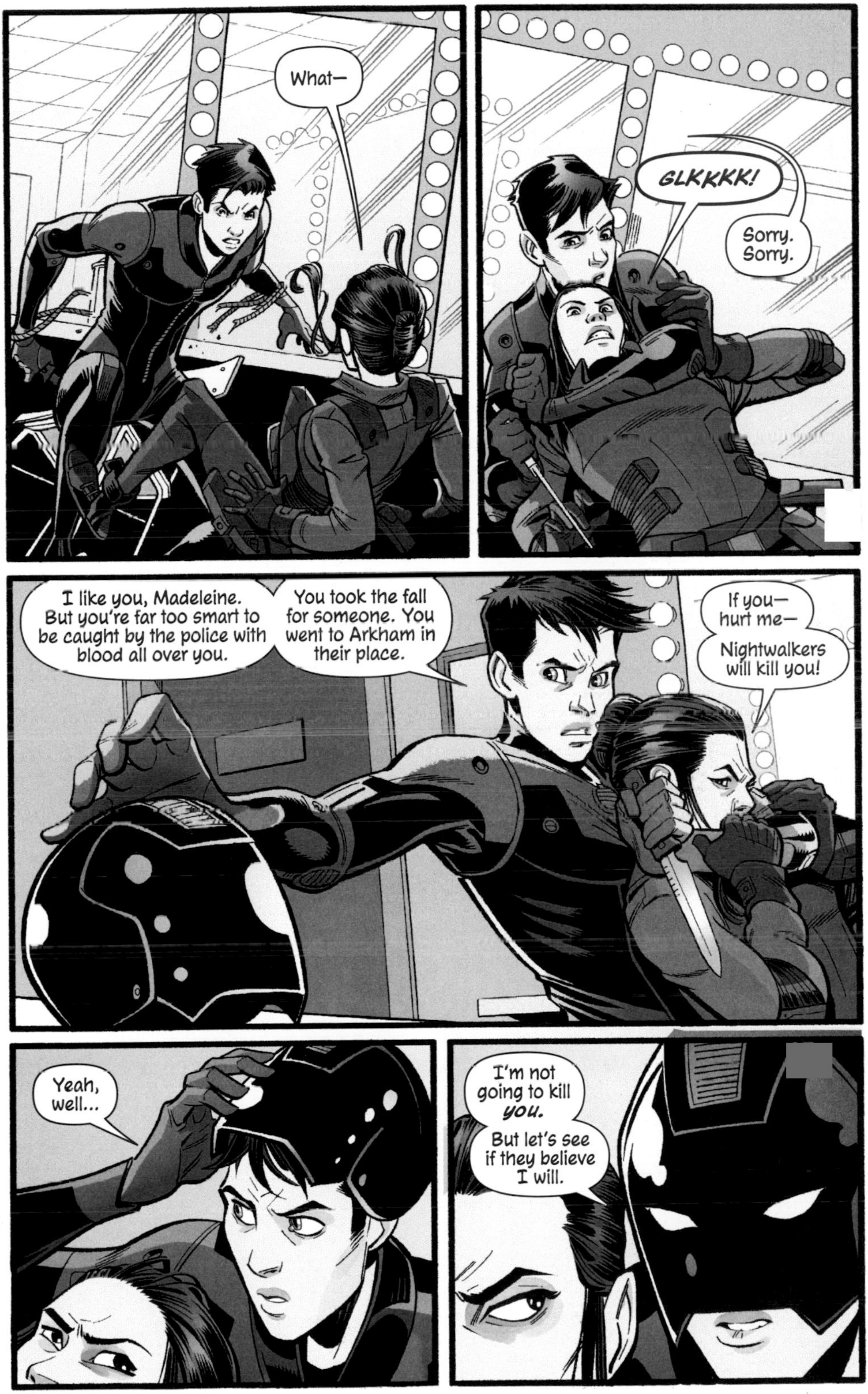
What—
GLKKKK!
Sorry. Sorry.
I like you, Madeleine. But you're far too smart to be caught by the police with blood all over you.
You took the fall for someone. You went to Arkham in their place.
If you— hurt me—
Nightwalkers will kill you!
Yeah, well...
I'm not going to kill *you.*
But let's see if they believe I will.

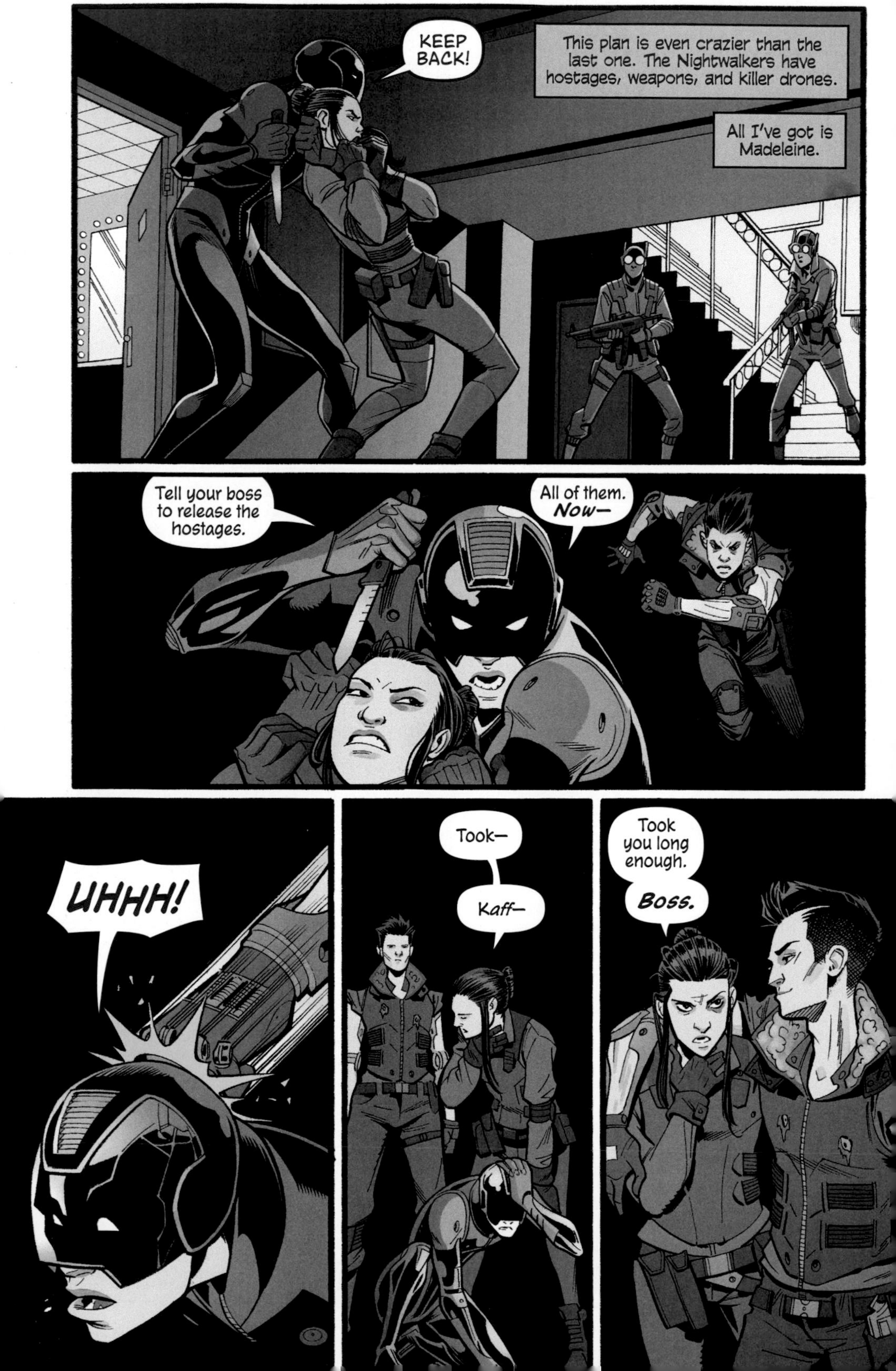
KEEP BACK!
This plan is even crazier than the last one. The Nightwalkers have hostages, weapons, and killer drones.
All I've got is Madeleine.
Tell your boss to release the hostages.
All of them. *Now—*
UHHH!
Took—
Kaff—
Took you long enough.
Boss.

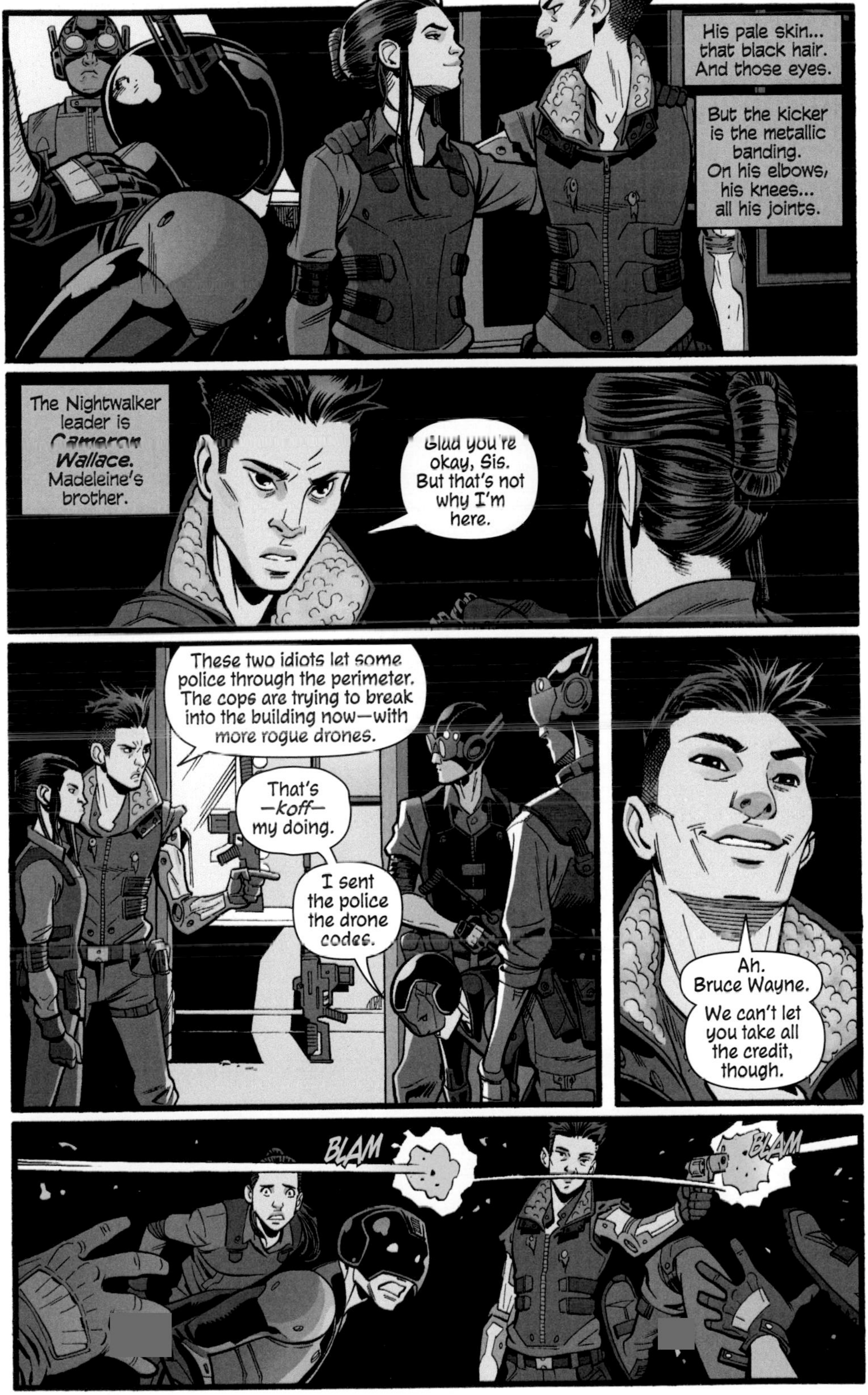
His pale skin... that black hair. And those eyes.
But the kicker is the metallic banding. On his elbows, his knees... all his joints.
The Nightwalker leader is Cameron Wallace. Madeleine's brother.
Glad you're okay, Sis. But that's not why I'm here.
These two idiots let some police through the perimeter. The cops are trying to break into the building now—with more rogue drones.
That's —koff— my doing.
I sent the police the drone codes.
Ah. Bruce Wayne.
We can't let you take all the credit, though.
BLAM
BLAM

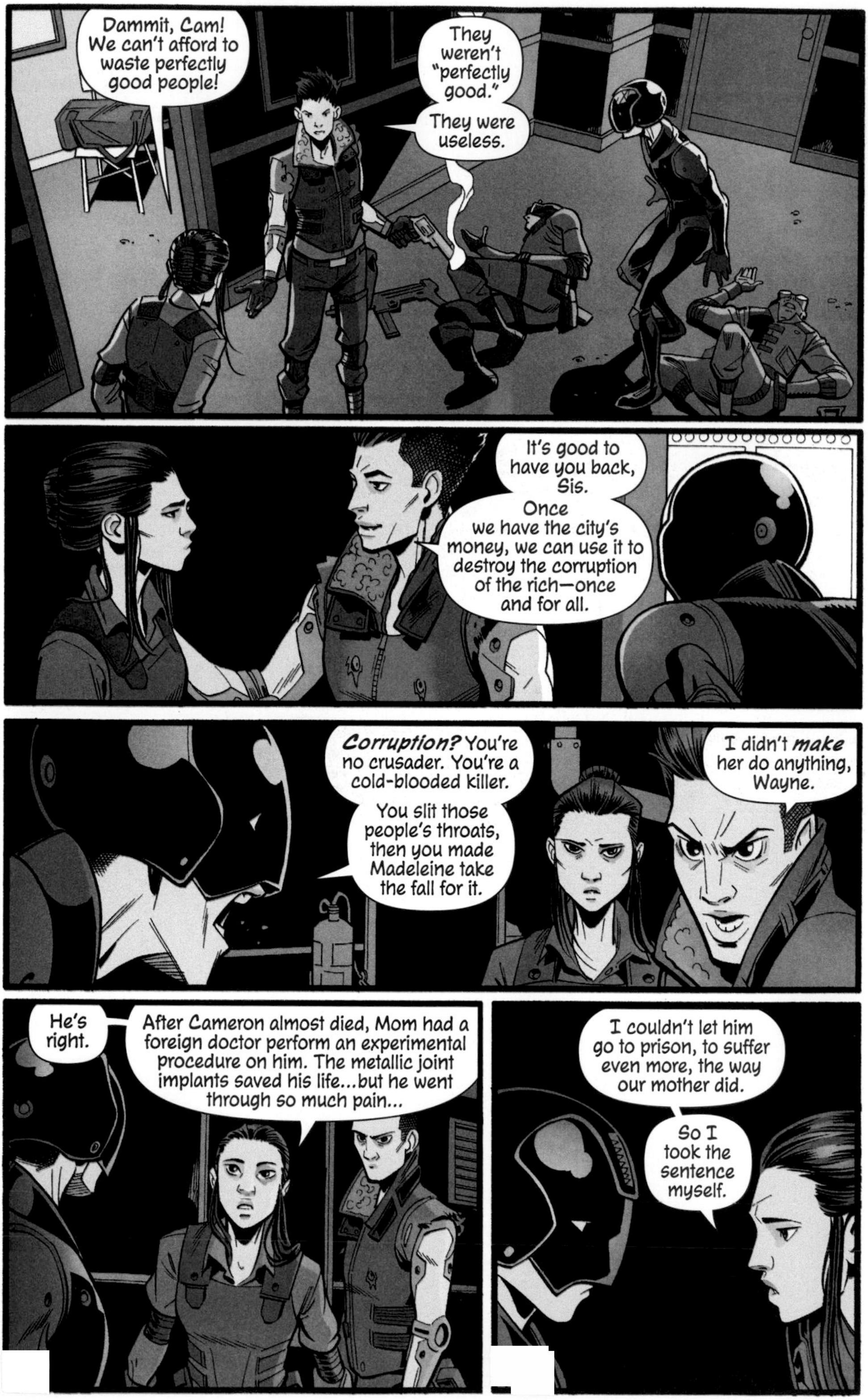
Dammit, Cam! We can't afford to waste perfectly good people!
They weren't "perfectly good."
They were useless.
It's good to have you back, Sis.
Once we have the city's money, we can use it to destroy the corruption of the rich—once and for all.
Corruption? You're no crusader. You're a cold-blooded killer.
You slit those people's throats, then you made Madeleine take the fall for it.
I didn't *make* her do anything, Wayne.
He's right.
After Cameron almost died, Mom had a foreign doctor perform an experimental procedure on him. The metallic joint implants saved his life...but he went through so much pain...
I couldn't let him go to prison, to suffer even more, the way our mother did.
So I took the sentence myself.

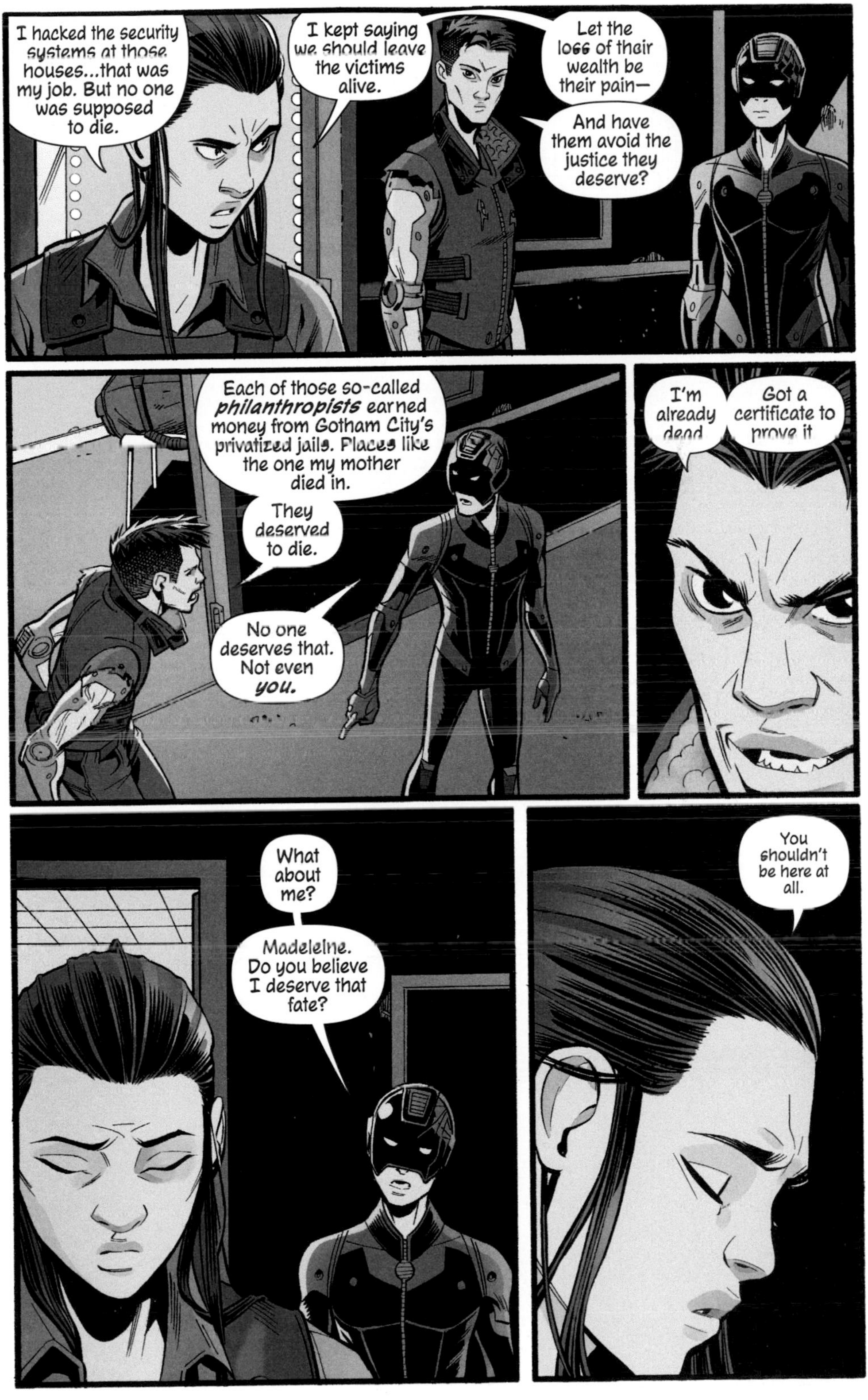
I hacked the security systems at those houses...that was my job. But no one was supposed to die.
I kept saying we should leave the victims alive.
Let the loss of their wealth be their pain—
And have them avoid the justice they deserve?
Each of those so-called *philanthropists* earned money from Gotham City's privatized jails. Places like the one my mother died in.
They deserved to die.
No one deserves that. Not even *you.*
I'm already dead.
Got a certificate to prove it.
What about me?
Madeleine. Do you believe I deserve that fate?
You shouldn't be here at all.

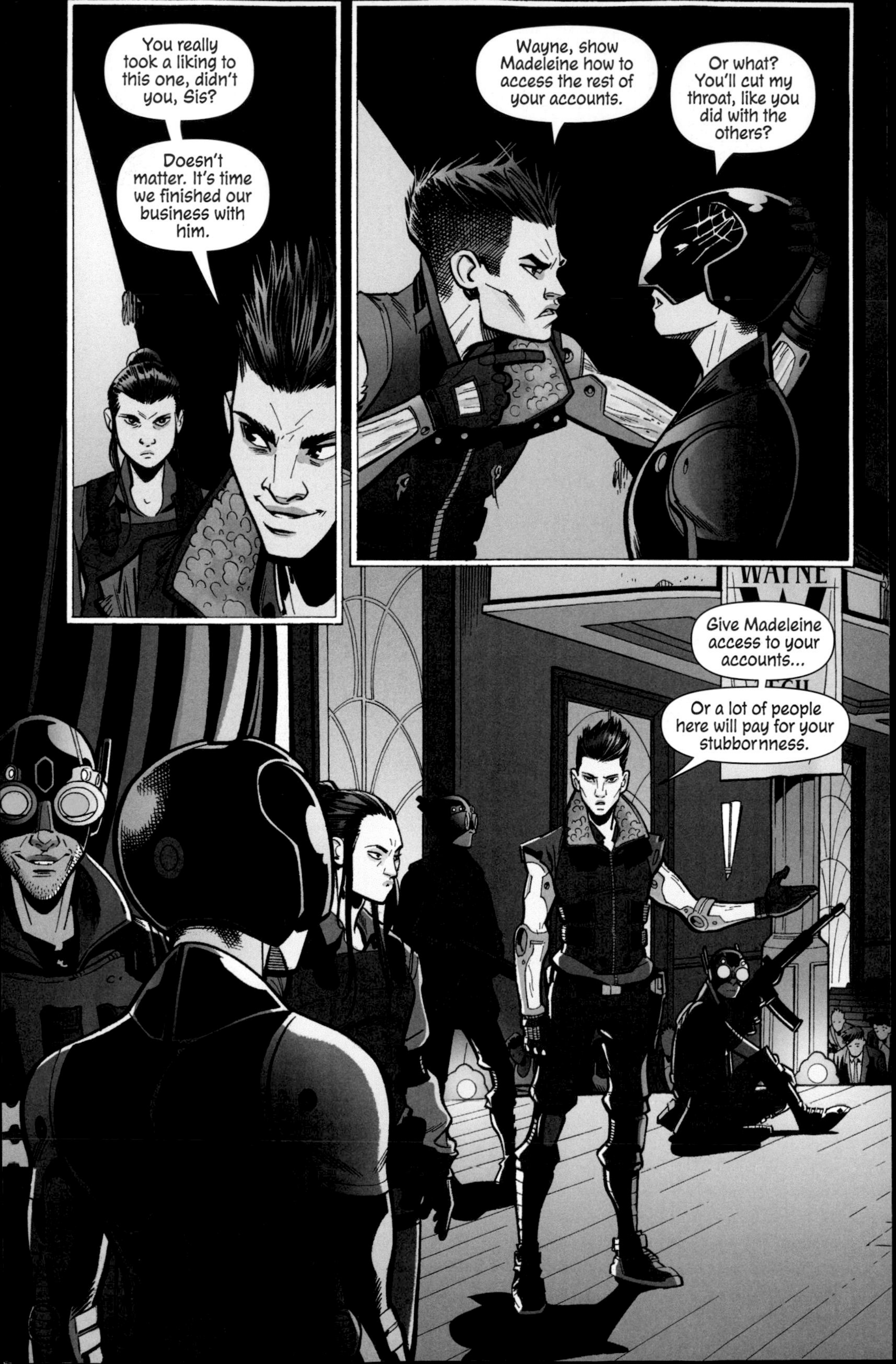
You really took a liking to this one, didn't you, Sis?
Doesn't matter. It's time we finished our business with him.
Wayne, show Madeleine how to access the rest of your accounts.
Or what? You'll cut my throat, like you did with the others?
Give Madeleine access to your accounts...
Or a lot of people here will pay for your stubbornness.
!

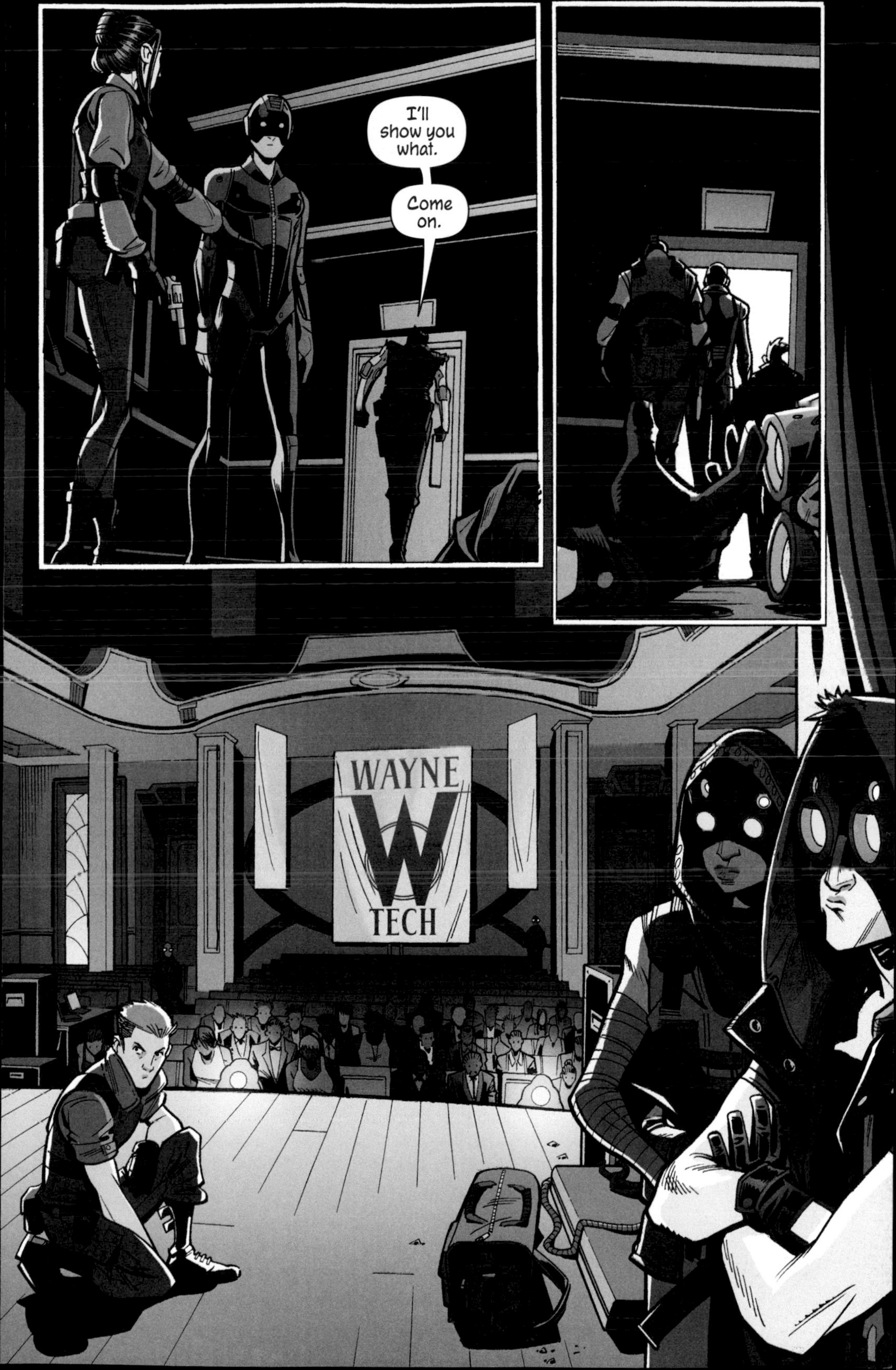
I'll show you what.
Come on.
WAYNE
W
TECH

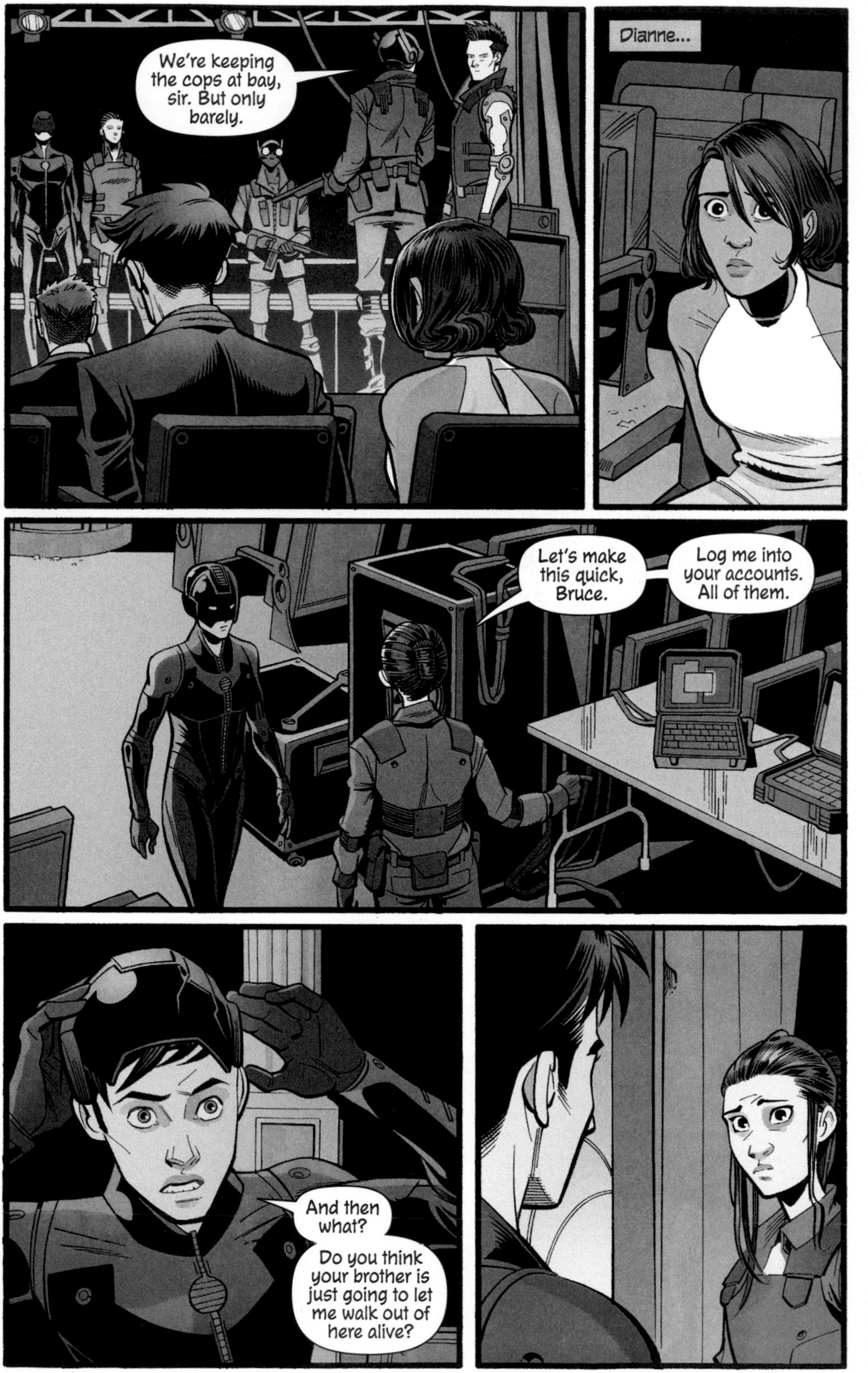
We're keeping the cops at bay, sir. But only barely.
Dianne...
Let's make this quick, Bruce.
Log me into your accounts. All of them.
And then what?
Do you think your brother is just going to let me walk out of here alive?

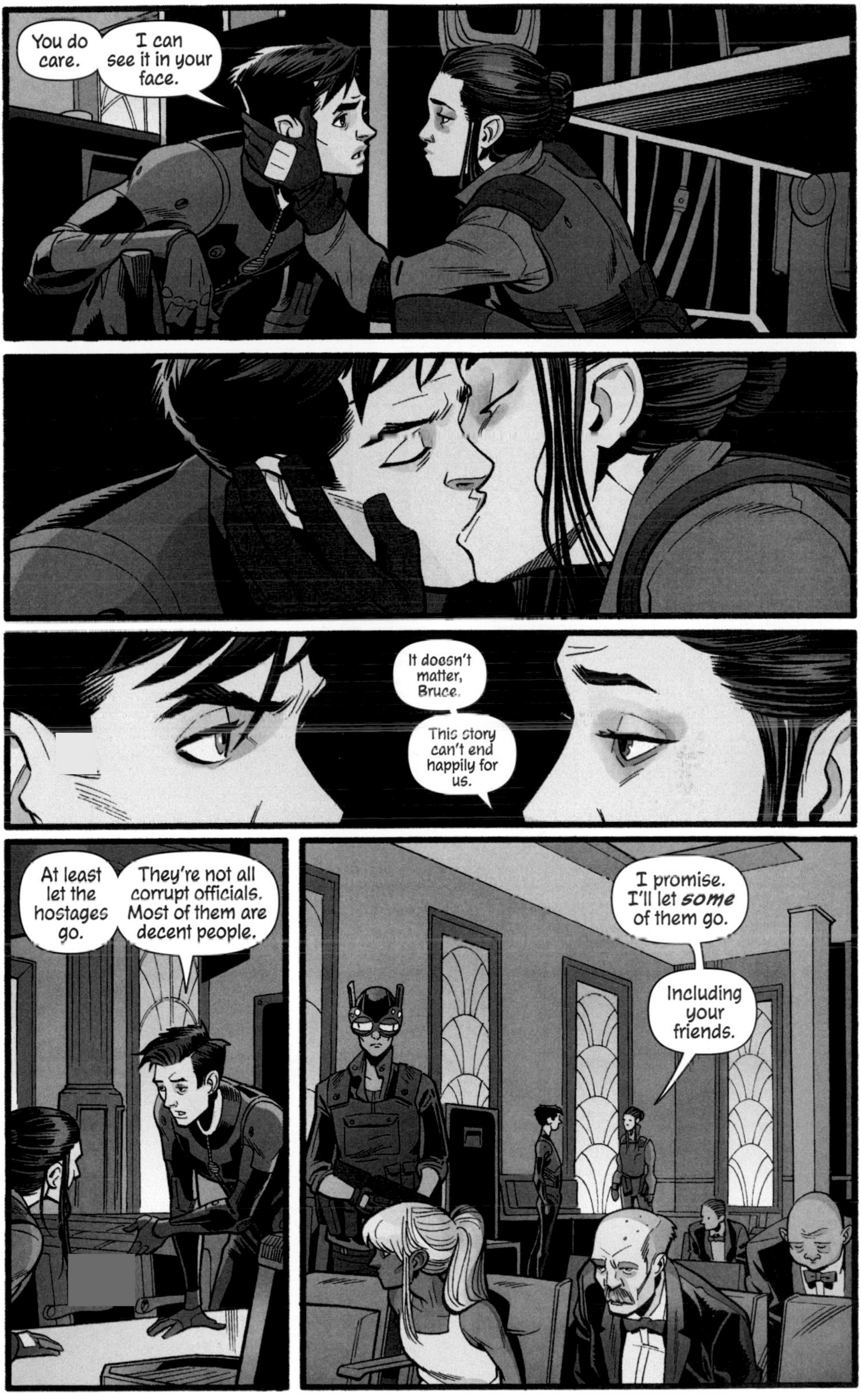
You do care.
I can see it in your face.
It doesn't matter, Bruce.
This story can't end happily for us.
At least let the hostages go.
They're not all corrupt officials. Most of them are decent people.
I promise. I'll let *some* of them go.
Including your friends.

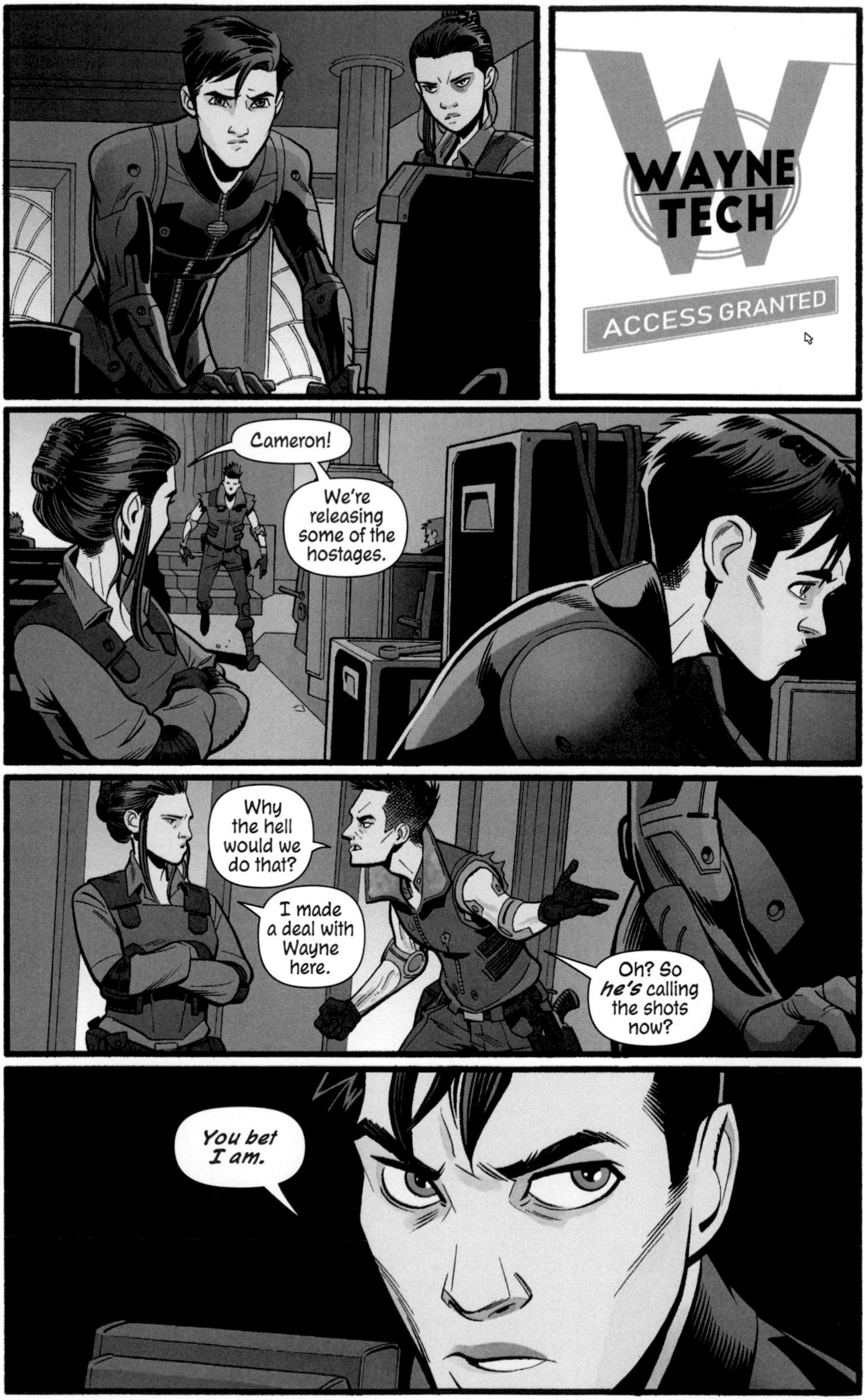
WAYNE TECH
ACCESS GRANTED
Cameron!
We're releasing some of the hostages.
Why the hell would we do that?
I made a deal with Wayne here.
Oh? So *he's* calling the shots now?
You bet I am.

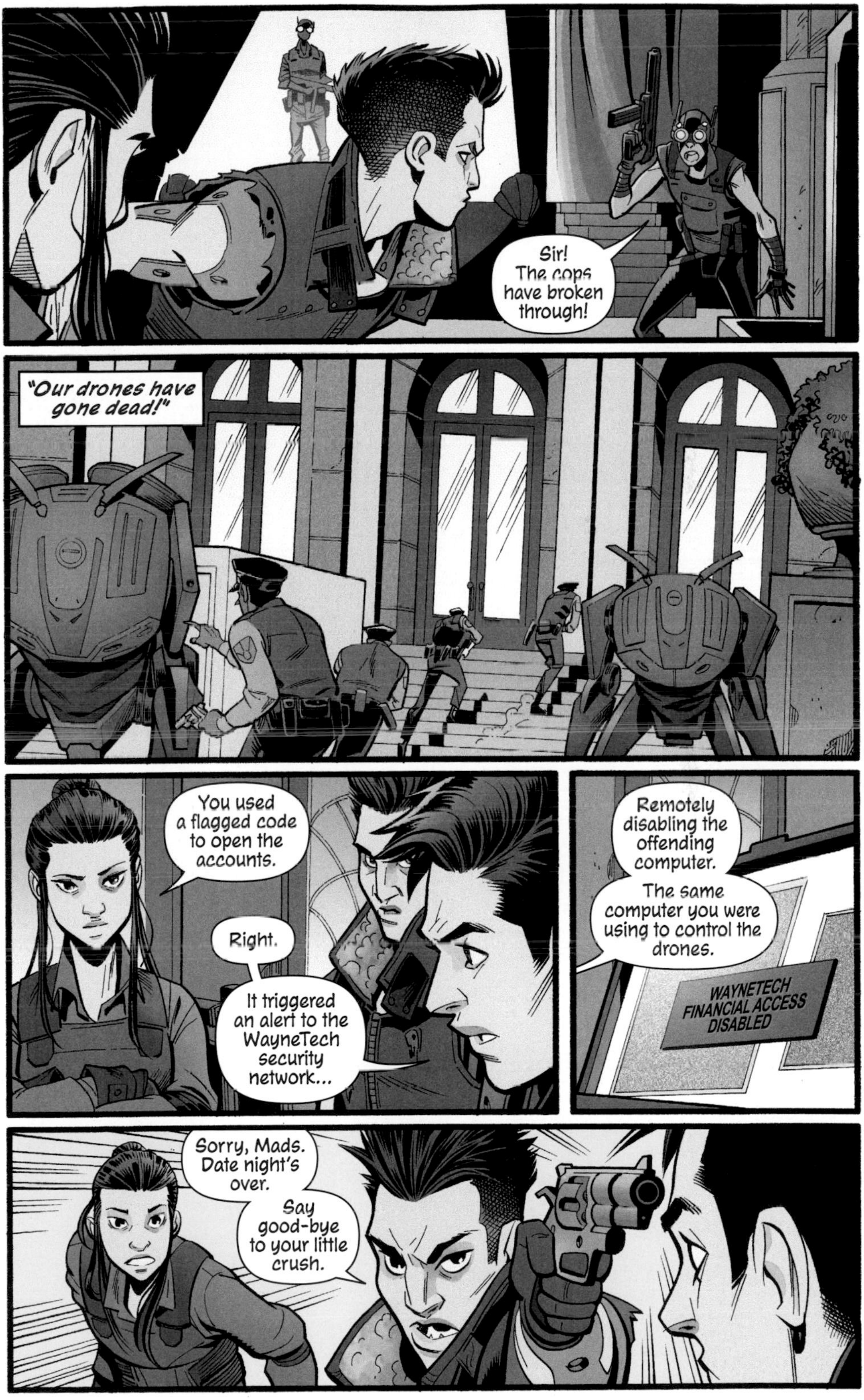
Sir! The cops have broken through!
"Our drones have gone dead!"
You used a flagged code to open the accounts.
Right.
It triggered an alert to the WayneTech security network...
Remotely disabling the offending computer.
The same computer you were using to control the drones.
WAYNETECH FINANCIAL ACCESS DISABLED
Sorry, Mads. Date night's over.
Say good-bye to your little crush.

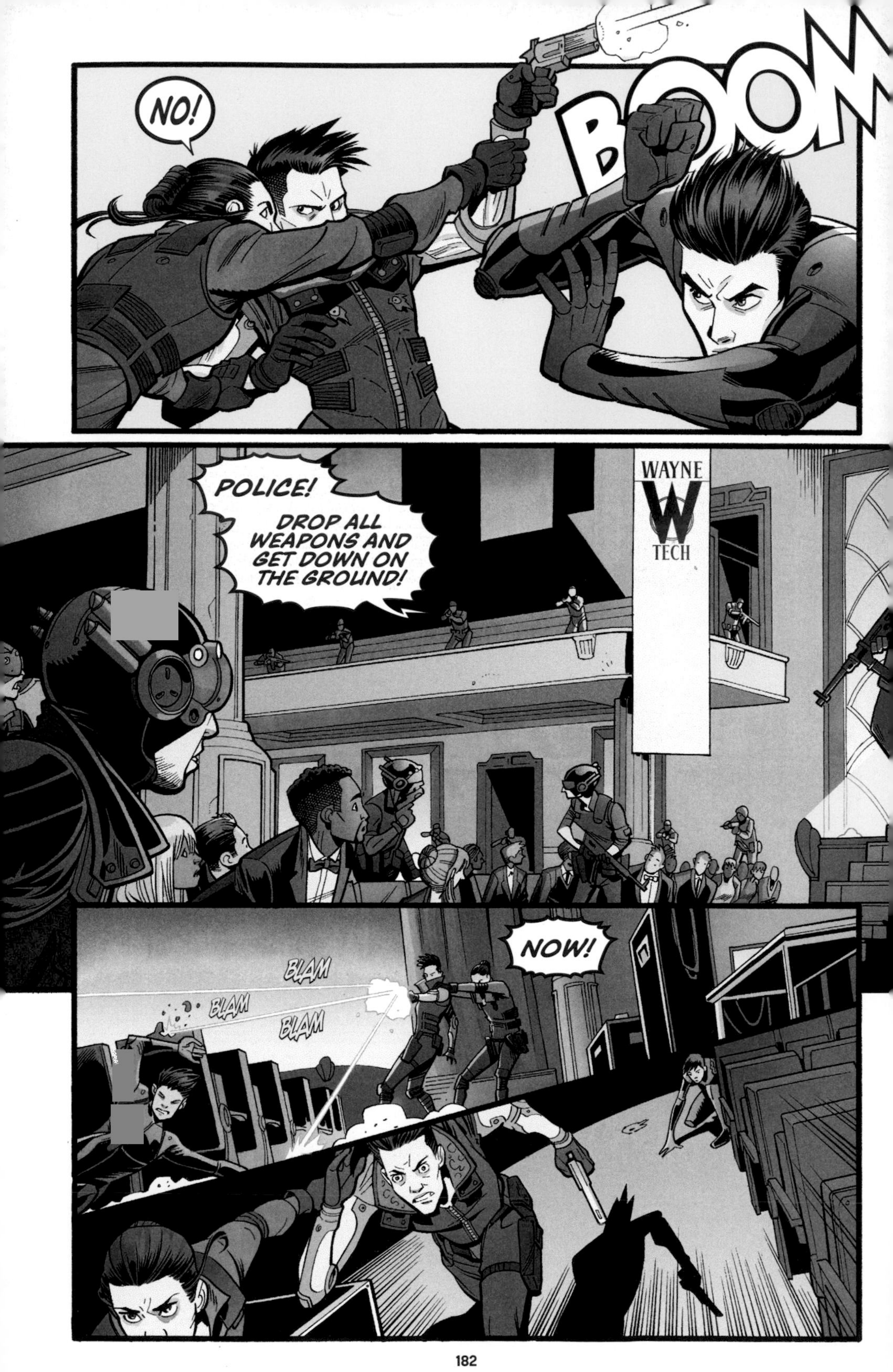
NO!
BOOM
POLICE!
DROP ALL WEAPONS AND GET DOWN ON THE GROUND!
WAYNE
W
TECH
NOW!
BLAM
BLAM
BLAM

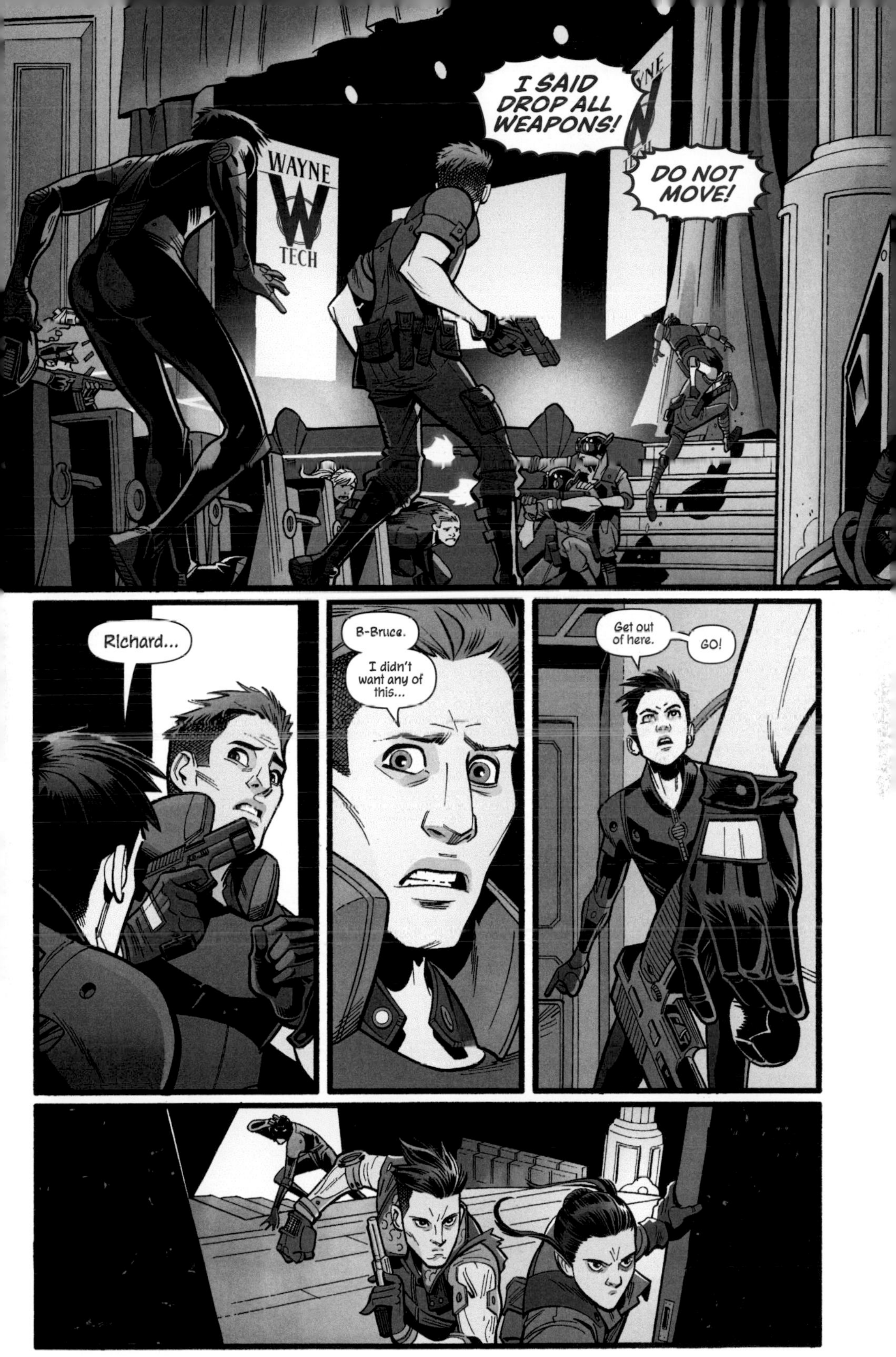
WAYNE TECH
I SAID DROP ALL WEAPONS!
DO NOT MOVE!
Richard...
B-Bruce.
I didn't want any of this...
Get out of here.
GO!

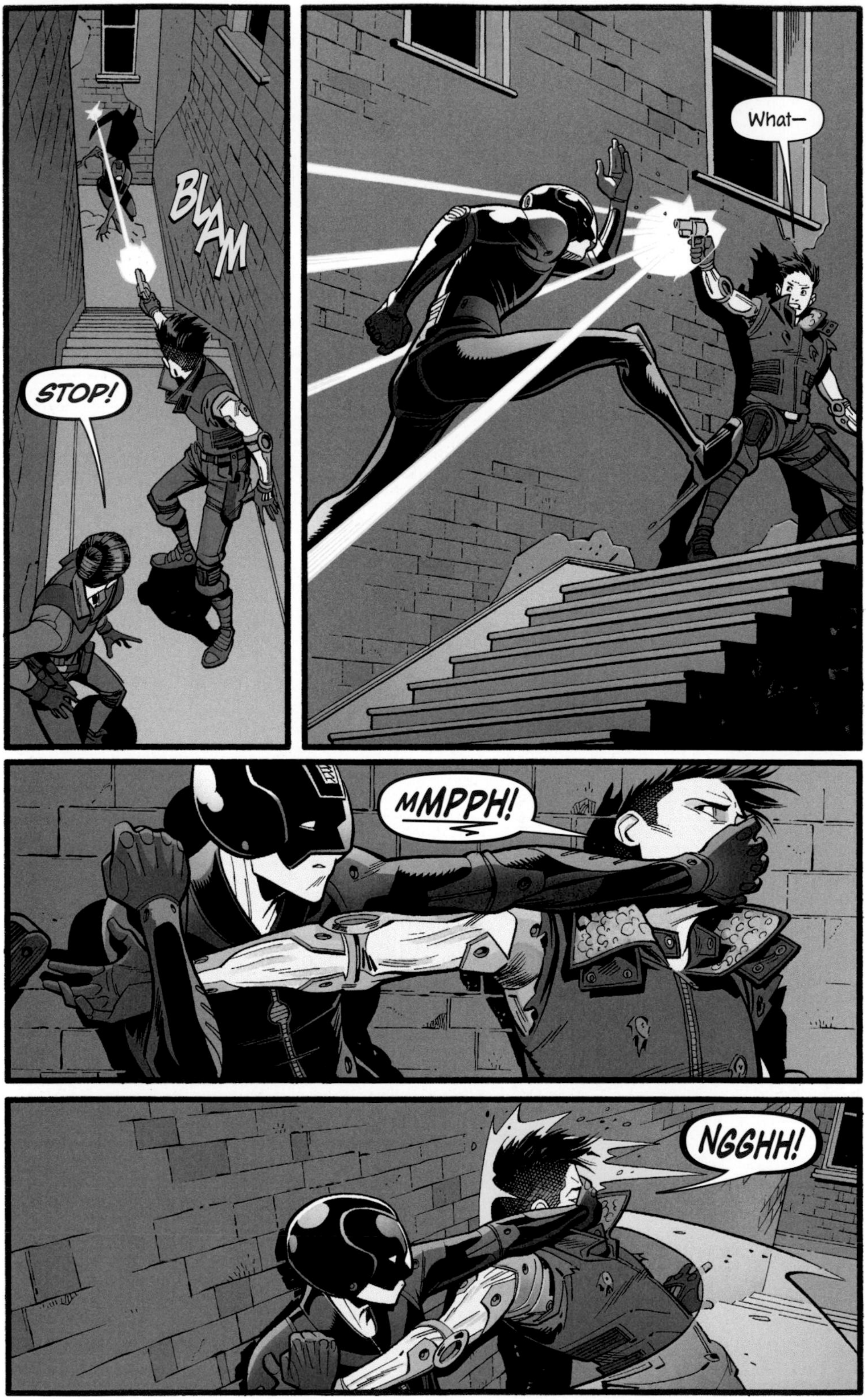
BLAM
STOP!
What—
MMPPH!
NGGHH!

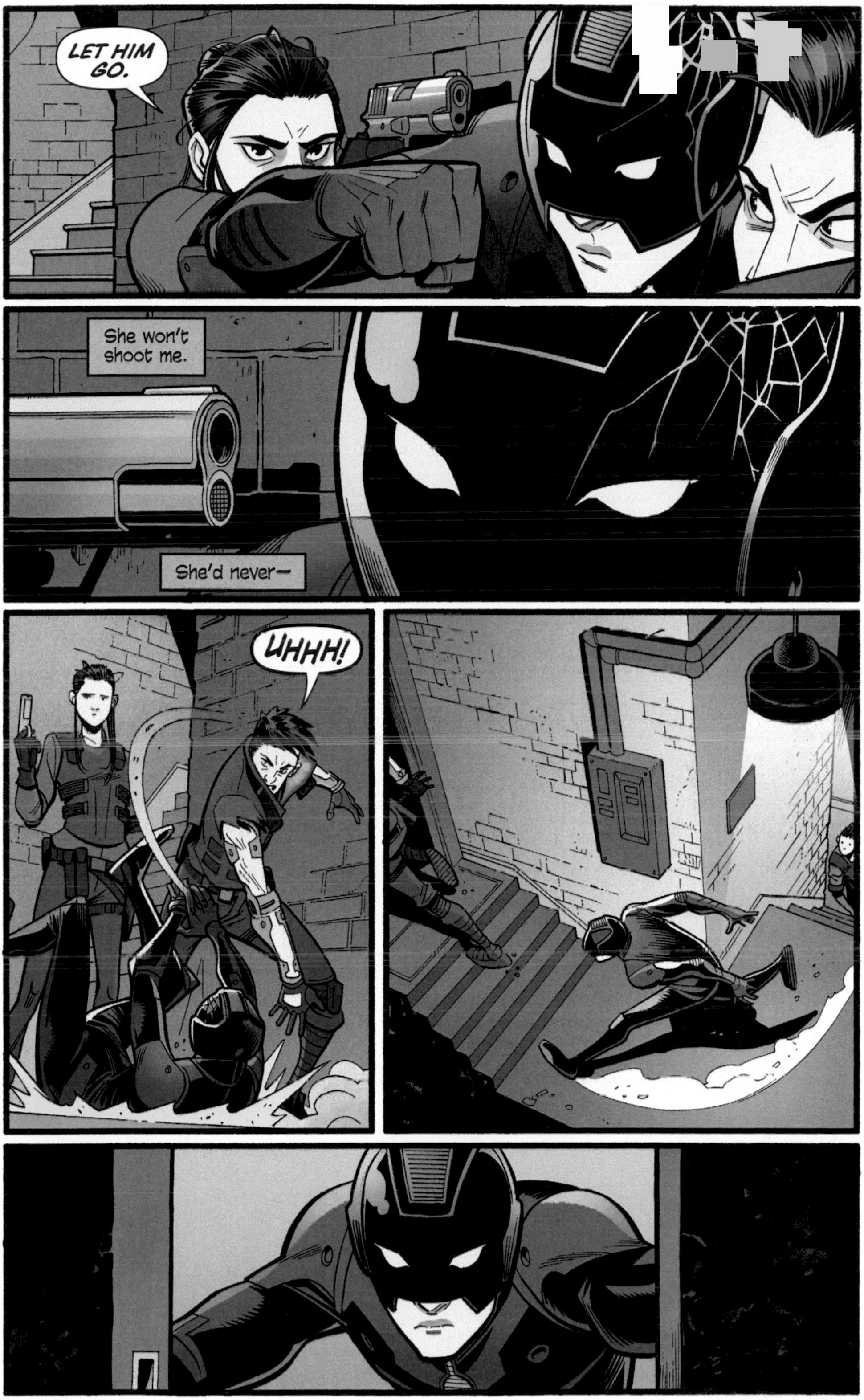
LET HIM GO.
She won't shoot me.
She'd never—
UHHH!

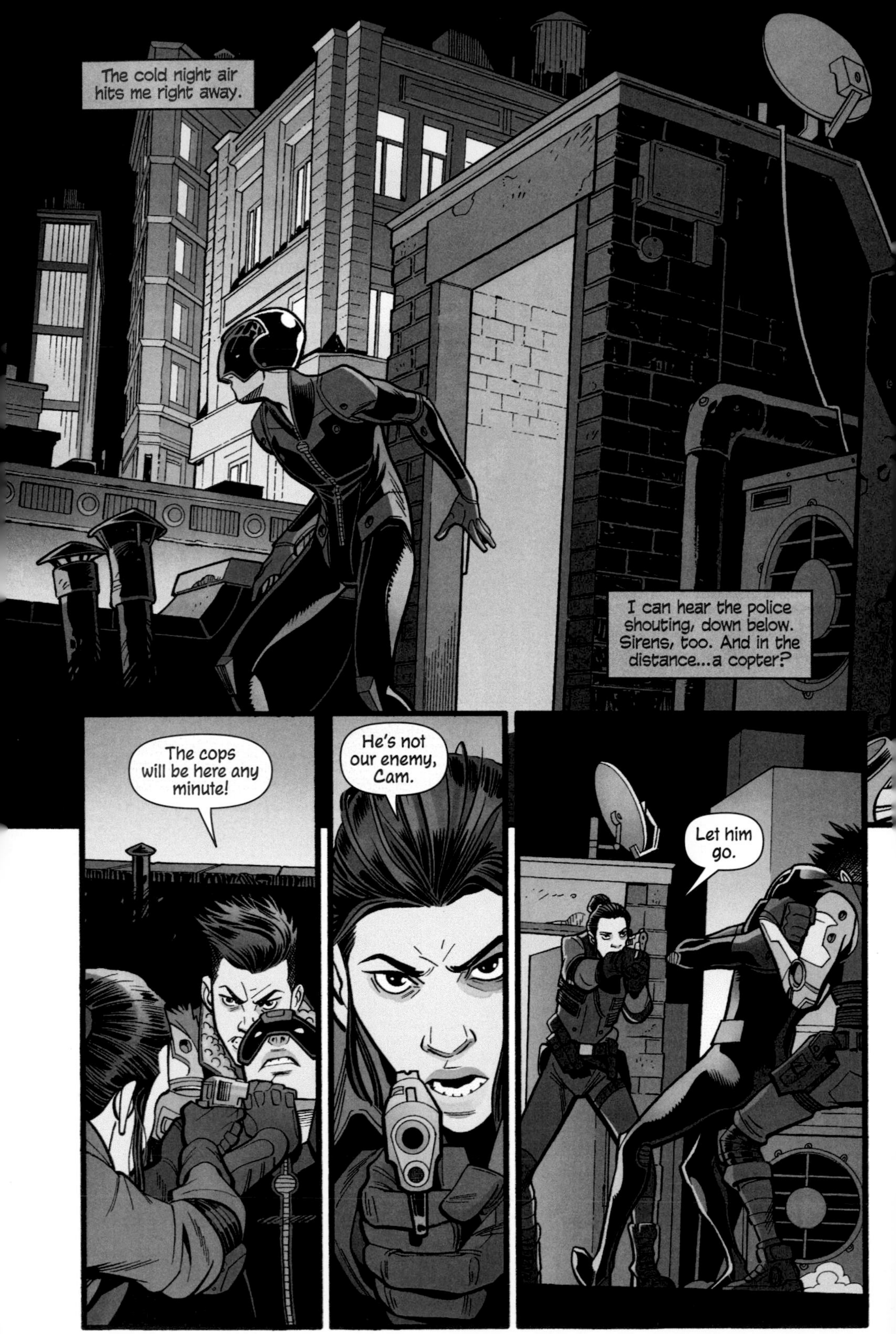
The cold night air hits me right away.
I can hear the police shouting, down below. Sirens, too. And in the distance...a copter?
The cops will be here any minute!
He's not our enemy, Cam.
Let him go.

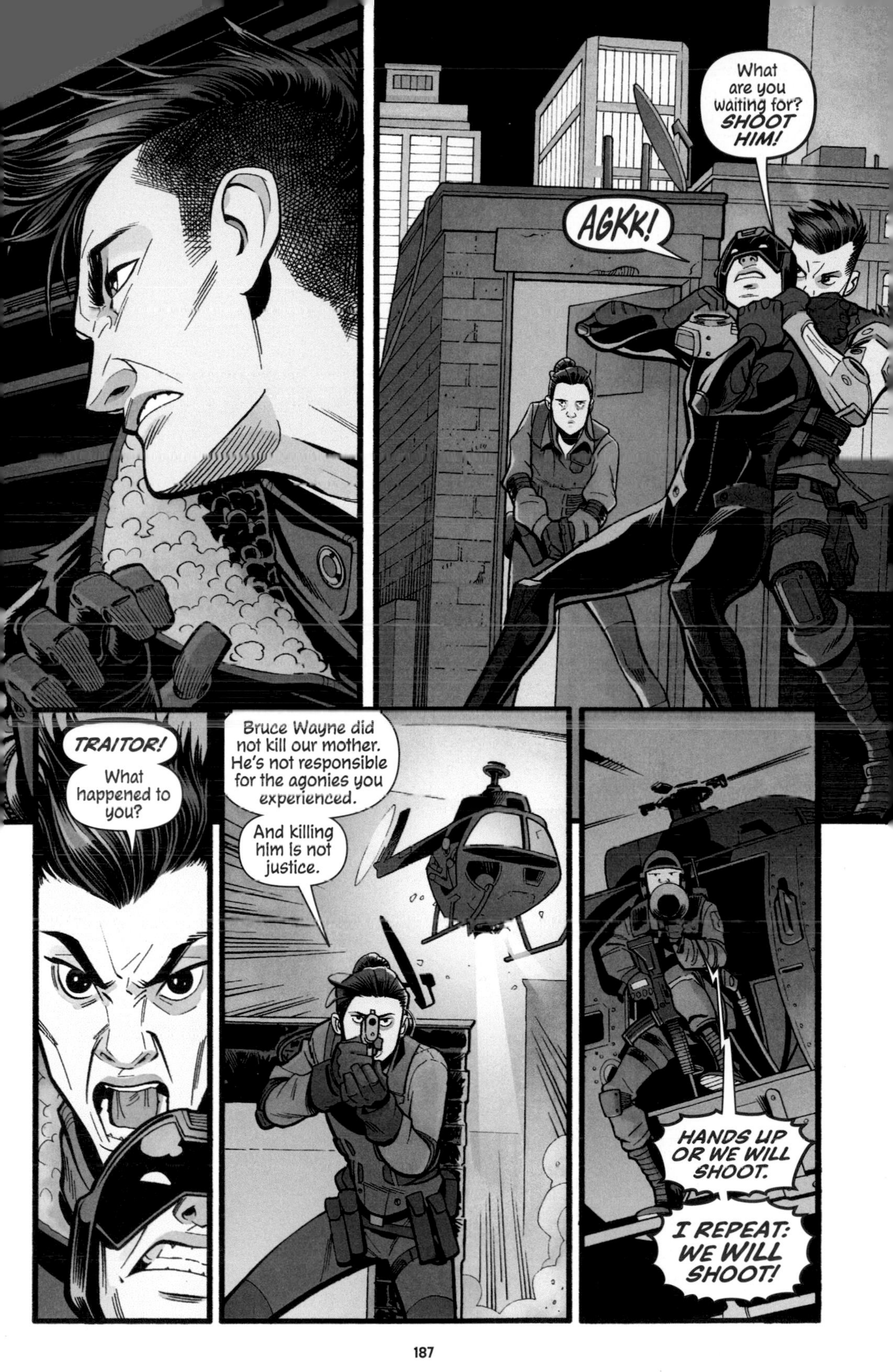
AGKK!
What are you waiting for? SHOOT HIM!
TRAITOR!
What happened to you?
Bruce Wayne did not kill our mother. He's not responsible for the agonies you experienced.
And killing him is not justice.
HANDS UP OR WE WILL SHOOT.
I REPEAT: WE WILL SHOOT!

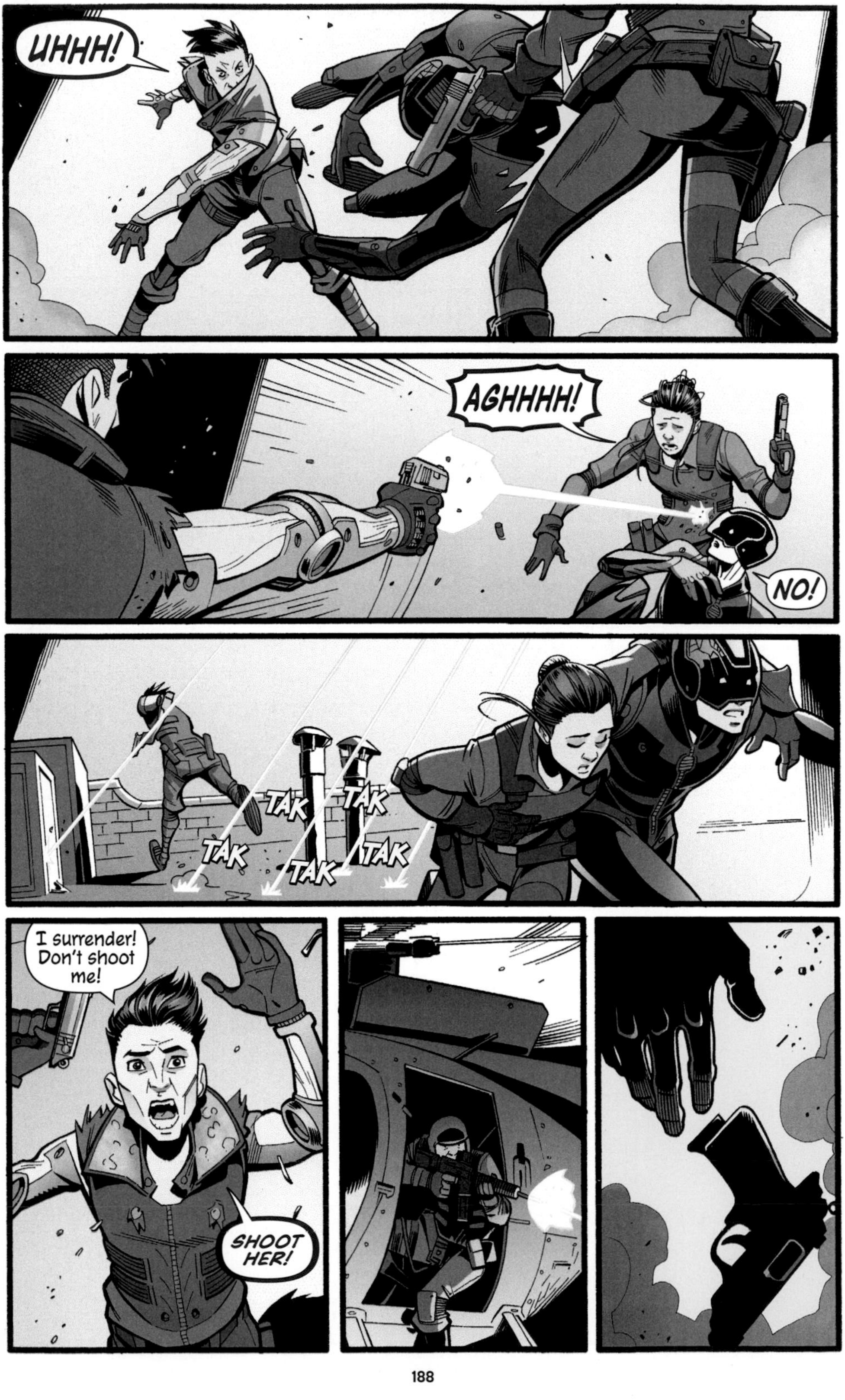
UHHH!
AGHHHH!
NO!
TAK
TAK
TAK
TAK
TAK
TAK
I surrender! Don't shoot me!
SHOOT HER!

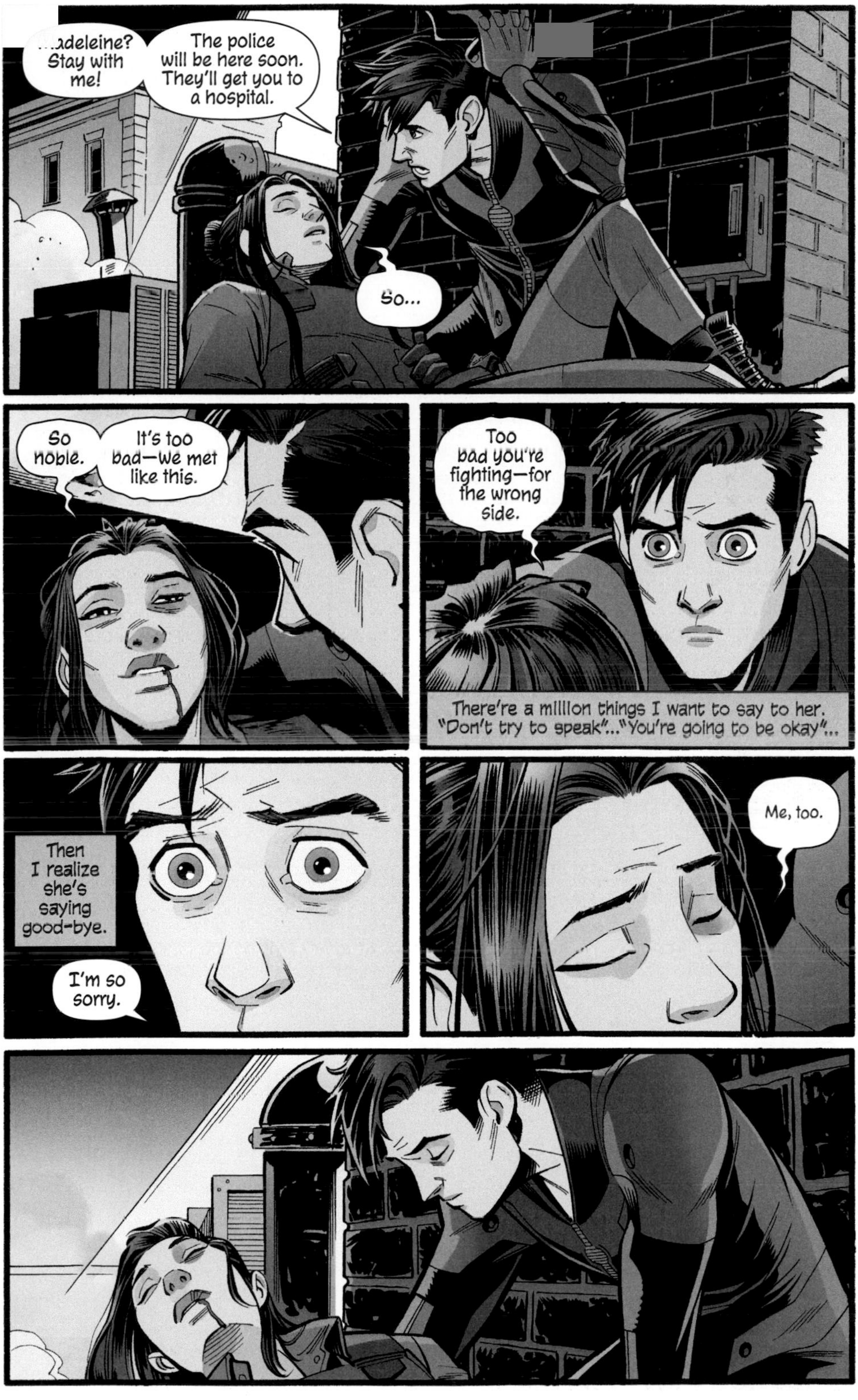
..adeleine? Stay with me!
The police will be here soon. They'll get you to a hospital.
So...
So noble.
It's too bad—we met like this.
Too bad you're fighting—for the wrong side.
There're a million things I want to say to her. "Don't try to speak"..."You're going to be okay"...
Then I realize she's saying good-bye.
I'm so sorry.
Me, too.

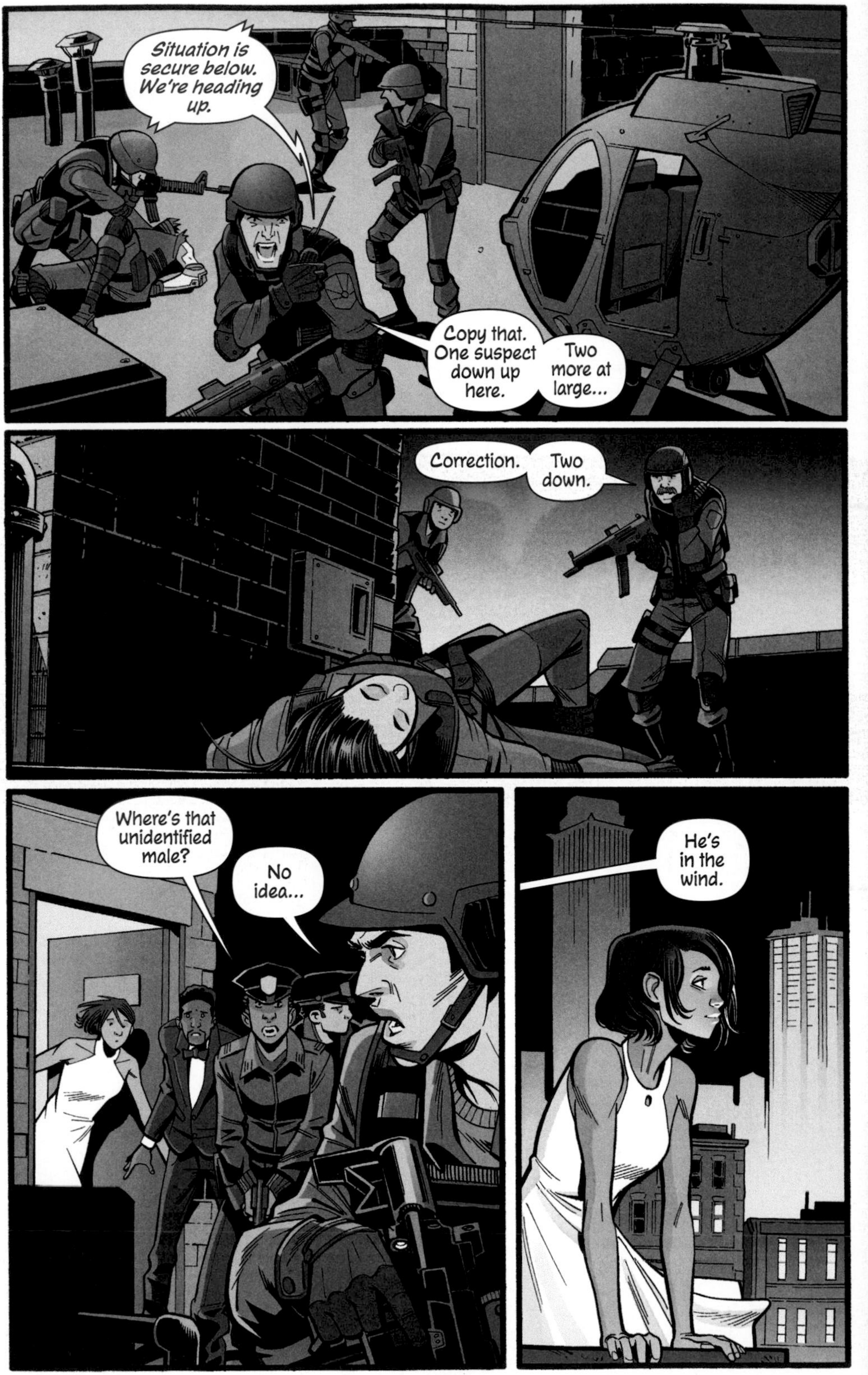

Situation is secure below. We're heading up.
Copy that. One suspect down up here.
Two more at large...
Correction.
Two down.
Where's that unidentified male?
No idea...
He's in the wind.

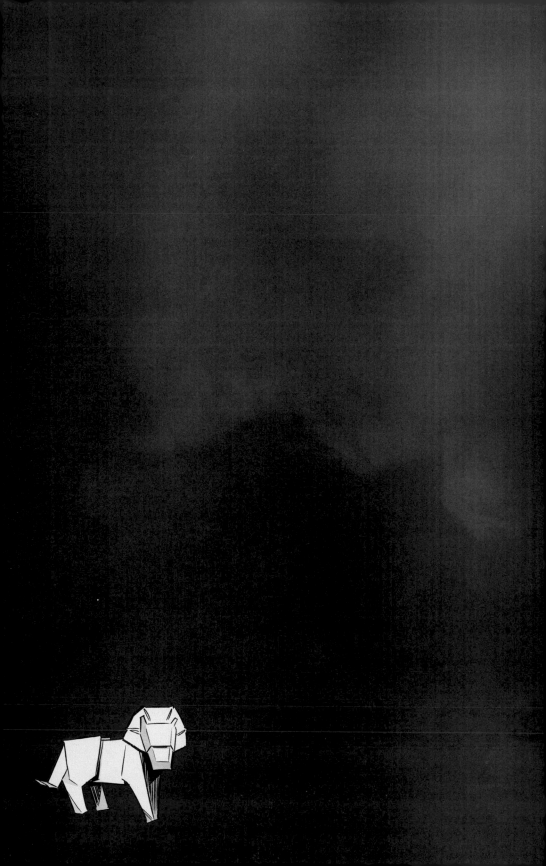

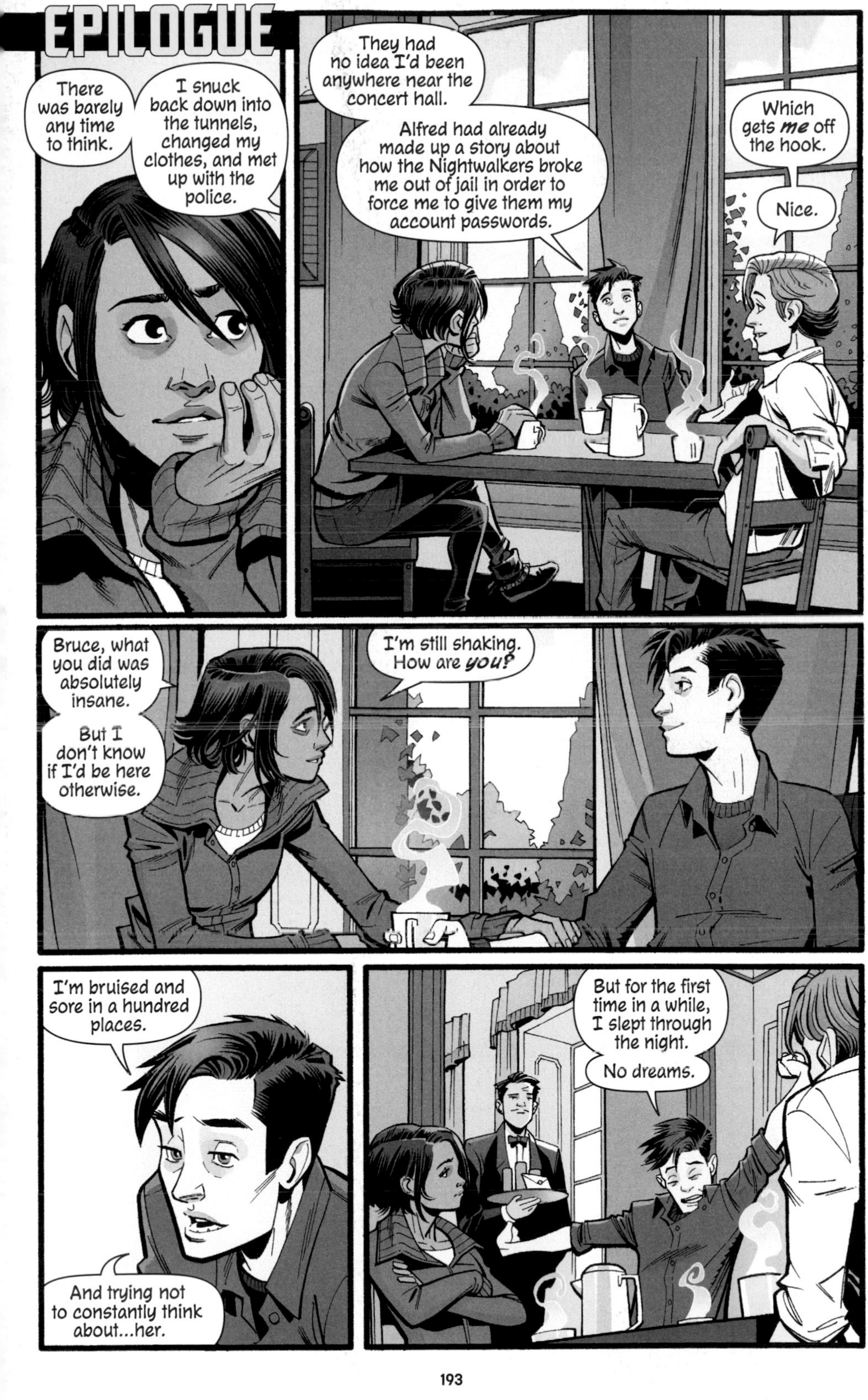
EPILOGUE
There was barely any time to think.
I snuck back down into the tunnels, changed my clothes, and met up with the police.
They had no idea I'd been anywhere near the concert hall.
Alfred had already made up a story about how the Nightwalkers broke me out of jail in order to force me to give them my account passwords.
Which gets *me* off the hook.
Nice.
Bruce, what you did was absolutely insane.
But I don't know if I'd be here otherwise.
I'm still shaking. How are *you*?
I'm bruised and sore in a hundred places.
And trying not to constantly think about...her.
But for the first time in a while, I slept through the night.
No dreams.

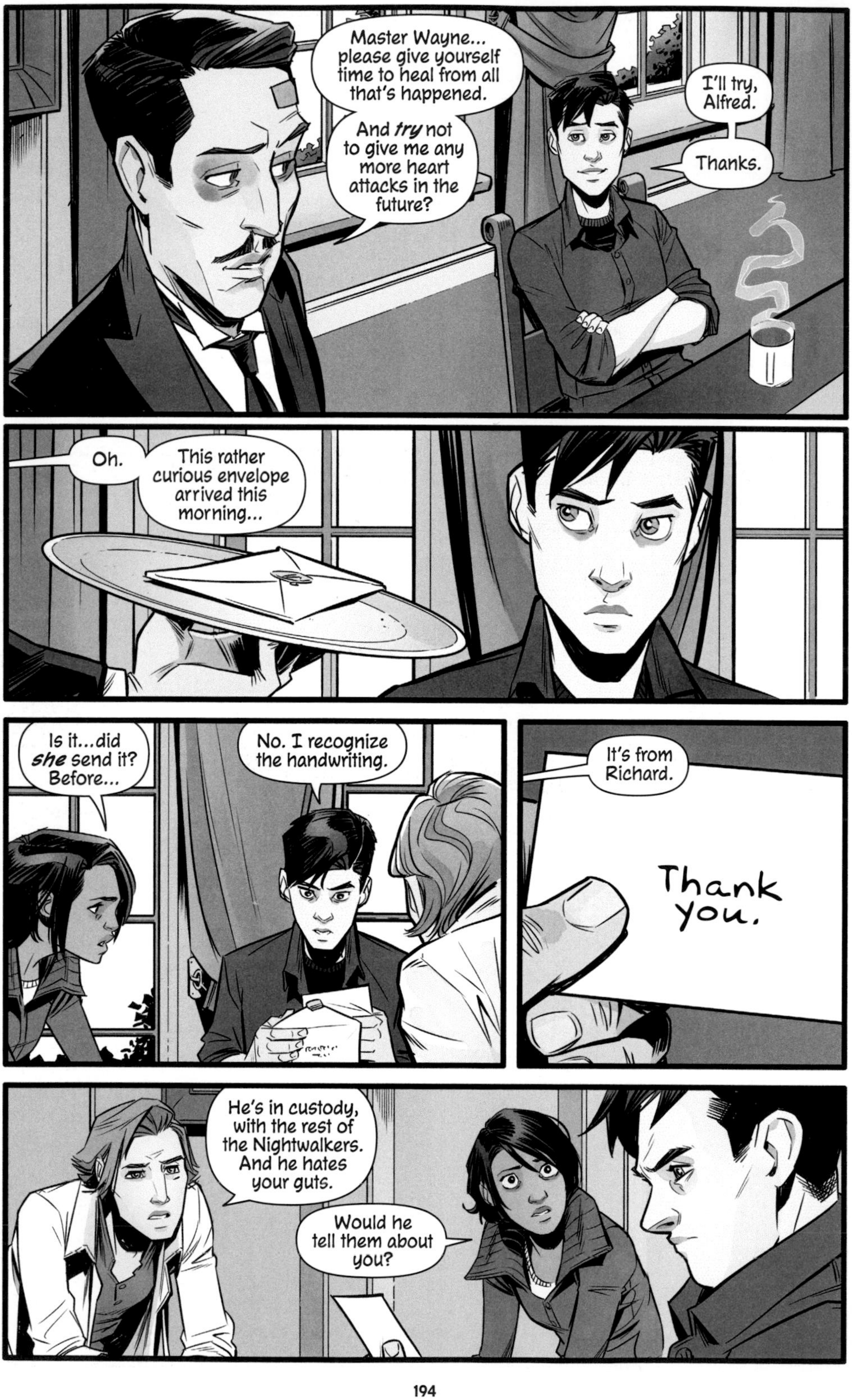
Master Wayne... please give yourself time to heal from all that's happened.
And *try* not to give me any more heart attacks in the future?
I'll try, Alfred.
Thanks.
Oh.
This rather curious envelope arrived this morning...
Is it...did *she* send it? Before...
No. I recognize the handwriting.
It's from Richard.
Thank you.
He's in custody, with the rest of the Nightwalkers. And he hates your guts.
Would he tell them about you?

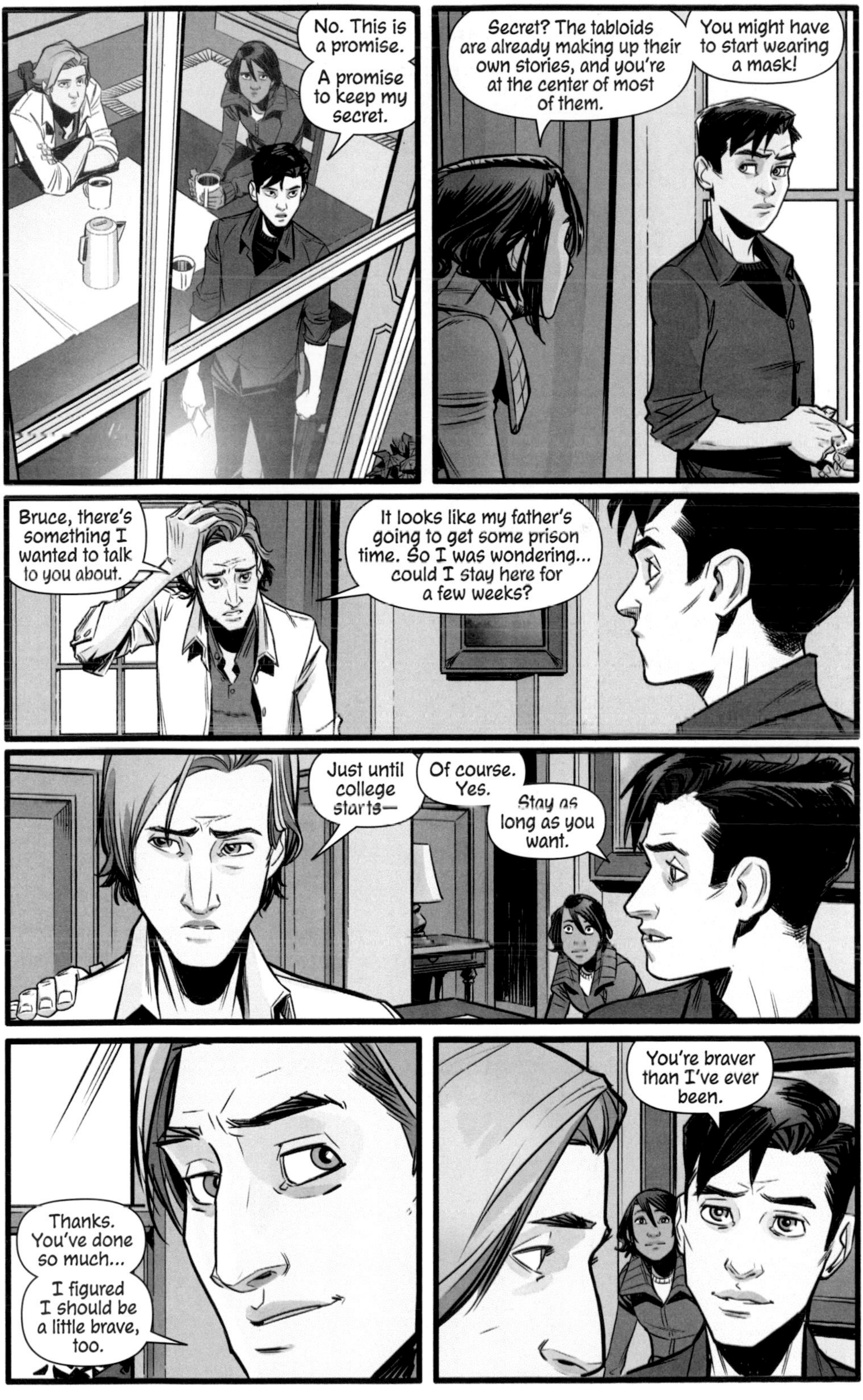
No. This is a promise.
A promise to keep my secret.
Secret? The tabloids are already making up their own stories, and you're at the center of most of them.
You might have to start wearing a mask!
Bruce, there's something I wanted to talk to you about.
It looks like my father's going to get some prison time. So I was wondering... could I stay here for a few weeks?
Just until college starts—
Of course. Yes.
Stay as long as you want.
Thanks. You've done so much...
I figured I should be a little brave, too.
You're braver than I've ever been.

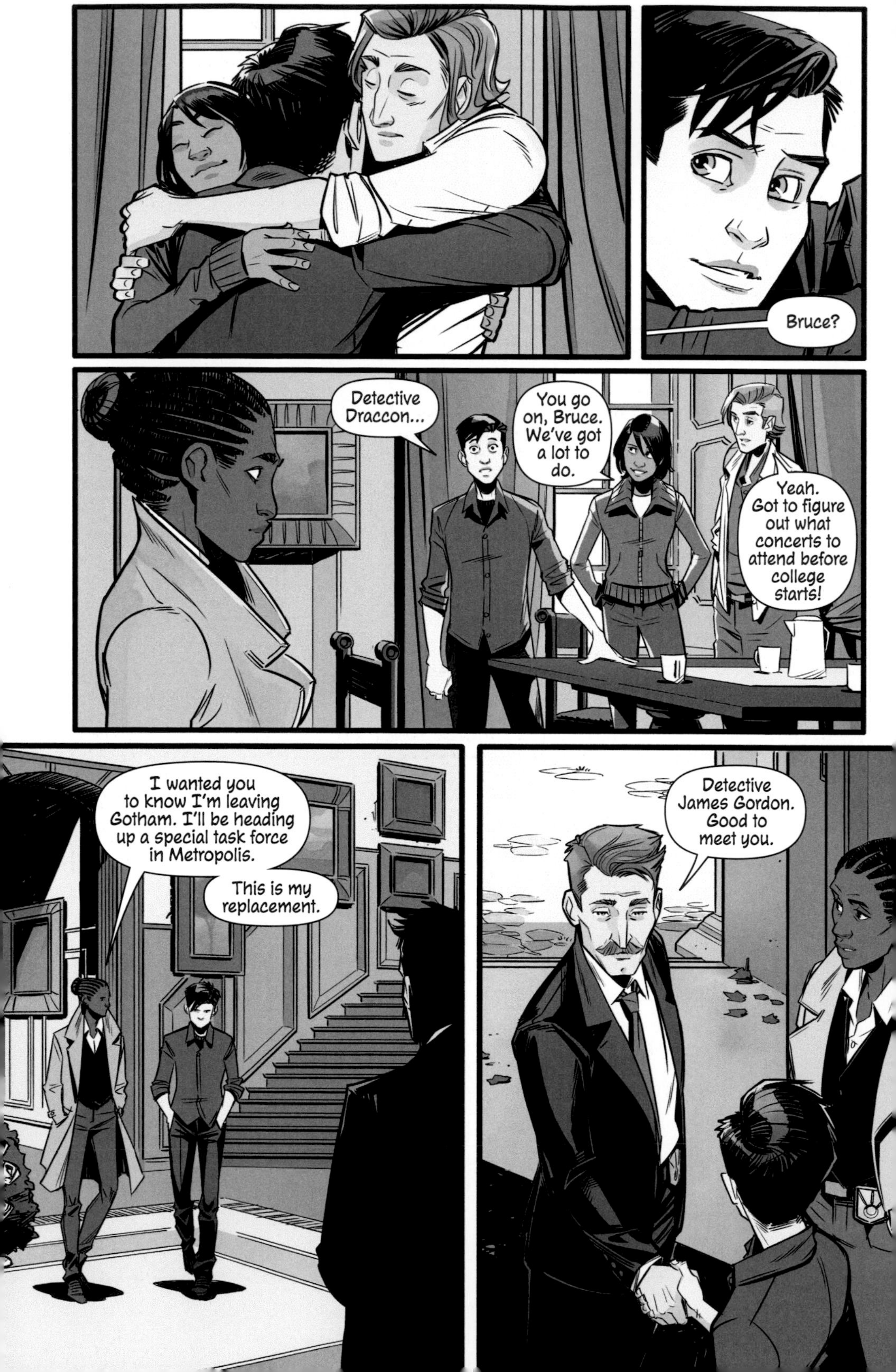
Bruce?
Detective Draccon...
You go on, Bruce. We've got a lot to do.
Yeah. Got to figure out what concerts to attend before college starts!
I wanted you to know I'm leaving Gotham. I'll be heading up a special task force in Metropolis.
This is my replacement.
Detective James Gordon. Good to meet you.

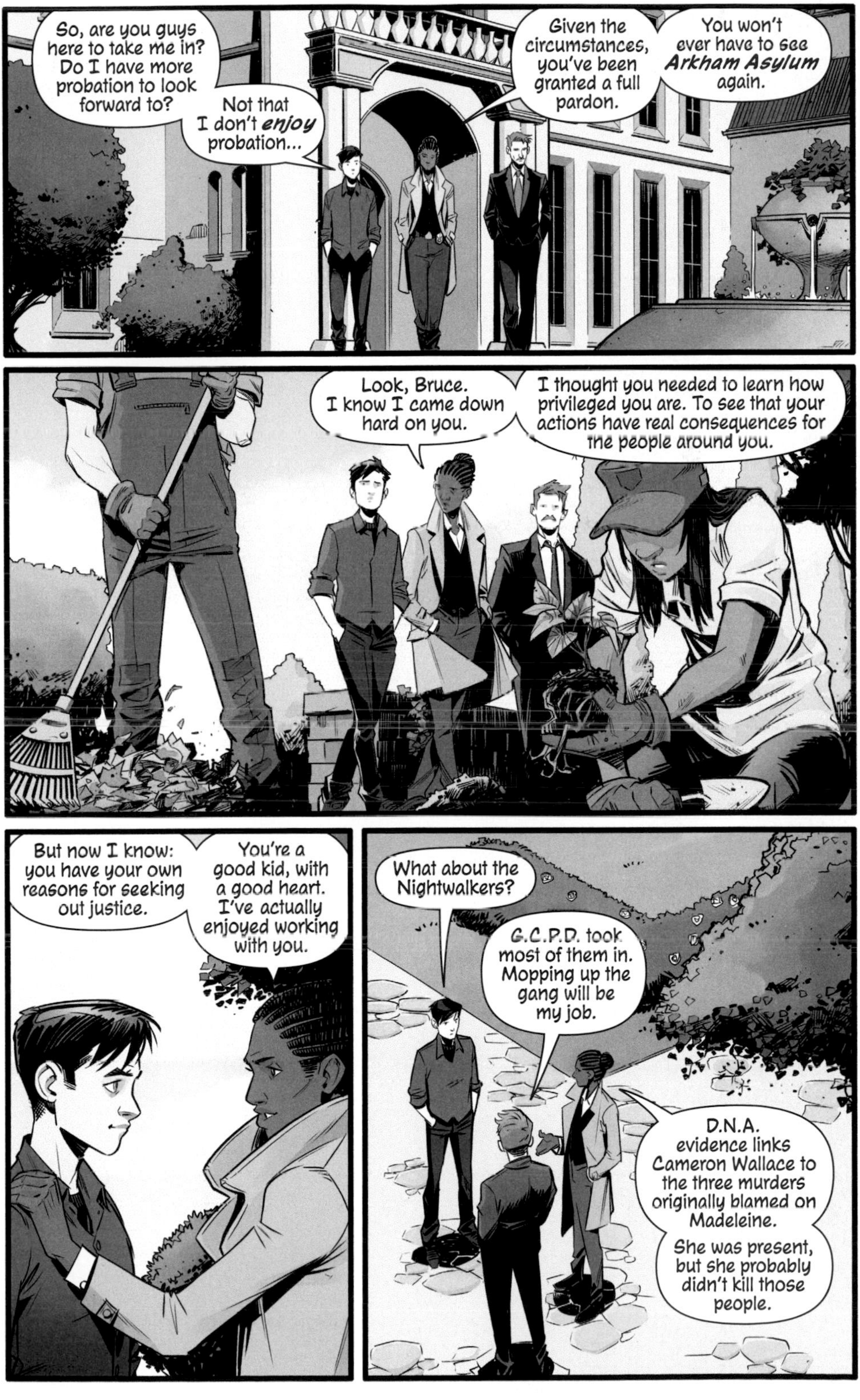
So, are you guys here to take me in? Do I have more probation to look forward to?
Not that I don't *enjoy* probation...
Given the circumstances, you've been granted a full pardon.
You won't ever have to see *Arkham Asylum* again.
Look, Bruce. I know I came down hard on you.
I thought you needed to learn how privileged you are. To see that your actions have real consequences for the people around you.
But now I know: you have your own reasons for seeking out justice.
You're a good kid, with a good heart. I've actually enjoyed working with you.
What about the Nightwalkers?
G.C.P.D. took most of them in. Mopping up the gang will be my job.
D.N.A. evidence links Cameron Wallace to the three murders originally blamed on Madeleine.
She was present, but she probably didn't kill those people.

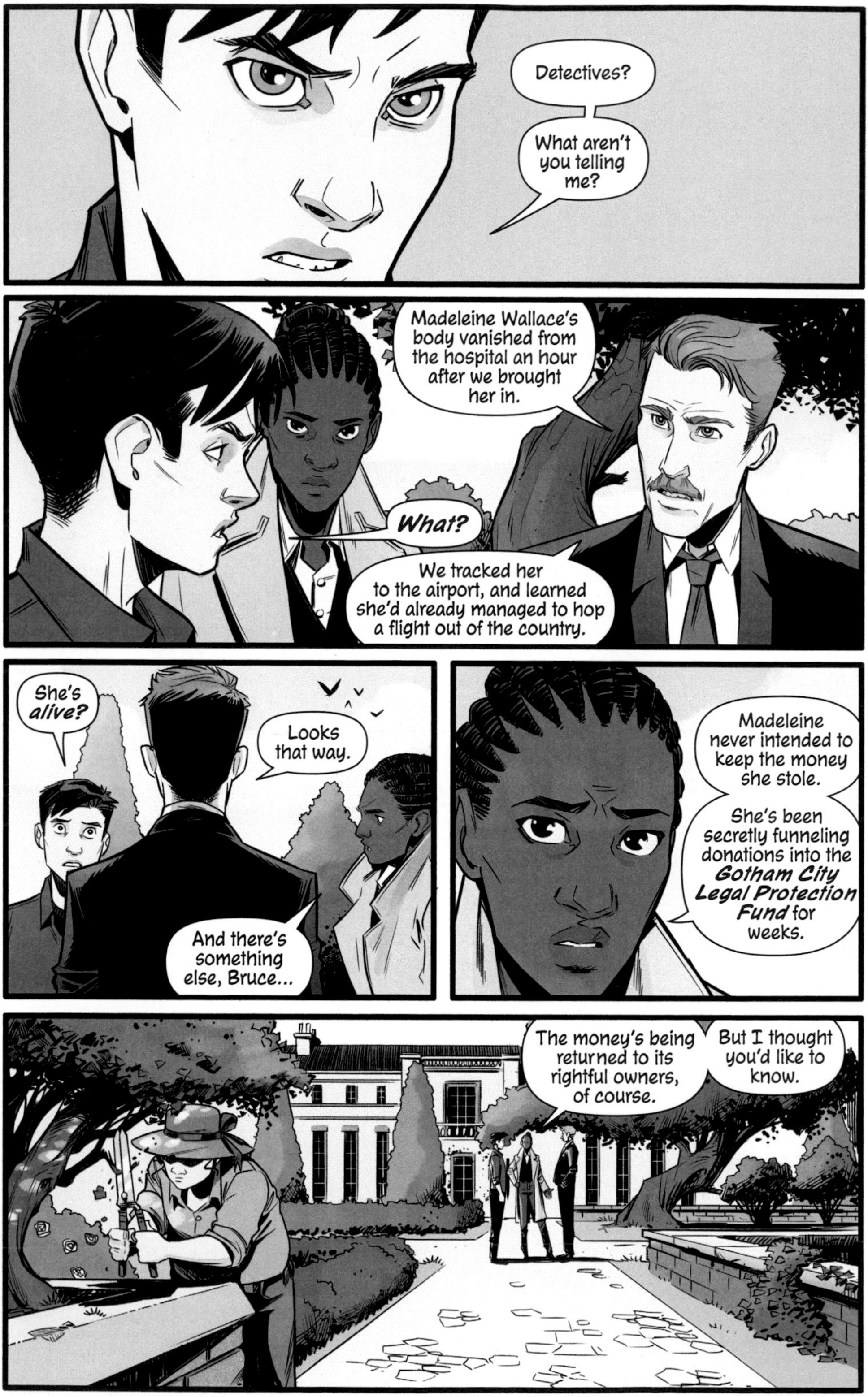
Detectives?
What aren't you telling me?
Madeleine Wallace's body vanished from the hospital an hour after we brought her in.
What?
We tracked her to the airport, and learned she'd already managed to hop a flight out of the country.
She's *alive?*
Looks that way.
And there's something else, Bruce...
Madeleine never intended to keep the money she stole.
She's been secretly funneling donations into the ***Gotham City Legal Protection Fund*** for weeks.
The money's being returned to its rightful owners, of course.
But I thought you'd like to know.

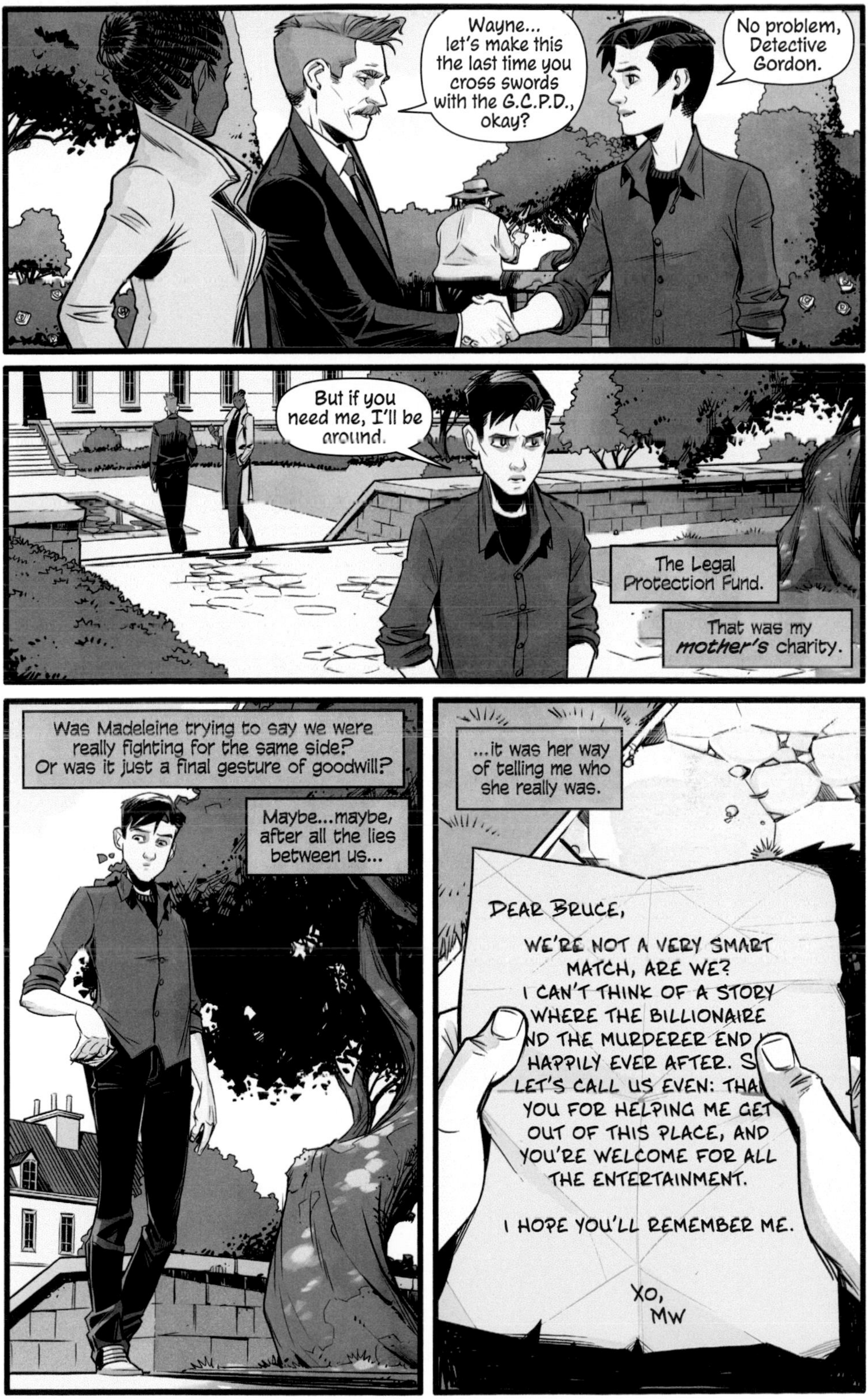
Wayne... let's make this the last time you cross swords with the G.C.P.D., okay?
No problem, Detective Gordon.
But if you need me, I'll be around.
The Legal Protection Fund.
That was my *mother's* charity.
Was Madeleine trying to say we were really fighting for the same side? Or was it just a final gesture of goodwill?
Maybe...maybe, after all the lies between us...
...it was her way of telling me who she really was.
DEAR BRUCE,
WE'RE NOT A VERY SMART MATCH, ARE WE?
I CAN'T THINK OF A STORY
WHERE THE BILLIONAIRE
ND THE MURDERER END
HAPPILY EVER AFTER. S
LET'S CALL US EVEN: THA
YOU FOR HELPING ME GET
OUT OF THIS PLACE, AND
YOU'RE WELCOME FOR ALL
THE ENTERTAINMENT.
I HOPE YOU'LL REMEMBER ME.
XO,
MW

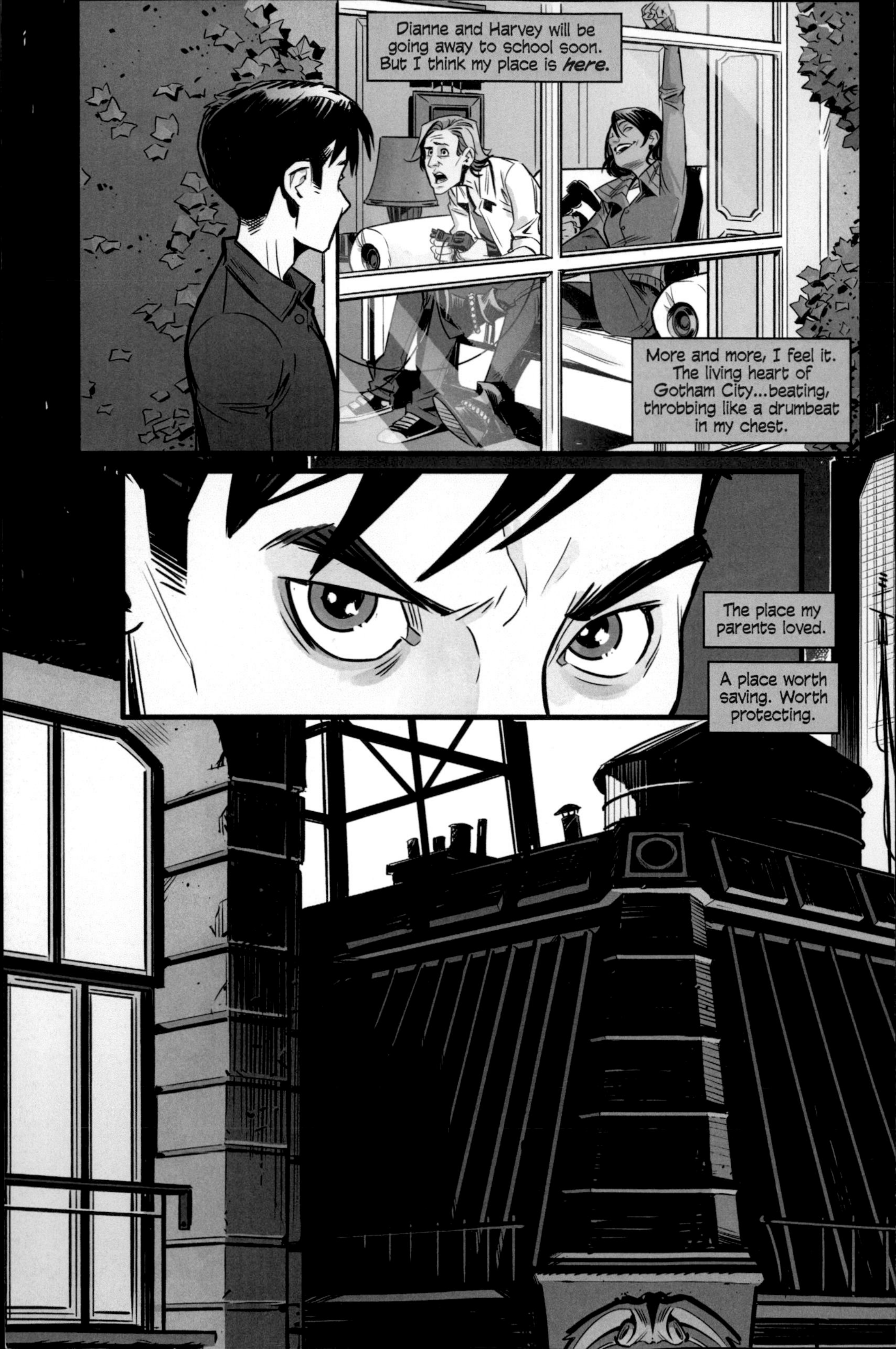
Dianne and Harvey will be going away to school soon. But I think my place is *here*.
More and more, I feel it. The living heart of Gotham City...beating, throbbing like a drumbeat in my chest.
The place my parents loved.
A place worth saving. Worth protecting.

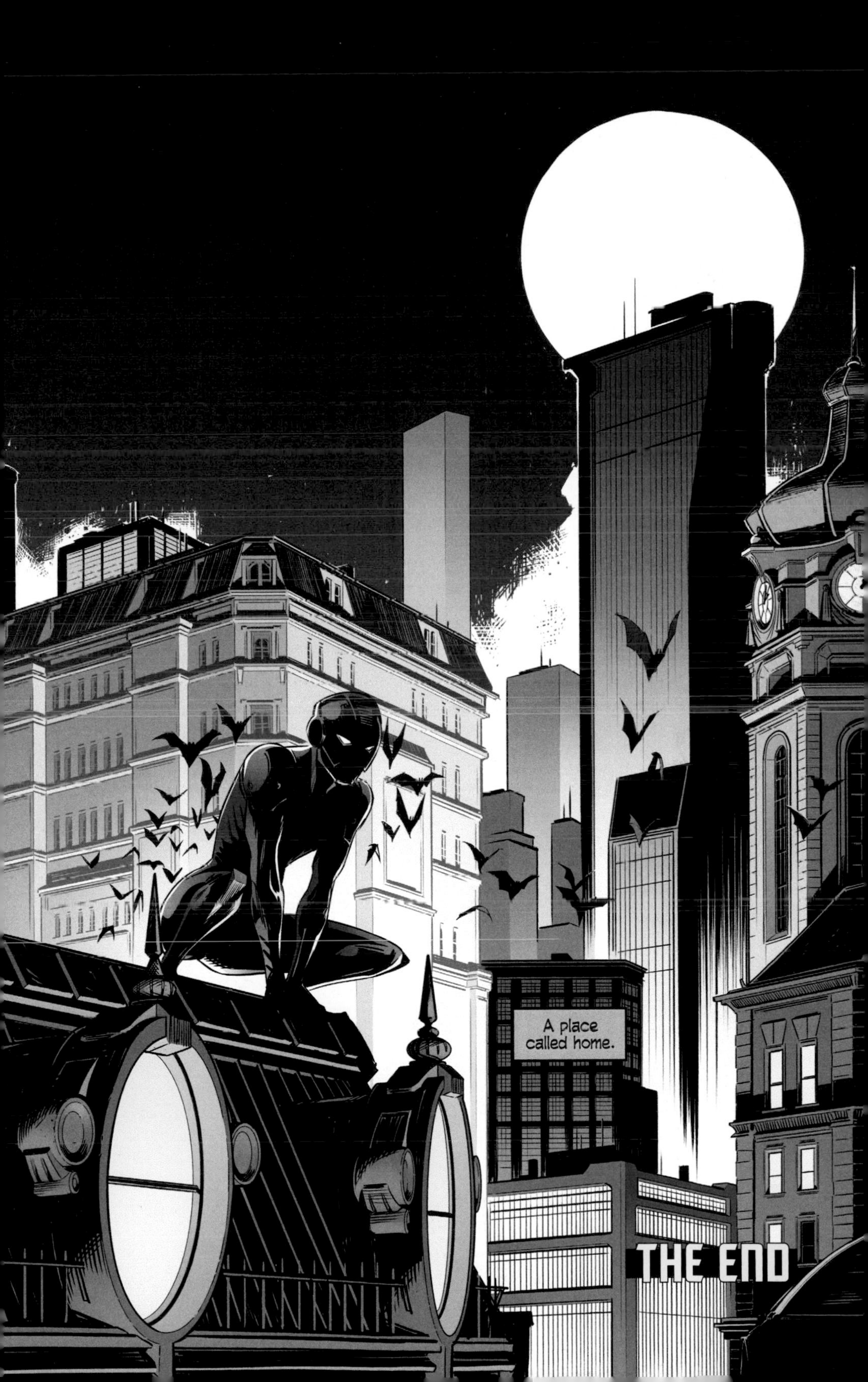
A place called home.
THE END

MARIE LU is the #1 *New York Times* bestselling author of *The Young Elites*, *Legend*, and *Warcross*. She graduated from the University of Southern California and jumped into the video game industry as an artist. Now a full-time writer, she spends her spare time reading, drawing, playing games, and getting stuck in traffic. She lives in Los Angeles with her illustrator-author husband, Primo Gallanosa, and their family.

STUART MOORE is a writer, a book editor, and an award-winning comics editor. His recent novels include *X-Men: The Dark Phoenix Saga* (Titan/Marvel) and three volumes of *The Zodiac Legacy*, in collaboration with Stan Lee (Disney Press); his comics writing includes *Captain Ginger* (AHOY Comics), *EGOs* (Image), and *Deadpool the Duck* (Marvel). Stuart lives in Brooklyn, New York.

CHRIS WILDGOOSE is a British comics and concept artist known for his work on DC's BATGIRL: REBIRTH, GOTHAM ACADEMY, and Vertigo's CMYK: YELLOW. He is the co-founder of the indie comics studio Improper Books and artist for their award-nominated *Porcelain* series. His publishers and clients include BOOM!, Dark Horse, Delcourt, Image, Paramount, Titan, Ubisoft, and Vertigo. Chris is based in the UK, where he lives and shares a studio with his awesome and equally creative wife, Laura.

MORE
FROM

BASED ON THE *NEW YORK TIMES* BESTSELLING NOVELS

BATMAN: NIGHTWALKER
novel written by Marie Lu
adapted by Stuart Moore
illustrated by Chris Wildgoose

WONDER WOMAN: WARBRINGER
novel written by Leigh Bardugo
adapted by Louise Simonson
illustrated by Kit Seaton

CATWOMAN: SOULSTEALER
novel written by Sarah J. Maas
adapted by Louise Simonson
illustrated by Samantha Dodge

Based on the *New York Times* Bestselling Novel by

LEIGH BARDUGO

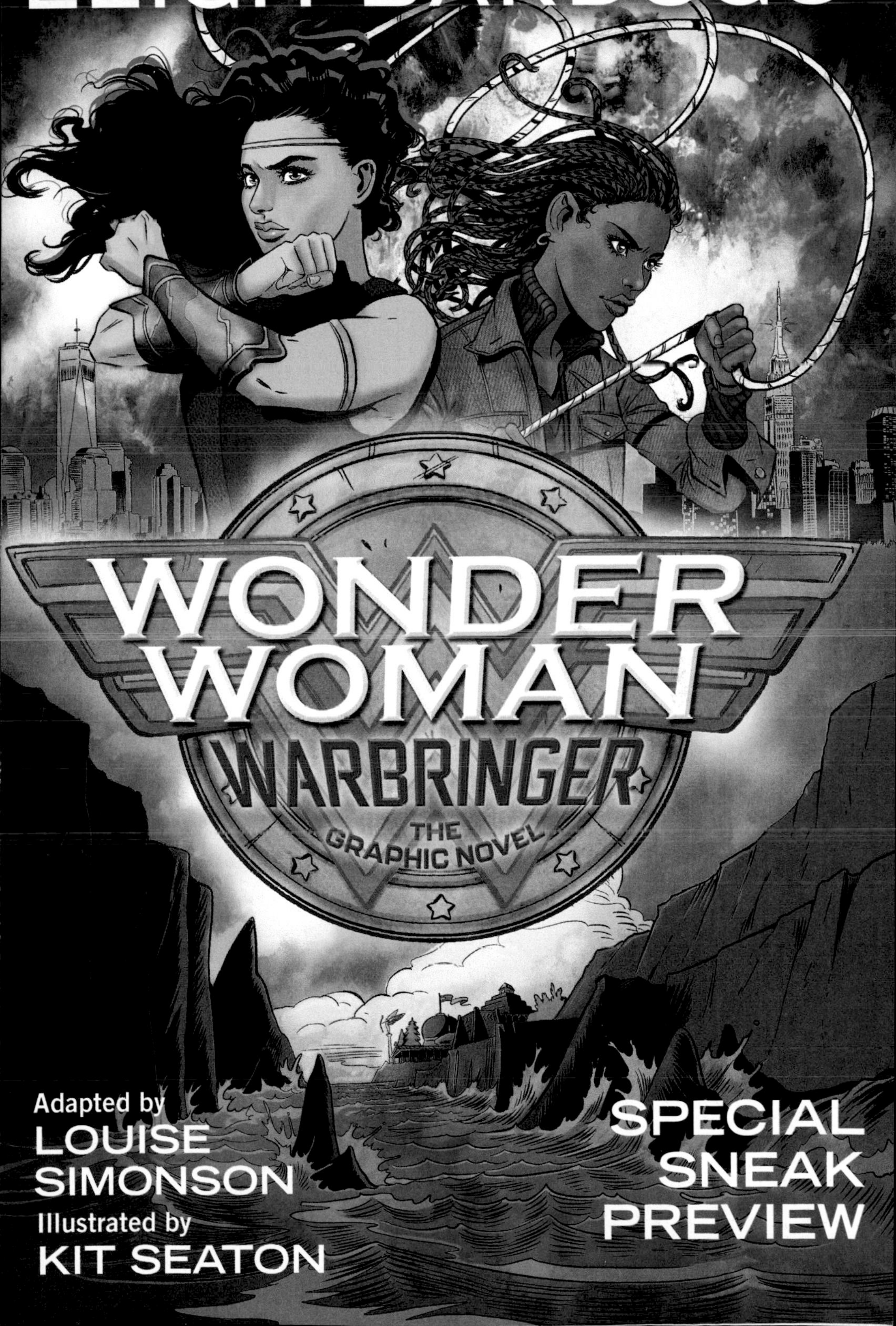

WONDER WOMAN
WARBRINGER
THE GRAPHIC NOVEL

Adapted by
LOUISE SIMONSON
Illustrated by
KIT SEATON

SPECIAL SNEAK PREVIEW

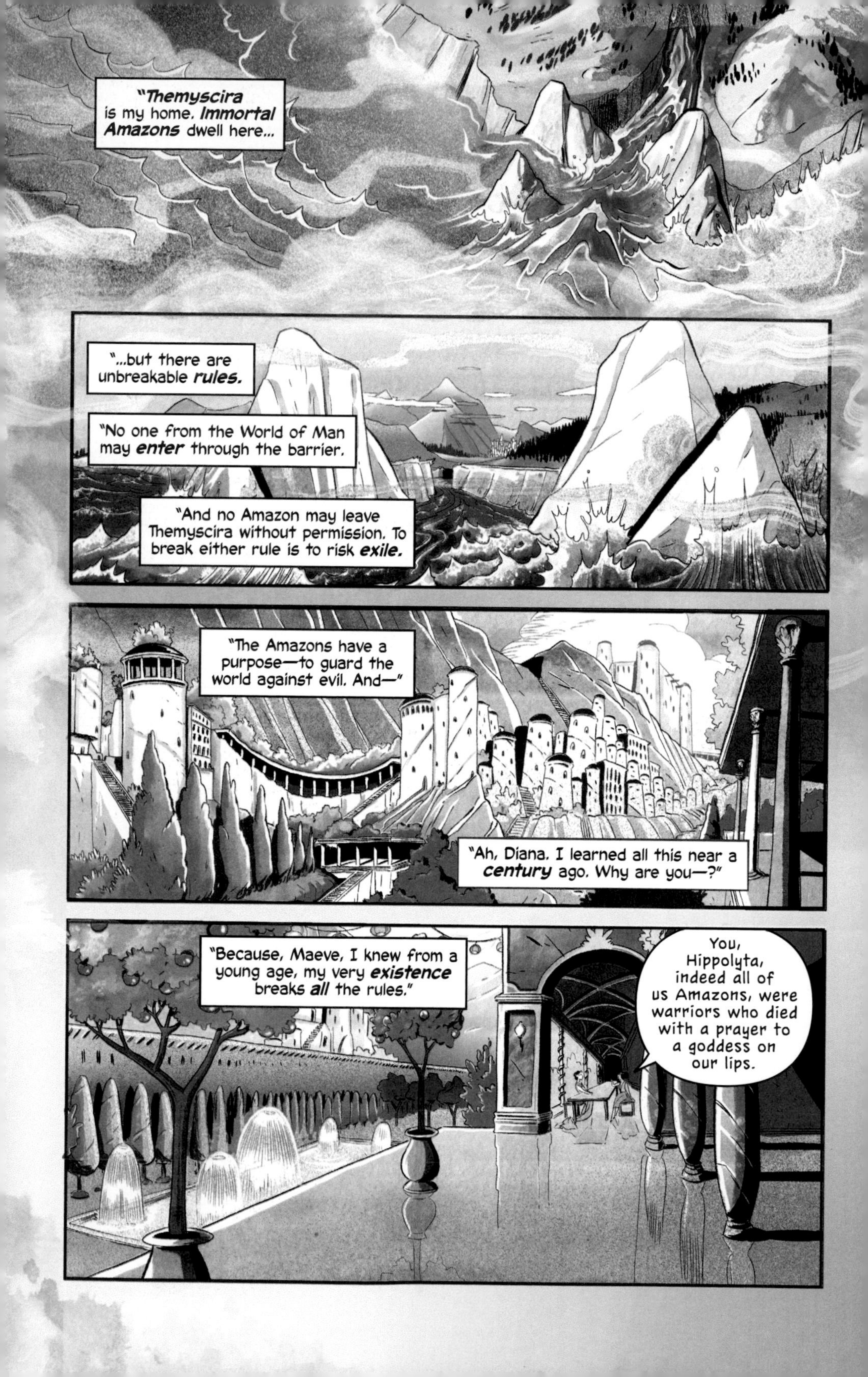
"Themyscira is my home. Immortal Amazons dwell here...
"...but there are unbreakable rules.
"No one from the World of Man may enter through the barrier.
"And no Amazon may leave Themyscira without permission. To break either rule is to risk exile.
"The Amazons have a purpose—to guard the world against evil. And—"
"Ah, Diana. I learned all this near a century ago. Why are you—?"
"Because, Maeve, I knew from a young age, my very existence breaks all the rules."
You, Hippolyta, indeed all of us Amazons, were warriors who died with a prayer to a goddess on our lips.

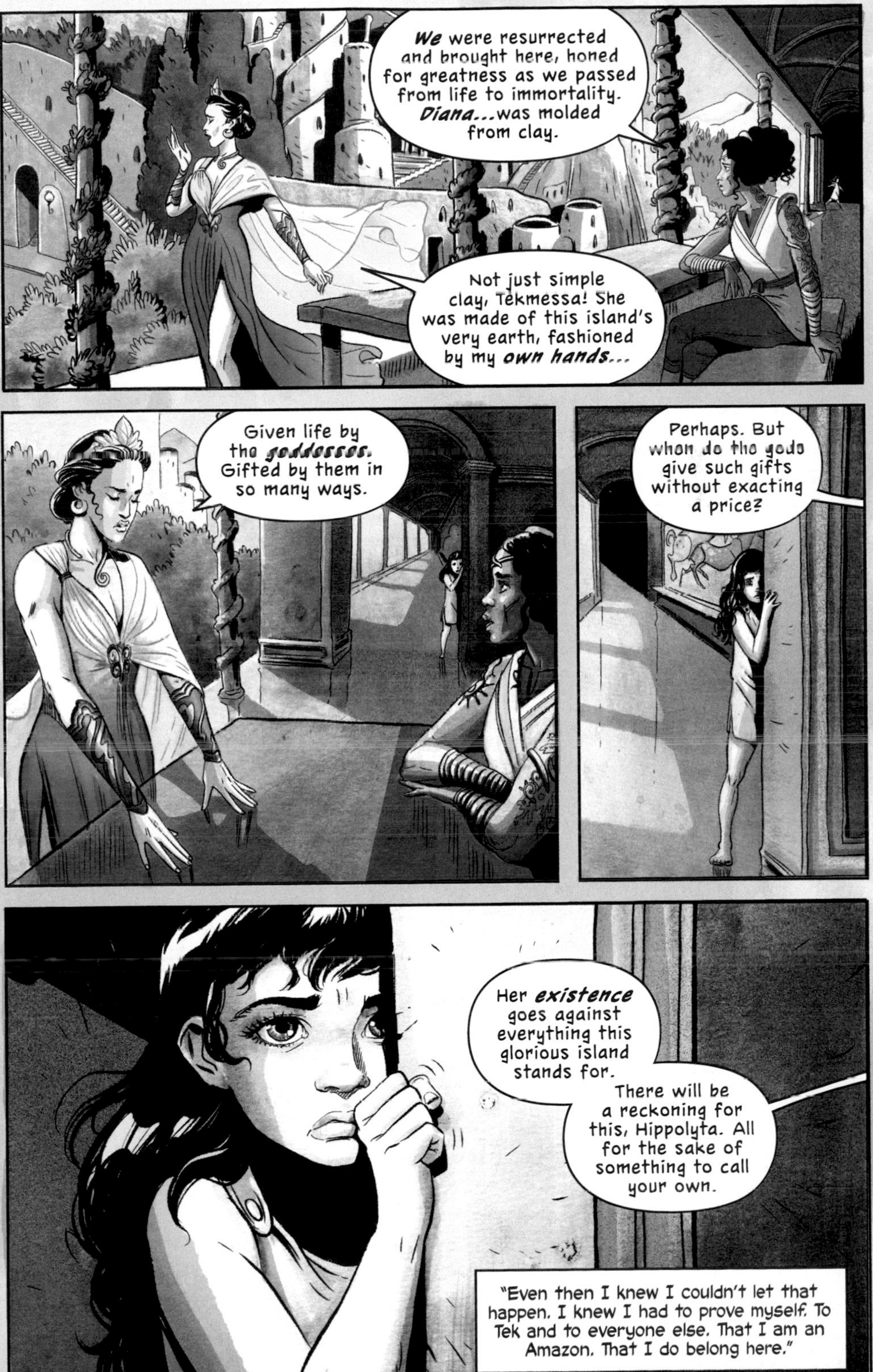
We were resurrected and brought here, honed for greatness as we passed from life to immortality. Diana...was molded from clay.
Not just simple clay, Tekmessa! She was made of this island's very earth, fashioned by my own hands...
Given life by the goddesses. Gifted by them in so many ways.
Perhaps. But when do the gods give such gifts without exacting a price?
Her existence goes against everything this glorious island stands for.
There will be a reckoning for this, Hippolyta. All for the sake of something to call your own.
"Even then I knew I couldn't let that happen. I knew I had to prove myself. To Tek and to everyone else. That I am an Amazon. That I do belong here."

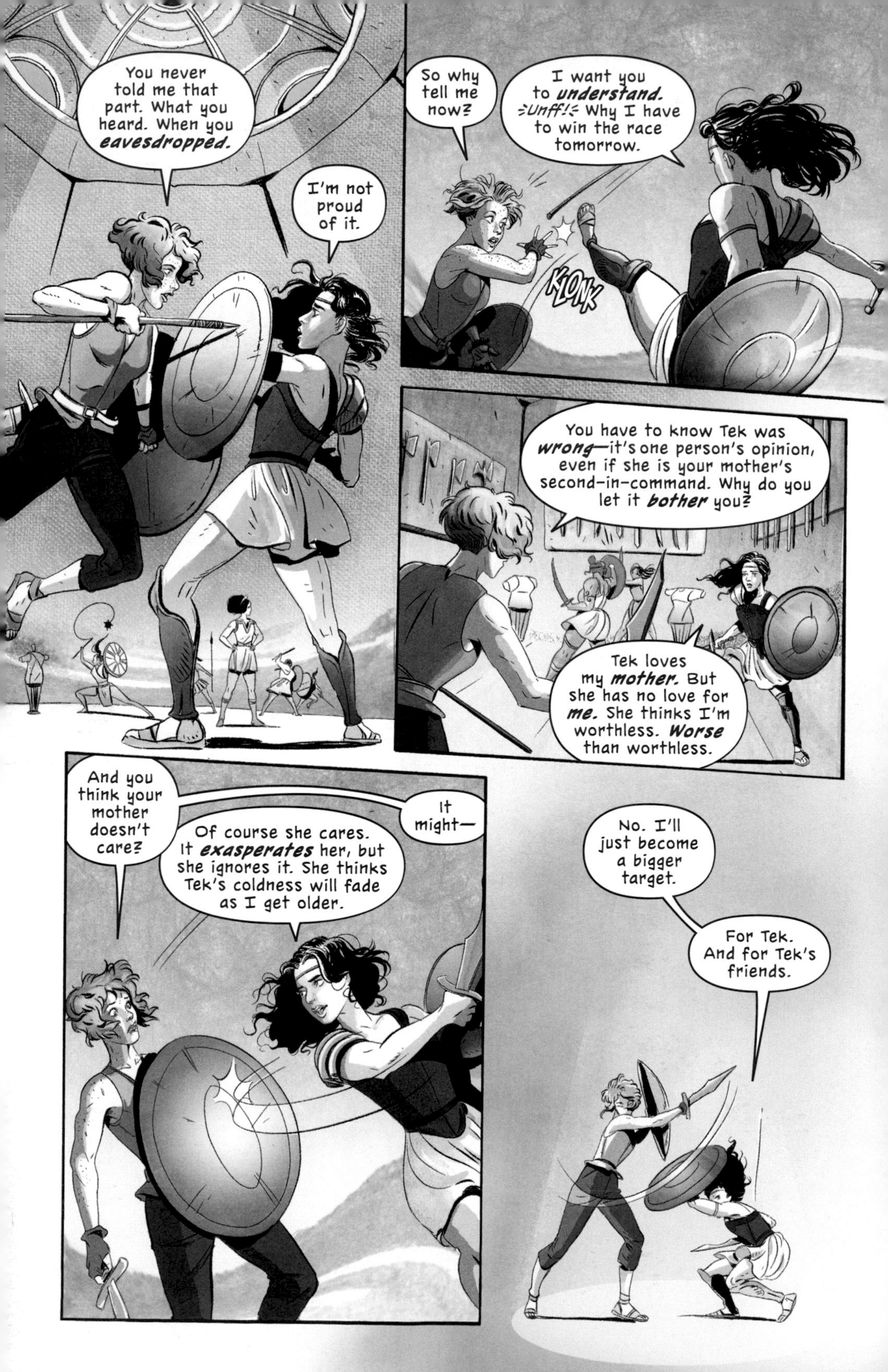

You never told me that part. What you heard. When you *eavesdropped.*
I'm not proud of it.
So why tell me now?
I want you to *understand.* =Unff!= Why I have to win the race tomorrow.
KLONK
You have to know Tek was *wrong*—it's one person's opinion, even if she is your mother's second-in-command. Why do you let it *bother* you?
Tek loves my *mother.* But she has no love for *me.* She thinks I'm worthless. *Worse* than worthless.
And you think your mother doesn't care?
Of course she cares. It *exasperates* her, but she ignores it. She thinks Tek's coldness will fade as I get older.
It might—
No. I'll just become a bigger target.
For Tek. And for Tek's friends.

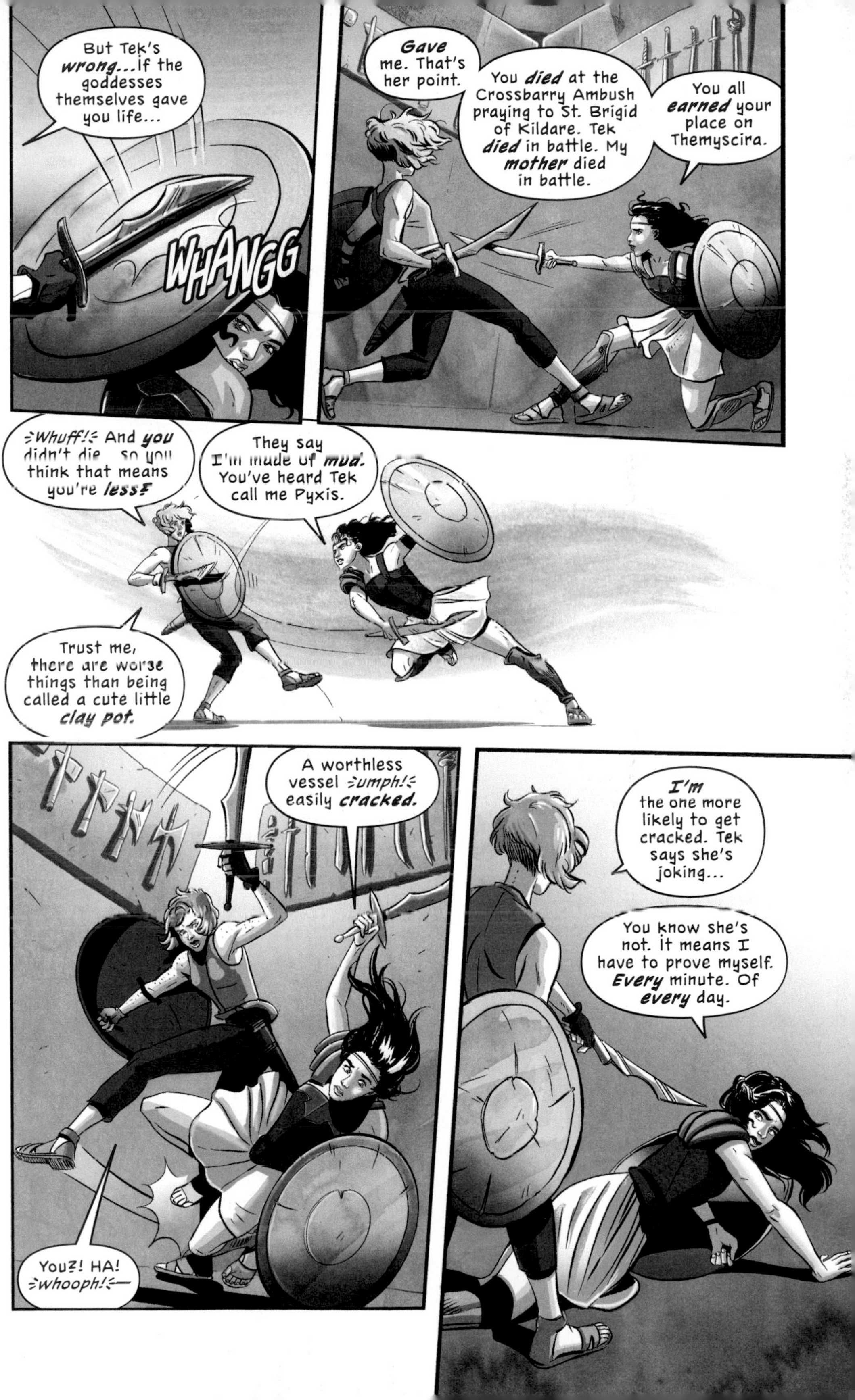

But Tek's wrong...if the goddesses themselves gave you life...
WHANGG
Gave me. That's her point.
You died at the Crossbarry Ambush praying to St. Brigid of Kildare. Tek died in battle. My mother died in battle.
You all earned your place on Themyscira.
Whuff! And you didn't die so you think that means you're less?
They say I'm made of mud. You've heard Tek call me Pyxis.
Trust me, there are worse things than being called a cute little clay pot.
A worthless vessel umph! easily cracked.
You?! HA! whooph!—
I'm the one more likely to get cracked. Tek says she's joking...
You know she's not. It means I have to prove myself. Every minute. Of every day.

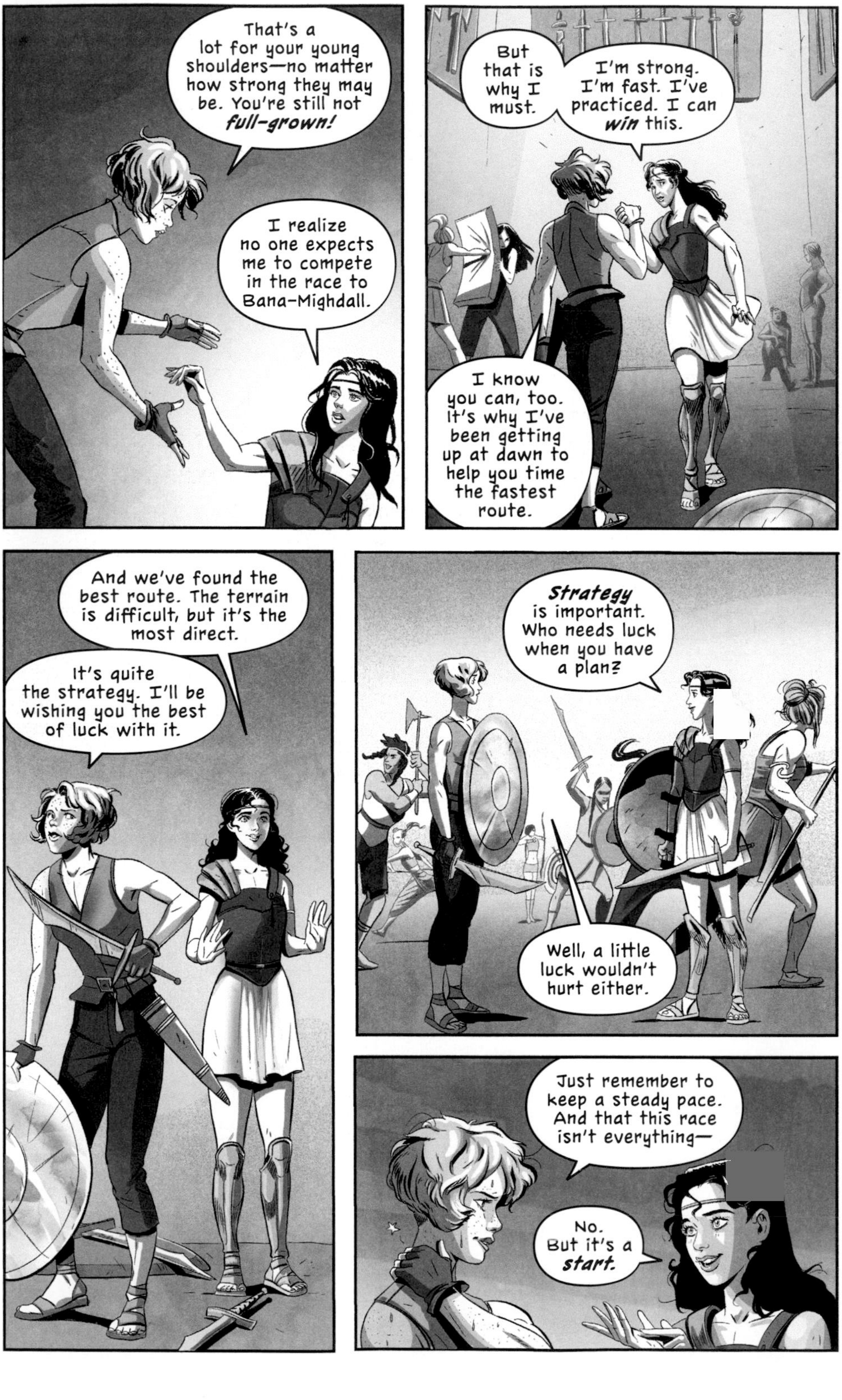
That's a lot for your young shoulders—no matter how strong they may be. You're still not *full-grown!*
I realize no one expects me to compete in the race to Bana-Mighdall.
But that is why I must.
I'm strong. I'm fast. I've practiced. I can *win* this.
I know you can, too. It's why I've been getting up at dawn to help you time the fastest route.
And we've found the best route. The terrain is difficult, but it's the most direct.
It's quite the strategy. I'll be wishing you the best of luck with it.
Strategy is important. Who needs luck when you have a plan?
Well, a little luck wouldn't hurt either.
Just remember to keep a steady pace. And that this race isn't everything—
No. But it's a *start.*

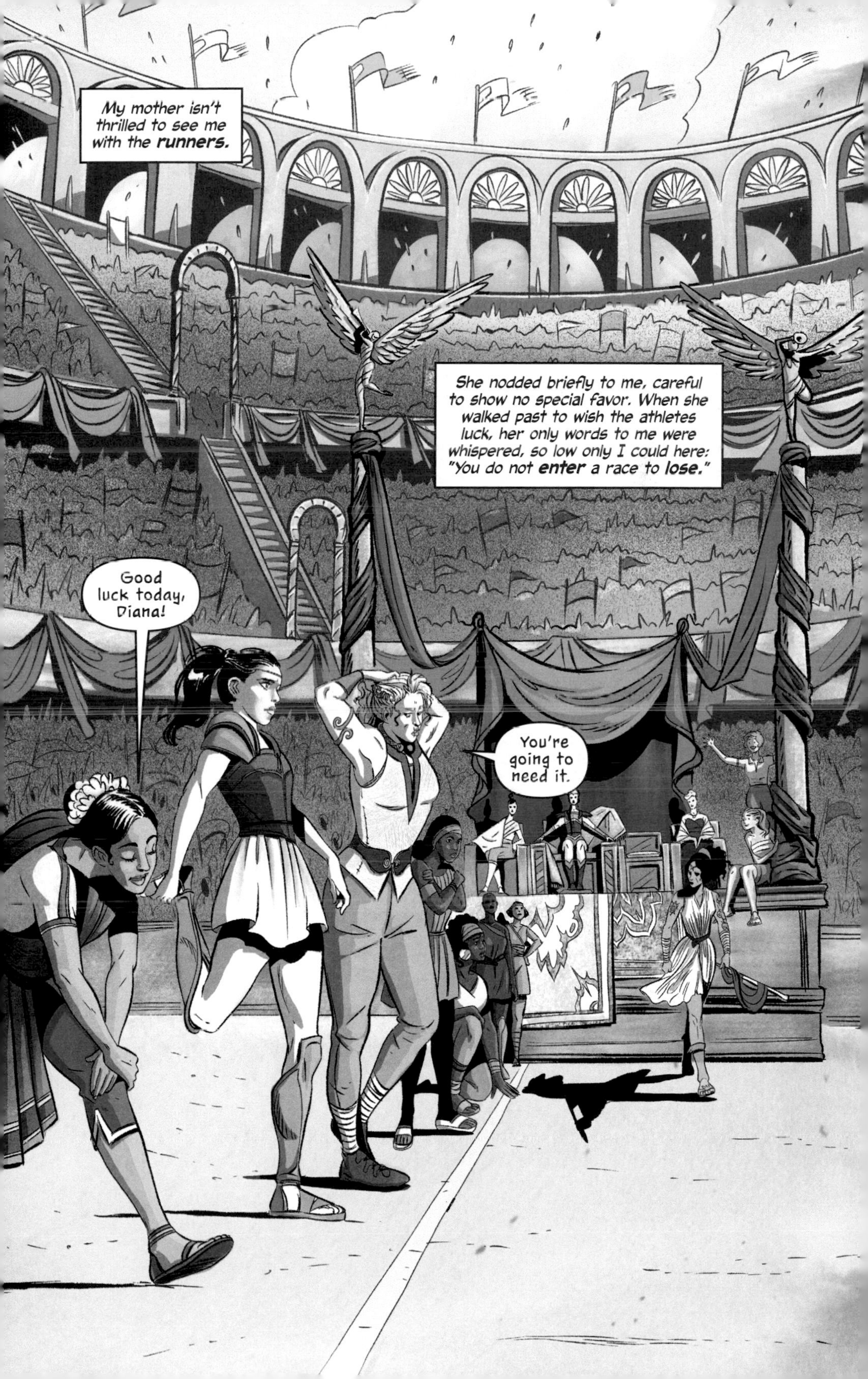
My mother isn't thrilled to see me with the **runners.**
She nodded briefly to me, careful to show no special favor. When she walked past to wish the athletes luck, her only words to me were whispered, so low only I could here: "You do not **enter** a race to **lose.**"
Good luck today, Diana!
You're going to need it.

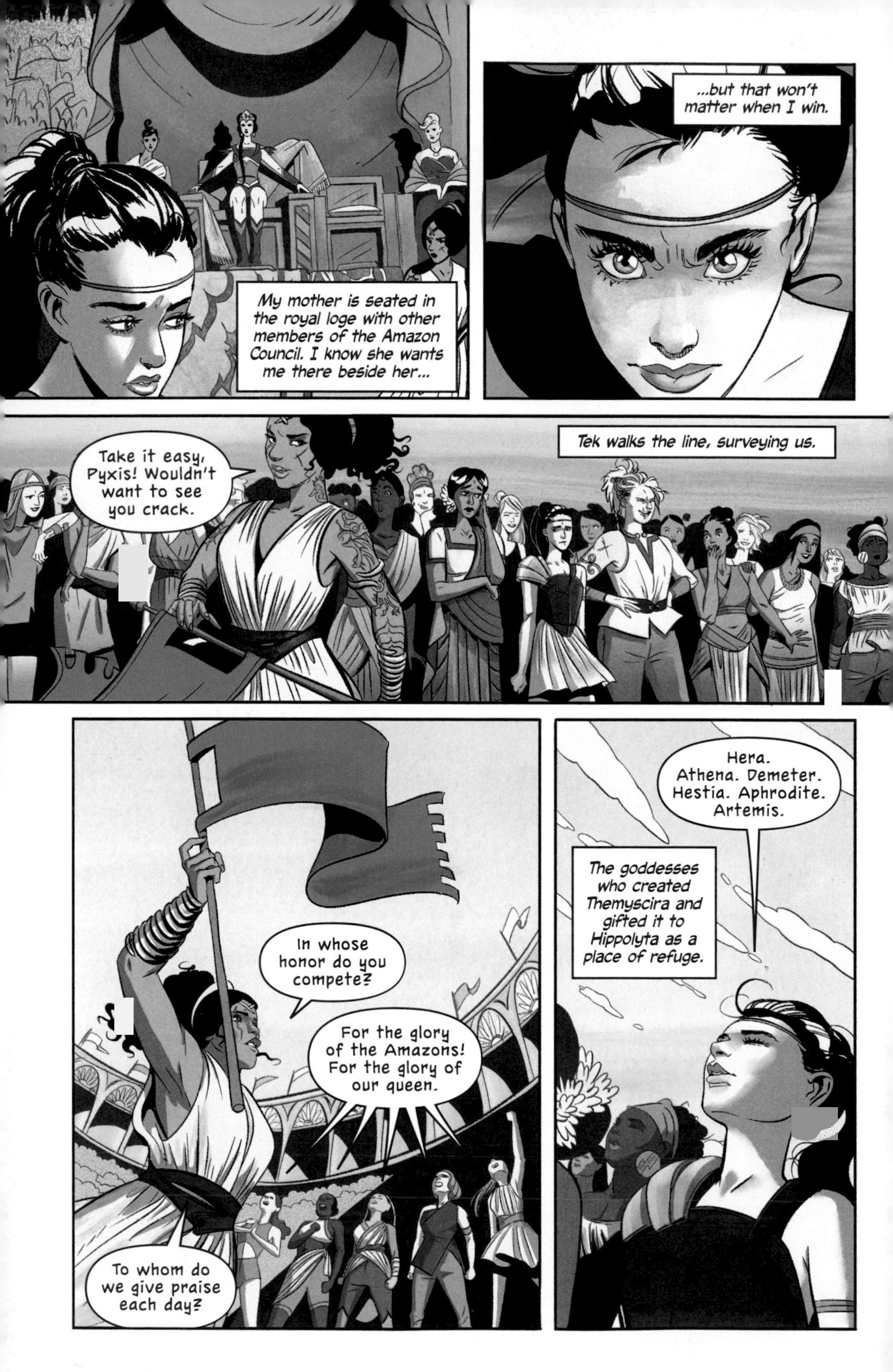
My mother is seated in the royal loge with other members of the Amazon Council. I know she wants me there beside her...
...but that won't matter when I win.
Tek walks the line, surveying us.
Take it easy, Pyxis! Wouldn't want to see you crack.
In whose honor do you compete?
For the glory of the Amazons! For the glory of our queen.
To whom do we give praise each day?
Hera. Athena. Demeter. Hestia. Aphrodite. Artemis.
The goddesses who created Themyscira and gifted it to Hippolyta as a place of refuge.

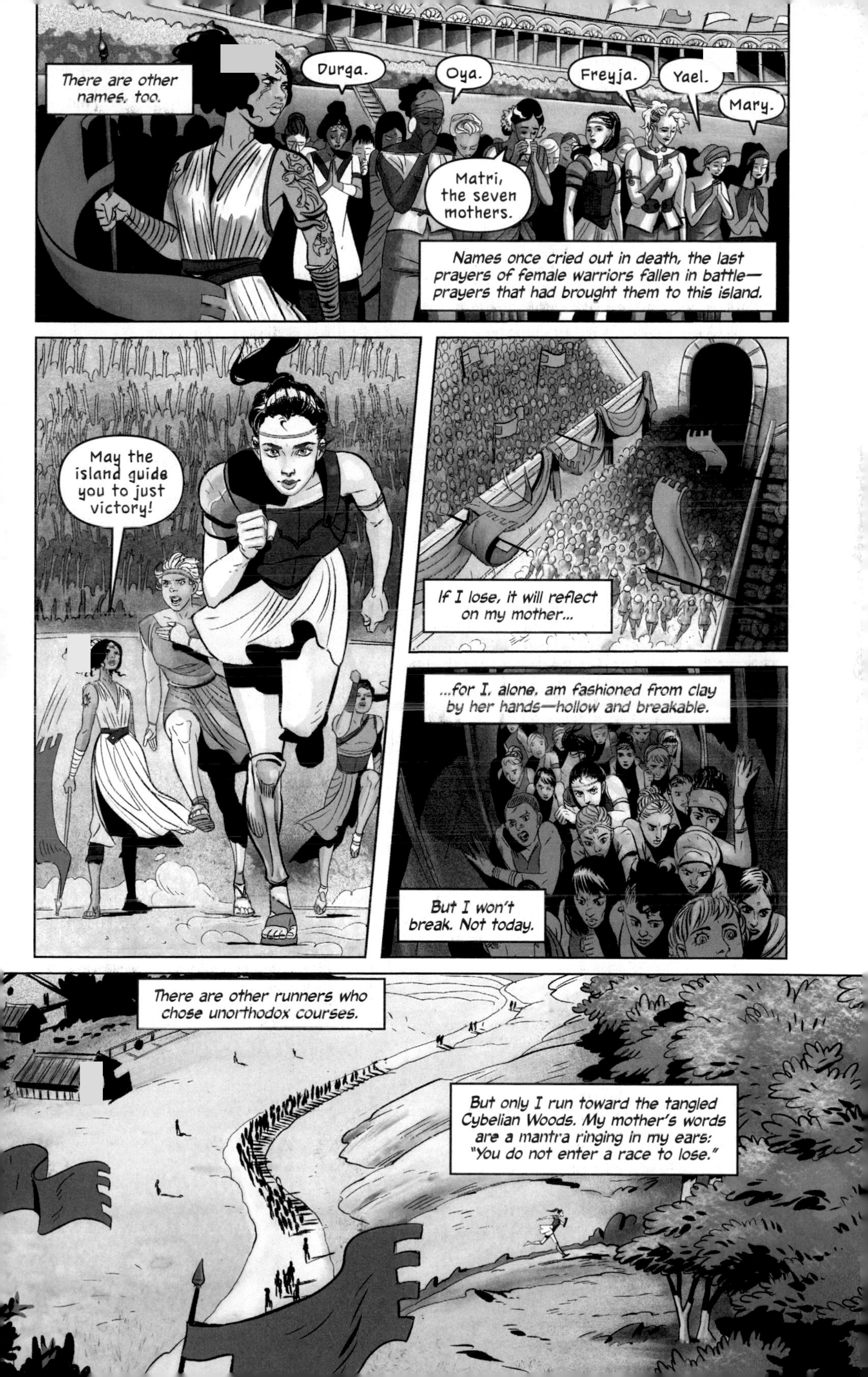
There are other names, too.
Durga.
Oya.
Freyja.
Yael.
Mary.
Matri, the seven mothers.
Names once cried out in death, the last prayers of female warriors fallen in battle—prayers that had brought them to this island.
May the island guide you to just victory!
If I lose, it will reflect on my mother...
...for I, alone, am fashioned from clay by her hands—hollow and breakable.
But I won't break. Not today.
There are other runners who chose unorthodox courses.
But only I run toward the tangled Cybelian Woods. My mother's words are a mantra ringing in my ears: "You do not enter a race to lose."

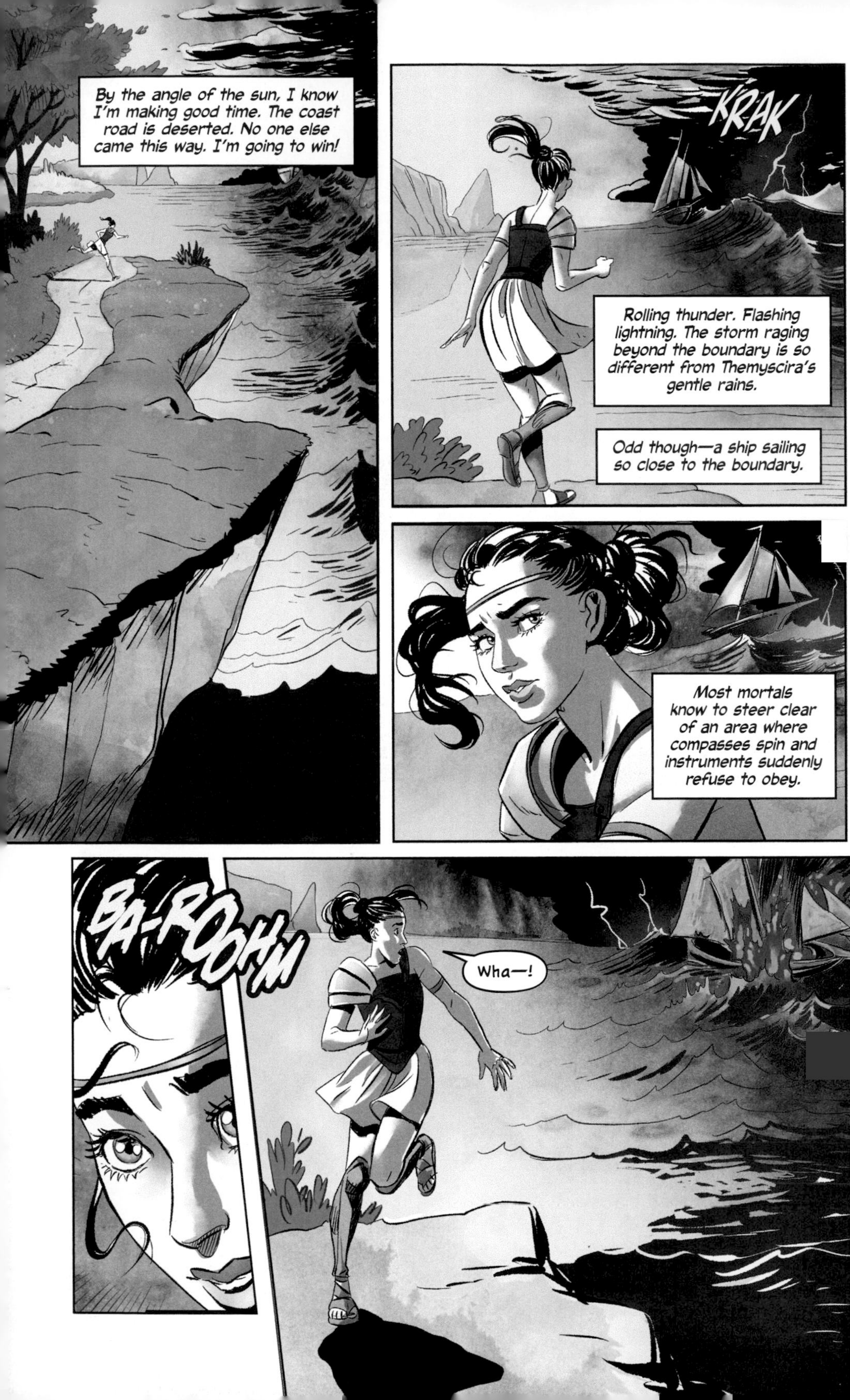

By the angle of the sun, I know I'm making good time. The coast road is deserted. No one else came this way. I'm going to win!
KRAK
Rolling thunder. Flashing lightning. The storm raging beyond the boundary is so different from Themyscira's gentle rains.
Odd though—a ship sailing so close to the boundary.
Most mortals know to steer clear of an area where compasses spin and instruments suddenly refuse to obey.
BA-ROOHM
Wha—!

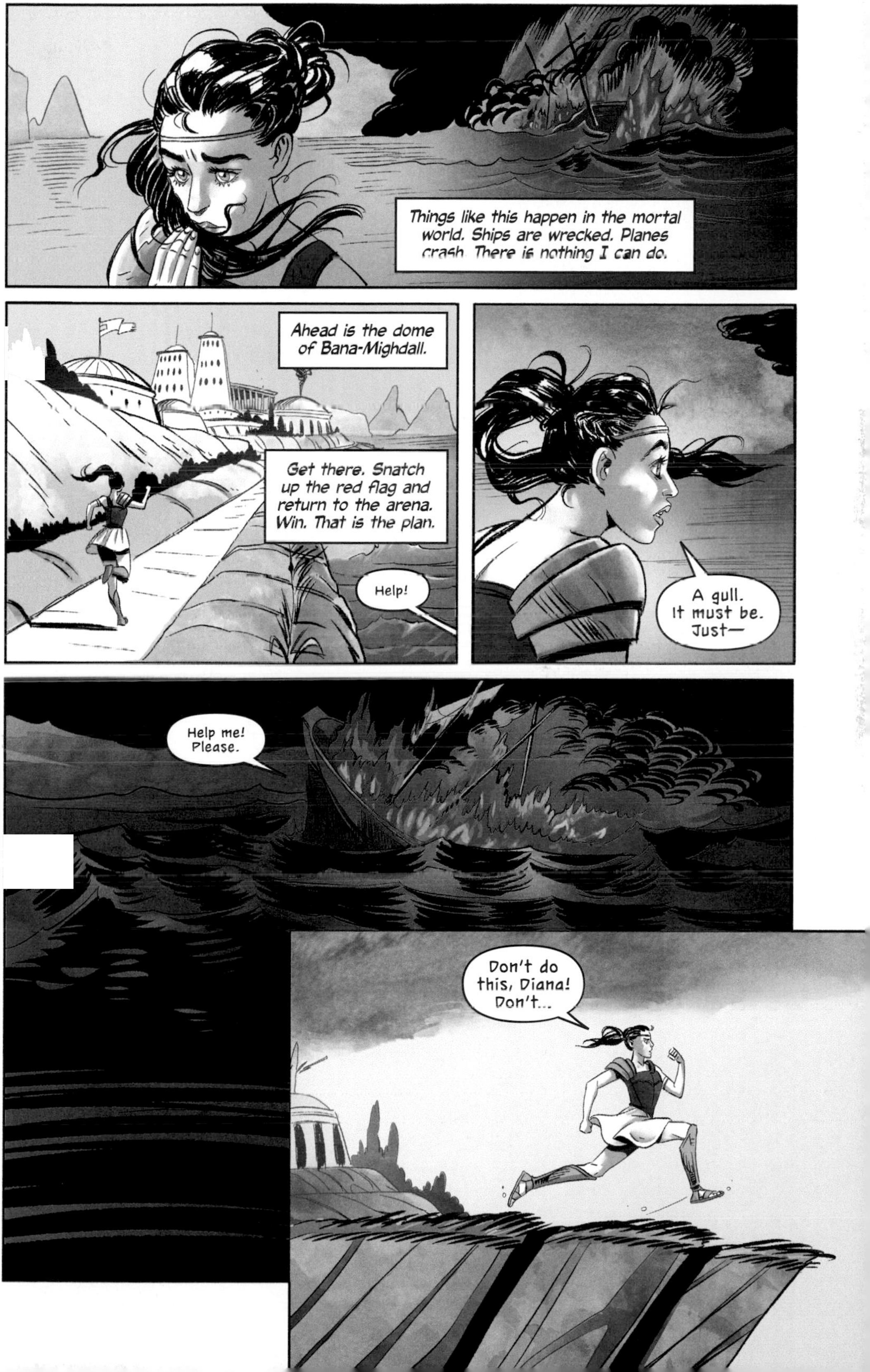
Things like this happen in the mortal world. Ships are wrecked. Planes crash. There is nothing I can do.
Ahead is the dome of Bana-Mighdall.
Get there. Snatch up the red flag and return to the arena. Win. That is the plan.
Help!
A gull. It must be. Just—
Help me! Please.
Don't do this, Diana! Don't...

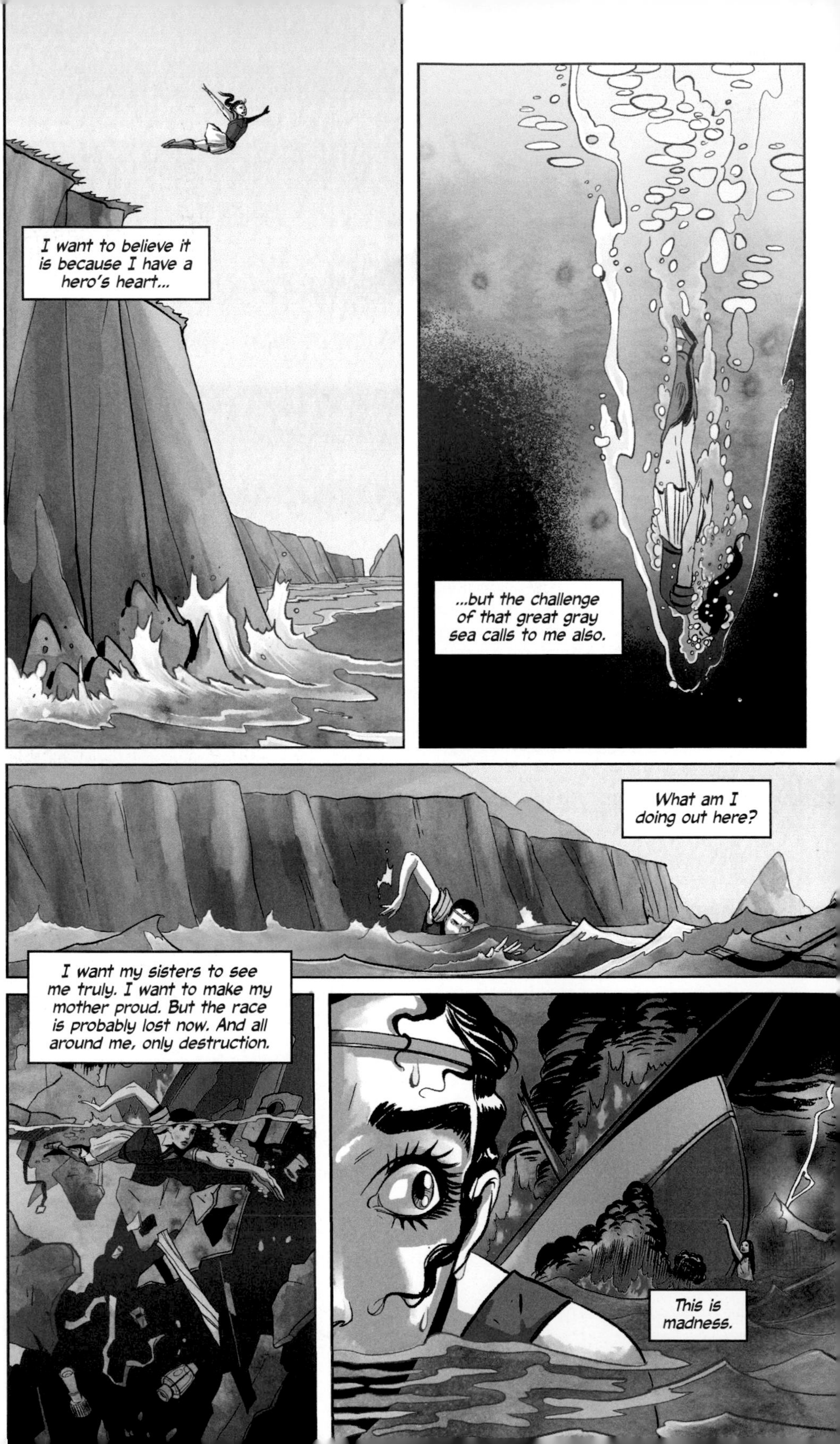
I want to believe it is because I have a hero's heart...
...but the challenge of that great gray sea calls to me also.
What am I doing out here?
I want my sisters to see me truly. I want to make my mother proud. But the race is probably lost now. And all around me, only destruction.
This is madness.

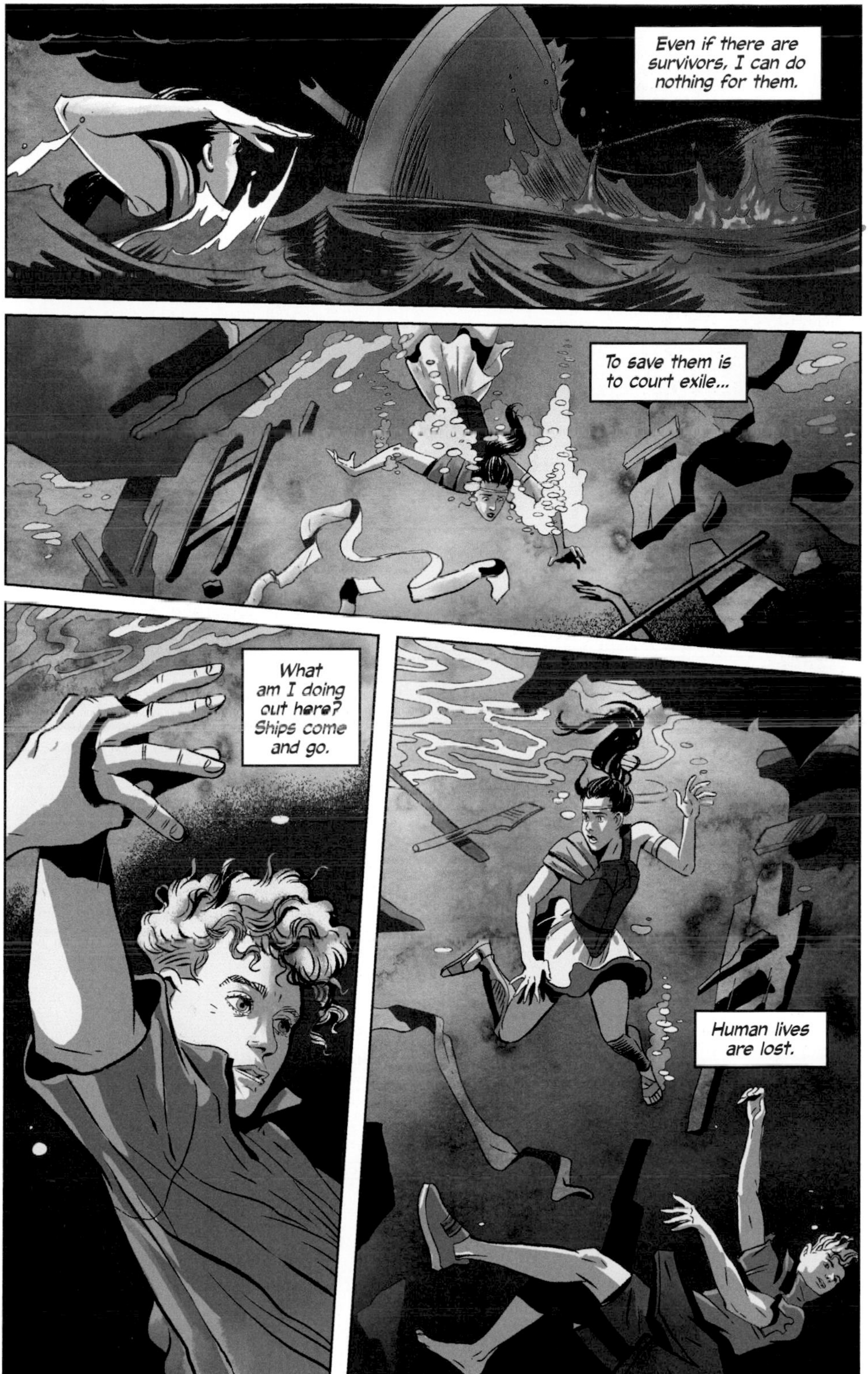
Even if there are survivors, I can do nothing for them.
To save them is to court exile...
What am I doing out here? Ships come and go.
Human lives are lost.

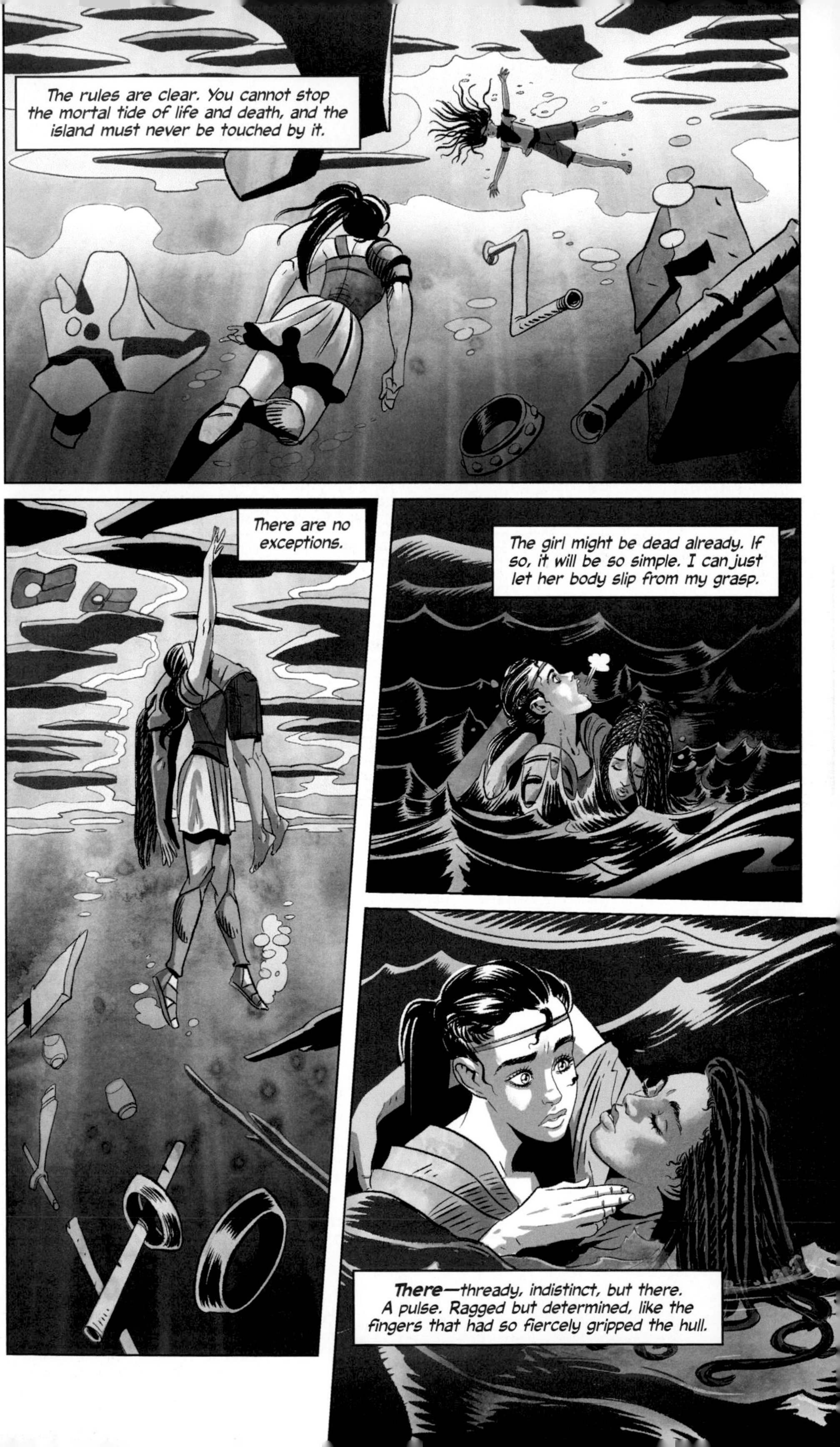
The rules are clear. You cannot stop the mortal tide of life and death, and the island must never be touched by it.
There are no exceptions.
The girl might be dead already. If so, it will be so simple. I can just let her body slip from my grasp.
There—thready, indistinct, but there. A pulse. Ragged but determined, like the fingers that had so fiercely gripped the hull.

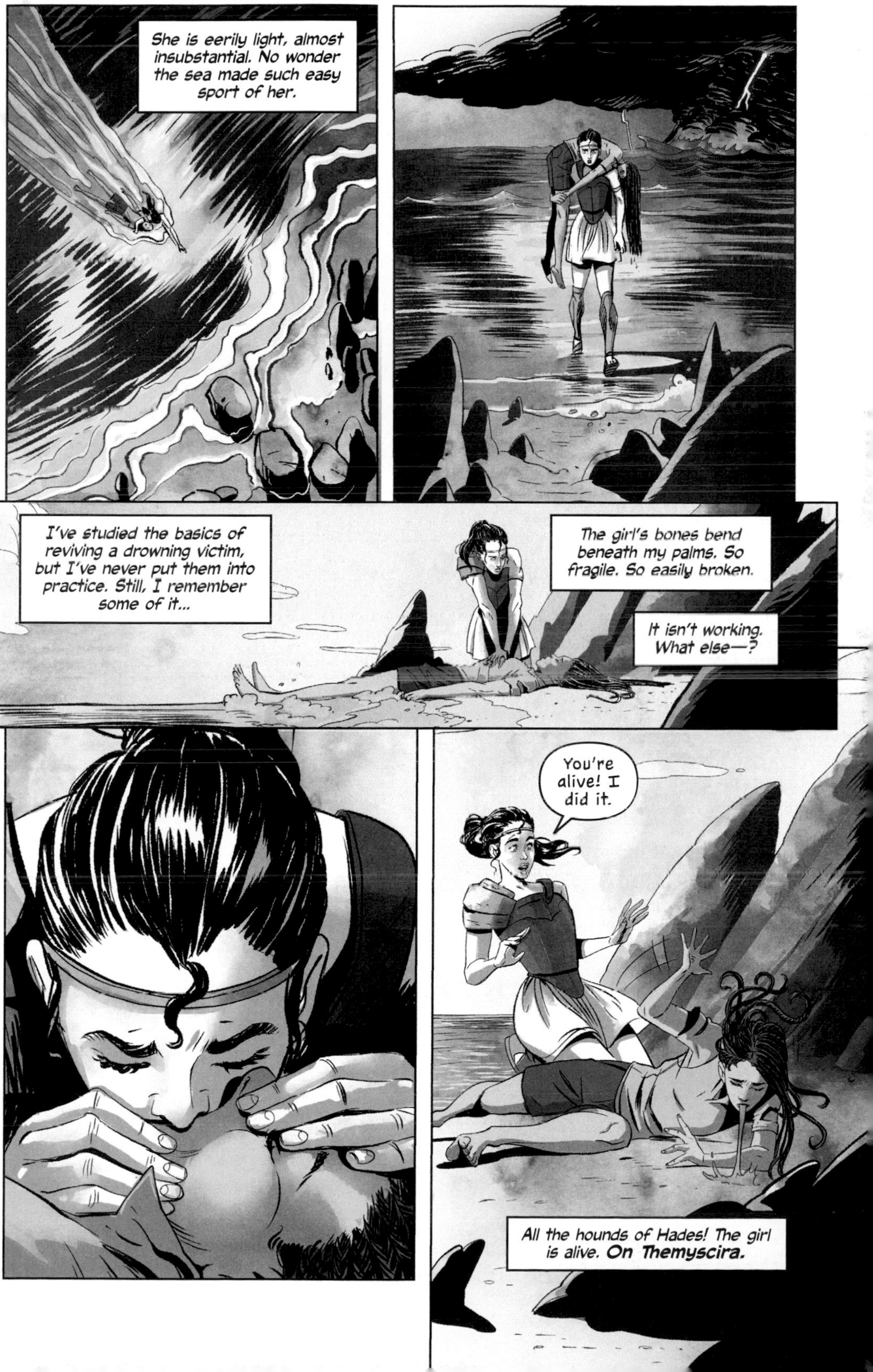
She is eerily light, almost insubstantial. No wonder the sea made such easy sport of her.
I've studied the basics of reviving a drowning victim, but I've never put them into practice. Still, I remember some of it...
The girl's bones bend beneath my palms. So fragile. So easily broken.
It isn't working. What else—?
You're alive! I did it.
All the hounds of Hades! The girl is alive. On Themyscira.

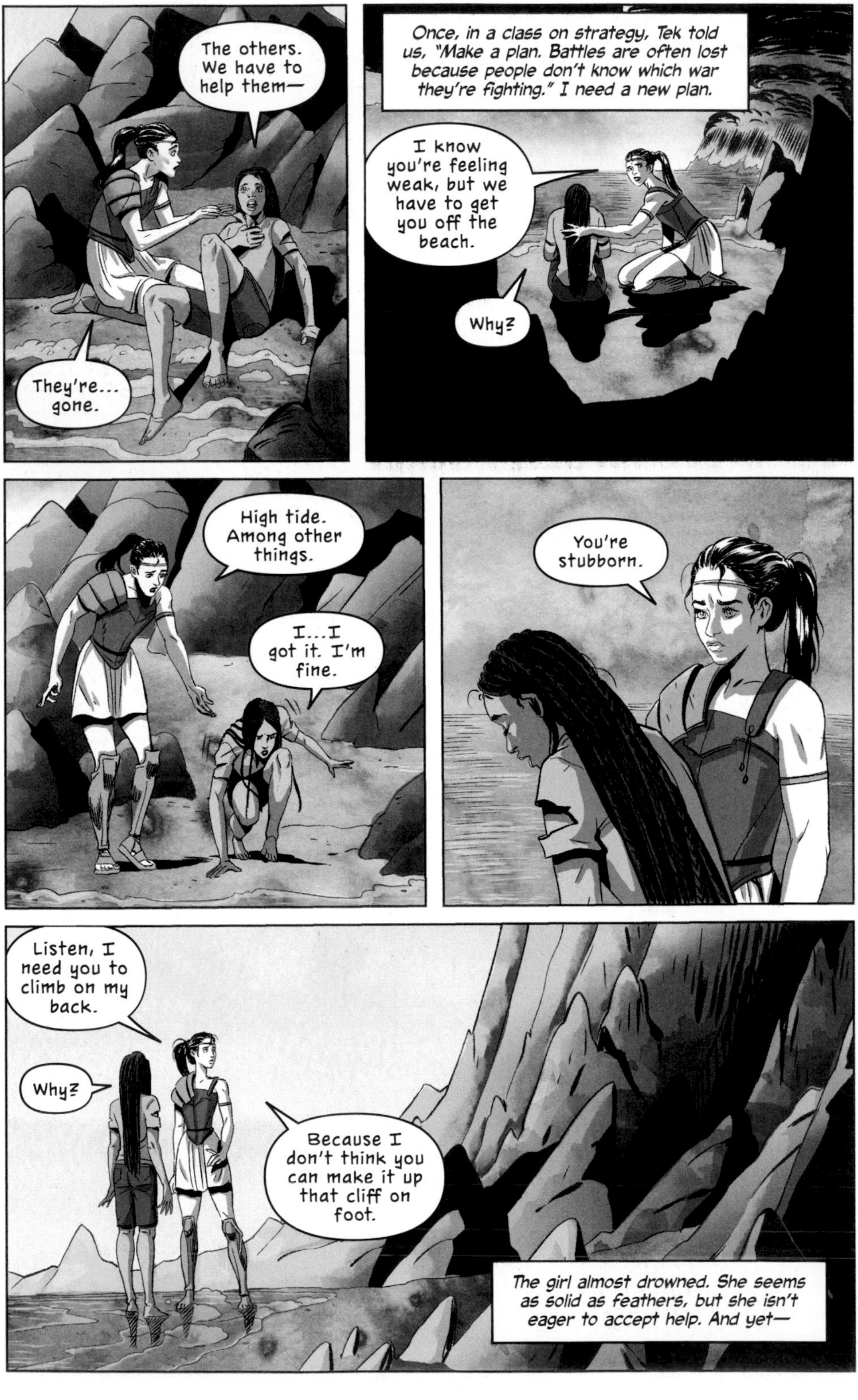
The others. We have to help them—
They're... gone.
Once, in a class on strategy, Tek told us, "Make a plan. Battles are often lost because people don't know which war they're fighting." I need a new plan.
I know you're feeling weak, but we have to get you off the beach.
Why?
High tide. Among other things.
I...I got it. I'm fine.
You're stubborn.
Listen, I need you to climb on my back.
Why?
Because I don't think you can make it up that cliff on foot.
The girl almost drowned. She seems as solid as feathers, but she isn't eager to accept help. And yet—

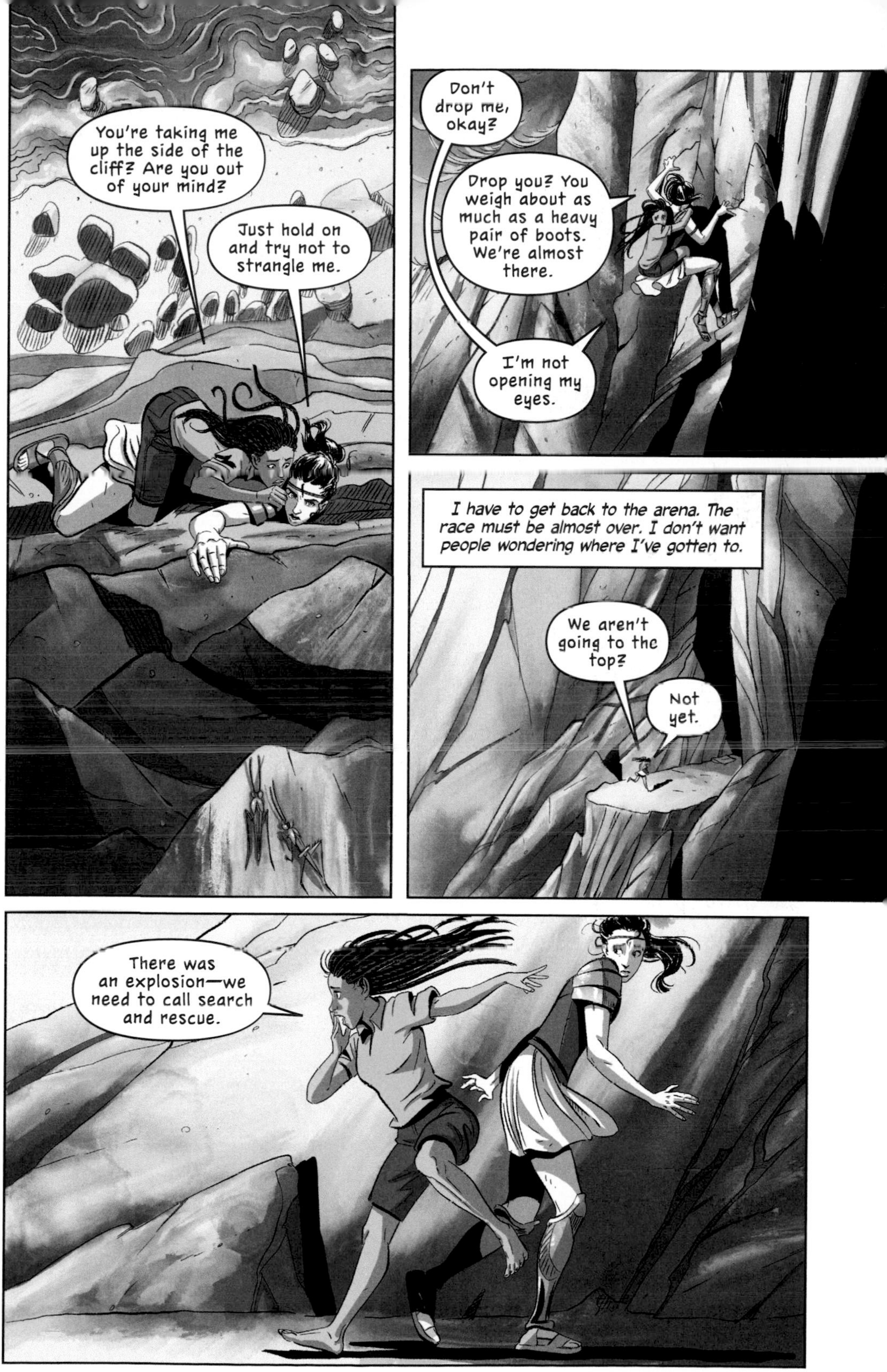
You're taking me up the side of the cliff? Are you out of your mind?
Just hold on and try not to strangle me.
Don't drop me, okay?
Drop you? You weigh about as much as a heavy pair of boots. We're almost there.
I'm not opening my eyes.
I have to get back to the arena. The race must be almost over. I don't want people wondering where I've gotten to.
We aren't going to the top?
Not yet.
There was an explosion—we need to call search and rescue.

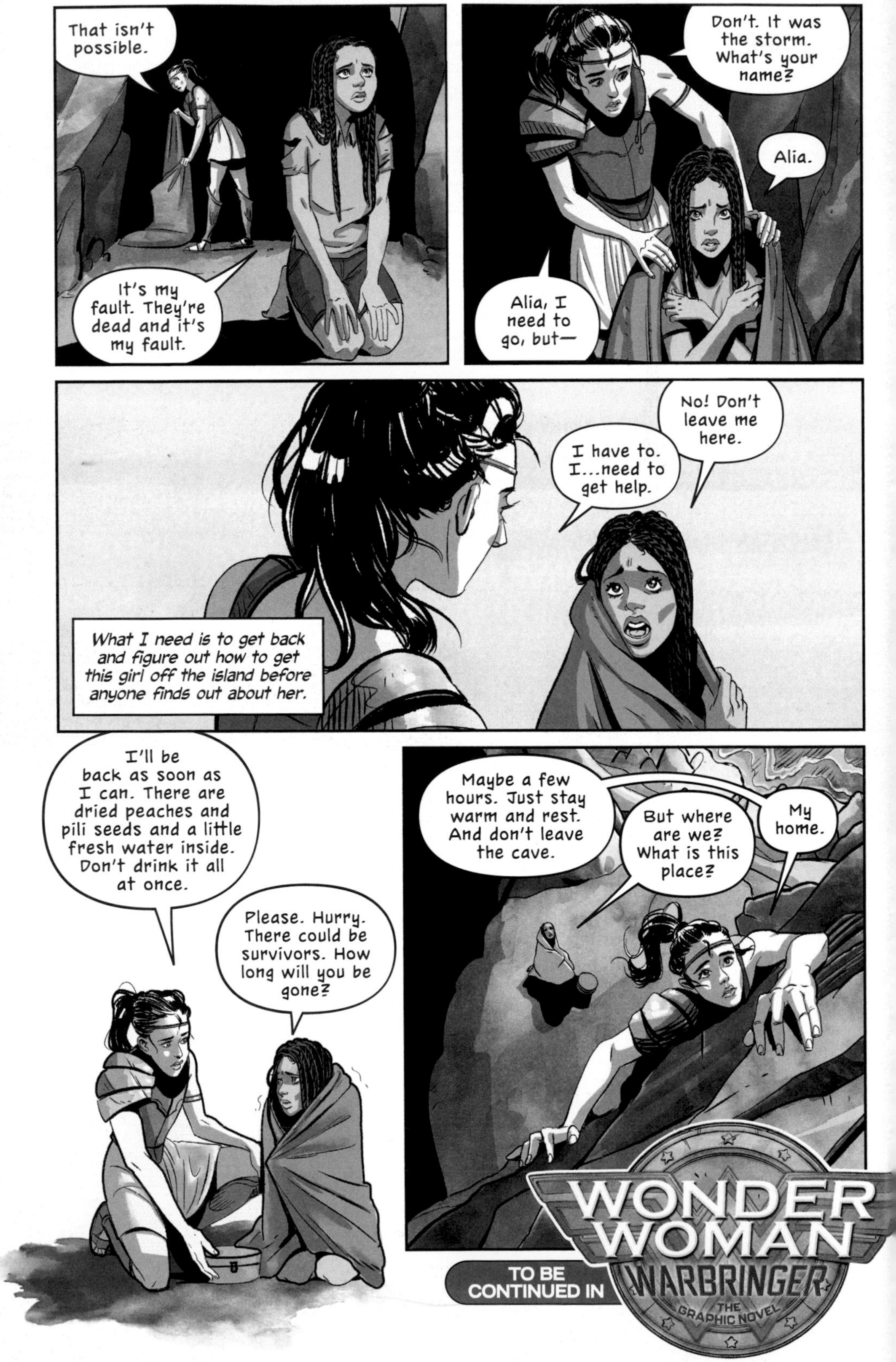
That isn't possible.
It's my fault. They're dead and it's my fault.
Don't. It was the storm. What's your name?
Alia.
Alia, I need to go, but—
No! Don't leave me here.
I have to. I...need to get help.
What I need is to get back and figure out how to get this girl off the island before anyone finds out about her.
I'll be back as soon as I can. There are dried peaches and pili seeds and a little fresh water inside. Don't drink it all at once.
Please. Hurry. There could be survivors. How long will you be gone?
Maybe a few hours. Just stay warm and rest. And don't leave the cave.
But where are we? What is this place?
My home.
TO BE CONTINUED IN
WONDER WOMAN WARBRINGER
THE GRAPHIC NOVEL

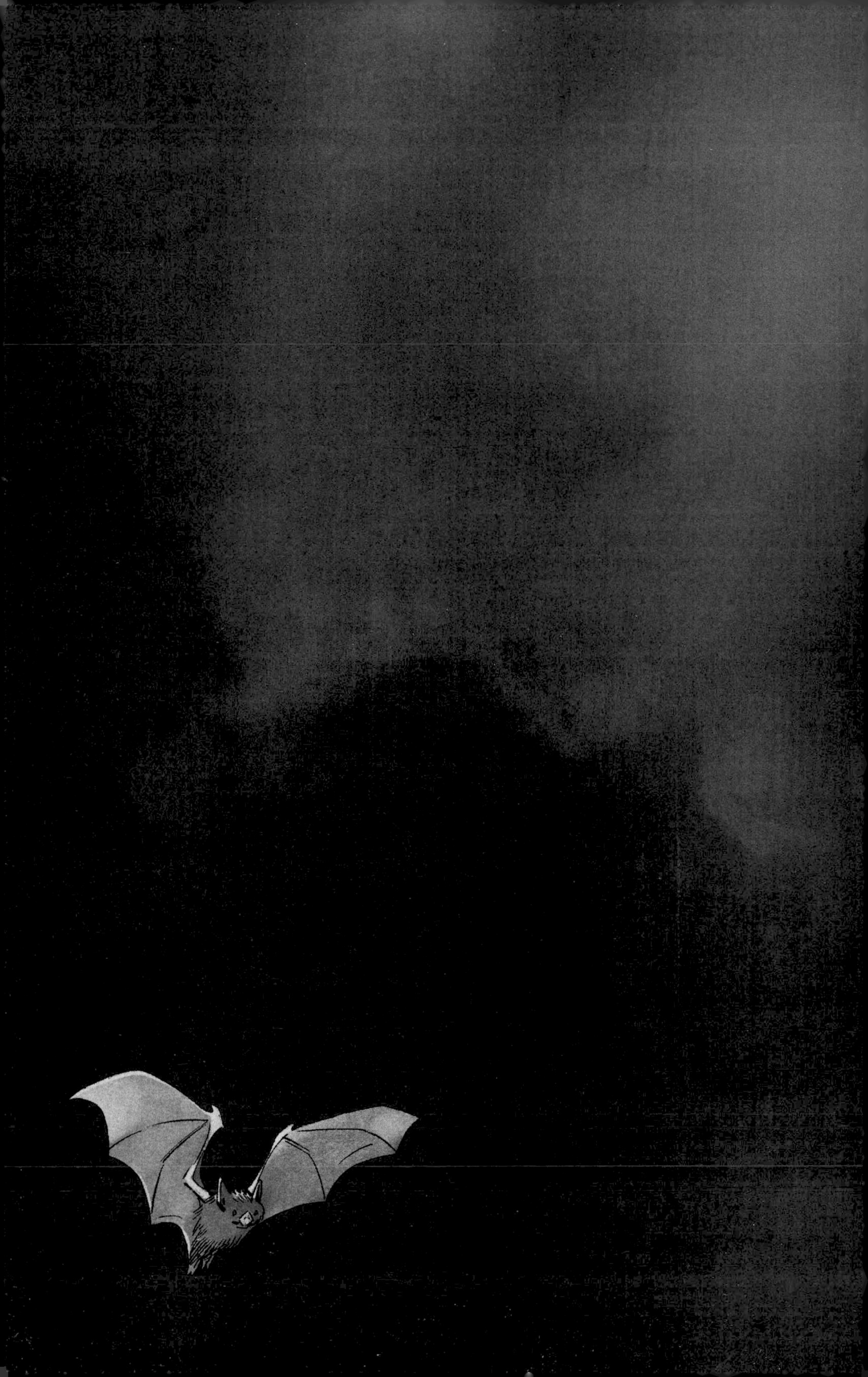